Check out A.J.'s books in AudioMovie format.

Listen to free tracks at

www.AJsAudioMovies.com

"Ditch the complex ticket and pick up this title for an instense, action-packed thriller."

—Audio File Magazine, on Vengeance AudioMovie

God's Eye

A.J. SCUDIERE

GRIFFYN INK

This book is a work of fiction. Names, characters, businesses, organizations, places, events, and incidents are either a product of the author's imagination or are used fictitiously. Any resemblance to actual persons, living or dead, events, or locales is entirely coincidental.

Published by Griffyn Ink
1409 Rivermont Cir N.
Gallatin, TN 37066
www.griffynink.com

Distributed by Emerald Book Company

For ordering information or special discounts for bulk purchases, please contact Emerald Book Company at PO Box 91869, Austin, TX 78709, 512.891.6100.

Design and composition by Greenleaf Book Group LLC and Alex Head
Cover illustration by Ruke (www.RukeStudios.com)
Cover design by Greenleaf Book Group LLC

Publisher's Cataloging-In-Publication Data
(Prepared by The Donohue Group, Inc.)
Scudiere, A. J.
God's eye / A.J. Scudiere. — 1st ed.
p. ; cm.
ISBN: 978-0-9799510-8-4
1. Demonology--Fiction. 2. Angels—Fiction. 3. Good and evil—Fiction. 4. Supernatural—Fiction. 5. Man-woman relationships—Fiction. 6. Fantasy fiction. I. Title.
PS3619.C82 G63 2011
813/.6 2011926665

Part of the Tree Neutral® program, which offsets the number of trees consumed in the production and printing of this book by taking proactive steps, such as planting trees in direct proportion to the number of trees used: www.treeneutral.com

Printed in the United States of America on acid-free paper

10 11 12 13 14 15 10 9 8 7 6 5 4 3 2 1

First Edition

This one is for my Dad, who taught me about the things I can't see and the importance of paying attention to them.

ACKKNOWLEDGMENTS

Special thanks go out to everyone who helped make this book a reality.

As always, huge amounts of gratitude go to Eli, Matt and Guy (and also James) who make all this possible.

I have always believed in "Ask and so shall ye receive". I studied Latin for this book and realized that I wouldn't get as far as I needed. I asked around to see if anyone could help. And Beau Henson spoke up. His fluent Latin gave Zachary and Allistair a voice from the other side. He spent hours translating and answering my questions about subtext and nuance. Just like everything else in this book, there's more than the simple translation in the Latin . . . I cannot thank you enough, Beau.

Thank you to Rosie Daniel and Andrea Hebert who did beta-readings for me . . . your red pens are forever appreciated.

JKSCommunications also deserves a shout-out here. They have had my back and are simply a fantastic team to work with.

Daniel Ruke and his considerable talent are responsible for the amazing cover art. You may have seen "Ruke" work on other AJ Scudiere pieces . . . Check out the Resonance Fan Pack on the Website. Thank yous to Dan for all that and more.

Of course, thank you to all the fans who kept this going and who already have their eyes out for Phoenix!

Let us sever the ties that bind the sky to the earth.
Tear asunder this gorgeous façade of cloud and blue.
And hide away the jagged pieces
in the scattered caverns of our souls.
We lift our faces up to the truth,
as though it is something we honestly desire to see.

With fine needles we sew together the fabrics of our fate

PINS

CHAPTER 1

He pushed his way through the synapse between the spaces. It required more energy than he possessed. It always did. Still, he always made it. For now, he paused and inhaled the searing air deeply into new lungs, holding it in despite the pain. His teeth clenched and his hands grabbed for the edges even though they offered no purchase as he forced his way farther through.

He stopped again to rest and wait . . . and feel. A small breeze from somewhere brushed his fingers. It didn't matter where it came from, only that it touched him, and that the sensation produced euphoria. All sensations did. Taking another gulp of air, he exulted at how the fumes trailed into his lungs and produced a raw, not unpleasant scream in his tissues. He pushed farther through the tear in reality he had fought so hard to create. It would last only as long as he needed it to; the fissure would seal itself behind him as he fell the last part of the way. But he wasn't there yet, wasn't finished yet.

He inhaled again, taking in the acrid scent of his own burned flesh. He always forgot just how painful it was. The edges sparked tiny friction fires as he forced his way. Tracers of smoke and greasy lines of soot marked his passage as he clawed his way into the abandoned subway station from somewhere most humans only imagined existed.

Zachary paid no attention to the evidence of his passing. He was too busy watching the changes in himself, and besides, he'd done this so many times before. He knew about the black ash that would drift down and pile up where he came through, just as he knew that there was nothing he could do about it anyway.

As he altered, his eyes watched the human skin of his arms knitting into a smooth, pale color that made him smile despite the pain. The color showed just how far he had come. When he reached up and pulled a short lock of his hair forward for inspection, it too was light—a translucent honey color that went with the skin and the mind-altering agony. He would bet on his eyes being blue or green, without the depth of blacker tones. He took immense pride in having earned the pale features he would display on this visit.

With effort, he turned his newly minted brain back to the task at hand and gave the final shove, birthing himself into the human plane. He looked for all the world like he was of it. Appearances were often not just deceiving; sometimes they were downright dishonest. He wondered what his boss would think of the thoughts in his head. He wondered if they were up to snuff. Then Zachary pushed that thought aside, too. His deeds would be what he was measured by.

. . .

Katharine didn't have a cat. Though the sleek, black creature she chased looked and acted like one, she wasn't sure it actually was a cat. Because of this, she doubted her own sanity as she chased after it into her bathroom.

The padding of her bare feet was ghastly compared to the ethereal cat. Shouldn't it have made some sort of sound in the silence of the night? Since that realization only added to Katharine's disturbing conclusions, she chose to ignore it. She also refused to question why she was running after a creature that she wanted to believe wasn't real. Without thought, her body followed .

Her long bare legs halted, toes digging into the plush carpeting as she came through the open doorway. Katharine caught a glimpse of the flick of a midnight tail as the creature slipped behind the toilet.

Her breathing stopped, her nose crinkled against the smell she did not want to identify as familiar. But her brain, usually so adept at pushing aside what she disliked, was hard-pressed to deny the odor.

Ash.

Cautiously now, she stalked her way around the toilet. It was the latest in plumbing innovations, a sleek, low-volume-flush model that sat directly against the wall. There was no place for the cat to duck out when she stepped around, no opening behind the bowl to dart through. She should have had the cat trapped—but knew she didn't. The smell told her what she'd see when she peered around to check the once-pristine carpeting on the concealed side of the toilet.

Still, Katharine stepped across the expanse. Blinking slowly, she forced in a full breath to fortify herself, then immediately wished she hadn't. The remnants of fire burned her lungs, but she pushed on.

As she had suspected—*known*—there was no cat. Katharine would have been grateful to chalk the experience up to a bad dream. But dreams ended when the dreamer woke. That was when hers had begun.

The small cat had been sweet, rubbing his unbelievably soft head against her hand, demanding the petting that was surely a cat's due. Katharine had obliged. Half-asleep, her fingers had stroked silky ears and spine, all of it overwhelmingly real, even after she had woken fully to the knowledge that she had no cat, that she had closed and locked all the doors and windows because she had feared something like this might happen. She had convinced herself that it had been her fault the last time it had happened. Her fault meant her fix, so she had sealed the condo before bed.

Tonight, when her brain had recognized the cat, she bolted upright, her nose already detecting the faint scent of fire that accompanied her visitors. Her lungs had gasped for air; she had known something was wrong. It was her movement as she awoke that had startled the cat into its mad flight.

Katharine blinked now. Her eyes might be deceiving her, but she had begun to doubt even her doubt.

Slashed across the bathroom carpet in the corner behind the toilet was a dark stain of soot. It was about a foot long, lighter at the end of the streak closer to her and thick enough near the wall that there was actually a tiny pile of burnt ash.

She didn't want to touch it, but some part of her was compelled to. For a while, she had believed she was hallucinating all of it, until her maid had asked what created the black messes. Katharine didn't know, but the maid's question told her that she wasn't the only one who saw it. The soot was on the deep, pale carpeting, not in her brain.

That was more disturbing than the thought that she was going crazy. If the things she had seen were real, then she was playing a game in which she had no idea of the rules or the stakes. Real meant that the cat had not been within the confines of her definitions. That she could pet and stroke the cat meant it wasn't merely a ghost, an idea she was pretty certain she could find a way to deal with. No, this was worse.

From what she had seen before, and from the way she had cornered the cat behind the toilet tonight, she had to believe that the creatures could pass through walls and floors. That would mean the large black dog of two weeks ago had passed through her closet into her living room, then somehow escaped from there. But she hadn't found him in her living room, or in the common hallway. Nor had any of her neighbors complained. There had been just enough time between the last visit and this one to make her believe maybe it had simply ended. Clearly it hadn't—the black ash on her floor now said otherwise.

If her previous theory was correct, this cat had dropped through the bathroom floor into the unit below. The soot was the remnant left as the beings passed through physical matter—the carpet or wall or barrier remained unchanged once the mark was washed away. But she didn't believe the dog had passed into the neighbors' unit, and she was certain the cat hadn't dropped to the condo one floor down, which meant that she didn't know where they had gone. Katharine didn't want to know.

Taking a deep breath, she let the smell be a reminder that she was no longer allowed the luxury of ignorance. Her only recourse was to learn what she could. So she knelt down and stuck her finger into the soot.

. . .

As she opened the door to her office, Katharine winced at the stab of pain and made a note to keep her finger from touching anything. Mostly it was an easy lesson—when she forgot and touched something, the pain served as a strong punishment even through the thick bandage.

It was also a constant reminder of what she had seen the night before.

Turning her thoughts back to the task at hand, Katharine slid behind her desk again, gingerly setting down the stack of files she had pulled from the library. Not much remained on paper at Light & Geryon. The library had been a constantly expanding force in her younger days, but the firm's computerized programs had slowly edged out the old paper filing systems. Still, her research required that she check all angles and see what had been invested in before, so she pulled paper and electronic files alike, wondering when her duties would change again.

She didn't have long to wait. The change came that very afternoon as she was wincing again at the pain in her finger. Katharine knew she must have bumped it to make it flare up, but she was just as certain that she hadn't hit it at all. The knock at the door distracted her and she stood as two people entered; she met her new trainee with her left hand grasping her right wrist, her bandaged finger held high, and her face scrunched in an expression her mother would frown upon even from heaven.

"Miss Geryon." The voice was crisp and modulated and the expression, much like Katharine's, was held steady, but Lisa Breu was clearly agitated. "Mr. Light has decided that you need an *additional* assistant. This is Mr. West."

Katharine rushed to assure her young associate that it was no failing of her own that brought about the second assistant. Though she couldn't be entirely sure that was the case, she didn't think Lisa was getting pushed out or passed over; her own position at Light & Geryon was held by the strong but slim thread of her lineage. She reminded herself to reassure Lisa before the day was out that neither one of them was at fault for this maneuver. "Thank you,"

Pushing Lisa to the back of her mind, she shifted her focus to the young man standing before her. He was of indeterminate age, but everything else about his looks was more easily definable: he was dark in every way. Katharine stuck out her hand and braced for the pain. "Mr. West."

"Allistair, please." He grasped her fingers firmly and etiquette demanded equal pressure.

The sting did not come. Somehow, Allistair managed the solid clasp without triggering the sensitive nerve endings in her finger. Katharine nodded, too impressed by the lack of pain to add that he should call her Katharine.

She spent the rest of her morning showing him around the building and ignoring Lisa's pointed looks each time they passed in and out of the office. Lisa sat at the desk situated just outside Katharine's door, but Mr. West was to have a desk *in* her office, an arrangement Lisa clearly considered an omen of her own replacement.

Katharine thought no such thing. While her office certainly had space enough for a second desk, the situation was demeaning. The first time Mr. West had excused himself for a moment she had called her father, demanding explanations. In hushed whispers, she argued with the man who held all the strings to her life. In his standard overpowering and dismissive way, he replied that training other, newer employees was merely the next step for her.

The next step in what? Katharine remained forever unaware.

As the last Geryon, she was supposed to take her father's place at the helm along with whomever the Light position was granted to. After her mother's death, though, it became more apparent that Arthur Geryon would not retire; he would have to die before he let another take his post—even his own daughter. So Katharine had been shuffled from position to position, following some grand scheme that had never been laid out before her.

She reminded herself that the money made the uncertainty far more than bearable, and that the top position should be hers when it was vacated. She was pointedly not thinking of just how it would be vacated when Mr. West returned. With a tight smile, she greeted him and returned to explaining the file system, using his computer to show him how to review old purchases and see the percentages assigned to particular stocks. She walked him through projections and statistical analyses, all the way through to the actual purchase of the chosen shares. The computer balked at the command to finalize the transaction. "We don't have access to actually put the order through," she explained. "That has to come from another division—acquisitions. It doesn't occur in research."

West nodded yet again, never asking any questions, and Katharine wondered whether he truly absorbed it all or only wanted to look like he did.

She set him free at 6:00 p.m., and then stopped by Lisa's desk on her way out of the building. Her reception was chilly. Katharine leaned low, bringing her face level to her underling's, a trick she had learned in one of the management seminars her father forced on some of his employees and always on her. "I did not ask for another assistant in any way, shape, or form. I believe the point is merely for me to train someone, since you seem to need no further training from me."

Lisa's expression did not change; her only acknowledgment was a slight nod as her fingers continued their rapid staccato across her keyboard.

Katharine had expected nothing less. She walked away, her heels clicking along the marble hallway. In her usual practiced movements and sure steps, she made her way down to the parking garage and slid into her BMW. A male employee in a full three-piece suit gave a small nod accompanied by a smile that did not reach his eyes, as he too climbed into his car. She knew what he thought, what they all thought. But, contrary to their belief, she didn't own the building or the firm. No matter how the security guards might bow before her, she was nothing more than Mr. Geryon's daughter. Indeed, it seemed to her that little had changed since she was in the pigtails and pinafores her mother had insisted upon.

Yes, the only true difference was that the employees no longer thought she was cute—now they thought she was competition. Which was about as wrong as they could be. She lacked the ambition required to wrest anything away from them, and even if they did try to compete with her, there was no way any of them could prevent her from becoming co-CEO.

As the only child the Geryons would produce, Katharine was both son and daughter—equally schooled in business and deportment. She offered her own tight smile in response to the guard's as she pulled out and down the ramp. She merely waved at the entrance, never having needed the ID required of other employees.

Making sleek, tight turns in the falling dusk, the car's dark color mingled with the night. Katharine's eyes blinked and scanned, paying minimal attention to the road. Her mind wandered, not wanting to worry about what might greet her when she arrived home, but she was unable to keep the thoughts entirely at bay.

The cat had come just last night, which would mean she was likely in the clear for a while. Then again, twice she had come home to find subtle disturbances. Her clothes would still be pristinely hung in her closet, just in a different order. Once, her bed had looked wrong, and only when she climbed in did she realize that the seam she always kept at the foot of the bed had been turned to the top.

Each time she noticed one of these abnormalities, there had been a streak of soot on the floor. She didn't come upon the first streak until a day after she noticed the disturbance, as it was under her desk and she hadn't gotten on her computer that night at all. The second had been square in the middle of the living room, nearly a foot wide and impossible to miss. Katharine didn't like to think how that correlated to the size of the mess the cat had left.

As she pulled up under the portico at her building, the uniformed valet appeared from the shadows to open her door. Quickly, she gathered her briefcase and purse and slid out. Nodding briefly to Rod, the security guard behind the desk in the lobby, she made her way down the plush hallway by routine rather than thought. Her thoughts were worth less than mush, as they usually were at the end of the day, and she was looking forward to a hot meal nuked in her microwave and an evening spent in sweats.

The elevator gave a soft ding and she stepped in. She waited out the short ride to the tenth floor, only to find the hallway in turmoil when she arrived. Katharine sighed. It just figured.

Movers were everywhere. Several large, blanket-wrapped pieces of furniture were propped against the wall, some identifiable, most not. Men in T-shirts and gloves hauled furniture into the corner unit next-door to hers. The freight elevator at the end of the hallway arrived and another pair of men spilled into the space with more wrapped items.

This was the second time in a month that her hallway had been overtaken by movers, and she knew from before that she would be able to hear some of it through the walls. She had only seen the elderly couple that used to live in the corner unit a few times during her three years in the building. In fact, she'd be hard-pressed to say who most of her neighbors were. But she hadn't recognized the man orchestrating the clearing of all the furniture, and as he'd looked a little strung-out, she'd eyed him warily. He'd explained that his parents had died. Together. In their sleep. In the kind of romantic, in-each-other's-arms death that Katharine, along with the rest of the world, longed for. Apparently, it didn't lessen the grief of loss. The unit had stayed empty for the five days it took to sell, and then didn't even get a full thirty-day escrow period. Not a wasted minute—here was the new owner, hallway full of possessions and all.

Without making any eye contact Katharine slipped her key into the lock and pushed her door open. She breathed in the scents of home—lemon and a hint of rose from something the maid used. She wondered if she had again been able to work her magic and get the soot out of the carpet.

"Wait!"

The voice jerked her back into the present and out of the folds of comfort. "Yes?"

She was every inch a Geryon daughter now, polite to the tips of her toes. She stepped back into the hallway, presenting herself to the speaker.

The voice belonged to a strikingly handsome man. Pale blue eyes looked warm under an unbrushed fall of gold-colored hair. His build was powerful, but more than that there was something magnetic about him. Katharine felt compelled to take a step closer, and another. As though he had an aura about him, she had to prevent her hand from reaching out and touching . . . something—his arm, his face.

Her eyes were wandering his features when she caught the twist at the edge of his mouth, so it was only her peripheral vision that caught the movement as his hand extended to her. "I'm Zachary. Zachary Andras. It looks like I'm your new next-door neighbor."

This time she did reach for him, and he clasped her fingers in a warm grip that radiated up her arm and into her core. It was all she could do to get the word through stunned lips. "Katharine."

He smiled fully now, the grin creating a glow in his features. It reached his eyes, crinkling the edges and transforming his entire face from stunning to unbelievable.

Abruptly, he dropped her hand and stepped back. "I have to go make a decision on where the couch belongs."

Just like that, he was gone, ducked back into his apartment amidst the voices of the movers. Now she could distinguish his from the other's, but that didn't matter much as she stood in the hallway, her own door hanging open, forgotten in the spell the man had woven.

. . .

Allistair lay back against the comforter. The bed took up a good portion of the small room. Land out here wasn't cheap. Light & Geryon paid well, but his salary wouldn't buy him space. In Los Angeles, he wasn't sure if there even was a way to buy space. At least he had a yard. Or what passed for a yard in this town.

Still, he had all the creature comforts he needed. And he loved his creature comforts just a little too much. His dinner had been line-caught halibut he'd bought from the pier on his way home. He'd stopped in a bakery for hot French bread and had been enjoying putting his nose over the bag and inhaling the fragrance when he passed by a farmers market that was folding up for the night. He'd haggled for the last bundle of asparagus. No detail of his dinner had been overlooked.

He had enjoyed the heat radiating from the stove top as he sautéed the vegetables and seared the fish. The bread knife sawed an easy rhythm through thick crust and soft center, adding to the already luscious smells wafting around his tiny kitchen. Putting out one setting of nice china that was soothing and cool to his findertips, he then loaded up his plate and sat down to eat, savoring every bite. He let his dinner roll and melt on his tongue as though it had been millennia since he had tasted anything so divine.

After he was done, he sat for just a moment and then got up to clean. There was simplicity in washing the dishes, in the repetitive circles and the flow of the water. Grace in doing for himself. Satisfaction at completion.

Then Allistair had peeled down to his boxers and laid himself across the cool bed. The boxers were still on only as a nod to propriety. He needed the practice with human niceties. So the boxers stayed on.

With a low thread count, the comforter wasn't the luxury model he could have gotten. The fabric was a little rough, slightly abrading his skin as he lay on the bed. But he enjoyed the sensation. Spreading his arms wide and running his hands across the texture of the cloth, he closed his eyes and merely *was*.

Thoughts tumbled low and long in his brain. There was only so much time to roll around enjoying the bed. Today had been only the start. He couldn't do too much too soon—he couldn't afford to look suspicious. But he needed Katharine.

And he needed her before Zachary got to her.

. . .

Katharine stood, hands wrapped firmly around her coffee mug, as she looked out her window at a good portion of the cost of her condo. The view of the marina stretched before her, still wrapped in the deep of night. The bar of rocks and seagulls that protected the small inlet from the waves obstructed part of her view, but there was still plenty to see. Leisure boaters were out every day, and this early predawn was no exception. Up close, she could make out boats leaving the marina with fishing poles stuck in tubes to keep them upright, waiting to get beyond the entrance and drop their lines. She'd heard there were sea bass and halibut out there.

A floating mist clung to the surface of the ocean. As thin as it was today, it still made it impossible to see where water ended and sky began. To her right she could see a finger of land that jutted out into the sea, buildings cluttering its surface and vying for dominance. She smiled at the winner. Farther out on the peninsula than the others and slightly taller than the rest, it bordered on garish. But it had won. Light & Geryon has staked its claim.

She didn't question why she lived within sight of the building. In truth, she didn't question a lot, not even the fact that there had been no animal visitors during the night. She had slept, deep and dreamless, all night long—which was surprising given the jolt she'd gotten from her new neighbor the evening before.

In her sweats, Katharine had pulled one of the Tupperware meals from her freezer. When her mother had died, her father had been left alone, unable to really take care of himself. He couldn't do his laundry or his cleaning, so Katharine had hired a service for him. He couldn't cook his own meals, so she'd hired that for him, too. Unless she quit Light & Geryon, there was no way she could find the time to take over what her mother had done. As she had no brothers or sisters, it all fell on Katharine's shoulders.

Katharine already had a woman who came to perform light maid work at her apartment every other week, but the food service she'd found for her father was worth the money. Now Katharine too had ten meals in Tupperware show up in her freezer every Thursday. She could even email if she hadn't liked a particular food, and it would never turn up again.

She had been eating the last container of the week when her doorbell rang. Though the sound itself was soft and lilting, it startled her out of her dinner, as Katharine was pretty certain she'd never heard it ring in the three years she'd been here. Her mother was the only one who visited her, and she was gone before Katharine bought this place. Deliveries came during the week, while she was at work. The service at the front door rang up before anyone could come in, and she was always waiting. So the doorbell was a shock.

Though she'd immediately jumped up and pressed her face to the peephole, she stared at the doorknob for a moment as if she didn't know what to do.

The small fisheye lens distorted his features, but the sight of Zachary still packed a punch. Without further thought, she'd flung the door wide. He planned to ask her out to dinner, she could tell. He had changed all his clothing from earlier, the new light sweater molding to him over dark jeans. His hair was damp and combed perfectly into place, giving him the look of a partially reformed rogue.

His light eyes had skipped around the room, taking in the wide maple table with carved legs and the Tupperware with her mother's silver fork sticking out of it. Only as those same eyes landed on her did she remember she was in sweats and an oversized T-shirt. Even now in the morning light Katharine cringed, remembering.

He'd changed whatever it was he had planned on saying and asked where he might get a sandwich this late at night. With a smile, she'd directed him to the deli on the corner and he'd thanked her.

When he turned away, she had pushed the door closed and ended the interlude. Not that anything could have come of it—she had duties and plans to fulfill. While a date with Zachary Andras sounded wonderful, it wasn't going to happen now. Not in L.A., where he could walk down the street and see fifty better-looking women. It was a shame, though. It might have been fun.

As she sipped at her coffee, the light around the ocean lifted a little from the sun coming up behind her. She gripped the mug and drank more. She had duties—her job at Light & Geryon, things she owed her mother, a new employee to train, and an assistant to soothe.

She drained the cup of the last drops of coffee and rinsed it before setting it down beside its twin from yesterday. Tonight she would hand-wash the mugs; she couldn't stand to see more than two sitting in the sink. She tugged the jacket of her suit down and skimmed her hands along the matching skirt. Best get to it.

CHAPTER 2

Allistair had given up early last night. Keeping form was difficult; the energy necessary to walk as a human was far too difficult to maintain, even for one as powerful as himself.

So he'd studied his shape in the mirror for a great length of time. When he came back, he would have to come again as the "same." Humans put too much stock in "same," paid too much attention to the surface. The surface could be so easily altered, but that was what they read, so that was what he would repeat.

He studied his face first. His hair was medium length—he couldn't go altering that; it would look suspicious to the people, even though it was everything else about him that should arouse suspicion.

Dark as midnight, the hair was a sign of where he'd come from. The color would be easy enough to replicate as it was now his natural color—he could force another shade into his hair, his eyes, his skin. But, unless he made a concerted effort, the shades would naturally alter as he shifted levels, and he hadn't messed with any of it on this trip. So he was dark. Dark hair, deep, deep brown eyes, and olive skin. He needed to remember to say he was of Italian descent, and southern Italian at that. It was what the people would easily believe, true or not.

Though his coloring was a mark he took pride in, it wasn't what he needed to study. He needed to know the shape of his hands, the breadth of his shoulders, the line of his nose. Where did his cheekbones sit? His eyes? His mouth? Those were the other cues, right after the colors, that the people would depend on. They had to. They had not been granted any further senses. Stuck with a pitiful five, and the occasional sixth, they used what they could, and Allistair would have to work within those boundaries. So he turned his face side to side, and he looked and he memorized.

He wondered if he was good-looking. In the human world a lot more would come his way if he were. But, like most humans, he couldn't tell if he was or wasn't. At least he knew he couldn't tell; people all seemed mixed up about it, which made him think maybe it shouldn't matter. But it did. Take Katharine: she walked like she owned the place—the world, in fact—but she didn't know what she looked like, how others saw her. She missed or dismissed every sexual cue thrown her way. Allistair could smell the want on the men and a few of the women as they went by her, not as well as he could in his natural state, but he wasn't quite human even when he looked it. And at the same time, many of the men in the office radiated jealousy. It was a bizarre combination, the want and dislike curling off them in discordant waves. Allistair wondered what it did to their insides to be so at odds with themselves.

The women were for the most part easier to read: it was jealousy, pure and simple. Some of it needful, some downright evil. Like tendrils, it reached out to Katharine everywhere she went, but she was oblivious to all of it.

Not all people were. Lisa, just outside the office, had a keen sense of those attracted to her; she reacted to what he could smell from others. Every time. Not Katharine. And because of that he would need to change how he approached her.

Allistair smiled at his reflection, frowned, opened his mouth, and peered inside. He studied every inch of his body, but concentrated on his face. If it didn't pass, the rest didn't matter.

When he'd done all he could, he closed the shades and lay back across the bed, this time completely naked. His last human thought was that Zachary was no stronger than he and had likely given up his form for the night as well. They would both have to claw their way back in when the sun came up.

Taking a deep breath and holding the sweetness in his lungs, Allistair was loath to give up the heightened five senses that humans so infrequently enjoyed. Though human inputs were sad in number, there was nothing wrong with them, only that their limits were so rarely tested. And to make matters worse, humans tended to look upon those who savored the tactile and sensorial as diseased. He made a mental note to try to appear disaffected the next day.

With that, he slid out of the plane.

In his true form he pulsed, felt all the pieces of life flowing within him. For a moment, he had watched through the veil into his own empty apartment, then slipped away. Moments later, in Katharine's bedroom, he watched her, watched his own energy reach out to lick at her as she slept. She mewled softly and turned when the energy built past a certain point. So she did have some sense of him, even if only when she was asleep. Her auburn hair spread across the pillow, and even now he longed to feel his human fingers running through it. But that would not be.

His goal was to keep her from Zachary.

Zachary had plans for her, and Allistair's only recourse—in fact, the only way to maintain his position—was to win her soul himself, to follow his own plans. He'd written his own devil's bargain on that one. He'd failed so many times before, they wouldn't let him back if he failed again. He'd known that Zachary was after her, and had proposed stealing her away as his personal means of salvation. He just hadn't counted on enjoying the process.

She rolled again, this time facing him, and he wondered if those hazel eyes opened would they see him through the night? He doubted it. Katharine was notoriously unaware. It was why they wanted her in the first place.

Her full lips moved against each other, pink tongue darting out to lick, and Allistair was hit with a bolt of need. Something so rarely felt in this form. Crap.

His feeling was a flare sent into the ether. Anyone on this plane would likely see the strange emotion. He could only pray they assumed it was a human in great want. Although that was unlikely. Though they were perfectly capable, humans didn't emote much.

Rather than send a tracer out to see where the spark had gone, he worked to rein it in. He had to stay here, had to keep Zachary from his prize. So Allistair watched and tried to make no comparisons to his own human form. Her long, slim fingers to his own thicker ones. The cut of her features was called "delicate" in the English language; his were rougher, sturdier, stronger. It seemed he was unable to look at her and not catalog the features.

Eventually, morning came and he left. She would wake, and things would be far better if she never saw him as he was. He had things to do himself, in his human form, before he presented the dark man to her again, as though he had not watched her sleep all night.

Once again over his own bed, Allistair began clawing at the veil. He worked talons into the fabric of the world until the tiny opening appeared. Pushing an arm through immediately, he managed to keep the hole from closing. His fathomless eyes watched from the other side as the dark skin burned and formed. Ashes, falling by gravity, added to the pile he created when he'd returned the night before. It was why he'd chosen this spot. Less cleanup.

He pushed the other hand through. Then a leg. Sensation, sharp and vicious, shot up his forming limbs him as he hurled himself into the gap. Like a live wire, a blue crackle of fire walked the edges, sending tendrils of hot smoke up into the air. As his head went through, the brain registered the feelings as pain and he clamped his mouth shut against the purely human scream that threatened to erupt.

His mouth opened, his lungs fighting for the oxygen he now

required, and he gasped, sucking in great quantities of air. Luckily, the scream could not get out while the air came in.

From the space above his bed, he fell naked onto the comforter, his skin still too raw to relish the textures and temperatures of the fabric and soot he had tumbled into. Muscles stretched and skin rippled as he flexed and curled the new body. But he couldn't stay and coddle it, no matter how badly he wanted to.

Trailing ash and leaving faint footprints as he went, Allistair dashed for the bathroom. He had to see if he'd done it. If he'd accomplished "same." If not, he'd have to go back and incorporate again, which would drain his energy further and interfere with his plans for this day.

As his feet carried him, his ears searched the sounds around him, grateful that he couldn't distinguish the overloud beeping that had occurred when he'd come into his new home for the first time yesterday. His passing had set off smoke detectors in three rooms, as surely burnt flesh should. He'd been grateful they weren't attached to an alarm system and that he wasn't in an apartment building. He'd disabled them all, first thing.

The mirror spoke to him even as he approached.

He'd done it. Allistair today would pass through the human world identifiable as the man he'd been yesterday.

The mirror also told him that his brand-new body needed a shower.

He turned back and gathered up the four corners of the comforter so as not to spill any more of the soot. With the blanket wadded up in his arms, he stepped into the shower and turned on the spray. Water hit him, cold as ocean depths, almost painful to his skin. But pleasurable all the same.

The temperature changed as he held the comforter up, letting as much soot as possible run down the drain bit by tiny bit. He didn't want to explain massive quantities of ash to a repairman. Wringing as much water as he could from the bulky blanket, Allistair then turned to the task of scrubbing himself.

. . .

The drive into the office was uneventful. A good thing, since Katharine's brain was off track.

Or maybe it wasn't. She had a duty to fulfill. Certainly one required by her mother and father. She wondered if therefore maybe she owed Light & Geryon as well. As the only remaining Geryon heir, it was her job to marry and produce another heir, preferably a spare as well—although that had been an oversight on her parents' part. At thirty-two, she wasn't getting any younger in the baby department, and the knowledge that her family was waiting was a force breathing down her neck. Never mind that her mother hadn't lived to see her first grandchild. The idea had been planted long ago, and she was required to see it through.

The problem was, most daughters were married off in their twenties to wealthy men from the right families. But Katharine wasn't just a daughter—she was filling in as son, too, entrenched in the family business. Her mother had once huffed at her marital lack, arguing that Katharine's father had surely accomplished what he had needed to: he had run the Geryon side of the investment firm and found a wife and fathered a child. Katharine had held her tongue, not pointing out that they'd fallen a little short on number of children. It wasn't just her fault they were short of options.

There were a lot of inherent problems with that comparison. No matter what her place in the company was, Katharine was stuck as a female. Short of a sex-change operation, there wasn't much she could do about that. And it completely changed the playing field. The men in high positions at the company had women draping themselves across the shoulders of their Armani suits and wrapping their silk ties in manicured fists. There was never a shortage of willing females—and therefore opportunities. Katharine had no such options.

Apparently, she intimidated the hell out of most of the men she met. She outearned them, and often outranked them. And the practically guaranteed co-CEO position rankled. There seemed to be only two categories of men who were interested in her. The first were gold diggers: male counterparts of the uber-blondes at high-end bars. Only these men worked. Hard. Their work was to woo her, and their goal was to build a future, a future resting on Katharine's place at Light & Geryon. Endless money, nonexistent responsibilities. The second type wanted her spot. Each figured if he married her, he would get the position at the firm—Katharine could stay home and make babies and run charity events. While she might have no ambition to actually run the family company, the thought of being a Main Line housewife like her mother was enough to make her dig some up.

Zachary Andras had come to her door a second time and asked her out. Perhaps at dinner tonight she would be able to figure out whether he belonged to either of those two categories. She harbored a faint hope that he didn't.

Her car dinged at her, telling her she was trying to get out with the keys still in the ignition. It was also telling her it was time to get her head screwed on straight. Yanking at the keychain, Katharine gathered her thoughts and her things and headed inside.

In her own hallway on Light & Geryon's twentieth floor, she made out Allistair hovering over Lisa's desk, a wide, telling smile on his face. With a sigh, she reprimanded them both. "Mr. West. Do not spend your time flirting with Miss Breu." She directed her gaze to Lisa next. "Even if she states that it is a job requirement. There should be no fraternization among employees."

Katharine stepped through her door with Mr. West hot on her sharp heels. "Is that a company policy?"

In her own office, feet planted on the carpet, she turned to face him squarely. "Not in print, but at any level of common sense, yes."

Ignoring him now, or trying to, she settled her things on her desk. It was hard to ignore the presence of another person in her space. There was plenty of physical room, but she'd been taking up all the atmosphere here for a while now, and Mr. West was an affront to that. Or maybe it was him; maybe *he* took up too much atmosphere.

He worked quietly over his desk, a smaller version of hers, in the corner he'd been relegated to. His dark hair was combed out of his face, letting her see all the planes and angles while he worked. His fingers marched across the keys in short bursts, alternating the staccato typing with scratching notes on a legal pad he had carefully set at his side. He used the computer programs she had first showed him the day before with almost the same ease that he used the fountain pen.

Her eyes seemed pulled to him, unable to look away or to concentrate on her own work. Finally she forced herself to open her programs and do something. She checked her emails first, returning those she could and finding out what was needed for others. That alone generated work for the first half of the day. But that was standard in her world. Researchers found what was needed for the other employees, and when that was done they dug up other investment opportunities.

Katharine was likely the most overpaid researcher the firm had ever seen. But she was a Geryon. So she didn't think about it much. It was, quite simply, what was.

She pulled files, sent Mr. West out on errands under the guise of his "getting to know the layout of the office," and showed him another path through the computer system. He hadn't seemed to have forgotten anything from yesterday, so Katharine amused herself by giving him a pop quiz.

He aced it. Much to her surprise.

After he left for a short lunch break, she pondered the possibility that West was her replacement. That would mean she was headed to a new department. Katharine pondered her options for the rest of the day. Her hands kept up with her responsibilities, but her brain was elsewhere. Even as she drove home, she wondered what her next department would be. She had held every position in the tax department. That had been kind of fun, trying to outthink the laws and find a legal place to store money for Light & Geryon's wealthiest clients. But aside from running that department, there wasn't much she could learn there. And Dean Geckhoff wasn't likely to kick the bucket anytime soon, which was the only way he was going to let go of the death grip he had on his job.

Client Relations was an option. She'd started there but hadn't learned the whole arena before her father had deemed her fit to move to another position.

Her key was in the lock of her condo door before she was able to jump from the runaway train her brain had become and bring her focus back to the present. She had a date with Zachary Andras tonight, and this morning she'd have willingly taken a bet that nothing would have budged her mind from that. But her brain had been absolutely hijacked by curiosity about her assistant.

Now she boldly walked into her own apartment, determined to be unafraid of what she might find. Her nose sniffed at the air, checking for a singed smell, but detected nothing out of the ordinary. The last thing she needed was for Zachary to show up at her door and see a wide streak of soot in the middle of her carpet. Worse, she wouldn't have a clue how to explain it. But she didn't find anything. Hopefully that was a good sign.

She changed clothes, noting that all her hangers were in the appropriate places. Her shoes stood in a sharp line across the floor of her closet. She rehung her jacket, slipped her pumps back into the space they had vacated that morning, and chose something suitable for a date with a man who could afford the corner unit in her building. A man who wore a suit to work but went out to delis in jeans and a sweater. Unconsciously, she emulated Zachary's look, pulling a "date" outfit from behind the other clothes. Throwing on a pair of "fun" shoes, she figured she could go anywhere, except maybe on a hike.

Katharine picked pins from her hair and brushed it loose while she waited. Unusually nervous about the date, she fidgeted around the apartment, checking her email and nibbling just a little. She couldn't recall feeling this hyped up about something as stupid as a date before. Then again, she couldn't recall a date where she hadn't already been close to certain which kind of predator the man was prior to the first course.

At seven sharp, her bell rang for the second time in three years. Katharine sprang up, again checking for soot around the room, or black animals, or to see if her sanity had wandered away while she wasn't looking. The one thing she didn't look at was the peephole. It had to be Zachary on the other side, right?

Throwing the door wide open, she startled him from a motion that looked like maybe he was settling into his skin for the evening. Blue eyes looked deeper than the surface of her, creating a buzz that she hadn't felt in . . . well, maybe ever. "You look ready."

It wasn't a question, and she didn't know how to respond. So she slung her purse over her shoulder and said, "Yes."

His smile made her want to follow him down the hall or into hell. And she wondered why she hadn't questioned the wisdom of dating the man next door and why, even after thinking that, she still didn't question it. Zachary didn't speak until the doorman had handed her into the passenger side of his car. There was a tiny thrill in his assumption of superiority. He *was* more than the other men in the room. There was something there; it radiated through his bearing and around him as well. It was also evident in the low-slung car they were cruising in—a wealthy man's toy. Turning to face him, Katharine asked him about his new condo, but not about where they were going. She'd been taught to hold her tongue on that one, and so she did.

Zachary answered with details about the move, and his story about something the movers had broken was enough to make her laugh. The way he told it radiated alpha male, but there was no mention of where he'd moved from, why he'd moved, or any of the other standard bits of information. Katharine tucked that observation away, knowing that she could deal with those issues later. Men loved to talk about themselves.

LeDieu was crowded when Zachary slid the car up to the entrance. Without a word he handed over the keys and pocketed the valet ticket so deftly it was as though it had simply disappeared. People standing outside the restaurant stepped back as they approached—as though Zachary were a war hero, or Moses. The hostess smiled at him, a soft, welcoming bend of mouth that told everyone in eyesight that she could take care of more than just getting him a table.

Had he not responded so coolly, Katharine would have taken more offense at the hostess, but Zachary brushed it off. Maybe he was used to such offers. He was, after all, beautiful. Katharine wanted to wonder what it was that interested him in her. But once they were seated, his attention turned full-watt onto her and she ceased to care. In the end, it didn't matter what interested him; it was enough that he was interested.

She spent the evening telling him everything about herself. Trained socialite though she was, she still wasn't able to get more than a passing comment or two out of him about his life and what he liked and wanted. By the end of dinner she knew only a small handful of facts: he was an only child, a lawyer, and new to L.A. by way of New York. In exchange, he knew all her deepest secrets.

Normally she would never have told such things, but there was something about him that made the words come tumbling out. About her parents, about their expectations, about her work at Light & Geryon, about the employees who weren't her employees but still treated her like the fire-breathing boss.

There must have been something in the wine—she bordered on feeling drunk. Although she couldn't be. She was too well schooled to let herself do something like that. Then again, maybe she'd been hit by the proverbial lightning that comes with falling in love. Or maybe it was just the kind of chemistry that leads to it. Never having experienced it before, she didn't know how to deal with it.

At least that's what she told herself later as she stood in her living room, Zachary's hands peeling her clothing and his mouth sending hot streaks of need through her. Before she could think any further, they were tangled on her bed, cool sheets twisting around limbs that reached for each other. She opened for him and his name fell from her mouth in a cross between a sigh and a moan as he drove into her. Countless minutes later an intense orgasm slammed into her, tearing the world apart before her eyes.

Later, as things slowly righted themselves, her brain returned to normal functioning. Although whether that was even possible with this intense man around, Katharine was unsure.

He stayed there in her bed for an indeterminate amount of time, lying by her side, barely touching her. And Katharine refused to look at the clock. She didn't want to time him, to know how long he waited. If he fell short, didn't stay all night, she would be disappointed. He'd been so perfect in every other way. So the time didn't matter.

She only knew that it wasn't very long. Neither of them had fallen asleep when Zachary stretched and stood. He said something about getting to an early case in the morning. But Katharine knew it was all the same regardless of the excuse. She forced a smile and a nod.

Planting a kiss atop her head, he said he'd call the next day. She was unable to muster the "Yeah, right" that rang in her cynical heart right next to the fervent desire to believe. Turning away, he walked naked from her bedroom, while her libido enjoyed the view. Through the open door, which they hadn't even taken the half-second to shut earlier, she could see him as he gathered his clothes and slid into them with a sinewy grace that belied his power.

Without turning back—maybe he didn't know she could see him—Zachary slipped quietly out the front door. Only when she heard the lock click shut did Katharine get to her own feet, her head swimming as she tried to think logically again. But logical thought didn't come. Only a cold flood of memories.

She circled the apartment, checking locks on windows. She checked all three bolts on the front door. Made sure everything was locked down tight. Then she sat, still naked, on the edge of the bed. It was the animals that occupied her thoughts, not the fact that she'd willingly fallen into bed with a near stranger on a first date. Somehow, that rang as perfectly normal—not like something she had never done before. But the possibility that the animals might come again scared her.

She lived on the tenth floor. If creatures got into her apartment up here, then it wasn't through the windows. She'd seen two cats and a glimpse of a large black dog—nothing that flew or scaled buildings.

The animals, this dread—it was the one one part of her life she hadn't handed over to Zachary wholeheartedly. It hadn't even occurred to her. The memories of the fear had receded in his presence and only returned when he was out of her sphere.

Unfortunately there wasn't much she could do about it. It wasn't like the animals were dangerous, anyway. They were more of a threat to the carpet than to her. And after that encounter with Zachary, she was nearly dead on her feet. Her body cried out for sleep.

Slowly, in an attempt to calm herself, she straightened the covers and went through her routine. Methodically, she brushed her teeth, washed her face, and ran her comb through her hair. She pulled on a satin sleep shirt—her only concession to the possibility of night visitors, but she didn't admit it even to herself. Katharine checked her alarm; each morning she turned it off, then immediately reset it for the next day. It was as it should be. Then she slipped beneath the covers, pulling them up tight beneath her chin, instantly drifting off.

Hours later, she woke, her eyes blinking in the darkness that didn't seem to recede. Still, she headed toward her bathroom. Half-asleep, she used the toilet, washed her hands, and dried them on the towel next to the sink.

When she opened the door, the wave hit her full blast. Unused to the sensation, she stood there buffeted by the feelings that came at her and pushed through her. Fury. Overlaid with despair.

And they were radiating from the corner.

Her eyes drew a sharp focus in the very thin light coming through the curtains. The back half of her room was bathed in shadow. But something sat there. Large and fathoms deep, it broadcast its feelings to her, the anger permeating the room. Katharine, for some unknown reason, perhaps anger of her own, took a step toward the creature.

The rage disappeared. Instantly, she was drenched in arctic cold, her quick gasp freezing in her lungs. Still, she took another step forward, some part of her brain demanding that she see what had invaded her space this time.

One hand came out toward her—emerging from the darkness that somehow seemed to continue beyond the borders of her bedroom. Silver claws the size of kitchen blades unfurled at the ends of its long fingers.

Terror, this time her own, smashed into every cell, and the dark in her room became timeless, spinning. Her eyes wilted shut as her vision was shot through with stars.

CHAPTER 3

Allistair had already seated himself and gotten comfortable at his desk when Katharine walked into their shared office..

He'd heard her heels clicking down the length of hallway as she approached, each tap on the marble radiating outward through the air and thick rock like a ripple on a pond. Each click reverberated in him, speeding his heart a little faster with anticipation, so by the time she appeared in the open doorway, he was as tightly wound as a spring.

Her hair was pulled up and away from her face, displaying cheekbones many women would be proud to call their own. She looked like she'd managed to pull herself together after getting a glimpse of him the night before. He'd seen her faint and hadn't been able to do anything without incarnating right there in front of her. Had she come around while he was climbing through, he would have been done for.

So he'd stood over her for a short while, seen that her breathing was even and strong, and had reluctantly left. He'd been waiting to see how she fared. From the outside it was impossible to tell—as he'd known it would be. Katharine was a master at the art of giving nothing away. If he hadn't been able to discern the slight waves of agitation and fear that peeled and curled off her, he would have thought she didn't remember it at all. He could see it was more like she didn't want to.

Her movements were the same as any other day—sharp, efficient, yet somehow still feminine. She was pretty enough, not truly beautiful on the outside, but like many women she was radiant when she smiled. He wanted to be attracted to the woman inside her, but he found he was attracted more to her humanity than to what was uniquely Katharine. It seemed so much of what he saw in her was merely the result of the expectations of others. Things she had transferred into herself without truly thinking about them. She did a good job of making herself into what those around her expected her to be. Only rarely did she share glimpses of the woman he thought Katharine might truly be—the person he thought she should be. And that was exactly why he and Zachary had been dispatched for her.

She was malleable, open, gullible, and swayable.

He only prayed Zachary didn't get to her first. But it was already looking like his rival was making headway with Katharine. Her attraction to something so completely the opposite of himself should have kept his feelings at bay. But it didn't. Though he wanted to keep tight reins on himself, and though he should have been able to, for some reason he had no control over the baser urges he felt. He could see his own want licking out at her as she passed by his desk, barely nodding good morning. In this, at least, he seemed to be like any real mortal man.

And this was the one way in which he was supposed to be *un*like mortals. The disguise was intended to be only flesh deep. For his brethren, it was. They walked among man, in man's skin, without man's needs. But Allistair had always enjoyed the feelings of humanity too much. Sharp smells and sweet sounds. Pungent tastes. Visions of earth as humans see it—solid and enduring, without the turmoil from beyond the veil. Right now his body craved texture.

He could feel the fabric of his button-down shirt as it wrinkled inside his suit sleeves. The chair pressed soft against his back; his feet were held tight by his shoes. But he longed for the sweet, cool feel of Katharine's skin against his fingers. His eyes saw her, already bent toward her computer screen, having begun her day's work. She didn't feel him over here, needing to run his hands and mouth along her hair. He needed to inhale her. Devour her.

He needed to not feel any of it. But it seemed he was incapable.

Forcing his features to disguise his thoughts—for he had already given in to the knowledge that he was lacking the will required to actually not think them—he got to the work that was expected of him at Light & Geryon. Still, his thoughts wandered.

Like the others at the firm, Katharine remained absolutely focused on her work, and had just as absolute a deficit about what she really accomplished. This was another reason why she was a prime candidate—why she was the game piece in this war that was being carried out between Zachary and himself.

Allistair pulled the files and researched data for the reports Katharine had handed him. He needed information on companies that would be good for the mutual funds or even individual investors to put their money in—maybe. It was her job, and now his, to determine the risks. The report packets were already started for a gem mine in Australia that was going public, a metal works that made pins, and a paper manufacturer. While he watched her, Allistair began the required work. He looked up stock analyses and productivity. He pulled past benefits and dividends. He charted the information they would present to the board of Light & Geryon. He didn't like what he learned.

The contrasts beneath his skin weren't visible at the surface, and only those few humans with special gifts would be able to see the manifestations in the energy around him. It seemed none of those special people worked at Light & Geryon. No one here would see his shortcomings. His goal this time, aside from claiming Katharine, and therefore a victory over Zachary, was to finally become what he was supposed to be. To not be so human. To not want, not need. If he failed this time, as he had so many times before, the punishment would be swift and likely fatal. A harsh dealing to a creature intended to be immortal.

It was afternoon before Katharine was called away. Aside from a break for lunch, it was the only relief he had from the tight grasp his emotions held him in.

. . .

Katharine wanted to run down the hall, but so many things were holding her back, the least of which was her pencil-slim skirt. Her heels were a hindrance. Her brain was churning too fast to pay enough attention to do anything other than have her crash wildly into the things around her if she achieved any speed at all. But mostly it was her upbringing, ingrained on every motor pattern she had, that kept her pace sedate. It was possible that, even in jeans and sneakers and with a clear mind, she would not ever be able to bring herself to run in the halls of Light & Geryon.

The summons to her father's office brought gut-churning sensations—anticipation of a new promotion perhaps and entwined through it all the fear that she was being reprimanded. Just because she had no idea what she might have done, it didn't mean that a lecture wasn't coming. It had happened more than once before.

With a sincere smile at Sharon—the woman had sat outside her father's office for as long as Katharine could remember—she walked up to the door, only to be brought up short by Sharon's sweet but firm voice. "He's busy, dear."

Hmmm.

Katharine waited outside. His damn dutiful daughter, who had given her life to his firm as thoroughly as if it were her own. His only offspring. And he summoned her when he already had someone in there.

Katharine pulled back, startled by her own thoughts. She had never before resented her father for making her wait. It was merely the way of the universe—she came when he called, she waited when he wanted her to. Taking a deep breath and settling herself on the sofa, even though she had a myriad of better things to do, she wondered if she was cranky because of last night.

She'd woken that morning on her floor and in pain. Her head had pounded to an evil cadence that had turned out to be the beeping of her alarm. Her legs were cramped, folded under her, and so was her arm. Her entire left side bore marks of carpeting and the ache that came with sleeping on a hard, flat surface. If that could be called sleeping.

She remembered the creature in the corner. The straight razor talons that were extensions of each finger. She knew she'd seen its eyes, but didn't remember them. And she couldn't be sure if she really couldn't remember them or if her brain simply refused. A voice at the back of her head told her to be grateful. She would have been doubtful of the whole thing, she *wanted* to write it off as a nightmare, but waking twisted on her floor in the exact place where she remembered falling was more than she could push her brain to just disregard.

Light had streamed in as she'd peeled herself up from the floor, even though her bedroom window didn't face the sun. The corner of her bedroom had been brightly illuminated. When she looked, she could see every fiber of carpeting, the line where two pieces of baseboard molding had been cut on the bias and seamed together, the lack of soot and ash on the carpet. There was nothing hovering at the edges of her room or reality this morning. She trusted that the place was clear more because of her feelings than her eyesight.

Katharine accepted the beast that had been in her room. She accepted the creatures that wandered through her space and disappeared from the world. She accepted that Zachary had simply landed in her lap—a man perfect for her needs who also drew her out and lit sparks in the best of her. She told herself she only had a hard time dealing with all of it at once.

Luckily, the door to her father's office swung open just then, snapping her back from her thoughts. Toran Light emerged, gray hair as impeccably groomed as the smile he pushed to his face when he spotted Katharine on the leather couch. "Miss Katharine."

She smiled back at him, her grin genuine even though his was tight. He had called her Miss Katharine since she was two. Something subtle in his demeanor gave a cue that he was bothered. "Uncle Toran."

His hug was firm and solid, and he spoke as he always had—directly into her ear. "You help your Daddy out now. We need you on this."

"Absolutely." The personal communication and trust he extended to her were more than her own parents had given her. Always had been. Maybe he knew it and maybe he didn't, but encouragement from him worked like a charm. Every time.

She went into her father's office, previous anger dissolved and gone, ready to face whatever challenge he set before her. Seating herself into a firm leather wing chair, she faced the man with the same hazel eyes she had inherited. His hair had been a thick, deep brown and was now liberally shot through with wire the color of steel. It aged him, but only added to his authority. He leaned back in his chair, not bothering to stand. His greeting was as impersonal as the rest. "Katharine." And the simmering anger came right back. Two could play at that game. Even as she wondered where the meanness came from, she spoke, as coolly as he had. "Daddy."

He didn't notice the icy endearment, and pushed a short stack of papers across the desk to her. "We have a problem. We are missing funds."

She almost blurted that she was in research, but then again, maybe she wasn't anymore. There was a very fine male sitting in her office right now already up to speed on how to do most of her work. She didn't know whether it bothered her more that he was so attractive—though she couldn't say why—or that he was so fast in taking over her spot. She pushed her thoughts and her impatience aside. And waited.

"Toran and I have worked on it as much as we can. We've chased paper and followed leads for a few weeks now. This is what we have." He pointed at the papers. "We suspect the payroll department is responsible for the disappearances—they have the greatest access and we have satisfactorily ruled out all other departments. If the culprit isn't in payroll, then they're working through that division."

Picking up the papers and leafing through them, Katharine nodded.

Her father continued dispensing information, and she listened while she looked at what he'd handed her. "You worked with all but a few of the newer payroll people. You hired a handful of the employees when you were in HR before that. And everyone here knows that you move around the company frequently. Being my daughter may be a hindrance, but the rest is a great advantage. They likely won't tell you all their secrets, but no one will be suspicious if you start checking records or pulling files. We have a prime suspect as well."

That made her head pop up, and for a brief second she met her father's eyes.

"Mary Wayne. She seems to be living above her means and is the only one in the department doing so."

Katharine started and her brain turned over her father's suspicion. She had hired Mary. Had liked the woman. Mary's background and references had been impeccable. That this must be a mistake was Katharine's immediate gut reaction. Then again, people changed.

"Get to work on this. We need it shut down as fast as possible. Use your assistant—he hasn't been with the company long enough to be the culprit."

With a final nod to her father, Katharine organized the papers and, tucking them under her arm, left the office. She had said only one word during the whole exchange. Sharon waved to her as she left but didn't say anything, and for the first time it occurred to Katharine that Sharon usually expected her to leave her father's office tense and preoccupied.

For thirty-two years, her life had progressed as expected. In a matter of weeks, great cracks and questions had appeared at the foundation of all she knew. But she had limited experience handling real questions, so Katharine did what she was good at and pushed it all aside. She had a thief to catch.

. . .

Zachary saw Katharine emerge from her father's office, but she didn't see him. He sat behind the veil, watching. Waiting. Making sure things didn't go horribly awry for her.

There was so much she did. So much she accomplished. He needed to show her the path to her own soul. She was so devoid of knowledge of herself, but he could set her free. She could join and do the work she was meant for. See all the things he could give her.

She walked down the hallway away from him, but he could detect no change in her from a week ago. Nothing that said she belonged to someone, even though he knew she had feelings for him. That was something that couldn't be helped. When one of his kind incorporated, while people could see and accept the brethren as human, there was usually still some tiny tip, some clue, that was picked up on. People flocked to Zachary's kind like moths to flame, wanting to be near something they barely sensed. There was little he could do about it. Her attraction to him was as natural as the doormen going out of their way, the clerks at the grocery being nice for the first time all day, the hostess in the restaurant having feelings for him.

He didn't return the emotions. He couldn't—he was a higher being. He could enjoy the interaction, empathize and placate the ones with feelings, but he couldn't be attracted to them the same way they were to him. Katharine included. Having sex with her had been a necessary evil. Zachary needed her bound to him. He needed her to listen and hear what he told her. Allistair would destroy everything if he got to her first, if he tied Katharine more tightly to him, if he swayed her away from what she was capable of becoming. So Zachary had been forced to move first, to protect what she could become.

His thoughts had wandered, his attention lapsed, and as he turned to follow Katharine he mistakenly ran into an employee. Mary Wayne. She was delivering the paystubs for the division chairs as well as for the payroll department. It was poor form for payroll to hand themselves their own checks, so it fell to Sharon to hand the payroll clerks the checks they had approved for themselves.

Zachary had taken one step when Mary had passed through him. That was an error.

He'd had contact with Mary off and on for several weeks, yet she was becoming a problem. Zachary decided something needed to be done. But as she passed through him, she stopped and shuddered as though she felt a chill.

Mary was developing a sense of the other side. Not that she knew it, but she was having minor reactions to things that were happening across the veil. Even though she clearly sensed something, she didn't see him, or even sense what he was.

He stood and stretched, his wings unfurling to their full length. This body needed to be used when he was in his own form. This was the skin that fit him best, and he'd spent so much time in human form lately that he was in need of his own shape sometimes. His back worked and he felt the motion as his arms, legs and wings pulled in and pushed wide several times. Large as his kind was in comparison to humans, several steps brought him into Katharine's office.

The wall was no hindrance; it existed solely on her side of the veil, a mortal device that worked only on mortals. Katharine gave no indication of recognizing his presence on any level. Even the time she'd spent with him, some of it humanly intimate, hadn't made her more aware.

But Allistair paid attention; he looked around as though checking out the office. He sensed Zachary's presence. Though Allistair's mortal form limited his perception, it did not entirely block it. Likely it was merely a tickle at the back of the reduced brain he now possessed. But Allistair had waged this battle. He was the one who had come along after Zachary and his lord had chosen Katharine. Had taken what was meant to be a simple offer and turned it into warfare. Allistair was smart to be alert, and he knew that a tickle was likely all the warning he would get that Zachary was nearby.

Not feeling the slightest bit threatened, Zachary laughed, a festive sound that again tipped Allistair's head. Poor Allistair, he was clearly enamored of Katharine, his human feelings much stronger than they should be. Katharine seemed unaware of all of it. She remained oblivious to the radiation her assistant was giving off. From this side of the veil, it was plain as day what Allistair felt for her. Need and want curled tendrils around him, pulled tight into himself by his own sub-par discipline. Every so often, several escaped his imperfect grasp and reached out for Katharine.

Allistair had always been a failure at this. He wasn't supposed to be human, but he had an insidious need to slide into them, to feel them. If Zachary had his way, this would be Allistair's last foray, last assignment, last chance. And so far, it seemed that Allistair would fail this one too, as he had so many others before. Even in this short mortal timeframe, he was already too entangled in Katharine. Zachary was grateful to her for being completely oblivious to the creature who presented himself as her assistant.

But Allistair was another story. The world would be a better place without him in it. He was a disgrace even to his own kind. And Zachary would be glad to help rid the realms of this interloper.

Even now he was standing in Zachary's way, having risen to his feet and concocted an excuse to look over Katharine's shoulder. Effectively, he placed his mostly mortal body between Katharine and Zachary, blocking Zachary's view of her. He could no longer read her feelings through the shield that Allistair provided merely by being what he was.

Zachary growled his frustration as he watched Katharine all but disappear behind the curling tendrils of thought and feeling that Allistair finally allowed himself to wrap around her. The second loss, which bothered Zachary more, was that he was unable to exert any pressure on Katharine with Allistair in the way. He needed to nudge her, to help her get uncoiled from Allistair. But that was an impossibility right now.

He turned away. He would make sure he saw her tonight and then he would undo the damage Allistair was doing now.

Zachary slipped away to wait.

. . .

Katharine tried to concentrate on the data retrieval program that Allistair needed help with. She didn't know why he needed the help;

he'd been going along just fine, seeming to never forget anything she told him. Then, suddenly, he popped up from his desk, complaining of problems with the advanced functions of the graph generator.

She could have sworn he'd already produced a chart for her using this program. She was certain she'd shown it to him. But she went through the steps again, patient as a lamb. He was her trainee, so she trained. His performance reflected on her, so she would show him whatever he needed. She was more than aware of his head directly over her right shoulder. Her entire body was reacting to the scent of him—or maybe just the nearness of him.

Heat radiated from his skin. The smell of him called to her, inviting her to lean her head back and test the texture of his crisp shirt. His voice, engaged in the simple task of asking questions, was a siren's song. He could break into "Row, Row, Row Your Boat" at any time and she would likely just sigh and ask him to sing it again.

Katharine forced her mind back to the task. With effort, she kept her own voice calm and modulated. She pieced together logical strings of words. She walked him through the program and tried not to notice his hand planted on the surface of her desk right beside where her own hand operated the mouse. He didn't notice that he hadn't left enough room for her to move it sideways—she had to pick the damn thing up and make short jerky movements to sweep to the right. But Allistair didn't move his hand.

Not that any of these problems shut down her want.

Katharine told herself it was because of Zachary. He'd turned her on and now she was . . . well, *on*.

The problem was, she was *on* for Allistair. She breathed in his scent, shivered at the heat and sound of his voice at her ear. And nothing else mattered at that moment. Her brain was clouded with this man, right here, right now. She wasn't lost in a high school fantasy about what would happen after school when she would meet up with her boyfriend. She wanted him now. Her glance slipped sideways without her permission and caught the movement of his mouth.

There was something deep and drowning about him. Something like the pull of quicksand or a vortex that drew the imagination, until you were stuck and there was nothing more you could do.

Her heart beat faster and she wondered if he could pick up on her rising body heat from where he stood. She glanced at his mouth again—it was likely he could sense all her thoughts, he was so close. Katharine considered squirming, but didn't think she could pull it off. It was too ingrained in her to never show discomfort. She could fake contentment, she could verbally turn unease back on the offender with an underhanded jab, but her mother had drilled into her to never let anyone see that she was anything less than at ease. For a brief moment Katharine almost laughed. Her mother should have played the world poker tour. Her greatest bluff would have been walking away without the other players realizing how crass she thought the whole thing was.

But Katharine was having an increasingly difficult time bluffing Allistair. He leaned and pointed, bringing his body in closer to hers again and again. He asked questions that bordered on repetitive, then immediately jumped to advanced issues that showed he'd already mastered some of the basics. He did it all while forming a cocoon around her that was slowly driving her insane.

She consciously regulated her breathing. She fought the rising heat in her face that was due both to her awareness of him and to her embarrassment that surely he was aware of her feelings. Resisting the urge to shake her head and see if physical movement could dislodge the sensations, Katharine missed most of his next question.

"—about the strip function?"

She did shake her head. Unfortunately, the missing moments weren't there at all. "What?"

She turned to him without leaning back, almost brushing his cheek with her nose in the process. There was a whiff of something, something eons old and distant as a sunset. She couldn't cover the gasp. Something about this man was getting under her breeding, and it was damned uncomfortable. There was no denying she didn't like it, even though she seemed to very much like him. And there was no denying she didn't seem to be able to fight it.

He didn't repeat the question.

It had happened. His brown eyes were staring at her, seeing far too much, certainly without her permission. Moving her mouth, but unable to form words, Katharine began to pull back. But Allistair followed, leaning in closer. "Katharine."

His breath played the word as a whisper across her mouth.

OhGodOhGodOhGod

Inside, her belly clenched as his mouth moved closer, his eyes searching her for something she couldn't identify and didn't want to give. At the same time she was desperately afraid that she would be found wanting.

The world melted away beyond the borders of her vision, her sole focus on his mouth as it moved to form more words. "Close your eyes."

Even knowing she was about to be kissed, she obeyed.

Moist heat from his breath touched her cheeks as his face neared hers. Her mouth lifted, just a fraction, waiting for his touch. But she jerked, imperceptibly, as his finger touched under her eye, lighting there for a moment and then lifting away.

Blinking rapidly, she slammed back to reality. This time she knew her face was flooded with red heat. And there was nothing she could do about it. She'd been so certain he was going to kiss her, and he'd . . .

"You had an eyelash." He held his finger just under the edge of her vision, forcing her to look down. But there it was. A tiny dark slash against the brown of his skin. Allistair even smiled, an infectious, engaging grin that once again altered her reality. "You get a wish."

He placed the tiny hair before her mouth and she took him at his word, wishing this would all go away. She blew softly, trying for something appropriate to the social setting of blowing on the finger of a work subordinate. But what was appropriate about it? She'd thought he was going to kiss her.

The eyelash didn't budge.

His grin widened. "You need a different wish or a stronger blow."

Katharine could only nod. She needed a workable wish. So she altered it: she wished she could find the thief and look competent to her father. This time she blew just a little harder, and thankfully the damned thing disappeared.

"Good work." He uttered the words as though he were the one training her and not vice versa, then gave a distracted look around the room and thanked her. Apparently she had suddenly answered every question he had. Or maybe his sole purpose had been to get her into that compromising position, make her think that he would kiss her, then . . .

Okay. That clearly wasn't it. Katharine berated herself for even having that thought. There was no way anyone would orchestrate that. No adult would get her worked up and then pull away just to prove that he could. No, that one had been all in her head. Instead, she found it took a surprising amount of effort to turn her thoughts back to Zachary and her work.

Needing to leave the office after that, she went in search of the payroll thief. The afternoon was spent talking to everyone in the division—ostensibly for an employee directory. She asked them questions about whether they wanted something like that, what should be included in it, and how it should be accessed. Most of the employees were open and forthright about their information. Even Mary Wayne had no issues with the entire working body of Light & Geryon knowing where she lived.

Katharine had seen her father's report. Mary had recently moved to a house twice the size of the one she had just left, one that cost more than what a person in her position in payroll should be able to afford. But there had been nothing obviously false in the woman's eyes at any time during the interview. Nothing that said she was embezzling company funds.

Katharine's gut tightened. The thief was stealing *her* funds. This would be *her* company one day. But Mary had looked straight at her and hadn't batted the proverbial eyelash. If she was the thief, then she was far better—far colder—than any of them had given her credit for.

If that were the case, this was no opportunistic swiping of spare funds but a calculated gambit by a pro.

By the time the day ended, and, more importantly, by the time Allistair had left her office and headed home, Katharine was exhausted. The other employees were gone. She had stayed as late as she could, not wanting to run into her assistant again and feel the needs slam into her as they had before. She had wandered the payroll division, checking out desk surfaces for stray paperwork and opening computer files that might lead her little investigation anywhere. All of that was legal, but she didn't dare open drawers or search anything the company didn't have a specific clause about sharing until she had a better plan and another investigator backing her up.

Still, it was fruitless. She hadn't really expected to find a computer icon labeled "How I stole the money" on Mary Wayne's monitor anyway.

With heavy heart and heavy eyelids Katharine made her way home and tumbled into bed. She hadn't been sleeping well these past few nights. She'd had only the deep, heavy slumber of the dead or a light and restless tossing, if anything at all. No wonder her body needed to catch up.

. . .

The alarm bounced sound off the walls the next morning, just as light was beginning to seep over the mountains in the east and filter around to her side of the building. Katharine stumbled out of bed.

In the mirror, she took stock while she brushed her teeth. Her hair was a mess—she hadn't brushed it the night before. Her face bore the wrinkles of the bedspread she'd bunched beneath her cheek in her sleep. She looked undead. But it was nothing a shower couldn't fix.

Against her will, her brain wondered what had happened last night while she'd been asleep. Bare feet padded into the living room, and eyes that were awake too fast scanned every inch of carpet for soot. Finding none, she moved on to the furniture and curtains. Nothing seemed touched or altered.

Good. Another clean night.

More awake, but now happier about it, Katharine climbed into the shower and cranked the heat up. She lingered as long as she could if she was still going to stand a chance to make it to the office on time, then at last took a deep breath and steeled herself to turn off the water. Stepping out into the shivering cold of the steamed bathroom, she reached for her towel and wrapped it around herself.

Only when she stepped up to the sink and grabbed the hand towel from its ring to wipe the mirror did she see it. There in the steam was a single word.

Cavē.

CHAPTER 4

Katharine was mad.

Who would write *cave* on her mirror? It was the stupidest thing she'd ever heard of. She wanted to be frightened. In fact, she figured she should be. But after all the creatures that kept appearing and disappearing and the beast with the claws the other night, well, the word *cave* on her mirror was hardly anything to scare her into a tailspin.

Who knew what it could be? Maybe it was some other language. But anyone who would go to the trouble to break in just to leave her a message would know that she'd only learned French in high school, and then not very well. Someone writing on her mirror in a foreign language? That made even less sense than the word *cave*. And she was more mad that someone had done it than that they had written a really stupid message. It just pissed her off.

Focusing on the questions the appearance of the word generated, Katharine tried to organize her thoughts. It had been written on the mirror, when? *During* her shower? That was unlikely. Probably it had happened while she was asleep. A finger dragged across the mirror would leave oils, ensuring that the word would appear while she was washing up—but no one would have to be here to do it.

And just like that, there went all her hard-won control. She had believed her night had been uninterrupted or, maybe more accurately, unvisited. Yet here was proof that she was wrong. Again.

She peered at the writing. Large but precise, there was nothing to distinguish it one way or another. Katharine had done this as a kid—written *I see you* on her nanny's mirror. Boy, had that not gone over well. But that meant she knew how the trick was pulled off. Probably every sixth grader did. Still she frowned; this was perfect. Too perfect. It wasn't in lipstick or some identifiable substance. There was no way to match the handwriting. There weren't even marks at the end of the line where the writer lifted their hand away.

She would bet her annual salary that the cops wouldn't be able to lift a fingerprint from it.

For a moment her blood ran cold as she wondered if the creature from the other night had written this. Not that it could have written anything with those long talons. Not that *cave* made any sense for any beast or man to put there, but . . .

Taking an involuntary step backward, Katharine bumped into something hard. Her scream froze in her throat and as she turned she fought desperately to keep her eyes open—to see what was behind her now.

Then she felt stupid. Really stupid. She'd bumped into the wall. Her own wall that had been there for the three years she had owned the unit. With that realization, she stomped off, her wet hair trailing down her back. She jerked clothing from her closet, not stopping to think about what was on her agenda for the day or what kind of image she needed to project. Mostly she didn't need to project "mad rage," and that was all she concentrated on.

But she couldn't put the suit on with her hair wet. So she stomped back into the bathroom and took her hairdryer to the offending word and cleared the entire mirror before turning the air gun on herself.

Later, Katharine figured she must have yanked out half her hair the way she had tugged at the snarls and hit it full blast with the dryer. As it was, she was lucky she was merely presentable. She was just on time, which was late for her. And she had to stop and take a moment to look down at her shoes and make sure that they matched each other and her outfit. She'd been late before, but being unsure which shoes she had on was definitely a new experience.

Allistair stood up to greet her as she came through the doorway to what she was now beginning to think of as *their* office. He smiled and the force of it knocked her back on her thankfully matching heels. That was enough to make her want to turn around, go home, and call in sick. For a brief moment she wondered if it was possible to call in sick after everyone had already seen her walk in. Could she say, "Ooops—didn't mean to show up, that was a mistake"? Instead she found a smile to answer him with, one she hoped didn't convey the heat that kept rushing to her face—her whole body, in fact—whenever he was in close proximity.

She had barely draped her jacket over the back of her chair when he came into her personal space. She wondered if he inhaled the scent of her when he breathed in this close, the way she did him. Then she wondered if the anger and fright from this morning had knocked her brain out of whack. Taking a deep breath to center her thoughts, she smelled him again. *Damnit.* That was not the way to calm herself. He smelled of the elements, rain and fire, wind and water. Something primal and necessary. But what was truly necessary was to listen to what he was saying and pay some actual attention for once.

He placed a short stack of files on the desk in front of her. "These are finished, but we need further research. I've done all I can do with the Light & Geryon databanks. I thought I might hit the library and see if I can pull up some archives or some connection between WeldLink and its parent company."

"Who is the parent company?" Katharine wanted to smile, but her mouth didn't want to work. It seemed her brain couldn't do much more than sort through her actions and make sure that she was making sense while her thoughts ran everywhere but where they should be. She had formulated a fine question; all the words worked together. She was sure, even though she was still too close to this man who made her head swim.

Allistair shrugged. "That's just it, I can't find it anywhere. So I figured I'd check the library as a last-ditch effort."

This time she did manage a smile. "I'll get it." It was just the excuse she needed. "What does WeldLink manufacture?"

Allistair looked at her. "Does it matter? They're making money hand over fist, and sharing it with their stockholders."

"Of course it matters." Realizing too late how the words had come out of her mouth, Katharine made an effort to sound less snappish and more civilized. She was his trainer after all. "We need to understand the market for the product. Whether it will still be there in ten years, why they've only come into our radar lately, and whether it's just a flash in the pan."

He nodded through her whole little speech, his dark hair framing sincere eyes that she couldn't look directly into for fear she'd get lost and never find herself again. His eyebrows rose. "Shouldn't I come with you then? See how it's done and all?"

"No." She shut that down as fast as she could. Where he was concerned, she needed space, not proximity. And she couldn't do what she needed if she had him hanging around. But that didn't change the fact that he was right; he should see how it was done. So she conceded a little. "Next time."

He nodded again but didn't step out of her personal space. Katharine was beginning to wonder what it would take to shake him when he asked, "Should I continue your work on the employee directory?"

She started to tell him no, but then decided it would appear more genuine if they asked the questions of more than just the payroll people. "Yes, get the acquisitions and purchasing departments."

But she found she then had to spend the rest of the morning explaining what questions she'd been asking the employees and how she'd been recording them. Katharine had no doubt that it would be done, and done flawlessly, when she returned. With two people performing her job these days there wasn't much left to do—Allistair just didn't require the expected training. She'd have to start thinking up assignments for the two of them or she'd have to, God forbid, go to her father and tell him she needed more work. That would cause problems when Allistair was removed from her office and she became overloaded.

It was several hours later before she was gathering her things to head to the library. Her intercom buzzed, but she was already on her feet and on the opposite side of the desk. This particular buzz meant that the caller was Lisa, just outside the door, so Katharine stuck her head out. "Yes?"

Her assistant lifted her almost too-blue eyes, the phone still held to the side of her head. Slowly she set it down and gathered a little dignity, pushing her platinum hair behind one ear, only adding to an already polished effect. "You have a visitor."

"Oh?" That stopped her, as it was unusual. In fact, she couldn't think of the last time she'd had a visitor at all,.

Katharine straightened. As she did so, she caught Lisa's eyes darting to her left, and that was when she saw his shoes. Shined to a high gloss, they practically reflected her face at her. The hem of silvery gray slacks broke perfectly across the top of the lace ties, and her eyes traveled the crease up to the belt and the front of a starched white shirt. She already knew who was in that shirt. She smiled all the way to her eyes. "Zachary."

This was what she needed: a reminder not to focus too much on her assistant of indeterminate age and only so much possibility.

Zachary's coloring was much like Lisa's—fair and wholesome. Briefly, Katharine looked back and forth between the two and thought what a fine couple they would make, but then brushed the thought aside. For now, at least, he was here to see her.

His hand extended to take her fingers, the contact sending electric shivers up her arm. Caught in the sensation, she almost missed his words. His voice ran over her, smooth as honey, "I was hoping to take you to lunch today, but my case ran late. Please tell me you haven't eaten yet."

When she'd gathered her things to go, she'd had no intention of spending her lunch hour actually eating lunch. But she answered automatically, even as her brain registered somewhere in the back that he hadn't asked if she *wanted* to go. "I haven't eaten lunch."

"Excellent." His fingers tightened around hers and he pulled her down the hall. The only consideration she made was that her purse was already over her shoulder; the rest could wait. After a few steps she abruptly turned back. "Lisa! I'm—"

"At lunch. Got it." Her assistant gave an appreciative grin at Zachary's retreating backside. *Well, at least I have Lisa's approval,* Katharine thought. If not fully her own.

His car awaited them at the front of the building, giving her a rare opportunity to pass by the front desk. The two employees there nodded and offered a respectful "Miss Geryon."

At the restaurant, he procured the best table, seated her, and fed her scallops that melted in her mouth along with words that melted in her brain. He was smooth, but never came across as the standard player. He seemed to genuinely think she was beautiful, perfect. Since she'd been played that way before—and more than once, given her trust fund and her future—Katharine figured she could spot the insincerity if it were there. In truth, she was relying on her instinct on this one. But it screamed at her that she was safe with him, that his words were only what he meant, and not a calculated gambit on his part.

His actions added to that faith. He didn't look at other women. He complimented her, and did it in a way that showed he'd been paying attention to all the details. And Katharine spilled the details, even grinned while she did it.

"I had to go to deportment classes. Every Tuesday after ballet."

"Is that like charm school?" He leaned back, but his focus didn't leave her.

"Heavens, no!" For this once, she let herself laugh out loud in a public place just to watch him smile. Just to feel that jolt to her solar plexus when he did. "Charm school is for tacky people. For girls who want to do"—she shuddered—"beauty pageants."

"So, no beauty pageants for our Katie?"

He'd just started doing that, calling her Katie. No one had ever called her anything so casual or endearing. She'd always been Katharine, even as a toddler. The feminist part of her spoke up, saying she should feel affronted by a man who simply took that liberty and didn't ask if she minded. But another part of her was enamored with the idea; that part of her felt coddled and cared for in way that seemed both silly and completely real. Still, while that back part of her brain nagged at her, her heart disagreed. Her heart was tugged at by this man, over and over.

He ordered them a dessert and dismissed the amount of time the waiter told them it would take to prepare. The end of her lunch hour had come and gone a while ago. But if she wasn't going to enjoy the perks of being the boss's daughter, then what was the point? So she listened to his tales of the courtroom this morning, about how he'd won his case—just barely.

Dessert slid down as smoothly as the rest of the meal, and Katharine finally made a decision, insisting that she could not take the rest of the afternoon off. She had to get to . . . wasn't there some errand waiting for her at the office? She was sure there was, but for the life of her, she couldn't remember anything that had gone on at the office that morning. That was how bad this man scrambled her thoughts. If she wasn't falling in love with him, then what?

He held her jacket out for her, leaning in to discreetly place a small kiss where her neck met her shoulder as he draped it around her. In the car, he agreed to take her back to the office if she agreed to see him again that night. Even before she could answer, he sweetened the deal by saying he'd bring dinner, not that she had even thought about saying no.

In a few minutes, they were parked in front of the Light & Geryon building again, and Katharine wasn't surprised at all by the gentlemanly gesture he made in opening her door. She was, however, surprised when he followed her up the elevator, insisting that he drop her off at her desk. Her heart lifted with the elevator as it passed each floor.

She tried to tamp down the thoughts that bubbled up. Images of weddings and babies. Corporate suits and swimsuits. Caseloads and cases of baby formula. She *had* to wait him out. She was just too smart to bank on anything this early. But she'd never felt like this before. Surely that counted for something. And maybe she wouldn't—couldn't—bank on anything just yet, but she could dream a little, couldn't she?

He walked her all the way down to Lisa's desk, where he kissed her lightly and whispered that he'd see her later. As he stepped back, her office door opened and the sight of Allistair, tall and almost menacing, slapped her with the sudden memory that he was there.

While she'd been out at lunch with Zachary she'd forgotten that her new assistant even existed. Eyes as dark as ocean depths focused on her mouth accusingly, as though he could see some kind of mark or stain from the kiss that Zachary had left there. Beside her, Zachary stiffened—it was the only thing that could have pulled her away from Allistair's riveting stare. Her gaze swung up in time to see Zachary's cool skin flush with what must be anger and his warm blue eyes turn to shades of ice.

Her own eyes felt large as saucers, until something finally snapped and she finally remembered the years of etiquette that should never have escaped her for this long. "Zachary, this is Allistair West . . . He's my new trainee." She offered up the explanation when she suddenly realized what Zachary must think to find another man waiting for her behind her closed office door. Why hadn't she thought to mention him before, to tell Zachary that she had a trainee who was taking over her office and her job . . . it was so big, how had she possibly missed it?

Scrambling for safe conversational ground, Katharine stumbled. "Allistair, this is Zachary Andras, my—"

Shit. She was at a loss on that one. She couldn't for the life of her think of what the proper term was, even though she had sat through specific lessons in introductions, and more than one on unusual or improper situations. What was he? She'd slept with him, gone out a few times. She would *not* say "lover," not on pain of death. But was he her—

"Boyfriend." Zachary supplied with smooth tones that indicated the steel behind the single word.

"Nice to meet you." Allistair's hand shot out, and though the gesture was appropriate, Katharine could see he really thought it was anything but.

Zachary merely nodded in return and clasped the other man's hand. Katharine would have sworn she saw sparks fly. She had a brief hysterical moment and considered jumping between them, tearing their grip apart. But she didn't have to. The handshake was disturbing but brief, and they pulled their own hands apart soon enough.

They were dressed like reasonable men, in ties and button-front shirts, but they regarded each other more like gladiators in the ring or lions who met at the edge of the territory each had marked. Katharine didn't like where that last analogy left her—didn't like the thought that she was an object to be fought over. Deciding the only way to defuse the situation was to remove the two men from each other's presence, she turned to Zachary and placed her hands against his chest. She tried for a light tone that belied the tension swirling in the hallway, "I really need to get back to work now. Lunch is over."

His grin wasn't as warm as it had been before. "I'll see you tonight." He said it loud and clear, staking his claim for any and all within earshot. Then he leaned over and pressed his mouth to hers, and for the first time it didn't feel warm and focused on her—it was definitely a show for the other alpha male in the vicinity. Finally, with another stare that would have withered anyone else, Zachary left.

When Katharine sighed in relief and turned, Allistair still stood in the doorway, his hands braced on either side of the frame, making it impossible for her to walk gracefully back into her own office. So she waited. Luckily, he didn't make her wait long.

"For the record, I don't like him."

Katharine cocked her head. "Well, I don't think he likes you very much either." She motioned for him to let her pass. At last he stepped back just enough to let her into the office, but there wasn't enough room for her to walk by without smelling him, without feeling the tug of his presence. She didn't think she could take much more of this. She felt like a ping-pong ball between the two of them, always waiting for the next hit.

Gathering the files into her arms, she turned around. "I'm headed for the library. I may not be back today."

Like hell I'll be back today, she thought. There was enough crap in her life without dealing with these two sniffing and roaring at each other. But she didn't say it. What she said was "I'll see you tomorrow morning" in her sweetest voice.

Only when she'd dumped the files on the passenger seat of her car did she finally allow herself to relax. With a deep breath in and a blow out, she tried to let go of all the tension, but only succeeded in releasing part of it. But part was better than none, so she repeated the breathing several more times; then she put the car into gear and headed out to the library.

Once there, she didn't even bring the paperwork in. She'd have to come back tomorrow. As she was still shaking off the bizarre showdown she'd just seen, there was no way the WeldLink research was going to happen now. Katharine didn't think she'd ever just blown off work the way she was doing today. She'd been good all morning until Zachary had shown up. Lunch had been longer than a lunch had the right to be. Then the confrontation. There wasn't enough time left for a proper library search, so Katharine did something new, something entirely against her better breeding. *Screw it*, she thought and went in through the wide front doors with her own agenda in mind.

After figuring out the basic layout of the shelves, she wandered into the reference section and started looking at dictionaries.

The *Random House Webster's College Dictionary* defined *cave* as a hollow in the earth. There was a secondary meaning: to give in. Is that what it was? A command? *Give in*. But what was she supposed to cave to? There had been no demands. It wasn't like Katharine had ever held out against anything in her life. There was no need to demand that she do what came naturally.

She couldn't find anything else that made any sense whatsoever in the other dictionaries. After half an hour she sat there on the aisle floor with all the tomes in a heap around her, thinking of everything and coming up with nothing.

As she stared at the gray, nubby carpet and tried to gather her thoughts, a pair of feet in cheap heels planted themselves next to her, and a voice more refined than the footwear floated down. "Can I help you?"

Katharine wanted to laugh, but simply shook her head. "I don't think so."

Still the woman insisted on squatting almost ungracefully, closer to Katharine's level. "I'm a librarian here. I'm Margot." She didn't hold out her hand. Her face was a shade too long, the patrician nose out of place on a woman and the mouth too full under such a nose. Katharine thought Margot's face suited her job, but her voice didn't. In practiced, cultured tones Margot spoke again. "I probably could help. I'm a professional researcher."

Well, everyone needs something to be proud of, Katharine thought ungraciously, deciding Miss Margot of the long fingers with no rings and her librarian pride couldn't fare any worse than she herself had. "All right. I got this message in the mail. It said *cave.* That's it, one word. I can't figure out what it means. It can't be a reference to an actual cave,I don't know anything about caves."

Immediately, Margot dove to the secondary definition Katharine had needed a book to come up with. "Does it mean 'surrender'?"

Tucking her feet up under her, Katharine set aside the dictionary cradled in her lap and shook her head again. "I already found that in the dictionary. I can't think of anything I even could give in to. No one is pressuring me. I'm not involved in any legal problems. No personal or corporate battles. At least none that I know of." She sighed and raked her hand through her hair, "I mean, wouldn't I have to know something to surrender it?"

"Sounds like you're right. That doesn't make any sense." Margot stood to her full height and tapped her foot in a way that said she was thinking. "It was just a note? With just the one word?"

She looked down long enough for Katharine to nod. It was only a semi-lie.

"Is it part of a series? Perhaps it will mean something after you have all the pieces?"

Katharine shrugged. "It's the first of its kind. And I have no idea what sort of message would start with *cave*."

"Then maybe it isn't in English."

What? She was opening her mouth to say all that. To say that she'd thought of another language, and already dismissed it.

But Katharine didn't get to say it. Margot was already at work, and besides, she was a professional researcher. She was probably going to make a fool out of herself. But first she told Katharine what she was thinking. Margot immediately dismissed the Chinese, Japanese, and Russian dictionaries out of hand. Katharine asked why.

"Nothing in them even could resemble the word *cave*. You would never have mistaken it for English." She turned her long face back to the shelves in front of her, her mouth pursed as her brain worked. She pulled down the German dictionary, then dismissed it too, only passing it over her shoulder to Katharine when she asked for it. But there was no mistake; the *C* section was barely a few pages, and the only thing even close was *café*. That wasn't it. Margot hadn't had to open it to know that.

The French dictionary actually had *cave* listed, but it meant "cellar." That was even less likely than the English meaning. Margot persisted. Italian had only *cavo*, meaning "hollow" or "rope."

Katharine's gut twisted when Margot tried the medical dictionary. If the word had meaning there, she wasn't sure she wanted to know. Luckily there was only *cavum*, meaning a recess. Which was a hell of a lot better than if the word *pox* had shown up on her mirror. Although at least she would have known what that meant. Then she had another thought.

Maybe she was dealing with a stupid beastie. There was no law stating that being paranormal meant being intelligent, right? Somehow her mouth got ahead of her brain and she blurted, "Could it be Aramaic?"

Margot frowned as Katharine scrambled for a plausible excuse for what she'd said—something that didn't involve visitation from black cats and creatures with razor claws. But Margot asked no such thing, just launched into another display of nerdy intelligence. "Aramaic isn't right. Again, the alphabet is so different, you would have recognized right away that it wasn't English. But it might be Latin."

Her long fingers snaked for a thick purple book, reminding Katharine of the talons she'd seen the other night. Deftly, the librarian thumbed through the pages, then stopped. "Did it have a bar over the *E*?"

Katharine scrambled to her feet for the first time since Margot had approached. "Yes, kind of."

Her heart scrambled in her chest, trying to get away from what she didn't know. She had been telling herself the mark was a glitch, an old fingerprint on the mirror, a smudge and nothing more. A bar over the letter *E* complicated things immensely.

Margot turned the dictionary toward her, one long, almost ghoulish finger pointing to the word just as it had been on her mirror that morning: *cavē*. Her voice was almost condescending, but Katharine's pulse was too fast for her to bother being offended. "It's not pronounced *cave*, it's *cah-way*."

Katharine didn't care about that, only what she read as her eyes traced the across the print.

In Latin the word meant "beware."

. . .

Zachary sniffed at the food on his counter. He'd ordered it from a nearby restaurant and wanted to claim that he'd made it himself. That would impress Katharine. However, when she caught him—and she would—the lie would not impress her. So he left the meal in the boxes.

He could have conjured it, could have simply conjured anything he needed. But the effort that act required would have taxed him. It was a great irony that in his true form he could obtain anything he needed and as many things as he needed, except the one thing he needed most:

Katharine's belief. He had to appear as she expected, as something she accepted.

She was very average in that respect. Humans in general had preformed ideas. It helped their brains deal with the world around them. But, though they had the ability to think beyond their immediate input whenever they wished, people rarely did. If you gave them what they expected, they didn't look further, didn't question. So it was far more important that he put his energy into being the Zachary she knew than making it look like he had cooked the meal for her.

His head turned. The high-end maid had left flowers in several places around the condo; he would grab one of the bouquets and take it next door to Katharine.

His mouth twitched, as though he were a real human. He wanted Katharine to come here, to his place, but that would require planning. Because she couldn't stay—he wouldn't be able to hold form long enough. If he was promoted after this task he would likely be granted the strength to do so, But again, his work was here now, and he wasn't of a high enough order to pull it off. Yet. He had to make do with what he had. So she couldn't stay. She couldn't be in his bed when he lost control of his form. Even if she slept through all of it, what if she woke in the night and he wasn't there?

No, he needed to be with her at her place—needed to be able to make his excuses, such as they were, and leave.

Wandering the unit, he looked for something to wrap the flowers in, before coming to the conclusion that he had nothing of the sort and would have to take the entire vase. He'd make sure she saw the bouquet as a sweet gesture rather than as a lack of planning. Tucking it under one arm, he grabbed the handles of the plastic sack with the stacks of savory-smelling Styrofoam boxes and turned his front door handle.

Zachary didn't bother locking it unless someone was there to watch. No one would enter his unit without his permission, and even if someone did manage to get in, once there they wouldn't steal from him. They wouldn't be able to; some deep, buried, innate sense would save them from the urge.

It was twenty feet from his doorway to Katharine's, and he prepared himself as he made the short walk. There were things he needed to do while he was there, information he had to get from her, if he was to save her from Allistair's plans.

She opened the door almost as soon as his finger lifted from the chime. Her smile was radiant, but the smell hit him like a slap across his face: she reeked of Allistair. But he couldn't say anything, couldn't react. Zachary forced a grin to his lips and greeted her warmly, even though she bore the scent of the other.

It had been clear for some time that she had been in contact with his opponent. When Zachary touched her he could pick up the tracers that Allistair left behind—he could smell the strong contact between the two, and initially he had wondered how his rival was interacting with her. But it had never been as strong as it was when he picked her up for lunch. The impression of Allistair, touching her skin, of his merely being near her, had threatened Zachary's composure throughout the entire meal.

Katharine hadn't given up any details. No matter what he'd asked, she had said nothing about Allistair. Zachary hadn't gotten a good look at his opponent through the veil the other day, but he'd been around long enough that he would recognize Allistair's eyes from the times they had crossed paths in the past. But when the sensations of Allistair's touches had been so prominent on Katharine at lunch, Zachary had been forced to follow her up afterward.

He had been so certain that he'd staked out prime territory, getting a unit next to her condo. She was easy to track and to follow. So he'd thought it would be as easy to protect her from Allistair, but that shifty bastard had actually gotten into the one place where she spent more time than her home. And Zachary was furious with Allistair for besting him, even in this slight way, and with himself for letting it happen.

During dinner, he kept a calm appearance for Katharine, and his mouth kept up with chatter and pretty compliments throughout the meal. He fed her, and part of him paid attention to the conversation and how her eyes darted to the flowers time and again. But there were more important things here than her childhood and her plans at Light & Geryon, and he needed to dig them up—needed to know what she knew.

After the meal, while they were clearing the dishes, he pushed his way in, reading her thoughts. He needed to be sure that she really didn't mind if he left her in the kitchen to clean up alone. It was ideal—he could check out her place while she was occupied. But humans were truly different from other creatures in one respect only—they were practiced liars, every one. Katharine would say she didn't mind if he left her with the dishes, but if she didn't truly mean it anything he gained in knowledge would be lost on other ground.

So he reached into her thoughts again, nudging her toward contentedness, pleased that she was so easily swayed. When he was absolutely certain she wouldn't hold it against him, he left to wander through the unit. It was a different design from his own but familiar enough that he could check the place discreetly while Katharine made noise in the kitchen.

He picked up Allistair's scent again in the living room and bedroom. But unlike the smudges on Katharine herself, it wasn't overlaid with the ripeness of humanity. His rival had walked this place often. Zachary trailed his fingers across the surface of the desk, as he had on previous visits, picking up visions and knowledge in a way that normal human flesh did not allow. He saw the creatures and faint outlines of soot, but most importantly he did not sense the human Katharine knew as Allistair.

Satisfied with his search, his feet took him into the bathroom, where he pushed the silver lever on the sleek new toilet, flushing it for effect. He washed his hands to get them wet and smelling of soap, to take up the required time. He couldn't afford any discrepancies nagging at the back of Katharine's brain. For all that she ignored the world and the cues around her, she was fairly intelligent. With the way things were going lately, she would start paying attention any day now—which was Zachary's first goal. Once she woke up, she could decide. And he had to make certain that when she did, she sided with him.

In the kitchen, Katharine was loading the last of the dishes into the washer when he planted himself behind her and wrapped his arms around her. She leaned back, enjoying the embrace she thought she knew so well. But Zachary had no guilt about her perception of him as a human lover. In the end, she would have so much because of this time with him. He would open the world to her, and give her so much more than she even knew existed. So he let himself be pulled into the want radiating off her, caught glimpses of her need enveloping him, and leaned her into the counter as she wished.

Katharine made love to him with a force he had not expected. And he took great satisfaction in the fact that their lovemaking left the tracers and the scent he needed. He would have to leave later, to recharge his energy, to change from this human form. Tomorrow when she went to work, when she went to where Allistair was, she would take this mark with her.

Only Allistair would see it. But only Allistair needed to.

CHAPTER 5

Allistair was furious and there was nothing he could do. Last night when he'd come to watch over Katharine, her bedroom had reeked—not only of Zachary, but of sex. Humans didn't truly understand it, didn't see the ties they knit each time they joined together. There was no such thing as casual sex. And Zachary, not being human, didn't knit those ties to Katharine, but she was surely binding herself to him.

Allistair forced his breathing to even. He set his hands on the desktop and, in a very human way, methodically pushed air in and out of his lungs in an effort to appear calm. He could sense her coming down the long hallway, so he straightened his tie and pushed his white shirt down his chest, smoothing it. He told himself it was all a game, that he should act as though he wasn't so invested. Not in her, not in the outcome. But it seemed he was unable to stop himself from thinking of either. This was life and death for him. If he failed . . . he likely would not be given another chance. And Katharine . . . if he failed, her life would be altered. However, Katharine's life was going to be altered either way. There was nothing anyone could do about that. It had changed—beyond her comprehension or control—the moment she'd been chosen.

The sound was the first human sense he noticed: the steady gait of a confident walk in a rhythm that was distinctly Katharine's. It should have soothed him. She was here, momentarily away from Zachary, momentarily in the sphere she shared with him. But the next thing Allistair noticed was the faint odor. Still she smelled of his rival. Still she wore a shroud of color that preceded her down the hall. Tendrils in the soft pinks of sex and—worse—infatuation reached through the doorway before she even came close.

He was losing ground rapidly if the colors came this far before she did. Already he was on the brink of losing it, just from the memories of wandering her apartment in the predawn. Against his will, he began to change. Allistair fought for control, but completely failed to gain it. His fingers lengthened while he watched, his jaw grew to support the long teeth that were one of the marks of his kind. Beneath his suit jacket, the skin of his back peeled, his shoulder blades sharpening into peaks, twin forms straining beneath the fabric.

The heels tapped closer, the scent of Katharine and Zachary and sex rolled in, and as though it had its own life or mission, it wrapped around him, angering him further. The seam down the back of his suit let out the zippery noise of stitching starting to rip as the sound of her shoes stopped just beyond the open door. He'd left it open because he had wanted to hear her approach, never imagining it would cost him this.

He took a deep breath, oxygen flowing into the lungs that still functioned. The core of him was still human, but if she walked in and saw this . . . she'd pass out, or scream, or . . . who knew? And then likely run straight to Zachary—which would surely spell Allistair's death. No matter what she was getting used to seeing at her own house at night, she wasn't prepared for this. For seeing so much of what he really was.

No, that could not happen.

So, as she came through the door, he fought for the one thing that had always been so elusive to him. Control.

He turned his head away, tucking his face down and to the side so she wouldn't see. He curled his claws into his lap and hunched over as she came through the doorway.

"Allistair! Are you all right?" Faster now, the heels clicked toward him. His eyes, no longer human, saw her feet and legs in shades of gray, her worry turning her energy from the flush of pink to a sickly yellow. It bothered him that she was concerned and he was unable to answer or signal to her. The sight of his hand or even just the sound of his true voice would give him away.

He chose to nod. At least the back of his head was intact. He'd managed to stop the change partway through. Still, he couldn't let her see him this way. There was every chance the bumps straining against the material on his back would give it all away anyhow.

When she didn't say anything, he steeled himself, fighting to reverse the effects of his anger. Anger he wasn't even supposed to feel. He was supposed to be impartial. He'd been dressed down for this sort of involvement time and time again. His kind stepped in, changed things, did their work, and got out. They didn't engage and they certainly weren't allowed to care. This was his greatest sin. His constant failing, his curse.

He saw the colors of her reaching for him before he felt the touch of her fingers through the fabric he wore. Flinching, he drew up tight, still unable to speak anything she would understand, as her hand caressed the back panel of his suit. Luckily it still held together, if just barely, though he didn't know how long he could maintain the half state he was in. Didn't know if he'd be able to reverse the changes that had already come.

This, then, was to be the end of him.

It seemed a shame to lose it all over something like this, after getting in had been so easy. Allistair had presented himself in HR as the perfect candidate. His resume was exactly what they'd been looking for, he'd made sure of it. He'd added a few things and made a few historical notes so as not to look too good to be true. But, in fact, he was. He'd interviewed with Sharon, and used what push he had to get her to convince Mr. Geryon that he belonged in here with Katharine.

Now he was exactly where he wanted to be, Katharine's hand on him, her thoughts focused on him, and it was all wrong. He was going to ruin the whole thing.

Allistair was resigned to his death just as her voice came again. "Allistair?"

His name from her lips washed over him. The word was only one facet of what he took in from her; the yellow concern had changed to the bright blue of fear. Her fear. For him. It pulsed into him, through the point of contact where her hand lay across his back, the very tenuous threads of his jacket the only thing keeping her from seeing what she truly touched. But the force of the feeling that Katharine generated was enough.

He couldn't die. He had to stay. He had to have Katharine.

From somewhere, Allistair conjured the will to force himself back into the form he needed. His eyes lost some of their ability to read the waves of colors coming off her, and the carpeting, her shoes, the worldly things he saw from his hunched-over position took on more color. His fingers shrank, the nails re-forming short and clean. His jaws clicked together as molars hit against each other, and he brought his new hands up to touch his face, feeling each part before he presented it to her. He rolled his back, the spine realigning as he did, his will a force of steel driving the changes beneath her unknowing fingertips.

At last able to look up at her, Allistair found his human voice again. "Something I ate."

. . .

Katharine figured frustration must be rolling off her in waves. She was glad her feelings weren't a tangible force—she'd bowl over everyone within shouting distance.

Allistair sat in his chair, squirming. He tugged at his tie, fidgeted his shoulders, and tapped one foot. She could easily believe that he felt her irritation, but he said he'd had bad catfish the night before and it had seemed to be bothering him all day. He wouldn't go home, though. He insisted he wanted to stay and work—and Katharine had to admire that.

Usually employees were the first to take off at any semi-legitimate ailment that presented itself. But shareholders and owners put in the hours regardless. It was a test of the worthy, her father had always said. Mr. Geryon had once wished out loud that he could drug new employees or find a way to infect them with a cold so he could see how they would fare in that situation. It would save him from having to wait until the illness presented itself, which was usually far too slow for his timetable. And God help him if he got a healthy employee. He had lamented the ethical problem of infecting people, not because it offended his morals but because he knew he was outnumbered.

Katharine secretly thought her father would be pleased if he knew of Allistair's commitment, although she personally questioned her assistant's judgment for eating catfish in the first place. It seemed like he had brought his own problems on.

She had planned to check her email and go back to the library this morning—to do what she'd been supposed to do the day before. Instead she did what research she could from her desk, mostly to keep an eye on Allistair. He'd looked pale and a little clammy when she'd first come in and, even though she was the first to admit she had no maternal instincts—from whom would she have inherited them?—she didn't want to leave him alone. She had yogurt and a granola bar at her desk for lunch, and still hadn't been able to learn anything new about WeldLink except that its parent company was called MaraxCo. Unfortunately, that name meant less on the Internet than WeldLink.

That in itself wasn't a red flag. Unless the company was actively courting new investors or selling off a greater portion of its privately owned shares, old-school businesses often weren't represented on the web very well at all. Sometimes there was a reference in another story or a byline, but that was usually it. Metalworks sold to other industries, not the public, so there was no reason to advertise or create a visitor website. Katharine would have to go back to the library and look for public records.

But not today. Not while Allistair said he felt fine but didn't eat or drink anything in the five hours they'd been here. And she'd offered.

He'd turned her down each time with a forced smile that kept some of the green in his features at bay. Then again, maybe it was better he didn't eat today.

She put him on research on the Australian gem mine—something he could do from his desk. But she was done with her standard busy work, so Katharine decided to get back to tracing Mary Wayne and the missing cash. She started with the payroll department.

An hour later she'd been up and down the elevator and in and out of the payroll files regarding the last year. Mary Wayne had gotten a raise. Not too substantial, but a good percentage. Still it was nothing that would buy her that new house. Even if she had managed to save a good portion of her pre-raise paycheck, she shouldn't have been able to do it. Not in L.A.

Also damning was the fact that Mary's was the only name on the mortgage. Since the woman had inked the deal on the place more than a month ago, the sale price was now public record. Katharine could not figure out a single way that a Light & Geryon payroll clerk could afford that kind of property. Even if she were stripping on the side—every night—she likely still wouldn't earn what she'd need to buy the spread at the edge of Brentwood. The price of the land alone was astronomical, and the closing price didn't include any homeowner fees. Katharine was sure there had to be monthly dues for the neighborhood, as there was an ornate gate and keypad for entry as well as a rock garden complete with waterfall welcoming you to Falcon Ridge.

While she'd pulled files, Katharine had kept up a steady stream of petty conversation with Brenda Hayes, the woman who manned the front desk for payroll as well as kept the employee records for the department. Well-trained in the art of small talk, Katharine easily steered the topic wherever she wanted. If Brenda realized that she was being maneuvered, she didn't let Katharine know—the woman simply spilled the beans on any topic Katharine brought up. Mary hadn't mentioned a new boyfriend. Hadn't gotten married. Neither her parents nor some wealthy distant relative had died leaving her a Brentwood-sized windfall—not that Brenda knew of. And Katharine could see from the personnel files that there hadn't been an absence for a funeral or even a vacation.

Nor had Mary shown up. Her desk remained empty the entire time Katharine was sorting through the files and chatting with Brenda. Katharine had chosen a spot with a view of Mary's cubicle. A sweater graced the back of the rolling chair. A brown leather purse listed to one side next to a potted plant with small white blooms. Mary was here. Today. But she'd been gone from her desk for over an hour.

Katharine felt she'd pumped as much as she could out of Brenda. They'd gossiped about almost everyone in payroll and a few from other divisions, just so it didn't seem that Katharine had an inordinate amount of interest in Mary Wayne. But she had to admit, it seemed her father was on to something.

As she made her way back down the hall, Katharine felt something akin to sadness wash over her. She'd liked Mary Wayne—had never in a million years expected anything like this. But that didn't change the facts, and the facts had Katharine headed straight to the ground floor and the surveillance department.

The entryway to the Light & Geryon building had high ceilings, green-veined marble floors, and a well-lit front desk. The overly designed entry also concealed the high-tech security division behind the Light & Geryon sign that made up the wall backing the front desk. Katharine slipped around behind the façade, using her employee access tag in one of the few places it was required of her. The scanner read her card, and the clear glass doors, like those in a hospital, parted to let her through.

Jeff Grason caught her first. "Miss Geryon!"

She smiled back at him. The opening of the entry doors triggered alerts all over the division, so every security employee was aware when someone came in. "Mr. Grason. Can you spare someone to help me view some tapes? Maybe see some current surveillance sometime before the day is out?"

"Of course. I'm free now. What can I do for you?"

He led her back into another room of glassed-in walls. Here, everything was visible except the safe and the division bathroom. At the touch of a button, a door slid back, allowing them access to a wall of monitors where another two employees sat drinking coffee and watching the flickering screens. Both glanced up at her and did a double-take before sputtering something to the effect of "Good morning, Miss Geryon." Each of them discreetly set down his coffee, straightened his chair, and began fiddling with something. The boss's-daughter treatment made her want to smile and cry at the same time. But she pushed the feelings down in favor of action. And she ignored the two security clerks to focus on what the cameras all over the building could tell her.

Anyone with an office door had privacy at Light & Geryon; everything else was monitored. Which meant Katharine couldn't check in on Allistair to see if he'd turned another shade of green or maybe pinked up a little in her absence. But she could watch Lisa at the desk just outside. And she could pull up tape of Mary Wayne. All day. In the employee room. The file room. The hallway. Everywhere but the bathroom.

Katharine asked for the payroll division. It only took a minute for Jeff to commandeer a few blank monitors and call up the appropriate cameras. Screens blinked to life, showing Brenda at her desk where Katharine had just left her, typing away and fielding calls exactly as she was supposed to. Another angle popped up and then a third. But Katharine's gaze was riveted to the second.

There sat Mary Wayne, at her desk, exactly where she was supposed to be. Mary made a call, entered a few things into the computer and turned back to her file. All of which she should have been doing while Katharine had been fifteen feet away talking to Brenda.

A frown marred her forehead; Katharine could feel it. Did it mean anything that Mary was away from her desk for the entire time Katharine had stood and chatted with Brenda—more than an hour—then reappeared within moments of when she left?

Jeff Grason must have spotted her frown, because he looked over from his seat and asked, "What do you need to see?"

She pointed to the screen, "Mary Wayne, for the last three hours."

"Normal speed?" He was already skipping the recording backward, keeping an eye on the clock, looking for the start time.

"Oh God, no. But I do need to see all her activities."

With an understanding nod at what she wanted and no questions as to why, he started the video. Just as rapidly, he took it from real time and clicked through a few options, speeding up the action a notch at a time, until Mary Wayne looked like a shaky version of herself. She sat at her desk for long stretches of time. Her hand, in rapid fast-forward, would dart out, grab the phone, often replacing it almost as quickly. But she didn't leave her desk. Not once.

Not until almost the exact moment Katharine appeared in the scene. "Wait. There. Go back?"

Jeff nodded and rewound a small stretch, then played the portion just before Katharine's arrival in normal speed when she asked.

Katharine watched with avid curiosity. There was no change in Mary's demeanor that she could discern. Mary simply got up and left her desk—as though she had to go to the bathroom or was hitting the snack machine in the employee room. But she did it just before Katharine arrived at the opposite door. In fact, Katharine had missed Mary by mere seconds.

Mary returned the same way—no pretense, no furtive looks, nothing out of the ordinary. It was as though she'd only been gone a minute, when in fact it had been far, far longer. Then, just a few seconds after Katharine left, the payroll clerk reappeared.

So the question was, would Katharine have seen Mary if she'd stayed a few more minutes making small talk with Brenda? Or would Mary have still arrived back at her desk moments after Katharine left?

Thanking the guys in security, Katharine headed back to her office to figure out how to test that point. The sound of her own steps down the hallway created a rhythm for her thoughts. But her thoughts didn't manage to get anywhere meaningful before she arrived back at her own office door. Allistair still sat at his desk, but he looked decidedly better than he had this morning, and he agreed with her assessment when she told him so.

"I think I need to eat something now. Something green and healthy. And I need some fresh air."

He hadn't taken a lunch break, so who was she to deny the man some real food? "Sounds like a good idea."

She'd only meant it was a good idea for him, so she was startled when he asked her to join him.

. . .

Allistair was surprised when she agreed to go out with him for the late lunch. He hadn't expected her to; he hadn't pushed her. He hadn't tried at all to alter her thoughts, even though he could have. So when she cocked her head to the side and shrugged, he wasn't quite prepared. He didn't know what to say and he wasn't sure how to turn the tide on whatever was swelling inside him. He'd like to say it was pride at the score, but he knew that wasn't the case.

"Do you know where you want to go?" Katharine glanced back over her shoulder from the office door, her jacket already slung on.

He shook his head. He'd intended to go by himself and get out of her sphere for a short while. He'd only invited her along because it seemed like the right thing to do.

No, that wasn't right. He'd invited her because he *wanted* her near, even if he *needed* to be away for a bit to gather his thoughts into something coherent. He'd imagined going alone to the little burger stand at the end of the street, but he'd told her he wanted something green to counteract the imaginary stomach upset of earlier. So he didn't know where to go.

She took pity on him. "How about Salami's? They have great salads and lots of green veggies. It's only a block away."

Katharine had already started out the door and toward the elevator when he nodded in agreement, throwing on his own jacket and straightening his tie. His feet sped up in an attempt to catch up to her. But she was easy to find. Colors, thrown from her thoughts and feelings, followed her down the hall, leading to where he found her—standing at the elevator bank, having pushed the call button, and waiting for him.

At this time of day, the hallways were virtually empty and he had Katharine to himself in the elevator. He didn't want to read her, didn't want to know what she'd done with Zachary the night before. It was bad enough that he had to see her feelings coming through the office door before he saw her; he didn't need graphic memories of touch to accompany them. But he did need to read her.

And he needed—desperately—to keep it together when he did. There could be no more errors like this morning. He had a good idea what he'd see when he looked: memories that showed him just how far Zachary had come and just how much he, Allistair, was losing. He was as upset that he wasn't the one Katharine chose as he was at falling behind in the game. Bracing himself for the onslaught, he let the back of his hand casually brush against hers.

It was a good thing he'd braced himself, but he still wasn't prepared for what came.

Though her gaze stayed straight ahead and her stance was steady, her thoughts wandered all over him. There wasn't a trace of Zachary anywhere. It was as though she had shed him as thoroughly as her nightclothes; Allistair's rival was nowhere to be found in Katharine's mind. It was Allistair himself that occupied Katharine's thinking. She thought he looked better after his bout of stomach flu this morning. She'd worried about him all day. She was disappointed with an employee named Mary, but Allistair was arrested more by the fact that Katharine found him compelling than by anything else going through her brain.

She thought him handsome. Attractive. Admired his work ethic this morning and liked the way he held himself. Allistair held himself a little straighter. From that single touch, mostly because he'd been looking for it, she had poured herself into him. And it was like nothing he'd ever experienced before. Maybe it was because he was stronger than the last time he'd tried that on a human. Maybe it was because her thoughts were about him. Whatever it was, it was heady, and he wanted—needed—another shot of it.

The elevator slowed, but they were still a handful of floors up. The last thing he wanted to deal with was another rider, but there was nothing he could do about it. Spontaneous combustion of a Light & Geryon employee wasn't in the playbook. Katharine smiled and stepped back as a woman stepped through the silver doors dragging a small crate on wheels stuffed with papers. The newcomer was too busy looking him up and down to prevent the wheels from dropping directly into the crack between the elevator and the floor.

From the corner of his eye, Allistair saw Katharine dive for the button to keep the door open. He dove, too, covering her hand with his as though it were accidental. He enjoyed the feel of her skin beneath his. Human contact was something that was supposed to happen only when necessary, but he'd always craved it when in form. Katharine's thoughts did nothing to curb his addiction.

This time he was prepared for, hoping for, the want. After the initial lightning bolt of touch, it flooded him—pictures, thoughts, feelings, all rushing from Katharine into him at the point of contact. Images from the past few moments pulsed through him. The woman pushing into the elevator, Katharine's irritation. A shocking picture of him and Katharine, clothes askew, pressed against the mirrored wall of the elevator.

His mouth went dry as blood flushed his skin.

Still touching Katharine's hand as the unwelcome woman finally got her cart across the threshold, Allistair saw Katharine's eyes.

They gave away nothing of what he saw inside her. She was completely unaware of his knowledge and it was a stark reminder that she hadn't given it freely. He wasn't supposed to be here, had no right to what he was seeing. Slowly, he pulled his hand back from hers.

Katharine smiled an innocuous smile at him, and before he lost contact, he got a fast flash of her inhaling his scent and thinking he smelled good. Just then the doors closed, sealing him in with the woman, Katharine, and the images he had stolen from Katharine's mind.

He needed the quiet of the remainder of the ride to find some equilibrium.

Katharine had touched him before. He'd touched her. Granted it had been few and far between. He hadn't gone looking for her thoughts before. But he'd not seen anything in her like what he'd perceived just now. Flashes, images, and sensations hovered, lingering at the edge of thought. Nagging him to go back and touch her again, to take more, to put action to want.

Allistair did none of that. He stood quietly, hands clasped in front of him as though he didn't know what he knew. He nodded politely at the other woman as she exited ahead of them, ignoring another long perusal. Even her nearly blatant invitation couldn't compare to the flashes of heat he'd received from Katharine, who stood as prim as the Main Line bluebloods she was descended from.

Out on the sidewalk, Katharine led the way to the restaurant, strolling casually between the clumps of people walking the other way, Allistair keeping pace beside her, his thoughts in a jumble. Perhaps there was another way to fight Zachary. Katharine was just as attracted to him as she was to his rival. And why not? The more Allistair thought about it, the more it made sense. Humans were always attracted to his kind. There was something there, just below the senses, something wild and feral that people were drawn to even though they were clueless as to why.

He couldn't help but enjoy the added benefit of cuckolding Zachary. He hated Zachary.

"What are you grinning at?" Katharine had read his face before he realized she was even looking at him.

He lied. "I just caught a piece of that couple's conversation as they went by. It was pretty racy." She didn't ask anything further and Allistair kept his silence.

That changed when they sat down in a booth at Salami's. Katharine began speaking. "Look, I hadn't intended to tell you this, but I need someone else's help and I trust you."

Here he'd gone thinking he'd had all his surprises for the day. He fought his own tongue to keep from asking her why she trusted him or from telling her that she shouldn't. Just look what he'd stolen from her not ten minutes earlier. But her faith in him was probably like the attraction—merely a side effect of what he was. Since he needed her trust, he cocked his head and waited for her to continue.

"There's a thief at Light & Geryon."

He blinked, surprised again, but just then the waitress showed up and there was nothing Katharine could say. She leaned across the table to him, the smell and heat of her swamping him when he needed to pay close attention to what she was telling him.

Her lips moved. "Can I come sit on your side?"

Allistair nodded before he even comprehended the question. She intended them to look like lovers; sadly, it was so they could speak without being overheard. Her reasons didn't change the fact that she switched to his side of the booth and pressed herself against him shoulder to shoe. That she didn't intend them to actually be lovers didn't stop them from brushing against each other, or stop him from thieving her thoughts. Each time they touched he got his own jolt as well as hers—and he tried his best to keep his mouth from curving into a satisfied smile.

"The embezzling has been going on since well before you arrived. So if you're the thief you are far too clever for us. The directory we've been working on is just a way to get information. There isn't going to be a final product—although maybe we should make one. It was an attempt to gather more about the embezzler without anyone getting too suspicious." She sighed. "I have no idea how dangerous our thief is, so you're welcome to say you're not interested, and it won't affect your job at all."

"Dangerous?" He'd been forcing himself to pay attention, but that—at last—caught and held his interest.

With a shrug in answer to him, she accepted the food that the waitress set down. When the woman became confused by their switched seats, Katharine offered a smile that was both polite and secretive. When she was gone, Katharine turned back to him, her mouth nearly in his shoulder. "It's white-collar crime. Embezzlers usually aren't dangerous. But over time it's added up to a large sum of money. The thief may get violent trying to protect what was taken."

Allistair grinned. He was hooked. Here was humanity at its very best: stealing from each other, ferreting out details, and trying to be superior in the name of justice. "I'm in." Danger didn't mean anything to his kind, but he didn't dare tell Katharine that.

Laying out the plan for him, she explained that she wanted him to go through back records and see if he could locate the thief, either by person or department. She didn't like the suspect they had already found. There were aspects that were incriminating but other parts didn't seem to fit. Allistair agreed to all of it. Katharine would be able to get back to her real job of researching the stocks that Light & Geryon was considering.

For the remainder of the meal, she didn't move. They spoke of the searches they would have to do. How he would gain access to the files he needed for his hunt. Unfortunately, she offered nothing that would make them the lovers they looked to be. He almost wished Zachary would come in and see them—although that would likely lead to another silent pissing match like the one they'd had in the hall the other day.

On the walk back he lost his focus on Katharine. Finally, she wasn't touching him, wasn't launching thoughts at him, thoughts that turned him inside out. Which was the root of all his problems. He'd been accused of liking human form too much. It was true, he did. There wasn't much he could do about it, though he did try. But it didn't stop the craving.

He'd almost been turned out after his last assignment. That final conversation still lingered in his thoughts, reminding him that it wasn't his involvement that got in the way; it was his liking of it that did. The reprimand had been harsh: *It is your ambivalence that is the problem. You are neither here nor there. And you are just as likely to find human form and walk away as to stay and continue your work. I cannot depend on you, cannot predict you, and therefore cannot trust you. For as much as he pains me, I'd rather have Zachary. At least I know where he stands.*

Though it was only words, the slap still stung, as it had been intended to. The knife twisted inside him; Zachary, who was clearly at odds with all of them, was preferred to Allistair because you knew what you would get. Perhaps it hurt more because he knew it to be a true assessment.

Allistair had sucked in air and clenched his teeth, making the effort to not retaliate. His rash responses and tendency to react rather than merely worship constantly irritated his betters. Even if he never managed to get the words out, the other still knew the thoughts were there. Allistair fought hard for control.

Then you do not need me. He had pushed the words calmly past his mouth.

Of course not.

Though it was the response he had wanted, he'd had to fight down the bitterness. *And therefore, I am not assigned. So if I bring you one, then you will give me another chance.*

Silence.

Allistair had posed the issue. Whether it would be allowed remained to be seen. Whether Allistair would follow dictates also remained to be seen. That was a total crapshoot. Both of them knew it.

I suppose.

Knowing that was as good an answer as he was likely to get, Allistair had set to dissolve himself out of the situation. But he was beaten to it. Without even a shimmer of air, the master was gone. Allistair had been left alone with only the thought of leaving still dancing in his head.

There was really no decision to make. If he simply brought another into the fold it would mean next to nothing. The lures and traps were already out there and humans fell—willingly—into them. They tended to stay within the fold and even set out to display the riches of their association, going so far as to recruit others. No, there was no glory in capturing what threw itself into the boat.

He needed to get one already devoted to the other side. Or pull one out of the opposing trap. That was where he could earn his stripes. How he would save himself. Why he desperately needed Katharine. And why he needed to remember it was all just a game. Katharine could be nothing more than a pawn to him. No matter how he craved her or how he burned for her. For he would surely burn if he failed.

CHAPTER 6

Katharine had gone to sleep feeling good. Zachary hadn't come over, but somehow she wasn't as concerned about that as she would have expected.

Normally, when she was involved with a man, she worried. Her thoughts would turn negative before she stopped them. Why hadn't he called? He was just next-door! If he was busy, was it with another woman? Why didn't he want to see her? Didn't he feel what she did?

With Zachary, it wasn't that she didn't care. Quite the contrary; she simply believed him. He said he wanted to spend the evening with her but had to catch up on work since he'd been missing so much time lately. Of course he couldn't work with her around—they'd end up having sex and he wouldn't get anything done. Though she had blushed when he'd said it so bluntly, she'd known he was right.

So she had watched some TV and had an overly casual night like she hadn't had in a while. She pulled a Tupperware from the freezer and heated one of her frozen meals, noting that her supply wasn't dwindling as fast as usual. She had sat around in her cotton pants with her hair pulled back in a ponytail, even though she knew it made her look like a teenager and all she'd ever really wanted was to be taken seriously. But suddenly none of that had mattered. Zachary was just next-door and he'd be back tomorrow—he'd said so. She had Allistair on her side at work and that was great. She held out hope that he would greet her in the morning by saying that he'd found the real crook. He would give her an unfamiliar name, and Mary Wayne would go down as a suspect who didn't pan out.

Katharine had smiled as she'd eaten ice cream straight out of the carton, for once not afraid that her mother was frowning down on her from above, concerned even in heaven about her daughter's poor manners. She had crawled into bed content as a ladybug on a rose and had fallen into a deep and soothing sleep of the kind she'd been lacking for a while now.

But sometime in the night, she sat straight up, screaming into the dark. Only no sound emerged from her throat. It couldn't. Her mouth and her vocal cords couldn't be made to work. The black was like a thick blanket wrapped around her and smothering her. As though her eyes were closed in the dead of dark, nothing helped push back the darkness. She blinked several times, noting the movement and finding no reassurance that even though her eyes were open, she could make out absolutely nothing. There was no edge of light at the seam of the window and the shade. No glow from the bathroom, where a tiny nightlight usually gave her a goal in the dark.

Growing more terrified as she discovered her absolute inability to see, Katharine tried again to scream, and again nothing came. She gave no care to waking her neighbors. She wanted them to come running, to help. So she worked her throat, having no concern for anything other than finding a response, a sensation. In a desperate bid for any kind of sensory information, her hands groped for the bedcovers beside her. But she found nothing—no covers over her legs, no sheets in her grip, no bed beneath her. As her lungs sucked in air, she heard the faint noise of her muscles moving oxygen into her system.

There was only a moment's relief in the knowledge that she had heard her own breath, that she was somewhere and she was alive. As soon as she relaxed, even as slightly as she did, she sensed it. There was something in the room with her. To her right. Against her will, her head turned, as if she might see it, as though it were safer to face it, unseeing, but head on.

She knew with certainty that it wasn't human. And, with the same clarity that came from somewhere she had never acknowledged, she knew that it could strike faster than she could think and more harshly than she could begin to imagine.

It breathed beside her, not moving air at all, but waiting, watching her. In her blindness, Katharine could sense its curiosity at her fear. She turned her head, knowing she would be looking right into its eyes were she able to see. Her heart, too terrified to speed up, maintained a slow steady rhythm that she knew the beast could hear from where it sat. The creature was unbelievably large and yet would still be stunningly swift. She perceived this with a new sense from somewhere deep in her, someplace far more elemental than she would have ever believed she possessed. The beast was fatal when it chose to be, and it had killed before, without remorse.

Still, Katharine longed to see her captor. Even knowing it wasn't human, her brain believed that if she could only see, she could stand a chance. Part of her mind nagged her, reminding her that she didn't stand the slightest chance at all—sight or not.

So she sat and breathed and waited.

Slowly, as eons passed, she felt, even if she couldn't see them, the changes that took place a hair's breadth beyond the reach of her fingertips. The beast's breathing became oxygen-based, its movement shifted air, it began to take shape and take up space. So she blinked, again and again, until finally cracks of blue came to her in a square to her left. A yellowish rectangle formed in the distance. Her brain worked, frantically testing and discarding ideas until she recognized the blue outline of the window shade, leaking light from the marina beyond. The yellow was the glow in her bathroom from the partially open door.

Grasping in abject fear, she found her hands were wound into her blankets in a death grip. She hadn't moved her hands at all; the covers must have been held tightly all along. But she only just now felt them. Slowly she breathed the room into focus. Corners and outlines formed as she watched, as though the mantle of darkness over her had thinned enough to see through and then, finally, had disappeared.

Katharine looked around the room, afraid of the last turn of her head, but she did it anyway. As she looked back to the right, back to where the beast lay waiting, she finally saw him. What must've been over two hundred pounds of lean muscle flowed under thick black fur. The mouth parted for the movement of air, stark white teeth gleaming in the faint light. Lean legs sat poised, deceptively looking almost relaxed, but ready to spring at the slightest signal. Green eyes, so deep they bordered on black, looked directly into hers. Watching her. Waiting.

Katharine didn't move—or at least she tried not to. But she was human, solid, of the land in a way she had never comprehended until she faced this beast that wasn't. It had changed while she couldn't see. It hadn't wanted her to know anything of what it really was, and this wolf that sat before her was more like a projection than a being. It wasn't real; this was only the image *it* wished her to see. But only minutes before, it had sat a breath beyond her in its true form. Whatever that was. Katharine still didn't know. She fought with herself over whether she did want to know. And whether she was better off if she didn't.

She was more than certain it could hear her heartbeat, and maybe her thoughts.

Nothing in the steady stare gave away anything she could use. Knowing nothing else to do, Katharine stared back. She held herself motionless, her breathing so shallow that she verged on passing out. Still she didn't give away more than a blink. Still, the creature watched her with knowing eyes and Katharine waited, wondering when she would die, but not how.

The teeth revealed the source of her death. She'd seen wolves before, but this was more like a hell hound. The teeth were whiter than any feral animal's could possibly be. They were longer than anything the Nature Channel had ever showed. And what little she remembered of biology told her that all this creature's long, sharpened teeth, not just the canines, were for tearing flesh. Its coat was a shade of ink that caught no light. What little there was in the room should have gleamed off the thick fur; instead, light disappeared into the animal, never to return.

But it was the eyes that were most unnerving. The green eyes were the only thing that reflected light, and they did it with an eerie glow. They held an intelligence far beyond her own.

Then, she must have done something—breathed too loudly, moved slightly, something—because the beast took a step toward her.

An untamed cry tore through the room as the beast's jaws widened. Only the sensation she felt in her throat told her the sound was her own. With the noise, the spell was broken. Katharine was suddenly terrified, and her body broke free of her control. The whimpering began in earnest, pleading noises leaking from her lungs into the preternaturally still air. Her hands twisted at the covers and her feet scrambled for some kind of purchase that would propel her away from the beast.

Still it approached. One thickly padded paw after another, each placed meticulously on the carpet, it came toward her. She slammed into the wall behind her, she was struggling so hard to get away. But she had come to the edge of her space. Unlike this creature, she was defined by her physical world—and therefore trapped by it.

In tracers and rushes of heat, she felt its breath slide across her. At last she gave in, gave up, and squeezed her eyes shut, not wanting to witness her own demise, not wanting to participate in it at all. The teeth were near her skin, she could feel the breath so close, in and out, in and out against her cheek. Her body trembled, her jaw quaking, and she didn't fight it. Couldn't.

Katharine.

It came to her—her own name on a sweet wind from somewhere beyond her terror. She wanted to open her eyes and search for the source of the sound. But she wasn't sure it was a true sound, only that she had registered it. Someone had whispered to her, her own name, in a dulcet silence. But the sound had come from far away and the beast was close. Too close to ever find out who had called to her.

She felt the thick tongue rasp at her skin, her cheek recoiling from the touch even though the other side of her face was pressed firmly against the wall. Her breath escaped her in a final bid to flee the death that was coming.

But it didn't come.

Katharine waited.

Her body took over, lungs heaving great breaths of air. Her eyes stayed squeezed tightly shut. The wall behind her pressed into her flesh where she tried to absorb into it but failed. The presence of the beast remained at her side. In a way she could only hope to achieve, it remained perfectly motionless.

Finally, she let her eyes slide slowly open. She was tired of waiting for her death, at last ready to make a small stand and look directly into its green eyes. With one last breath of oxygen, she turned her head, opening her eyes as she went.

It watched her, head cocked to the side like a puppy, a questioning look in its eyes.

Before Katharine could assimilate the expression, the beast sank quickly into the floor, leaving only a pile of soot where it had stood.

Katharine still couldn't breathe.

. . .

Though it was the middle of the night, Katharine called to leave a message for Allistair at the office, hoping he would get it in the morning. She wasn't completely certain why he was the one she felt compelled to call, but he was. In the past she would have notified Lisa, but for some reason it didn't sit well with her that Allistair would learn about her absence through someone else.

His voicemail picked up on the third ring, the timbre and cadence of his words soothing even on the recording. In spite of the comforting sound of his voice, loneliness folded itself around her, and she jumped at even the tiniest noises, though they were perfectly normal in the night.

Katharine was no longer normal. She clutched the long kitchen knife tightly in one hand, the phone in the other, and fought to make her voice sound merely tired rather than butchered.

"Hi, Allistair. Listen, I'm not feeling well. I think I'm going to sleep in; maybe I've got that stomach bug you had yesterday. I'll be late."

She didn't know what else to tell him, and was shocked that she desperately wanted to tell him that she needed sleep because of the hellhound that had visited the night before. She brandished the knife against another phantom noise and fought for something else to say. "I'll call you if I'm not going to make it in at all. Please let Lisa know. Thanks."

Out of words, she hung up.

Every light in the place was on. Her blanket and pillow were draped across the couch. The knife stayed tight in her grasp. As though any of those things was a match against what had been visiting her. Though they were small comforts, and false ones, they were comforts. She clung to them like they were worthwhile. Sinking into the couch, she picked up the remote and turned on the TV. The woman on the screen urged her to call in and purchase gaudy crystal jewelry. Katharine didn't change the channel.

Sliding down into the only kind of security she could find, Katharine pulled the covers tighter and fought for sleep amidst the noise and light that was her imaginary salvation. It was a long time coming.

Several hours later, Katharine woke in fits and starts. She'd been dreaming of the hellhound, but even in the dream she had known it wasn't real. In the dream, she'd been able to examine the beast without the cold terror of knowing she was going to die. In the dream, her fear had been something ethereal rather than the tangible hand around her heart she had suffered during the night. But the dream hadn't changed anything. It hadn't changed the fact that she was on her couch, her back pressed into the upholstery, the couch itself pressed against the wall. The knife was still firmly in her grip, her need for defense following her even into her sleep. And when she got up and forced herself to go into her bedroom, there was still a pile of soot so close to the bed that the dust ruffle was smudged with black.

Katharine stepped over it, unable to clean it or even think about it, focused entirely on getting dressed without passing out from thinking something had come up behind her. She was buttoning her shirt when her cell phone rang, the shrill tones nearly scaring her out of her skin.

After a few moments she got it together enough to answer without sounding like she'd just finished the Boston Marathon. Picking up the phone, she smiled at the ID. She sighed his name. "Zachary."

"Hey, baby, where are you?" It was a whisper that reached into her and made her feel safe. Almost beyond her control, her knees threatened to give way and her heart settled into a steady rhythm. His voice sank into her like old wine. "I called the office, but I've been getting voicemail all morning."

She almost lied. Almost said she'd been at the library doing research, that her cell had been off too. But something inside her clenched at the thought of lying to him. Her tongue spoke the truth. "I stayed home this morning. I'm only heading in now."

"It's eleven thirty." He seemed shocked by the time. Then again, probably everyone at the office was wondering if she had the Ebola virus. Katharine was never absent. She liked that Zachary seemed to know that about her even though she'd never said it. "You aren't ill?"

She opted for a combination of lie and truth. Since she'd already told the office that she thought she had a stomach bug, she went with that, just a little. "Not anymore. I had a really bad night last night. I wasn't going to be of any use to anyone until I got a little sleep." Ultimately a little was all she had gotten. But it would have to do.

"Were you sick?" His concern ran deep in her, as did the same clenching feeling that she shouldn't lie to him. But this time she did anyway.

"Maybe. I had a really bad dream; it kept me up half the night."

"Bad dream, huh?" He seemed to be mulling it over. Something in his voice made her wonder if he'd heard the lie. She was truly a bad liar. But what reason would he have to suspect anything other than what she said? She was a great girlfriend. Other than a few wayward thoughts here and there, she didn't want anything to do with anyone other than him. The only reasonable thing she could be covering up would be another man. And it wasn't that. It was just that what she *was* covering up wasn't reasonable.

She couldn't tell if he was trying to catch her in a fib or just trying to be helpful. But he offered to come over that night, and insinuated that he could help her sleep better. Katharine laughed and accepted. He would help her sleep better, but probably not the way he was intending. His presence alone would allow her to rest.

The thought pressed into her mind that maybe he could stay all night. That way the thing likely wouldn't come; Katharine had developed the creepy idea that it wanted *her*. After all, it hadn't presented itself on any of the nights when Zachary had been here. And if it did get brave and show its face again, Zachary would see it. Then she would know she wasn't crazy.

She told him she couldn't wait to see him, but that she would have to work late to make up for missing the morning. She'd come knock on his door when she got home. She then hung up before he could say anything else.

Katharine thought it might be the first time she'd ever taken charge with a man.

A sense of the inevitable settled over her as she finished dressing and did her hair. She couldn't call it peace, but the tension that had held her tight enough to snap under her own stress had ebbed away during Zachary's call. She was in a better a state by the time she went down to her car. She hit the drive-through window at a fast-food restaurant on the way into work and brushed the crumbs from her skirt as she stepped out of the car.

She faced her coworkers in the hallways as they headed out to lunch. She could tell a few were disbelieving that she was coming in so late. Others had perhaps assumed she was just coming back from lunch. Katharine didn't say anything.

She picked up her messages from Lisa and entered her office, where Allistair stood up to greet her. He came around from behind his desk and planted himself directly in front of her. Deep dark eyes looked her up and down, slowly assessing. She wondered what he saw.

His voice slid over her like honey, setting off a flare of heat she hadn't expected. "You look good." His finger came up and her breath caught as he traced her cheekbone. "But you look tired. Rough night?"

At least that was a question she could answer honestly. "Yes. I needed more sleep or I wouldn't be good for anyone."

He nodded, his eyes cast down. "I'm sorry."

"What?" But she understood the words even as her mouth asked. What she didn't understand was why he was sorry. "It wasn't your fault."

"I thought you might have had a touch of my stomach flu from yesterday." Too late, she remembered the lie she had spun, standing at her counter with the kitchen knife clutched in her fist. It had been a good lie, but she hadn't remembered it when it counted, had she? "Maybe, but I don't see how it's your fault. It wasn't like we were kissing or anything."

The sudden flash of heat in his eyes was unmistakable. Her body answered back by dropping the bottom out of her stomach and making her insides flutter. But he hadn't said or done anything. Though she wanted to, she couldn't respond to something unsaid or ungestured. As quickly as it had come, it was gone, and Allistair turned away, saying he was glad she was feeling better.

He pulled a stack of files from beside his computer, turned back to her, and followed her around behind her own desk. He was now definitely in her personal space. Did it mean anything? She flicked a glance at his face, but he was all business, the fire of a moment ago entirely gone. His voice was steady and even as he told her about what he'd found that morning. Katharine was forced to turn from her wayward thoughts and try to concentrate.

Stopping himself mid-sentence, Allistair then went to close the door, saying he'd found something important. Something that even Lisa shouldn't overhear. Katharine waited, intrigued.

Though the door was closed, he came back to stand behind her desk, right beside her. She fought the frisson of energy that shot through her at his nearness. Just that one look and she was turning to jelly around him. What was wrong with her these days?

His voice again broke into her thoughts. "I found only one person who looks like they're embezzling funds from the company."

Katharine waited.

"It's entirely possible that there's an alternate explanation, because I can't figure out *how* she's doing it. Also, a really good embezzler wouldn't show off what they'd stolen. She's hardly doing that, but she is living well above her means with no visible other income."

Katharine's heart sank.

He handed over a thick file on Mary Wayne. "She's in payroll, so she has access to everything she needs to get the job done. She also got a more thorough security check because of the payroll job, so we know a little more about her than some of the other employees. I don't know if you know her—"

The touch of Katharine's hand stilled his tongue, or maybe it was her slumped shoulders. "I hired her when I was in HR, then I trained her for her current position."

Bending at the knees, Allistair lowered himself until he squatted beside her chair, his gaze searching her face until she finally looked at him. "You like her."

"I did," Katharine admitted.

"It isn't your fault." His hand settled on her bare forearm, the skin-to-skin contact at once both very casual and far too personal. Heat flowed from him into her. And with it came the belief that maybe it wasn't her fault. It was the first time she had admitted that she truly felt responsible. She had hired Mary Wayne, over a few other choice candidates. She had liked the woman personally. Although they had never been friends—Katharine knew it wasn't proper to allow herself to be friends with an employee—she had thought she understood Mary Wayne.

She had clearly been wrong. Two separate searches had brought Mary to the forefront of the investigation.

Allistair had been watching the thoughts cross her face, and Katharine decided it was past time that she packed up her personal concerns; she could take them out later in a personal space. His hand slid across her skin as he removed it from her arm, the touch electrifying even though it had been accidental.

His voice only added to the rush of heat in her. The heat was followed quickly by confusion. How was this man affecting her so much? She seemed to have a schoolgirl's crush on him—the way he just looked at her and she felt it to her toes. But the feelings were far hotter than anything she had known as a teenager. There was something magnetic about him, and he was in her office leaning over her desk, his voice a brush of hot sweet air against her ear. She was helpless in his gravitational pull.

She pushed the words she needed past her lips in an effort to appear as though he wasn't having any effect on her at all. "What do you recommend we do?"

He sighed and something low in her melted. Katharine fought to ignore it.

"I think we should keep looking through our files, see if we can find where the money is going, or how it got out in the first place. And I think we should hire a private investigator and have Mary Wayne followed."

"A PI?"

"I assume she's the same suspect that you came up with. That's why you haven't mentioned anyone else. It would explain the look on your face."

Katharine nodded. "She's also the same suspect that my father and Toran Light came up with."

"Then I would guess that you checked for extra bank accounts that were linked through Light & Geryon but held by Miss Wayne."

Again Katharine nodded.

"You checked around to see if she had a boyfriend or renter or someone else on the mortgage to that house she shouldn't be able to afford?"

"All that, and, as best we can tell, there haven't been any deaths in her family to give her an inheritance, nor did she win the lotto."

"Yeah." He ran his hand through his dark hair in a thoroughly masculine gesture. Katharine wished she hadn't noticed. "I looked for those, too. But a professional is going to have much better access to her personal information than we do. And that way, if she catches someone following her, she won't come up to the car and say, 'Miss Geryon, what are you doing sitting outside my house at night?'"

Katharine had to laugh at that one. She actually giggled at the image of herself on a stakeout, cold coffee in one hand, binoculars in the other. As stupid as the image was, it drove home a point: she had no idea what she was doing when it came to gathering personal information on someone. "You're right."

They spent the afternoon calling two PIs they found in the phonebook, another her friend had used once, and a fourth her father recommended. They managed to interview two of them and finally went with the one her father had requested. Patricia Sange was a great choice. Katharine and Allistair agreed that Mary would be less likely to suspect that a woman was stalking her than a man.

Finding the PI took up most of their afternoon. Allistair stayed late even though Katharine told him he was excused. He said he was new to the area, and what else was he going to do anyway? She didn't say it but she appreciated the company. The building was mostly cleared out by six thirty, and those that stayed did so because they wanted to work uninterrupted. So the place was a ghost town after seven. Usually it didn't bother her, but after last night she would have likely invited the janitor in to play solitaire on Allistair's computer just to have someone else in the room.

Truth be told, if she had her choice of someone to stay with her she would have picked Allistair anyway. He wasn't the biggest or brawniest guy she had ever met, but he was solid. He looked like he knew how to throw a good punch. More importantly, he looked like he wouldn't shy away from things he couldn't just hit. The hell beast wouldn't visit her with him here.

Of course, when she went home she'd be—

Her brain cut off mid-thought. She'd be with Zachary, that's what she'd be. Her *boyfriend*. The one she'd completely forgotten about while taking the measure of the man across the desk.

She studied Allistair—he was working hard, typing and reading like there was no tomorrow. For a moment she wondered if he was faking—just tapping keys while he was really looking at porn. She wondered if his facial expression would give him away. But just then, he looked up at her and flashed her a grin that blanked out her mind again. Lord, that smile was devastating. Katharine quickly averted her eyes, trying desperately not to be pulled into whatever gravitational force the man held sway over.

She turned back to her own research. Allistair's work had yielded a few good leads on the gem mine as well as the info they needed to dig further into MaraxCo, WeldLink's parent company. They had to have the reports with recommendations to the board in two days. She was uncovering the last of what she needed on the mine. Tomorrow she'd have time to make a pretty presentation out of it.

The gem stock research was turning out to be fairly cut and dried. The mine had cheap local labor. The best anyone could tell, the gem source ran deep. But mines were always a gamble that way. This one looked like a good bet. She gathered data on the number of workers and the wages they were earning. Then she added her stamp of approval on a large stock purchase before Allistair's voice once again broke into her thoughts as he recommended Chinese delivery.

Half an hour later, they were taking a break with cardboard cartons and chopsticks—which Allistair used very well and Katharine used to make a fool of herself. But she tried to keep it together and eat while Allistair regaled her with his research between bites.

"The reason we were having trouble finding the info is that we were looking in the wrong direction. Metal works of MaraxCo's style do not make sewing fripperies."

"Fripperies, huh?" She couldn't help but grin, even though the chicken smelled delicious and she just couldn't seem to get a single bite to her mouth. The chopsticks thwarted her at every turn. Her mother's insistence on proper etiquette mandated that Katharine would never be so uncouth as to eat Chinese food from a box. Katharine's own sense of pride recoiled just as much at the thought of giving up the proper hold and using the ends of the sticks to stab the little suckers.

Allistair seemed not to notice her struggle. She didn't know whether that was a blessing or not. His voice pulled her away from her thoughts of chopsticks. "The pins that MaraxCo produces are firing pins."

"Like in guns?"

"Exactly. And they just patented a new method of pouring the molds that uses only two-thirds the metal and produces the pins almost twice as fast."

Katharine mulled that over for a minute. "Then MaraxCo could take a big chunk of the market."

Allistair unknowingly taunted her by taking a huge bite of his sweet and sour pork. "Does the company frown on purchases like that?"

Katharine blinked. What did he mean? "Investing in new technology that will likely make the stockholders as well as Light & Geryon a ton of money?"

"No, I meant firearms."

"Oh . . . no." She tried again for another bite.

"Then I guess we'll all get rich." He grinned. "How long before you ask for help with those things?"

She sighed. "That obvious?"

With a perfectly straight face, he answered, "Of course not." Then proceeded to take the chopsticks out of her hand and mold her fingers around them correctly.

Katharine wanted to pay attention to what she was learning, but it was as though the rest of the world disappeared into clouds beyond the two of them. When she tried the new hold for herself, her fingers slipped and again she dropped the piece she was after. Allistair demonstrated, but instead of watching his hands, she watched his mouth. Only for a moment did she even consider yanking her thoughts from the foolish path they had wandered.

She watched his lips as they curved into an angelic smile and, because she was watching his mouth, she didn't see the flash of sun in his eyes or the movement that brought him closer. Her body responded, sending its own flare of heat to the heavens, as he entered her space.

Still sitting against the edge of her desk, she leaned forward, reaching for him as surely as he was reaching for her. Their mouths met, devouring each other in their need. She felt him slide between her legs, his body pressed up against hers. She could feel him, hard and heavy, moving against her. His hands searched out the edge of her blouse and slipped up underneath. He was everywhere, and she wanted to respond in kind, wanted to touch him, feel the man beneath the skin. But she was held in place, her hands flat against the desk behind her, the only way to stay upright under his touch. He tasted of ambrosia and his hot touch brought her skin to life, his name escaping past her lips like a prayer.

It must have been the sound of his own name that snapped him out of whatever spell they were under.

"*Katharine*" was the only sound he made as he jerked away—almost as if by an unseen hand.

She went cold with the shock of it. In the split second it took him to mumble an excuse and leave her there, she saw that the buttons on her shirt were undone. Her skirt was pushed up nearly to her waist. And tendrils of hair had fallen from where she'd pulled it back.

She was draped across the front of her own desk, open to God and man. If anyone had walked in on her right then, there would have been no doubt about what she had been doing, only whom she'd been doing it with. Allistair was long gone.

CHAPTER 7

Zachary pushed through the veil. His wings folded in, disappearing as he became the Zachary that Katharine recognized—as he became, for all intents and purposes, mortal. He didn't really notice the loss of his wings, nor that his fingers had shortened, his legs straightened, and his size shrunk to that of a human. He was too busy gritting his forming teeth and waiting through the intense pain.

He would have bet that he'd eventually get used to it, but he didn't bet. A good thing too, because he would have lost that one. Each time it was worse than he remembered it, like a human trauma. Although he figured it was *like* human trauma because it *was* human trauma—it faded with distance. Just enough to almost be a shock each time it hurt so bad.

But he pushed through and lay panting in the middle of the floor in a huge pile of soot in what should have been his home office. Katharine had seen him haul the steam cleaner into the unit a few days ago, not that she had any clue what it was for. He was waiting for her to ask to borrow it—had schooled himself against the irony, that he owned the damn thing to clean up after his own comings and goings, but she would need it to clean up after Allistair. Well, and himself.

He couldn't very well be around all the time in his human form. He was already doing a fair job of that. But Allistair had been a sneaky little bastard; he'd gotten himself that job right across from her desk, and he had clearly been in her condo a number of times, even though Katharine wasn't aware of that. Zachary had been forced to do a little recon.

His keen hearing picked up footsteps in the hallway beyond his door; Katharine was home. So he finally dragged himself up off the carpet and out of the ash he was lying in. Pushing haphazardly to his feet, he nearly stumbled into the shower. He was in a hurry. Katharine was waiting for him. A few minutes later he was clean and more energized—as usual, the pain and effort of coming through had already faded somewhat from his memory.

He dressed hastily and proceeded to vacuum the floor. He could explain the open space in the apartment and the unused spare room since he'd only recently moved here. But given what had been happening at Katharine's lately, there was no way she would let him talk his way out of that big heap of soot. Especially when it had a Zachary-shaped dent in the middle of it. He got every last bit that he could before putting the wet vac away. He then picked out a few flowers from the stash he'd gathered earlier and grasped them into a bundle for Katharine.

Locking his door behind him, he carried the cluster the few steps down the hallway to her door. After he knocked he stepped back and waited, then knocked again. But still nothing. He had decided she must be in the shower when the elevator dinged behind him and he smelled her.

Turning in confusion, he looked down the hallway.

"Hey, Zachary." She looked exhausted, but inquired about him anyway. "What's wrong?"

"You didn't answer. I could have sworn I heard you coming in about fifteen minutes ago."

She shrugged, the movement looking like it took almost all the effort she had. "It wasn't me." She moved past him to put the key in the lock and he barely got out of the way in time. He had been so certain he'd heard her that he'd come over even though she'd said she would call when she got in.

Katharine brushed against him on her way through the door. The smell reached up and tickled Zachary under the nose. Then it grabbed him in the gut. Allistair.

It wasn't sex, but it was sexual. He'd been all over her. And this was far more threatening than what Zachary had read off her in the past. It seemed they hadn't actually had sex, but Allistair had sent her back to him reeking of intimacy. Likely, he'd known he was doing it, too.

Zachary fought the surge of anger that welled up and pushed back the desire to look around, through the veil, to see if Allistair sat, smirking just on the other side. Slowly, Zachary pushed the bile back down. He was better than this. Better than Allistair. And he deserved to win. There was no question of that. Katharine was perfect for him. He'd known that from the start. Allistair was only after her because Zachary wanted her, not because she was wanted or worthy or anything like that.

Zachary couldn't lose her. Not in that way. Not when it would be so unfair for Katharine to have to serve Allistair. She would never fit in there. She belonged here, with him. Zachary needed her. And she needed him.

Even though he had shoved back the anger and managed to hold it at bay, it still grabbed at him each time she came near. His eyes flared when she shed her jacket, and he offered to take it, using the opportunity to make certain his hand touched her skin. He saw the flash of an image: Allistair laying her across her desk. Zachary turned away so she wouldn't see the burn in his eyes.

Driving it down again, he didn't give in to the mirthless laugh that threatened to erupt when she said she needed a quick shower. A shower wouldn't wash away what he smelled. Zachary was going to have to spend the evening with her while she smelled like his opponent, which made it even more important that he didn't lose his head, or duck and run off. He'd have to tie the bonds between them a little tighter—to keep her safe from Allistair.

Sitting and waiting while the water surged in the shower, he mused that while he might have to smell Allistair on her tonight, when she went back tomorrow Allistair would smell him. Zachary would make certain of it.

. . .

Allistair was mortified. If there was one thing he wasn't supposed to do, that had been it. He fell back onto the bed, still somewhat in his human form, unable to change completely while he was so conflicted.

He moaned, and the voice that left his body told him that he was already more creature than human. Good thing he was alone. If Zachary saw him this way, he would . . .

Well, it seemed Zachary was bound to crush him one way or another.

And if his own kind saw this . . . well, they would just call the game over, laugh while they danced around his funeral pyre, and forfeit Katharine to Zachary. His teeth clicked together and his long claws nearly raked holes in his pretty, human face when he reached to cover his eyes in an oh-so-human gesture.

The feel of the comforter against his skin was a small consolation that he basked in for just a moment. The smell of the sheets, the smell of softener, fake though it was, was heavenly. There was even something beautiful in the plumes of red energy that danced off him into the darkness of the room.

He'd never opened the shades in here, lest someone see him change. All it took was once, one solid eyewitness or one person suspicious or bored enough to wait outside with a pair of binoculars. They could rouse a good modern-day witch hunt right here in Marina del Rey. It was easy to think that the Los Angeles area, of all places, would be most open to his kind. But when he was human, or even partially human, torches could burn him as surely as God's wrath.

And here he was, lying on his bed, half human, half beast, sore to his bones over what he'd done. He was failing. Maybe worse, he was failing in the same way he always did. If he failed differently, he could at least say he hadn't made the same mistake again. But, no, that consolation was denied him, too.

His plan had been to bind Katharine to him with sex. Fight Zachary's fire with fire. But the plan was to remain unattached, to keep control. If he didn't have control, what did he have? And, clearly, he didn't have control —of the situation, of Katharine, or even of himself.

Allistair hadn't altered her thoughts, pushed her to believe, or made her remember or forget anything. He didn't need to. Katharine could so easily fit in with him and his. He wouldn't push her into the bond. But he'd seen it in her thoughts, the thoughts that had rushed into him when he looked—the one time he had looked. He shouldn't have done it—knew it was wrong— but he was weak. Her longing had flooded him, surprised him, made him feel powerful and wanted. And he had easily fallen prey.

When he went to kiss her tonight, it had been worse. He had simply lost all control. Her mouth had met his, infusing him with all her thoughts and needs. He should have shut down the connection. Shouldn't have looked into her. But he didn't have to look. She'd handed it all over so freely, even if it was unknowingly.

Though he'd fought it, his human form had reacted. He had fallen prey to the urges, and there was nothing he could do. He'd wanted her so badly before he kissed her. But once he had, it had become unstoppable . . . a hurricane he'd been caught in, helpless. One he was unable to command or even navigate. And he'd almost taken her there on the desk.

He moaned again. It had been so . . . *human* of him. He was a more powerful being than they were . He was supposed to have full control. He wasn't supposed to feel like they did, and on those rare occasions when it surprised him, he was supposed to override it. That was the rule: walk among humans, but don't *be* human.

Only nothing was working that way. For him, nothing ever had. The feelings didn't just surprise him, they bombarded him. Day in, day out. It was getting so he felt them even when he wasn't in human form. He wasn't able to control them. Sometimes he could manage to maintain himself in the powerful wake the emotions left, but he'd never been able to rule the feelings themselves.

He had *wanted* Katharine. He had *needed* to drive into her. To own her, possess her, consume her. Still he longed for the feeling of her naked skin next to his. Or, better yet, under his mouth.

He didn't understand why he wanted her so badly. Even with all he knew of human feeling and the way that it dominated him, he still didn't understand how she alone was a stronger tide than all the rest. Once, he'd done heroin. He'd been assigned to a group of homeless men, and he'd needed to be trusted. He'd shot the drug directly into his human veins and felt . . . nothing. He'd had no side effects, no cravings, no addiction. But *Katharine* . . .

It wasn't just her, either. There was something about this incarnation that was worse. The sheets beckoned to him, always begging him to lie down on their cool softness, to skim his hands along their soft yet rough texture. The window shade allowed the neon light outside to seep in around the edges, and the play of the glow on his retinas fascinated him, too. Beyond the window the ocean was four blocks away, calling to him even now to dig his toes into the shifting sand, to sink into the cold water, to feel the push and pull of the tides.

A human would have been invigorated by all these feelings. But he wasn't. Though he loved them, they didn't make him feel better. He wasn't supposed to have them, let alone enjoy them.

He had to face Katharine again tomorrow—had to find a way to apologize and yet still leave the door open to connect to her even more strongly than he had. And to attach to her more strongly than Zachary had, too.

Still, he wanted her in ways he couldn't comprehend—in ways that would have left a mortal man invigorated and in pursuit. Instead Allistair just felt battered. He would likely die of it and wash up like so much flotsam on heaven's shores.

. . .

Katharine woke to confusion. No one had visited her last night. Well, no *thing* had visited her. No creatures came; there were no mysterious soot stains. She'd fallen asleep in the arms of a man—a man she was falling in love with. Wasn't she?

Regardless of those feelings, she still hadn't really slept. She'd gotten as little sleep as she had the night before when the hell beast had appeared.

Zachary had come at her with a vengeance. It was as though he knew she'd been with Allistair, even though she hadn't truly *been with* Allistair. She was a bad liar, and she counted herself lucky that she didn't have to say anything. Ultimately, she hadn't had to act guilty or secretive. Which was a good thing, because she'd been too shell-shocked to try to hide anything. But Zachary didn't ask. He was just a complete gentleman. Still, he'd made love to her until she screamed out his name. Three times.

Then he'd left. Said something about needing to get up early and not being able to actually sleep beside her. Her bed was too small, his body too cramped.

After being so wrung out, Katharine had mumbled what he took as an agreement. Assuming it didn't matter whether he was there—she was at the very edge of an exhausted coma, anyway—she let him go. Part of her raised the battle cry that he should stay. But she didn't know how to tell him why she needed him, didn't want to cling, and was still fighting generations of breeding that believed unmarried women should not have overnight guests. In the end, she said nothing, and he walked out the door with a sweet kiss to her forehead just before Katharine fell bonelessly to the mattress.

But she hadn't slept.

At first she had stayed awake, caught up in her thoughts. Zachary couldn't have known about Allistair—or he would have stayed, right? That concern volleyed in her head about three times before the memories of Allistair caught in her throat and took over, bombarding her with images and flesh memories of being pressed up against her desk and kissed with abandon.

She shook with need. She wanted Allistair. How could she? After this evening? After Zachary?

She was terrible. What kind of girlfriend was she?

Her head swam. Zachary had been wonderful. She'd been fully there, with him, the whole time he'd been making love to her. But now her thoughts were somewhere else.

At about 4:00 a.m. the thought came to her that, while Zachary didn't know about what had happened with Allistair, Allistair knew about Zachary. He knew she had a boyfriend. One serious enough to come to her office and get her for lunch. One serious enough for the two of them to have that silent pissing match in the hallway.

At that, she'd sat bolt upright. The men had already circled each other once. There had been something even back then, when she couldn't see it. And Zachary knew that, too. He knew she went to work every day with another man in her office. Yet he hadn't said a word. Did he think it wouldn't come to anything? Did he just trust her that much? Because clearly he shouldn't. She rarely even thought of him when Allistair was around. And the opposite was true, too.

Two men.

Either of them perfect in some way. After that long dry spell she'd had, she should be happy to be wanted by two men. But she sure as hell didn't need all of this at once. An embezzler in the company, two men, strange animals in her room, and an even stranger animal living under her own skin. She hardly recognized herself.

That made it hard to get up and get dressed for work, but she forced herself to do it. She'd been skipping out and living by a crazy and unpredictable schedule these past few weeks. She needed to be at work whenever she could be.

As she brushed her hair, she thought that looking at her face in the mirror was like looking at herself for the first time after she'd lost her virginity. She wanted to see if she looked any different on the outside. Because the Katharine she was on the inside wasn't the same woman who had lived there just three weeks ago. In fact, Katharine now didn't even know who that woman had been.

In a fit of restlessness that continued on the drive in to work, she stopped at a fast-food joint for breakfast. She'd done that twice now in the past week but couldn't remember when she had eaten fast food before that. The first time had been out of necessity. This time was out of want. She pulled up to the speaker and ordered a syrupy sausage biscuit and side of hash browns that ultimately amounted to deep-fried tater tots. Then she added a Coke.

She ate in her car in the restaurant parking lot, not wanting anyone she knew to see her, and not wanting to taint her indulgence with the hassle of driving. She ate every last bite, her body rebelling against the change from a small serving of granola and yogurt.

At last she sat amidst the trash and wrappers and stared out into space. Katharine Geryon had just completely snarfed down a fast-food breakfast in her car. But she didn't snarf. She didn't eat fast food. And she'd always kept her car immaculate—the only thing she drank in the car was water, just in case of a spill.

Now there were crumbs everywhere, as if the foil and waxed wrappers weren't evidence enough of her excesses. She took two deep breaths and began shoving all the papers down into the bag. She wadded it up before throwing the car into gear and tossed the bag into the trash can as she drove by it. She was barely going to make it to the office on time.

The food hadn't helped her decide how to deal with the Allistair situation. And she needed an idea—a plan—and quick. If he wasn't there when she walked in, then he would be within minutes. There would be no avoiding the man who worked at the desk across from hers. The drive wasn't long enough to come up with a solution. Hell, a cross-country trip wouldn't be long enough. She was way out of her league. Apparently her entire life had recently gotten way out of her league.

She decided as she pulled into the parking lot with her usual friendly wave at the attendant that her league seriously sucked. Her mother had prepared her for high tea and cotillion. Her father had prepared her for boardrooms and contract warfare. Nothing had prepared her for anything she suffered now. There was not a single weapon in her arsenal that would help here. And she had only the three minutes it took, give or take two, to get to her office from the front lobby to figure something out.

Katharine walked down the long hall to where Lisa sat working diligently on . . . something. For once Katharine didn't know what her assistant was up to. Chalk up another new experience. At least Lisa still said good morning and handed over the stack of message slips like she always did.

Just beyond the open door, Allistair sat at his desk, working as though last night had never happened. For a brief moment, she wondered if it hadn't happened at all. Maybe she had simply imagined or dreamed it. Maybe it was some cologne he wore or something, because she was having the most vivid thoughts whenever he was around. Maybe last night she'd finally gone so far as to hallucinate.

Katharine said a polite hello and considered that regardless of the reality of the previous evening, nothing good could come of it.

"Katharine." He smiled. Her name rolled off his tongue and into her chest, catching in her lungs. Allistair stood and gently closed the door behind her.

For a moment, she panicked. Like a wooden puppet, she went behind her desk and sat arranging her coat and briefcase, as though there were protection to be found in the routine or behind the expanse of wood. Her brain roiled. What would Lisa think about the closed door? What would anyone think? While a lot of the employees around the office worked with their doors shut tight, she usually didn't, although lately she and Allistair had been closing the door a lot to discuss the embezzling issue. As her mind churned out a plausible excuse, Katharine began to breathe easier. And she waited and wondered.

How was he going to explain last night? She certainly couldn't.

He came up behind her as she sat down at her desk, the same way he always did, hovering over her as if to protect her from some threat above. His voice was low and melodious in her ear.

"Patricia Sange works quickly."

What?

He kept speaking. "Apparently, one of her employees works around the clock and is amazing at forensic accounting."

She found her brain again, at least the part that made words. "What's forensic accounting?"

"Following old money trails, basically."

"Ah." This was not the conversation she had expected. Furthermore, as much as she had dreaded the other topic, she found she was disappointed to be discussing the fabulous Patricia Sange and her talented employee.

"So, the Light & Geryon money is going into an account in Panama."

"Panama?" *Wow*, her conversational skills were seriously lacking this morning.

"Yes, we are truly neck deep in an honest-to-God fraud situation."

"Oh, shit."

Allistair didn't flinch, but she did. Now she was swearing, too. She didn't swear. Or maybe she did and she just didn't know it. *Fuck*.

He pointed to a file she hadn't even realized he was holding. Her teenage puppy dog eyes had missed a lot, it seemed. "With the access you granted to the company files yesterday, they already confirmed that the money is leaving through the payroll department. It appears that the first shuffle was about four months ago, and in that time the thief has managed to steal about seven hundred thousand dollars."

"Crap." This time she didn't berate herself for swearing.

"Katharine."

"What?" She hauled herself back from her mental calculation that someone was moving almost two hundred grand through payroll each month.

"I want to tell you that I'm sorry about last night. That it was a mistake. That I won't bother you again." His words played havoc with her insides. Again he had taken her completely off guard. She—who manipulated diplomats and businessmen like a true aristocratic woman, then got them to sign on the dotted line while she batted her eyelashes—was getting snowed by her own trainee. Worse was that she didn't like what he was saying.

She opened her mouth even though she had no idea what would come out of it. But it was his voice she heard.

"I can't."

"Can't what?" God, she was so confused.

"Can't tell you that." He took a deep breath. "I'm not really sorry. I'm only sorry that I stopped. That I took off."

"Oh, Lord." Her heart turned over in her chest. Her eyes were drawn to the fullness of his lips, and her brain was drawn to the wish that he would kiss her again.

His mouth pulled into a wry grin, and the shine of it reached his eyes. "That's exactly what I was thinking."

His hand came up behind her head, cradling the weight, guiding her until her lips touched his and lightning burned through her system.

CHAPTER 8

Allistair pressed his mouth to hers, already feeling his control washed completely away in the whirlpool they had created. He had other senses. He smelled the people out in the hallway, usually saw their tracers before they came in the door. He knew of the other side of the veil, of the creatures that moved freely just beyond the air. But all that disappeared into the void he created with Katharine.

For a fleeting moment, he wondered if this was what humans felt when they loved. Where he came from, emotion was always grand and simple, not this complex, consuming passion.

Katharine leaned into him, returning the kiss and wiping all other thoughts clear of his head. When she had walked in, he'd seen and smelled Zachary all over her, but now those tracers had all but disappeared, unable to cling to her in light of their mutual want.

Her hands worked the knot of his tie, gentle tugs that loosened the restraining silk. His fingers undid the tiny buttons at the front of her shirt, and he rapidly became frustrated with the barriers that kept him from her skin. When at last the material fell away, he was faced with her bra.

The lacy fabric hid little from his gaze. He wanted to touch the garment and make it melt away, yet that posed another logistical problem. It would take so little from him to do it. But as he assessed her, her eyes watched him with a wealth of trust and need. Even if she didn't realize what had happened, she would later, when her bra was literally nowhere to be found. And his Katharine had enough unanswered questions in her life these days. He couldn't risk her knowing what he was, or what he was capable of, until much later. So he peeled her blouse and jacket in one move and dropped them to the floor behind her desk, then pushed her gently, draping her over the arm of her chair.

His mouth found her throat, his tongue tasting the sweet pulse beneath her skin, the flutter serving as a reminder that she was human, where he was only human enough. He traced a wet path along her neck and down her chest, encouraged by way she moaned seemingly against her will. The smooth satin of her skin passed under his hands as he attempted to feel every inch of her. He dispatched with her bra, a quick flick of his wrist sending it against the wall.

A gentle tug came at his wrists, soft but insistent. In his surprise, he saw that she had his shirt undone and off, except for the cuffs clinging slightly at his hands. With a shake, he shed the last of the fabric and reached around behind her again. The frenzy in his brain led his mouth up her stomach to the soft peak of her breast. He lingered, tasting and testing, engulfed in the sweet and full fragrance of her.

Her hands searched him, feeding him her need and hot images of exactly what they were doing. Allistair felt the tide washing over him, her desire for him and her enjoyment of his touch spurring him on. Her fingers found his hair, a sweet caress against his head that became a pressure urging him to meet her mouth with his, press their naked torsos together and hold tight.

He lost even the most rudimentary of thought processes.

Their hands were frenzied, pulling and prying at each other's remaining clothes. They wound up naked on the floor, in the cramped space behind her desk, soft carpet rubbing against their skin. When their movement brought him around on top of her, Allistair pulled his knee up between her thighs. Her legs parted, then wrapped around him, urging him to do exactly as he wanted. With an uncontrolled gasp pushed from his throat, he entered the soft, wet heat of her body.

His senses bloomed, opening to all the sounds and smells around him. His vision went to shades of gray, with great peals of color showing the emotion pouring off the woman writhing beneath him. Quickly, he buried his head in the warm curve of her neck. Her pulse teased him with the hot scent of blood and want just below the surface of her skin. He moved within her and his brain was shot through with indefinable streaks of need.

He felt everything. The carpet, rough against his bare knees and feet. Her legs, silky to the touch but iron strong around his hips, urging him deeper inside. Her arms, brushing against his ribcage as her hands stroked his back. His shoulder blades, sharpening and trying to push through the skin that defined him.

Fear pushed him to move harder against her, into her. As she moaned against his chest in response, he moved his hands along the underside of her arms, capturing and guiding her hands up and over her head. Lacing his fingers through hers, he intended to hold her somewhat captive, to keep her hands from finding the changes being wrought on his back.

Instead, he had formed a circle.

There was a reason prayer was performed with palms pressed together. The link to oneself provided an energy few people were even aware existed. He had just formed that bond with another. She had no control over the flow of her own thoughts and needs into him, or of his into her.

So he buried his face against her. He couldn't let her see his eyes. She wouldn't comprehend the depths in them. She'd be frightened, and rightfully so. So he kept his face averted, moving against her, within her, while she arched to meet him, her face pressed to his neck, her voice becoming stronger as she neared her peak.

At last, he cried out himself, straining against her, releasing the last of his humanity into her. She cradled him, her legs entwined with his, her fingers gripping him tightly—for or against what, he couldn't tell. Blinking, he watched as the world slowly came back into standard color. The sharp pain across his back receded, and he could tell that his human body had righted itself.

With their hands still laced together, he pushed himself up a bit to watch her face. He could see Katharine's world coming into focus, could see the moment she realized she was pressed against the wall, spread out on the carpet behind her desk, completely naked. He could see the moment she realized who she was with, and he was unprepared for the jolt of pain that was purely his.

She had wanted him, clawed at him, then at some point had become a writhing, needing ball of sensation. So much so that she had misplaced herself. And had been surprised that it had been with him.

Allistair fought to disengage his feelings. He needed to get off her, off the carpet, and to pull back from the pulse they had created both together and within him. But he couldn't bring himself to do it. Instead, he lay down, heavy across her soft form, pinning her there. His fingers toyed with her hair, and he enjoyed the feeling of her breasts pressed against his chest while he thought about what he should do next.

. . .

Somehow the day had reverted to normal.

At least externally it had. Inside where no one could see, Katharine was put together backward and upside down. And she had to fight hard to maintain as normal an appearance as she could.

Allistair had eventually stood up from where they had rolled on the carpet like a couple of kids in a hayloft. Only it hadn't been that good when she'd had clandestine sex before. Katharine had stayed seated on the floor, shaking her head when he offered her a hand up. She figured the nap of the carpet was imprinted on her back and her butt, and no one needed to see that. So she sat there and pulled on her underwear and hose, straightened her blouse and slid her arms back into it. The nude lace bra was invisible underneath, and she was still too hot to bring herself to put her suit jacket back on. Somehow she managed to refrain from fanning her face.

While Allistair watched with a glint in his eyes, she managed to get her hair back up into something of its original form. He smiled. "That looks good."

Her eyebrows rose at his first words since . . . well, since. "The question is: is it good enough?"

He tilted his head, his hand coming up to catch her chin and turn her face from side to side for inspection. Her breath caught at the simple touch, and the smell of his skin warned her that whatever had brought them crashing to the floor was far from over. She still wanted him, and she wondered if she would survive everything turning inside out the way it was.

"I think so." His words were vaguely reassuring, even though he was certainly referring to her hasty hairstyle rather than her inner turmoil.

He hadn't said anything after that, just fetched her heels and knelt to slide them slowly onto her feet one at a time. Surely he was looking up her short, straight skirt as he did it, but he didn't say anything or even smirk. His hands had run gently up her legs when he finished and he had crawled the two paces in between her legs to plant a kiss on her forehead before nimbly pulling himself off the carpet and returning to his desk as though nothing had happened. As though Katharine usually sat on the floor in the corner.

There had been nothing to do but follow his lead and return to her work as though her life was all just fine and dandy. When it certainly wasn't. Hell, she almost preferred the creatures wandering through her condo at all hours of the night to dealing with this. At least she didn't think the animals were her fault.

Katharine settled herself at her desk without looking up at Allistair, even though she desperately wanted to sneak a peek. Only her rigid upbringing held her back from blabbering about the whole thing, from asking what the hell had just happened. She managed to keep her mind on task only enough to turn out the reports her father wanted on the potential purchases. Research was, after all, her technical title, although lately she'd been spending a good chunk of her time as trainer and investigator.

When lunchtime rolled around, Katharine felt the desperate urge to flee the room, to get out and away from Allistair and the memories of the floor behind her chair. Though she was considering when and how she could be near him again, it seemed he'd gotten her entirely out of his system. He hadn't shown so much as a hint that anything had occurred between them. Not that she could tell anyway, given that she was *not* watching him. Although she wanted so badly to leave, Katharine couldn't bring herself to do it. She'd whiled away a good part of her morning fucking on the carpet rather than working. Add in that she was already overpaid compared to the other researchers—apparently the "heiress" qualification was worth quite a bit—and because of all that, she figured she owed Light & Geryon another working lunch.

So the only relief she would get until Allistair left was the few moments it took to wander into the employee lounge and grab one of the yogurts she kept in the fridge. She lingered on the journey, stopping first by the ladies room to kill some time, and finally began to breathe deeply. Then she made her way into the lounge and pondered the snack machine for several minutes before choosing a granola bar and slowly fishing out exact change. After she grabbed a plastic spoon from the supply bin, she headed back to her office, back to her waiting assistant with the killer smile and wicked style.

He was at his desk, busy typing away, when she entered. If he felt any of the remnants of the morning, it didn't show. In fact, he looked up and smiled at her slightly, then looked back at his work, as though nothing were amiss. And maybe for him it wasn't. She didn't know his work history. Maybe he screwed all his trainers in their offices during work hours. He was certainly hot enough. Maybe he thought this was a standard Light & Geryon initiation. Maybe she was finally, truly insane.

But she had a report to file. So she got back to it. She wanted to ask if he would have the recommendation for the gem mine ready by the end of the day. But that would involve speaking to him—something she didn't trust herself to do. She had plenty to keep her busy without speaking to him. They were writing the first report, against investing in the paper manufacturer. The stock was climbing, but not at the rate

Light & Geryon would have liked to see. And there was nothing special about this factory or this paper or this process; it was likely a random event that had led to the climb in stock price. It probably wouldn't yield any real value to the portfolio, and Katharine couldn't find anything to indicate that they should put their money in it. Luckily that made for short work.

It was the MaraxCo report that was using up her day. She and Allistair had gathered reams of information on the company, once they'd found out who and what MaraxCo was. It all needed to be compiled into pros and cons—although there weren't many of the latter. MaraxCo was making money hand over fist. There was something unique here, both in the product and in the process. The fact that WeldLink was already partway through obtaining the patent for its method was even better. The stock would likely rise significantly when the patent was officially awarded. But Katharine was good at her job. She didn't need to wait for the patent. WeldLink was going to get it; they had everything in place. All that was left was for Light & Geryon to invest a huge sum of money in the company.

Her fingers worked rapidly over the keyboard, her yogurt and granola bar disappearing in small bits. The only thing she noticed was that Allistair hadn't moved much at all. Maybe he didn't need food. Maybe she'd hear his stomach growl in a few minutes.

An hour later, she was nearly finished, but she'd hardly moved a muscle the whole time. A moment's disjointedness perturbed her brain. Why didn't she move more? Wouldn't she rather have a job where she could be physically active? See the sunshine outside her window? Or even *be* outside?

Her brow furrowed and she forced her attention back to the finishing touches on the report. She'd never had a thought like that before in her life.

So she dismissed it now.

At last she had the final pieces in place and could avoid it no longer. "Allistair?"

"Hmmm?"

She sighed in disgust at herself. The sound, his voice between pressed lips, had vibrated her very bones. But she tried not to show it. "Have you finished the report?"

Picking a folder up from the edge of his desk, he nodded. "Right here."

The words escaped her mouth before she could corral them. "Then what have you been doing?"

He was on his feet and coming toward her, the small sounds of the office loud around them. The hallway was empty; only the occasional distant ping of the elevator broke the silence outside the door. Dark had descended beyond the window shades, and Katharine had a vague memory that Lisa had stuck her head in the door and said goodnight, although she couldn't have said exactly when that had occurred.

Allistair moved to close the open door, and Katharine's heart sped up a little more as he reached to turn the lock. "I've been waiting for you to finish."

Suddenly on her feet, she came around the desk to meet him. There was a tinge of anger in her brain, something she needed to tell him. But the thought dissolved, sifting through her grasp the moment his hand came up and touched her face. Something lingered in his gaze; something in the slight caress told her she was precious to him, though she couldn't fathom why. Something deep, beyond her comprehension, pulled her toward him, though she knew for certain she should say something to keep him away. But she'd forgotten what she needed to tell him.

She forgot her own name as he pulled her closer. This time, when he kissed her deep, she sank willingly against the edge of her desk. She shifted her weight and helped when his hands cupped her and lifted her against him to settle her on the edge. Katharine clawed at her own clothing, wanting to be free of the restrictions.

They didn't make it all the way to naked, somehow more frantic this time than they had been before. Her skirt was rucked up to her waist, her hose destroyed and dangling from one foot. Her blouse was open and pushed back, the cuffs having caught at her wrists, effectively binding her hands behind her.

Allistair's hands were not restrained; his shirt merely dangled open, allowing her to nuzzle at his exposed flesh, to kiss along the line of his ribs and up his neck as he struggled with the bindings on his pants. Her mouth was still on his skin when he groaned and pushed into her again. His weight and advantage bore her back over the desk, pressing her down onto her papers, making it impossible to avoid full-body contact with him.

She didn't want to avoid it. Katharine breathed him in, writhed against him, cried out with each delicious push and drag of him inside her. She strained to free her hands, wanting to touch him as he touched her, needing to hold his face and turn his eyes to hers. But she couldn't. She was captive beneath his strength and held by the shirt she would gladly rip if she could. His body moved against hers, making sparks she hadn't known existed, but his face stayed averted.

His mouth touched her neck, her ear, her shoulder, as her tension built. The sounds she couldn't help but make surely told him she was almost there. She heard her name in her ear, in a version of Allistair's voice. Deep and almost guttural, it sounded as though it had crossed some great distance to get to her, although she could feel his breath on the side of her face.

One last time he pumped into her, his voice repeating her name in waves. *Katharine Katharine Katharine Katharine Katharine*

At the last moment, she fell over the edge he had pushed her to. Her head dropped back, over his arm, and her body rolled to the rhythm of his voice, until the waves subsided and she was deposited back in her body, atop her own desk.

. . .

Something was wrong with Katharine. Zachary frowned at her as she stood in her doorway, but he made his voice as soothing as possible. "Katie."

She backed away, into her condo, but her face told him not to cross the threshold. "Don't come in. I'm sick."

It was a bald-faced lie. She wouldn't have even been able to pull that one off with a human male. To him, the lie radiated out from her, screaming that it was untrue. The problem was that he only knew that she lied; he didn't know what the truth actually was. And calling her on her lie was a bad idea at this stage of the game—when she stood in her doorway telling him to go away as she oozed the scent of everything she had done with Allistair so recently.

He tried again. "Tell you what. I'll bring you chicken noodle soup, and warm blankets . . ." Zachary trailed off. She was already shaking her head. "Katie?"

She made her voice sound deeper and scratchier, the notes ringing false all around her. "I feel really sick. I don't want you to catch it. I think I'm just going to sleep all day tomorrow."

Only the last line held a grain of truth to it. Whatever else was going on, she actually intended to go right back to bed. "Will you call me when you feel better?"

She nodded, but even the simple movement was another lie.

Still, he had to push what he could. "I'll see you tomorrow then, baby."

With a small shrug that was a cross between a nod and a head shake, she closed the door on him.

Katharine was done with him?

No. It wasn't possible. There was no way that Allistair had taken her and won her over by that simple act. Only the strongest could manipulate like that. Allistair didn't have that kind of power—he barely had control over the power he did have. Certainly Allistair and his ilk were very charismatic; it was where the idea of thrall had originated. It was the spark for the idea of human hypnotism. And Zachary too had it in spades.

Or he thought he had—somehow that had changed. It seemed now he couldn't even get Katharine to open the door to her boyfriend. Never mind that she'd been with another man since she'd seen him last. He couldn't hold that against her. It wasn't the way she usually operated. He knew that. They all did. Katharine had lost every single secret long before this game had even begun. She was being pulled now, tugged between him and Allistair like a toy. That was why she had been acting this way. She was behaving like what she was: a pawn.

Zachary walked back down the hall on mortal feet, letting himself in through his front door. But when it closed behind him, he began to change. His skin lost some of the pale beautiful color he had earned. His eyes grew in size and depth, his jaw expanded. Lean, solid muscle flexed beneath his slick new skin. He had to get back into Katharine's home. Back into her head.

He couldn't let Allistair have her.

In his own shape, he walked the confines of his condominium, thinking. Perhaps Allistair had been on his way over to play with Katharine some more.

All the better. If Allistair arrived to see her, he would have to look human. In keeping form, he would lose some of his senses, some of his strength.

So Zachary would sit and wait like this. As himself, he'd know of Allistair's approach long before his opponent sensed him. He'd hear all the movement and what words they said on the other side of the flimsy barrier.

He settled in, snug against the wall, waiting for the vibrations that would tell him what he needed to know.

. . .

Katharine knew the pounding in her head was merely the exaggeration of her heartbeat. That didn't keep her from feeling like someone was beating her skull with a mallet. And it didn't look like it was going to get better anytime soon; the day was getting progressively worse.

That wasn't a good thing, since the trouble had started when she arrived home Friday night.

Fresh from her second tryst with Allistair, she had snuck into her own unit, not wanting to run into Zachary. She was pretty sure she'd succeeded, too. Until he showed up at her door just after she'd settled into her couch in her sweats. It wasn't until she heard the knocking that she decided she needed the weekend to herself. And rather than saying so, she'd lied—straight to his face—which was just another sign that her life was going to hell.

Wasn't that what she liked so much about Zachary—his trustworthiness? He did what he said he'd do. Zachary wasn't out tomcatting when he wasn't with her; she didn't doubt what he told her. But she herself was another story these days. Sweet Katharine, who always did what she was supposed to and didn't lie, had full on cheated big time on the best boyfriend she'd ever had. Then she'd lied to his face.

She might have felt better about lying to him if she'd suffered a good dose of guilt about it. About *any* of it. But she didn't. She couldn't dig up any shame. She felt bad about cuckolding Zachary, but mostly she was upset that he'd be upset when he found out. Not that she felt bad about it. Her brain certainly knew that what she'd done was wrong. But she couldn't conjure a single *feeling* about it.

Her only consolation regarding the lie was that later the next day she decided she actually was sick. Maybe a brain tumor, pressing on some vital decision-making part of her cortex.

In the end, she'd accomplished nothing. Katharine hadn't called Zachary all weekend, hadn't left her condo, hadn't even ordered food in. She'd heated up her Tupperware meals that had been accumulating since Zachary had taken to feeding her. She hadn't gotten dressed at all; she'd sat on her sofa, eating and watching CNN.

All the while her brain had wondered *why?*

Why hadn't she told Allistair that she couldn't? Sure, she had been befuddled, but couldn't she have uttered, "I have a boyfriend"? Then again, Allistair *knew* she had a boyfriend. There had been that meeting of the lions circling her like fresh meat in the hallway. Had it been some kind of superiority fuck?

Just the thought of that made her wince.

She didn't even try to deny to herself that there was every possibility that she didn't stop him simply because she didn't want to. Her brain had been fueled by images of the two of them tearing at each other's clothing for over a week now.

Allistair hadn't called her all weekend. Not to ask how she was, whether she wanted to see him again, or even to apologize. Zachary hadn't come back either. And there hadn't been any animals visiting. Maybe there was some cosmic awareness that Katharine needed her space. That, if you confronted her, she'd just as likely rip you a new one. So no one came around. And Katharine settled down.

In the end, she'd done what she always did. She ignored what she could and got on with her life.

She had curled into her bed, her back pressed into the far corner against the wall, and grabbed what little sleep she could. Monday morning, she woke up with her alarm and checked her apartment for soot. She dressed for work and ate a bowl of granola. When she went down to her car, she looked straight ahead and didn't admit to herself that she hoped she wouldn't run into Zachary.

She arrived earlier than Allistair and was glad that things were back on track. This was the way it was supposed to be. Or so she thought, until her trainee arrived, right on time, and casually closed the office door behind him.

As if it were perfectly natural, he came around her desk and used his foot to scoot her chair back while he perched on the edge of her desk. His arms came around her and pulled her out of her chair, positioning her body flush against his, his mouth finding hers and seeking every corner.

Some deep part of her thought she ought to be offended at the way he invaded her personal space, at the assumptions he made. But that part sat back and watched the greater part of her lean into him and forget everything else around. It was a mystery how much time passed while they necked on the corner of her desk. It was the ringing phone that brought them both out of their daze.

His mouth and his voice found her ear. "Answer it."

Strong arms rotated her to face the phone while warm lips found the base of her neck and placed small, sweet kisses there. Her arm snaked out for the handset, the distinct sound of the ring finally penetrating her brain and telling her that someone was calling her desk directly, bypassing Lisa. She stiffened in Allistair's grip as she answered. "Katharine Geryon."

"Patricia Sange." The voice was smooth and professional, and Katharine took a moment to be grateful that the door was already closed. Inside three minutes Katharine had all the information she needed.

"Thank you." She set the phone back in the cradle and turned to Allistair, who had loosened his grip on her as he sensed the importance of the call. "The account in Panama traces back to Mary Wayne. The original payout has an authorization code that was never assigned, but that Mary Wayne certainly had access to."

He only nodded.

There wasn't opportunity to respond further, because the phone rang again. Again the ring was indicative of her private line. She picked it up, still trapped within the circle of Allistair's arms. "Katharine Geryon."

"Katharine," her father barked. "We have a problem with Mary Wayne. I'll see you in a minute." With that, he hung up.

She turned to face Allistair, "I have to go see my father regarding Mary Wayne. Come with me."

Her eyes searched his face and found no trace of artifice. His fingers tucked a stray strand of hair behind her ear, lingering on her skin and settling himself a little deeper into her soul. This time, she did remember Zachary, waiting for her somewhere beyond the boundaries of Allistair's arms. But it didn't affect her at all; nothing penetrated this bond when he was near. He nodded, agreeing, and slowly let her go. His fingers trailed down her arms, briefly twining their grasps before breaking the contact.

With a subtly flirtatious smile she didn't know she owned, Katharine led him out of the office.

CHAPTER 9

Both her father and Toran Light had frowned as Allistair entered the CEO offices right behind her. But her assistant hadn't seemed to take as much offense as she did at the gesture. It was Katharine who directed Allistair to a seat, playing the hostess and being gracious despite the ire of both the older men.

For just a moment she toyed with telling her father that she was sleeping with her new assistant. On her desk. During work hours. She stifled the smile that fought to escape and made formal introductions even though she was sure either her father or Uncle Toran had met with Allistair previously to hire him. Then she settled gracefully onto the couch beside Allistair as she smiled at the two owners of the firm.

"Allistair has been assisting me with this search ever since you were able to rule him out as a suspect. He knows as much as I do about the Mary Wayne issue." She didn't pause to let them voice any concerns; she wasn't stupid. "What can we do to help?"

With a breath in, Uncle Toran started. Katharine was grateful that he addressed his statements to both of them.

"Mary Wayne just gave us one month's notice. Her letter of resignation was tendered yesterday. It showed up on my desk this morning.

We need to know where she stands in this investigation. Is she still a suspect?"

Katharine's eyes darted sideways at Allistair, as if for confirmation. Which was ridiculous. She had never needed confirmation on this kind of thing in the past, but now automatically she looked to her assistant? She shook it off and started speaking. "She is no longer on the suspect list; she *is* the suspect list."

"Explain." Her father sat back, his arms extending along the top of the sumptuous leather sofa, as if he knew he was in for a long and unpleasant story.

"The private investigator we hired traced the missing money to a single account in Central America. We found out this morning that Mary Wayne is the sole holder of that account. Also, the money was moved using a pay code she had access to. It's either an excellent frame job or Mary is our thief."

She quit speaking and waited. One of the men would say something; it would just take a minute. Allistair was smart enough to stay quiet too.

Uncle Toran formulated words first. "Maybe she *is* being framed. She moves all that money into a single account with only her name on it. Seems a little obvious for a smart thief."

Allistair opened his mouth at this point. As it appeared none of them had expected him to actually participate, his voice startled all of them. "Really the name on the account isn't an issue."

"How so?" Arthur Geryon took the bait but didn't move forward, didn't budge.

"That's not how she hid the money. We weren't supposed to find the account at all. At least not until it was too late, so her name being on it doesn't matter. And she was right about that. It was very well hidden; we would never have found any of it without Patricia Sange's company. The reason Mary Wayne used her own name on the account is that she did such a good job of getting the money out of Light & Geryon that she didn't think she needed to hide it anymore."

"Well, we did find her, so she wasn't that brilliant."

Somehow she knew what was coming, and Katharine wondered if she should stop Allistair. But she couldn't bring herself to do it. So she listened.

"With all due respect, sir, you didn't even know that she was taking the money until a few weeks ago. She's been at this for months with no one the wiser. And without some serious professional help, we would never have found that account." He leaned forward, his elbows resting on his knees in a casual position that conveyed he was comfortable, even among these people who probably only had a Webster's definition of the word.

She watched while her father absorbed the idea that his employee had bested him. Then they all discussed what to do. Mary Wayne needed to be confronted. Charges needed to be pressed. Katharine voted to give her one opportunity to defend herself, with the head of security present, of course. After a little badgering, her father and Uncle Toran agreed.

Afterward, she and Allistair went back to their office and tried to come up with a good excuse to talk to Mary Wayne without making her run.

. . .

Jeff Grason stared at the video footage, just as perplexed as Katharine was. For three days now she and Allistair had been trying to get Mary Wayne in for a meeting. For three days they managed to miss her—just barely miss her—each time they tried. She left work early. Took lunch at an odd hour. Went to the ladies room with an uncanny knack for timing. Yesterday evening Katharine had hung out in the lobby, waiting for Mary to pass by on her way out. She was going to pretend to have run into her. But Mary Wayne hadn't come by.

Katharine had waited and waited, but as time passed, her pretense of work at the lobby desk wore thin. This morning she had arrived early and tried again. At ten thirty she had given up and gone to the security division to ask them to keep an eye out for her.

Jeff Grason had agreed to keep an eye on the cameras. As Katharine had been leaving, he hollered to her retreating form that she should come back.

Typing in any employee's name would bring up the nearest video surveillance. In Katharine's case, this was the hallway outside her office door, and for Mary Wayne, who had a cubicle, it brought up a clear frame of the woman's desk.

Mary Wayne was sitting in her chair, working away.

Katharine's brain stuttered. "How did she get there?" There was only one way in and out of the Light & Geryon building that wouldn't set off serious alarms and security checks. "Unless she just didn't go home last night."

Grason shook his head. "That couldn't happen. Security would have found her, and someone would have been notified or it would have been logged."

Katharine was sure her face must have shown her confusion. Security was certainly the next division she needed to learn, as she clearly didn't understand all that was going on.

He explained. "Night shift makes a sweep. Security logs everyone in and out. Last year an employee was investigated as part of a hit-and-run investigation. He claimed he was working late that night. We showed the police his computer logs, and it was clear that someone with his access codes had been doing his work on his computer at the time of the incident. We even had footage of him entering and later leaving his twelfth-floor office. It made for a pretty airtight alibi. We can also show you that Mary Wayne wasn't here last night."

While Katharine watched footage of the darkened office in fast forward, she could see that there wasn't any activity around Mary Wayne's desk all night.

"Maybe she stayed in a different part of the building." Then she groaned. "Would that require watching every video camera, all night, for signs of movement?"

He shook his head and offered a slight smile. "It's not so bad as all that. But it would be a pain. So let's not do that unless we have to. Still, you might want to pull up a chair."

Katharine nodded and then settled in and listened as he explained what he was doing. First, he checked for when Mary Wayne's computer activity had stopped the night before. Then he used that time as a starting point for monitoring her desk. Sure enough, she stood up, grabbed her bag, and headed down the hall. A few camera switches allowed them to follow her all the way to the lobby—and right past Katharine.

"Go back!" Katharine almost apologized for the outburst. It was so unlike her. But Jeff Grason didn't seem offended, and he was already reloading the footage she wanted. As she watched herself on the video, her own eyes seemed to look right through Mary Wayne. The woman had walked blatantly in front of Katharine, as though she didn't have a care in the world.

Son of a bitch. How had she missed that?

Katharine shook her head as Jeff Grason rewound the footage again. The third time through she was able to voice her disgust. "I completely missed the one person I was looking for. And then I stood there for another two hours waiting for her to go by."

Jeff Grason seemed like the other security employees she had met at the firm—he wasn't fazed by anything. He just offered a kind smile and a suggestion. "Let's see when she came in this morning."

Twenty minutes later Katharine was seriously pissed.

She fumed her way up to her office wondering if Jeff Grason was watching her in the security cameras and if she was leaving a trail of smoke behind her. Twice she had stood at the front desk, pretending to work. Twice Mary Wayne had walked right by and Katharine had been totally oblivious.

How? How had Mary done that? How had Katharine missed the one person she was looking for?

She wanted to stomp right up to payroll—Mary Wayne had been sitting at her desk when Katharine left the security division. But Katharine was smarter than that. She'd blow everything if she went up there in a huff. And given her thief's ability to be absent at just the right times, she would probably just make everyone else nervous.

Instead, she went to her own office, upset about the whole thing. Lisa stood abruptly and asked if she could help, but Katharine refused. That earned her a sour look. Though she wanted to soothe the hurt feelings, there wasn't much she could do about it. She couldn't tell anyone about the investigation, certainly not her assistant. And she and Allistair had been locking the doors so much to talk about it . . .

She looked at Lisa. "It isn't what you think it is."

Lisa sat back down, but her eyebrows declared Katharine a liar. Katharine closed the door and sagged back against it. She *was* a liar. It was a lot of exactly what Lisa thought it was. As she spotted Allistair looking up from his desk, her hand reached back and clicked the lock on the door.

His look was sympathetic. "Baby, what happened?"

But Katharine shook her head. She didn't want to talk. She just wanted to feel.

Perhaps she had gone crazy. Zachary had come back to her after the long weekend. He'd come to her condo every night. Each night they had made love and he had left. That meant he wasn't there to see her getting dressed in the morning. He didn't know that she had put on an old camisole with straps that wouldn't stay up. With her gaze on Allistair, who was still in his seat, she shed her jacket and pulled her strapless bra out from under the silky material, just the way she had planned this morning.

She had worn a garter belt today rather than panty hose. She'd pulled her underwear over the top of the garters, telling herself it was easier to use the ladies room that way. Which was *true*. It just wasn't the *truth*.

Allistair's breathing was heavy by the time she reached his chair.

She was a fiend.

She was likely going straight to hell.

. . .

Allistair lay on his back in the sand. He was completely naked and breathing heavily, with Katharine curled at his side. Just as naked and just as sated.

He had convinced her to come out with him tonight, to walk on the beach, to talk with him. As usual for them, one thing had led to another, and another—right there in a little secluded piece of beach they had found.

He had kept her on top, his eyes enjoying the sight of her in the moonlight, his skin savoring the twin bites of brisk air and cold sand abrading him from either side. There wasn't enough of her to have. She was nearly enslaved to him, a servant to the drive that bound them.

Which was a good thing.

The fight for Katharine's soul had devolved into attempts to monopolize Katharine's time. Clearly at this point neither he nor Zachary had the advantage of being her lover—her only lover. She was sleeping with both and had no real loyalty to either. Zachary did have an advantage over him, though. Allistair knew. It was as he had suspected from the beginning—Zachary didn't get himself involved. He stayed beyond, above, unattached, while Allistair fumed about having to share Katharine with his rival.

He was angry at her for betraying him even though he knew she hadn't—she had promised him nothing. He was angrier at himself for wanting that promise. Not that it mattered; he couldn't have her anyway. All of this was temporary. Even Katharine herself.

He pressed his anger down to a controllable simmer. He had her right now, so for this moment he had the advantage. Unfortunately, he couldn't hold form long enough to keep her. He knew she would stay with him if he didn't leave—just as she would stay with Zachary if he never left either. She was a captive of the pull they exerted on her, and she was drifting back and forth like the tide. And, like the ocean, she was following without thought or aim.

That was another reason Allistair was mad, though this part was directed at her. Katharine was drifting. Even with everything that was going on all around her, with all the things she had seen and was experiencing, she was questioning so little. When she did question things, she seemed to stop as soon as she received any answer—right, wrong, or incomplete.

He wanted to rattle her, shake her awake to the world around her. She didn't see it, like a child who believed that if she closed her eyes no one could see her. At the least, it was foolish. At the most . . . well, for Katharine, it could prove deadly. But if she just looked . . .

If she opened her mind to see what awaited her, she could have a life she'd never dreamed of. He could offer her so much. Then again, so could Zachary. If the consequences weren't so dire, Allistair would have been tempted to force the decision. To just tell her it didn't matter what she decided, only that she did.

As the days passed by, he was losing ground. By merely staying still, he was falling behind Zachary.

He was also losing form. Making love took a large store of energy, just as it did for humans. The expenditure of effort was part of the binding process, but humans just required sleep and food to restore themselves. For him, he needed to cross over. His skin twitched, itched. He was running out of time.

Tenderly, he urged Katharine up from their hiding place. He offered a feeble excuse and helped her dress. She smiled at him like it was all okay, but he wanted to scream at her that *nothing* about it was okay. His immortal soul was on the line. And so was hers.

She gave no indication that she was upset that he didn't walk her up to her door, that he just dropped her at the door to her building and told her she'd see him tomorrow morning. The fact was that he *couldn't* walk her up. He was about to be overcome by the change. He couldn't risk running into Zachary. In Allistair's weakened state, Zachary would have all the advantage.

There was nothing more he could do in this form anyway except hold on to Katharine for another few seconds. She still wouldn't look up, still wouldn't see what was right in front of her face.

All the clues and cues were laid before her. In the end, it made her no different than any other human. It was the way of the earth, something God had put into place eons ago. If they looked, truly *looked*, people would find all the answers they needed. But they didn't look. So no one saw what Allistair really was, though he passed countless souls on the way back to his small house. Any of them could have—*should have*—seen the truth. But there were old beliefs in place and, if you never looked beyond them, the partial explanations stood. The blindness remained. You saw what you expected to see.

And if Katharine wouldn't start looking around for herself, he would have to force her to.

Unfortunately, Zachary probably had a similar idea.

. . .

Katharine sank back into her couch. The weekend was upon her, and again she had told Zachary she didn't feel well. Again she was holed up in the one place where she felt the least safe—her own home.

She stuck her soupspoon into the Tupperware and tucked the dish up against her chest to keep the casserole noodles from dropping onto her sweatshirt. As usual, she wasn't sure what the greater sin was: eating on the sofa, eating directly from the container, or using a soupspoon instead of the proper fork. She could feel her mother frowning down on her, could practically hear the voice urging her to get up and set a place at the table, to plate the food to look like she'd cooked the meal, even if the extent of her effort had been waiting the three minutes while it microwaved.

Fuck you, Katharine replied to the imagined mother-voice in her head.

That alone almost gave her pause. She *loved* her mother. That the woman had been overbearing had been almost a welcome relief in the face of her father's missing emotions. Her mother only wanted the best for her. Katharine had known this—better, she had *believed* it—from when she was old enough to understand. She had never said anything so vulgar to her mother. All through her teenage years, she had never even *thought* anything like that.

Her teeth worried at her lip as she wondered if maybe she really did have a brain tumor. Her thoughts and emotions were running rampant these days. She was like a dog in heat around two different men, and no matter how she resolved to refuse either of them, she never even made the most basic of motions.

She wished her mother were here now to talk to, although nothing in the woman had ever surprised Katharine. Her mother had always held to her party line regardless of the situation. So Katharine could, at this point in her life, basically recite what her mother would have said in any given scenario.

But the litany held no comfort. The thoughts and worries scattering through her brain were so far out of the realm of things her mother had dealt with that Katharine wasn't even sure the woman would ever understand. Certainly not when she herself was so far from any kind of comprehension.

In an effort to clear the thoughts she didn't like, Katharine ate another bite of her dinner and picked up the remote control. The TV surged to life. A shellacked brunette hairdo framed a face that spewed news while bright tickers ran in every direction, revealing the absolute latest news on sports, stock prices, and the war.

The anchor was talking about the case of a veterinarian who had been abusing the animals he was supposed to humanely euthanize. Katharine couldn't care less and lifted the remote and changed the channel.

The screen flickered but the brunette popped back up, ending the sentence that should have been cut off.

Katharine pushed the button again.

Again, the television flickered but remained on the same channel. The light on the remote had blinked red, indicating that it had sent the signal. Another button brought up the channel and program title across the top of the screen, so that part was working fine. She turned the television off and then back on before trying to change the channel again, and wasn't surprised when nothing more than the same slight flicker occurred. It seemed the TV thought it was changing the channel. Only it changed to the channel it was already on.

Well, she was smarter than the TV, right? Katharine tried typing in the digits for a different channel, and the numbers appeared on the screen as she pressed the buttons. She smiled, but when she hit "enter," they were immediately replaced by the digits of the same news station she was already on.

Maybe the number she'd typed didn't correspond to a channel she got.

Katharine tried again, this time inputting a number she knew was part of her programming.

Again, the channel stuck right where it was. Only the tiny ripple through the picture and sound acknowledged that she'd even tried to change it.

Half an hour later, Katharine had checked every wire, called the cable company, and waited on hold for ten minutes only to be told that service in her area was just fine and any problems she was having were likely due to her remote. She tried using the buttons on her set, even though she didn't think they'd been used before. It took her five minutes to find them, but when she pressed the tiny "channel up" button, the channel remained unchanged.

She couldn't play any of her prerecorded shows. Couldn't swap the inputs. All she could do was turn the set off and on.

She sighed. She'd be lucky if anyone would come out to fix it on a Saturday. Certainly no one would come out tonight. And what if she was incredibly unlucky and the repairman had the same effect on her as Allistair and Zachary? What if she started having random affairs with every guy she met?

Katharine wanted to laugh at the thought, but it really wasn't funny.

She thought about just turning the set off, but her dinner was cold and she was hungrier now than when she had sat down. She re-nuked her food and settled on the couch again, grateful that at least it was stuck on a channel she often watched.

Stories of far-off floods and earthquakes dominated the screen while she ate the casserole one small bite at a time. It wasn't the best programming for eating, but it was clearly all she was going to get. The field reporter turned the show back over to the brunette, who briefly thanked him, then promptly changed the subject again.

"A series of gun accidents has killed over twenty U.S. residents in the past three months."

Great, Katharine sighed to herself, another great dinner topic. She watched because she had nothing better to do.

"Misfirings are causing the weapons to explode at the handler rather than toward the target. This is occurring only in the latest model of the weapon, meaning that the vast majority of those harmed have been law enforcement officers, who upgrade and receive new arms at a far higher rate than the average gun owner."

Katharine chewed methodically and went for another bite without looking down at it. Her spoon scraped at the bottom of the plastic until it found a piece of pasta in the corner and captured it while she watched now with rapt attention.

"In related news, many of these same weapons are turning up in Sudan and Zaire, where fighting has escalated drastically in just the past week. The recent influx of cheap, faulty weaponry has not only increased the death toll, it has given peacekeepers a harder time maintaining any semblance of order in the area. Efforts to extract asylum seekers as well as workers for various peace organizations have ground to a halt. The African contingent of the Red Cross alone has suffered fifteen related deaths this week. Lieutenant Craig Seger, a military weapons expert, has joined us here in the studio. Welcome, Lieutenant Seger."

The camera cut to a man with quarter-inch hair that stood straight up from his head. Muscles bulged from his olive green T-shirt, and his mouth didn't budge from its grim, straight line, even as he talked. His hands moved as deftly as his words, taking apart the gun while he spoke.

"We don't know why, but some sort of cash surge occurred somewhere along the way. We know the weapons we are seeing were intended for sale in third world countries, as most of them have never borne serial numbers or any identifying marks."

The brunette's smile was out of place, but the scene had Katharine leaning forward.

"Would you say that's unusual?"

"Absolutely. Most of what we see in Africa are laundered weapons—guns that came from some legitimate source initially but were stolen or rerouted from their intended path. African guns often come from misappropriated weapons seizures or caches of guns that the U.S. Army has deemed unfit and sent to be destroyed. Or possibly from weapons holdings of now-defunct governments. But that's not the case here. These guns are new. And they're cheaply constructed."

He started showing the various parts of the weapon. "The barrel looks like a standard gun, but the metal composition is poor, meaning it's more likely to crack or degrade. The grip often isn't secured to the mechanics of the gun properly, so the gun can literally fly apart as it fires. And the firing pins we are seeing are made of a new metal composite and are constructed in such a way as to save material. Unfortunately, that means they don't last and often fail right at the critical point—as the user is trying to fire the weapon."

His voice kept going on, but Katharine's eyes were riveted to one spot on the screen. He held up the pin, pinched between his beefy fingers.

She had been looking at those pins for weeks.

All of the Light & Geryon portfolios had poured money into MaraxCo. They had even moved it from other funds. Shuffled all kinds of things to get as much as possible into MaraxCo. Was this how their expected profits were being generated?

She hadn't once looked beyond the bottom line. She had been quite satisfied that the pins were selling well. Hadn't asked where and how WeldLink was selling them.

But how could she have been so stupid?

At her request, Light & Geryon had fed money into WeldLink. So that WeldLink could make firing pins. There was only one thing a firing pin was good for.

The brunette had handed the program over to another reporter while Katharine sat there, her eyes glazed and her brain churning. The Tupperware still clenched tightly in her hand, Katharine jerked herself off the couch, upsetting the remote as she did. It hit the floor, jarring buttons and making the red light blink.

The TV channel popped over to a cartoon.

. . .

She didn't sleep. Hadn't slept. Hadn't spoken to anyone. Didn't know what to do other than roam her own apartment aimlessly and lie in her bed, twisted up in her covers.

She reminded herself that she hadn't pulled the trigger.

In general, she thought guns were okay. Her family—her father in particular—had always believed in every man's right to bear arms. Katharine had agreed. But she was beginning to see merit where she'd never seen it before. That your guns never stayed just your guns. That maybe outlawing firearms was safer.

The truth was, she didn't know. She didn't know what to think or what to do aside from being grateful that she hadn't been visited in a while. But the creepy animals would almost be welcome at this point.

What she did know was that she hadn't looked any further than those blindingly beautiful profit margins. While WeldLink may or may not have been selling their guns to third world countries directly, that's exactly where their guns were going. They were the only ones with that firing pin technology. The weapons had reached Africa with such speed that Katharine would like to point to that evidence to let herself off the hook. She desperately wanted to be able to say that Light & Geryon money hadn't been responsible, that this had occurred before they had been involved. But the fact was that MaraxCo had opened themselves to investors. Investors who would make these massive transports possible. Light & Geryon had jumped to fill that spot. At her request.

Her bed mirrored the pattern of her thoughts. The covers were scattered and hanging off the edge; the pillows looked abused and worn. Katharine herself looked no better. She'd swum in the haze of her own stupidity for two days. She hadn't showered or dressed, had merely eaten and scoured the Internet for whatever she could find about MaraxCo's guns.

After two days, she had a lot of information.

It was all right there at her fingertips. It had been there weeks ago, too. Only this time she didn't limit herself. She tracked the product far and wide, and she didn't like a single thing she saw.

When she became too upset researching the firing pins she switched gears and tried the gem mine she had also recommended investing in.

Her heart twisted with each new thing she found. It was just as ugly. If she had dug back a little further the first time, she would have seen articles that not only suggested, but held explicit evidence, that the mine had been discovered by an Aboriginal family that had met with a vicious accident. Katharine wanted to believe it was just that, an accident. But the more she followed the breadcrumbs, the seedier it got.

Local families were working the mine without any benefits or health care. They were cut off if they became ill or were injured. And injuries were common. Kids were dropping out of school to cover for parents. And no one was paid the minimum wage. Sure, there were laws, but because the company was providing housing and food, legal loopholes allowed wages to be much lower.

One reporter had followed through after a particularly nasty cave-in that resulted in the families of five dead men being kicked out of their homes—housing units that should have been condemned long ago. There were often a handful of families in only a few rooms. The food was scarce and half rotten. The outback, where the majority of the Australian mines were located, was rugged and hot. There were no buses no nearby towns, nothing in any range. And no one visited or monitored the owners. Because everything was flat and open, the few visitors they did get were spotted from miles away, giving the businesses enough time to put up appearances and make nice. Even worse, when the families were kicked out of company housing, there was literally nowhere for them to go.

Katharine couldn't breathe.

She had stared at her jewelry box for an hour, wondering where her pretty baubles had come from. Wondering whether anyone had died for the emeralds her mother had cherished. The collection in the safe set into the wall held sapphires, rubies, topaz, amethysts, plenty of diamonds—and maybe a thousand lives.

Finally, on Sunday night, she had packed herself off to bed, praying for sleep to rescue her and afraid of what she'd dream. But she hadn't dreamed. She'd lain in bed, wide awake, eyes fixed on the ceiling. Her peripheral vision followed the arthritic sweep of the minute hand on the old wall clock, once around every hour.

At five in the morning, the world beyond her window offered the faintest change of color, signaling the new day. She slid from bed and headed to the bathroom. Her eyes narrowed and she stopped in the doorway.

When had she last been in here? Only a little while ago. Her research had been fueled in large part by candy and Cokes, so she'd been up and down all night.

And the one thing that had pleased her was that she hadn't been visited.

But now even that was beyond her—because she had been visited.

This time the words didn't need steam to appear. The letters were red, like lipstick. Except she had never owned this shade. Again there were no smears or smudges to give away the writer.

Katharine walked right up to the mirror, too tired to be anything other than stupid. She pushed her left finger into the first word and rubbed, destroying its perfection. It felt like lipstick, although there was every possibility that she had just put her hand directly into something toxic. But it didn't burn. Her breathing was remarkably normal considering how ominous the words looked.

daemon te venatur

HAYSTACK

CHAPTER 10

Katharine decided she had a far better chance of bumping into Mary Wayne somewhere random than of finding her at work. So she didn't go into work.

Besides, she needed to know what the hell was on her mirror this time. So she went straight to the library. She'd go to work later, face Allistair, and attempt—yet again—to figure out what the hell was going on in any one part of her life.

Katharine pulled up in front of the Santa Monica Public Library, as always, surprised at how busy the place was. L.A. just didn't seem like that literary of a city. Inside, the reserved Margot sat behind her desk diligently clicking keys as though she were doing something important.

Katharine made it to the reference section without seeing Mary Wayne. Since, apparently, she wasn't likely to run into the payroll clerk at work either, she hadn't really missed anything by coming here instead. Tipping the big purple dictionary off the top shelf, Katharine wound her way back to an empty study carrel and pulled out the slip of paper she had copied today's message onto.

Fifteen minutes later she had hoped to be getting somewhere, but the three little words had been a bit harder to decipher than she had expected. *Te* was easy—"you," "thou." *Daemon*—"devil." Disturbing, yes, but not surprising.

Venatur took more work. It wasn't there. *Vena / venae* meant "vein." *Venalis* meant "for sale." And none of that made sense. She looked everywhere, tried alternate spellings, and wracked her brain, but nothing worked.

Soft footsteps pattered up behind her, and Katharine wasn't sure if she should be surly or grateful for Margot's presence.

"Did you get another message in Latin?" The voice was as soft as her feet had been, nearly completely unobtrusive. Katharine could have ignored her, except she really couldn't afford to.

"Yes. I have 'you' and 'devil,' but I'm hung up on this last word." She pointed to *venatur* and waited.

Not a full minute later, Margot had showed her all the words with that base and their various endings. They were all versions of "hunt." Katharine sighed. "So it says I'm hunting devils."

This whole thing was getting uglier by the minute. With a deep sigh Katharine thanked the librarian again and headed for the door. Margot followed. By the time she exited, Margot had talked Katharine into copying the message and leaving her cell number—just in case the librarian could figure something out. And she'd done it, not because she thought it was a good idea, but because Margot had pestered her.

Glad she had finally shaken the librarian, Katharine slid into her car and realized that it was time to head to work. But she couldn't do it. She just couldn't walk in and face the man who made her rip off her clothes and pant his name when she couldn't figure out why. She also didn't want to have to explain to her father that she hadn't managed to find Mary Wayne in any format other than video playback for the past three workdays. The investigation was going nowhere. Even the wonderful forensic accountant had hit a brick wall. The transfers had been made in the middle of the night and from the mainframe. Of course the surveillance showed no one was there or even logged on at that time. No, that would be too easy. And Katharine was getting absolutely nothing in the "too easy" category these days. Except maybe herself.

She was rapidly discovering a new flexibility in her work ethic as well. So she bought a fashion magazine and made herself at home tucked into a back table at the coffee shop around the corner from the Light & Geryon building. If anyone spotted her she would claim she was . . . well, the excuse of waiting for Mary Wayne would only work on her father, Uncle Toran, and Allistair. God help them all if Allistair found her here.

She managed to monopolize the little table at the Coffee Bean for a full hour and a half. She had finished the largest, most calorie-laden drink she could get and had read the magazine from front to back. She had no more plans and no excuses left. She had to get to work.

Katharine threw out her coffee cup and left the magazine for the next person who felt the need to veg at the table. She took a few deep breaths intending to find a little steel for her spine. It was 11:00 a.m. on a Monday and she wasn't yet in her office. She hadn't called anyone to let them know what she was up to, or even just that she'd be late. And she didn't care.

She really didn't recognize herself anymore.

So she did what she knew to do. She forced herself to head to work and waved at the parking attendant, as usual not needing to show her badge. At least he still recognized her. She took the elevator directly to the top floor and walked into her father's office. He glanced up at her, startled, and for the first time she saw that the streaks of gray were gaining prominence in his hair. He'd always had a slash or two the few times she'd gotten close enough to see. But these were visible from the doorway. The distance did nothing to ease the slight rocking of her world. Yet another fundamental truth—that her father was ageless—had slipped and cracked its façade.

"Katharine!"

She composed herself at the sound of his voice and forced a smile. She did not want to have to tell him what she'd been thinking. So instead of replying, she merely nodded.

"Tell me this unexpected visit means you have news of Mary Wayne."

"No, I don't." Katharine settled herself into the couch even as her father's earlier momentum carried him to his feet before his disappointment could completely register. Katharine gave her best attempt at an explanation without trying to explain anything she just couldn't. "I haven't been able to pin her down for a face-to-face meeting. She's not avoiding me per se, I'm just having very bad luck meshing our schedules."

"Then you can drop in at her house."

Katharine thought that was a horrible idea, and possibly a dangerous one, but her father pushed. After only a token resistance she partially caved. She said she agreed it was the right thing to do—a small lie on her part—but never agreed to do it. That was only an omission, a fine distinction she was starting to not only recognize but depend on. "Actually, I came up for an entirely different reason. I screwed up the research and recommendations last week."

This time her father seated himself partway on the corner of his desk, one leg cocked over the edge, his hands resting, folded on his thigh. He frowned at her. "How so?"

"We shouldn't have bought the WeldLink stock or the shares of the Bedourie mine in Queensland."

"What are you talking about? We've already seen an increase from both those investments. The board couldn't be happier."

"Dad." Just the one word sounded ominous, even to her own ears. Katharine couldn't remember the last time she had called her father Dad. "WeldLink makes firing pins for guns that are going to Africa."

"So?"

"Do you know what's going on over there?"

"I have a general idea." But he still didn't seem concerned about it.

"We used all our money—all our investors' money—to fund a war. We're funding *genocide*."

"Baby." Her father used a tone she hadn't heard since she was very small. He hadn't called her "baby" in forever either. She knew what he was going to say. Still, she needed to hear the actual words. "Our money doesn't make those people kill each other. They are going to do it no matter what we do."

She nodded. He was right. But for the first time in her life, her father was wrong. Didn't he see that? Still, she knew when she was backing a losing horse. In this office, money was king. Her father was a smart enough man that he could see things his way whether it was right or not. No amount of arguing from his baby girl would sway him. Anyone who disagreed with him merely had no sense. And Katharine knew she could be added to that list in short order.

So she left the top floor with a forced smile and pretended everything was okay. She headed to the one place she thought she would be listened to: her own office.

By the time she stomped past Lisa, she was fueled into a righteous anger that had her shoving the door wide with a flat palm and Allistair jumping to his feet.

He had barely closed the door behind her before she found herself engulfed in a hug of epic proportions. He whispered "*Shhhh*" and "*Baby*" over and over while he rocked her there on her own feet, in the middle of her own office.

Her head found his shoulder, a safe place to land, and she didn't know how long she stood there being held like an injured child and finding comfort in nonsense words and a soothing touch. Finally he lifted her face and asked, "What's wrong?"

Her breath sucked in and her eyes blinked, wetter than even she had known. "My TV got stuck."

She couldn't finish the thought, but he didn't look at her like she was an idiot. He just waited. Another deep breath and a near hiccup later, she managed to form words. "I saw what we put our money into."

When he frowned because he didn't understand, Katharine launched into an explanation of the story she had seen on TV and her subsequent research. Still feeling safe in the circle of his arms, she grew more upset as she spoke. "And then my father didn't even acknowledge that it wasn't right. He says we aren't responsible for what other people do."

"He's right."

With that, she jerked away. Her hands pushed hard against his chest, nearly toppling him. She felt heat behind her eyes again. "He *isn't* right. We shouldn't give our money to this."

Allistair cocked his head to the side. "He *is* right. But you're right, too. We aren't responsible for what other people do. We can't control it. But," he emphasized the word as her anger with him was peaking, "we are responsible for our own parts. The question is: what's our part?"

"We gave them the money to do it. We funded a portion of this war."

He shrugged. "If it hadn't been us, then someone else would have."

"But if we all stepped back we could keep the guns from going there."

He shook his head. "We help a company that makes guns. We don't advocate killing. People get killed by . . . baseball bats and kitchen knives. Should we stop the manufacture of those, too? Or better yet, cars."

"Allistair, those things aren't made for killing. These guns are. They are produced without serial numbers or identifying marks just for this purpose."

"Maybe the right people are buying them for protection."

"These firing pins, they backfire. They make the gun explode in the shooter's face." She was pacing the office now, waving her hands in rapid gestures that punctuated her words.

"Then maybe that's a good thing."

"Allistair!" How could he not see? How did no one see? Katharine was surprised by how alone she felt suddenly and how disappointed she was. She had expected him to understand.

"Fine then. But there's no way everyone would pull out of this. If not us, then *someone* would have come along and all the same damage would have been done." He stood looking at her, his expression unchanging.

"But it wouldn't be *us*. We would be able to sleep better at night."

He actually laughed at that. "I don't think either your father or Toran Light will miss a moment's rest over this one."

Her feet planted, her back straightened and she stared him in the eye, some kind of brave new Katharine. "I haven't even started to tell you about the gem mine. So tell me you're just playing devil's advocate. Tell me that you understand. That it's wrong to get rich from other people's suffering."

She stayed there rooted while he smiled. Didn't move when his arms came around her, or when his mouth neared her ear. "Of course, baby."

Only then did she let herself sag against him and lean on his strength.

. . .

"Doesn't it seem wrong to make money off their deaths?"

"We're not profiting from their deaths." Allistair protested. Though she rested within the confines of his arms, he needed to push her to see how far she would go. Her morals were finally being decided, and he needed to see where they landed and whether he could alter them. And whether Zachary could alter them.

"Yes, we are!" Her hands pushed against him as her anger radiated from her center. It slapped at him with more force than he'd expected, unintentionally letting him feel that she wasn't merely angry at the situation. She was furious with *him*.

Startled by the impact, he stopped for a moment, catching the rays of righteous anger coming off her in great peals. The woman was irate, and in the middle of the waves, bright and dark, she was beautiful. Magnetized by what he saw in her—by her newfound bulldozer mentality, by the fact that she had decided she was right and anyone who disagreed should get out of her way—he was pulled again to her.

He'd told himself, even when she'd started this tirade, that he was going to let her see it through. She needed it. It was part of her growth in the direction he had to see. It would lead her to the end, to either him or Zachary, but it would be the next step. That was so important when she had been standing still for so long. Though her fury pushed at him, he pushed back, attracted to her on a level he'd never thought to protect himself against—not from the formerly biddable Katharine. Now she was a valkyrie, a siren, and he was helpless.

Her hand flew by in an impatient gesture necessary to her berating his lack of morals. It was both gorgeous and ridiculous; Katharine had no right to berate anyone else's morals. Also, hers had only come now, suddenly and with great conviction. Allistair snatched her hand from the air as it passed again and used her gesture to propel her in his direction. "What, Katharine? Do you know what's right? Is this right?"

He dragged her flush against him, both waiting for and hindering her reply. But her breathing was ragged, her face awash with her new ideals, and her mouth didn't speak, merely beckoned him.

Within moments he had torn aside her clothing and was inside her, engulfed in the way she moved with him, against him. Katharine was a wash of texture both along his skin and in a place low and resonant. She was the drug he should refuse, but never could. She would be the death of him. But at this moment, he didn't care.

Her fingers dug into his shoulders, hopefully feeling only sinew and bone. His breath came from somewhere deep and distant, but Katharine was too far gone to realize it. She leaned into him, into the last push that would bind them together. For the moment her anger at his lack of morals had been set aside. She let out a last gasp and slumped against him.

It was the same old story—Allistair and the feelings he couldn't let go of. The sex they were both helpless against—even though he knew the way he had done it was wrong. Even though it violated all Katharine's basic beliefs, the few that she held. Only here, now, there was something more. The start of Katharine. The start of what she could be. She had finally found something and latched onto it. She had held firm—well, at least until he had caved and started the sex. But he forgave her for that lapse.

He craved her all the more when she spoke, still half naked, still cradled in his arms and joined with him. "It's wrong. What I did was so wrong. I didn't look any further than the money. I should have looked."

Her tired anger called to him. He fed on it. Let it drain from her and into him, where it soothed him. He was making progress. She needed to be in her anger for a while.

For a moment, he held them there, as suspended in time as he could keep things. But he was only so strong, especially when he had been drained by yet another altering experience with Katharine. In the end he failed at this, too.

Her cell phone rang, and for some reason it worried her. She couldn't seem to ignore it, though his soft words urged her to. She pushed against him, as if she was only just realizing what she'd done. There was something off-putting about the gesture—as though she hadn't done this before, as though it was an affront to who she was.

Cold fear gripped him deep inside. Had he pushed too hard, wanted too much from her? Had he led her to turn back to Zachary?

She completely extracted herself from his grip and managed to both straighten her clothes and grasp at the phone before it quit ringing. Her voice was soft in the sudden stillness that had pervaded the room. "Hello?"

Allistair waited.

"Really?" Her features lost their animation, and only because he could see the colors did he know it was due to fear. Katharine thanked the caller and hung up.

"What's wrong?" He leaned over, searching for her gaze, for contact. But she wasn't giving it.

"Nothing."

Her blank face told him that, whatever it was, for him it truly would be nothing.

. . .

"It doesn't say you're hunting devils." Margot had been waiting at the back table before Katharine arrived at the coffee shop.

On the way down she'd had several fleeting thoughts. The first was to wonder if she had gotten herself put back together correctly. She knew that at least Lisa suspected what was going on. So it was reasonable to think that others might be putting two and two together as well. And, truth be told, they should get four.

But her skirt wasn't hitched up into her underwear, and for now that was as far as she could get her concern to extend.

The second thought was that she'd hardly worked at all this last week. And that recently the only thing she'd actually accomplished was to get Light & Geryon to invest in the firing pins and the gem mine. The world would be a better place had she not done that work. She knew she should feel guilty about how she was handling things—skipping work, not caring—but she couldn't conjure the emotion. In a way, her father's disappointing, if expected, reaction had been a bye, allowing her an emotional opt-out from her responsibilities. If he didn't have any morals about killing people, then why should she have any about something as insignificant as doing her job?

As she entered the coffee shop, she was considering what skills she had that would be marketable if she left the family fold of Light & Geryon. A small terror skittered through her at the thought of so radically altering her life plan, but then she spotted Margot tucked away in the back and used the more immediate concern on the table in front of her to push away the ones she'd just dug up.

Katharine nursed the tea she had bought just to be polite. Never able to quite shake the hostessing rules her mother had drilled into her, she had done a velvet badgering job on Margot until the librarian had told Katharine what to get her.

Now, after all the niceties had been taken care of, Margot was finally able to make her point. And her point was the same as many others today: Katharine was wrong.

She wasn't hunting devils.

"The translation is different . . . Latin isn't like English. The placement of a word in the sentence doesn't determine the meaning."

Not being a total geek, Katharine was at a loss. Unfortunately, the look on her face must have conveyed this to Margot, who took it as a cue to launch into an explanation.

"In English, 'The boy loves the dog' is different from 'The dog loves the boy.'"

No shit, Sherlock. Katharine felt the uncharitable thought slide through her head as though it belonged. But Margot was speaking again before she had the chance to really berate herself.

"The sentences are different because of the word placement. In Latin, the words have different endings that you have to translate; you can't just feed the word meanings into English grammar. So, your 'You hunt devils' translation is incomplete."

Katharine merely waited.

"Once you put the correct endings into place, you get 'The devil hunts you.'"

Well, maybe the fact that Margot was a geek wasn't so terrible. That wasn't such a bad explanation, after all. Then the meaning sank in. "Oh shit. Well, that is different."

Margot nodded. "It's disturbing. You got this in the mail?"

Katharine nodded in return, a lie in movement if not in words.

"You've gotten two of them." Margot sipped her tea like she was thinking, but Katharine could see that a point was coming and she took the high road to wait the librarian out.

Margot didn't play around. "That's why I called your cell and asked you to meet me here. I looked up the laws, and these are threats. You should report them."

Katharine shook her head. The feeling of again flat-out disagreeing with someone was at once still uncomfortable and yet growing on her. "I'm not reporting it. No one has threatened my person." *At least not in writing*, but she didn't add that.

Margot leaned over the small table. "They don't have to say, 'I'm going to kill you,' not outright. There's a threat in those notes. It's implied, but as soon as you get an officer to agree that there is a threat, it's an offense."

Katharine opened her mouth to protest, but Miss Margot had another layer of frosting for that cake. "And it's actually a felony because they are using the U.S. Postal Service to do it."

Yeah, about that . . . Katharine thought. As the librarian leaned back, her poorly cut suit shifting so the lapels no longer stayed quite flat, Katharine tried to find a polite way out of this mess she had made. Her mother had told her that lies would come back to haunt her, and here was the smallest—that the notes had been mailed—smacking her in the face.

She could not get the police involved. They would lock her in the loony bin. Her father would quietly fund a padded room for the rest of her life. She would lose her future of little blonde babies named after Zachary. And her mother would die a second death, this time of embarrassment. "I'm not reporting it. It's not really a threat."

"Just because it isn't in English doesn't mean it's not real."

Katharine opened her mouth to protest again, but Margot beat her to it. It seemed the librarian had a bit of pit bull in her. "Even if you don't log it as a threat, you really should tell the cops. That way, if you get another one, or if something happens, there's already a record. That's the kind of thing that they ask later—why you didn't report it."

"I'll think about it." It was all Katharine could say, even though it was as bald-faced a lie as any she had told in recent days—and she had been laying out some whoppers lately.

She started to stand to excuse herself, but Margot stood first. "Thank you for the tea. I don't want to take up your whole day, but I didn't think it was really a conversation for the library either." She smiled and held out a small, glossy business card. "I put my cell number on the back so you can get to me if you need another translation."

Then she left so fast that it was almost as though she'd disappeared.

Katharine leaned back in her seat. Her world was getting weirder and weirder. She sipped at the tea while she thought. There was no point in going back to work. Who knew what she might suggest the company do with its money today? Maybe she could recommend blowing up a small planet, or making a few more species extinct.

Slowly, with concerted, simple movements to cover the magnitude of her thoughts, she acted like she was savoring the last of the tea. Instead, she was taking stock.

She was screwing her trainee. And he didn't seem to think there was anything wrong with that. She was in a relationship that seemed to grow more serious as the days went by. Zachary checked on her, asked about her, and behaved like the devoted boyfriend. But she was screwing her office mate. That put a bit of a damper on the seriousness of the relationship.

The animals had stayed away for a while. But the last visit, the black wolf, had been almost more than she could handle. If it happened again, her heart might explode from the stress if the animal didn't kill her first.

The latest message meant the visitations hadn't ended. And the meanings were disturbing in and of themselves. They also hadn't been in her mailbox as she had said. Nor were they tacked to her door. Someone—no some*thing*—had invaded her space and left them there.

Her heart was picking up speed, so Katharine forced herself to quit thinking about anything . She tossed the cup into a trash can and headed out the door. Allistair could wonder where she was. Her work could wait. Everything was less important than not thinking right now.

Fetching her car from the garage without entering the building, Katharine headed home. She ducked into the condo, not wanting to see Zachary, even though she doubted he'd be home.

She removed her suit jacket and skirt but nothing else. Drawing the blinds to shut out the afternoon light, Katharine tumbled into bed.

. . .

Zachary watched her through the veil. Katharine was deep asleep—like she hadn't been in ages. She needed the rest. She needed the deep dreams, too. It was one way that he and Allistair could get to her—to help nudge her along, to help her grow.

But Allistair was at his sham of a job, and would be there until the day closed. Zachary could look at him through the distance, could see his rival shifting at his desk as he sensed he was being watched. But he wouldn't know it was Zachary watching. He lacked so many of his senses while in human form that he didn't even seem to know that Katharine had left him.

Zachary wanted to laugh. He'd been upset that Allistair had gotten so close to Katharine through her work. Taking the job and getting inside her office had been brilliant. But there was a flaw. He was expected to show up and be human during working hours. Neither of them was strong enough yet to appear in two places at once. But soon Zachary would gain that strength. Because he was going to take advantage of the fact that Allistair had tied himself into this bind.

Katharine was safe from Allistair for now.

With a sigh of contentment that sent the air shifting on the human side of the veil, Zachary turned away from her. He had work to do.

He had been following Mary Wayne for a while now. He was trying to help her. She needed it. As a human on her own, she'd been on the wrong track. She needed him.

He found her quickly, and with a shift in his thoughts, Zachary reached across the barrier and into Mary Wayne.

CHAPTER 11

Katharine shrugged against the feel of skin touching hers. Her body burned. The man was dark. Thick black hair filled her hands as she reached to hold his head to her.

With a moan, she tried again to get even closer. He needed her as badly as she needed him. She could feel it deep in her bones. His touch enflamed her. Her head tipped back and she felt his mouth, hot and heavy at her throat. Teeth nipped sharply at her tender flesh and she begged for more.

His guttural groan answered her. Her breath escaped her as she had the sudden realization that she didn't know his name. In the same instant, the thought was ripped away from her, silently removed from her brain so that she wouldn't care. She needed him—whoever he was.

Her hands followed his slick skin down his back, tracing impossibly huge muscles as they went. Some kind of oil covered him, leaving her wet with it as he moved against her. He was larger than she had even thought him to be. But that didn't matter, as she was a writhing ball of need.

He teased her, bringing her to the edge of want, and Katharine thought she should give some of that back to him—even though she was certain that he was hard to tease.

She didn't know his name, didn't know him, and had no idea how she had the pieces of knowledge that she did. But she did. Still, these thoughts didn't stop her, and she ran her hands down his sides, up his back, across his sharp shoulder blades.

Her brain registered the oddity of that through the haze of desire. Still moving against him, still straining for more, Katharine slid her hands across his back.

She cried out at the pain that pierced her palm. The bony protrusion on his back had sliced her skin. While the hurt didn't destroy her want, it allowed her a tiny window through it.

Ignoring the pain, Katharine felt his shoulders as the sharp edges grew. Forcing their way out of his form, they spread and opened. Still his mouth ate at her, still she moved against him. Still she cried out with need that only he could fulfill. She wanted him. She just couldn't identify *what* he was.

The moan that hung on the air was her own. Deep inside, desperation tugged at her, begging for completion. But her brain had broken free of the storm-tossed moorings and she traced her hands—now slick with both his oil and her own blood—down his overly muscled arms. They were the size of tree trunks. He could crush her in an instant.

Somehow she wasn't afraid—though she knew she should be—and was just merely curious.

Her eyes followed the edge of his inky skin. Was it just the dark or was he really so deep a black? Beautiful and shiny like a widow spider, his skin didn't even show the blood she was surely trailing down it.

His arm ended in a hand as muscular as the rest of him. Long, strong fingers grasped her upper arm. She could see where his vice-like grip dented her flesh. The long blades that were the ends of his fingers brushed her delicate skin, leaving faint cuts as they passed.

The sight of more of her blood bothered her only on a cerebral level. She felt the pain, but for some reason, it didn't actually hurt her.

She looked over his shoulder as the air moved around him. Great black wings unfurled behind him and Katharine watched in awe. Her head tipped back to see and as she did, his face came up to look at her.

Katharine screamed.

The eyes were blank holes of evil and hate. The mouth she had begged for and writhed against was full of steel teeth sharper than the blades of his hands. His nose was merely a set of holes sunk deep into his face, and the air they breathed out over her stank of death and of a distant but powerful malevolence.

As she gasped she sucked in some of his breath, looked into his eyes, and for a moment she took in the evil that he was.

Then her brain shut down and the black enfolded her.

. . .

She came to with a start. Katharine sat up, sucking clean air into her lungs.

The dream had been terrible. But there was light outside—bright daylight coming in through the open window. The middle of the night already seemed distant, felt as though it had happened a long time ago. That she still remembered it so vividly was a testament to how afraid she had ultimately been.

Even now, fear and a healthy dose of shame at how she had begged it to touch her lingered in the back of her consciousness. Though she had done those things in a dream, Katharine still felt a measure of responsibility for her actions.

She laid back, pulling up the tangled sheets to cover her nakedness. She was glad it had been merely a dream, and an easily explainable one at that. She was afraid of the animals and the messages. And she had Allistair and Zachary both plying her with mind-numbing sex.

No wonder she'd had such a foul dream. With all that was going on lately, it wasn't surprising that her mind had learned how to make an image so evil and terrifying.

Part of her wanted to stay in bed, to roll over and go back to sleep, and hopefully replace this dream with a good one. She wanted to be lazy in a way that had always been forbidden to her, first through her upbringing and later through her own rigidity. But when she didn't slide out of bed, didn't act, her thoughts turned back to the dream.

Forcing them to something else was only helpful if there was something else to turn to. All of Katharine's something elses were just as difficult to get past: the writing on the mirror, her recent sex addiction, her growing lack of personal morals. On the other hand, where her work was concerned, she was finding new morals she didn't know she had. The problem was that those morals were going to cost her her relationship with both her father and Uncle Toran, the only family she had left.

So staying in bed was going to be a problem. Only when she rose was she finally able to push away the thoughts she didn't want to deal with as she pushed back the covers. Her feet found the plush carpet, and for a moment everything was as it always had been. She was getting up alone, in the early morning hours; she'd head to work . . .

It was only a momentary lapse in reality, this belief that all was as it should be. But she clung to it as tightly as she could. When her brain would start to wander, she forced it back to the task at hand—and buried her other thoughts behind the simplicity of picking out her slip.

Standing in front of her closet, Katharine skimmed her hose up her legs. She refused to wear her garter belt again. Today she was keeping it together. Today Allistair wouldn't see her slip, so she chose a slimmer one that was a little difficult to get in and out of. She chose her suit and laid it across the bed before turning to the bathroom to brush out her hair and put on some makeup.

Her brush was in her hand, pulling through a wave of her hair when she stopped dead.

Katharine would have thought the mirror could hold no more surprises for her. Simply finding more words she didn't understand wouldn't have unnerved her. Her eyes went wide as her own image made her wish there were words on the mirror.

As soon as she saw them, she began to feel them—the bruises on her upper arms tugged at her as she moved and turned to get a better look. She bore tiny parallel cuts on her ribs and the back of one arm. Her forehead pulled together as she frowned. It looked like she'd been in a bar brawl the night before.

Her face was clear of cuts and marks, but her neck bore a series of curved rows of punctures. As she leaned in close to look at the tiny wounds, she lost her curiosity and felt her heart squeeze in cold fear. The clusters of small cuts looked like teeth marks.

And the bruises on her arms were in the shape of a hand. A hand larger than any she had ever encountered on a human.

. . .

Katharine stood at her bathroom mirror and sighed—another message. She was scraping rock bottom and she knew it.

She had wandered through work for two days. She had lied through her teeth. And everyone had bought it. The whole thing.

She hadn't seen Mary Wayne, although she had run two other front-desk stakeouts. By the third time it had happened, she'd stopped asking security to run the tapes. Katharine had headed right upstairs, where she had been stopped by Bonnie at the front desk of payroll, who barely got her "Good morning" out through her nearly perpetual smile before she started into "have you heard?" and "isn't it sad?" and "oh, you just missed her, she just stepped out for a moment."

Of course she had. Mary Wayne was some kind of a ghost who could walk right in front of her and not be seen. Katharine wondered why the woman even bothered leaving her desk, when Katharine could so easily look directly at her and still miss her. It was caught on tape on more than one occasion. It seemed Katharine had developed some kind of Mary-Wayne-specific hysterical blindness.

But Katharine had just smiled at Bonnie and expressed her sadness over Mary's imminent departure, though it wasn't really even at the top of her concern list anymore.

No. She had been late two mornings ago, when she had discovered the bruises. Mostly because her brain had checked out rather than examine what the marks might mean. The last thing she saw in the mirror was her own eyes starting to roll back, and by the time she had come to on her bathroom floor, it was already close to noon. It was the ringing of the phone that had woken her, although she had been in no shape to move fast enough to answer it. She found out later that it had been Allistair calling, for the second time. Zachary had also left her a message. But none of it had budged her from her spot on the bathroom carpet.

As it was, she had barely heard the phone ringing for the third time over the pounding in her head. Of course, that had just been the sound of her own heartbeat, elevated to a level of pain akin to being battered by the surf.

For two days, she had been tossing back Tylenol and Advil like candy. It had lessened the hammering headache enough for her to attempt to go in to work and look normal. But if she had managed to look normal, she certainly didn't feel normal and was quite convinced that she'd never be normal again.

The bruises pulled when she moved in certain ways. She couldn't put her hair up because of the goose egg on the back of her skull. She was overheated from wearing long sleeves. And she had to pretend this was how she wanted it. There was no way to get into a discussion with anyone about her attire without giving away something that screamed she needed to be locked up.

And she probably did need to be locked up. She hadn't seen a doctor at all, though she could have used one to check out the cuts and scrapes. Even she knew that you didn't spend five hours unconscious on your bathroom floor and not get checked out. She was quite certain that she'd hit her head on the edge of the counter as she'd fallen when she passed out from seeing the marks. It wasn't the knock to the head that had put her out, but that was likely what had kept her out.

She also had to begin to think about the very real possibility of a brain tumor.

None of this stuff was likely. Seeing creatures in your room and finding soot. Thinking she had messages on the mirror. Passing out several times over a few weeks—when she had never passed out before, except once as a kid, when she'd stood still for too long in a church show, all stiff and starched out in the heat.

Her breath burbled out of her in a confused sigh. At this point she might have welcomed the brain tumor. That, at least, was an option of this world. But the maid had complained about the soot. So Katharine hadn't hallucinated that.

Maybe she had, in some altered state, placed the soot on the carpet herself. Like she had a second personality that was setting her up for . . . what? Paranoia? Maybe. But the other personality would also have to have written the messages on the mirror and therefore would have to know Latin—and know it well.

In the past two days, Katharine had surfed the web during work hours. She had convinced herself that she was doing the right thing, because she wasn't recommending that company funds be used to kill babies or destroy rainforests or any of the other things she'd probably put her John Hancock on in recent years. So she'd had plenty of time to read up on multiple personality disorders.

But none of it had been helpful. Usually, a second personality formed when a child was repeatedly abused. But Katharine didn't remember any abuse at all. Maybe the second personality had hidden it from her, but she had no missing gaps in her childhood memory, or even any of her adult life—until recently. She also had a handful of grown-ups, family, and help who had been around her throughout her whole childhood, so it was unlikely that they were all in on abuse so severe that it fractured her into multiple people.

There were a few odd ways that Katharine could create a scenario where it was still possible. Maybe Light & Geryon was a cover for some fanatical cult. Fine. But then why was she only experiencing these things now? The second personality was supposed to shield the major personality. It was supposed to take the abuse and hide it so the first personality could live a normal life.

Katharine shook her head to herself. If that were the case, then her second personality was doing a really shitty job, because all that crap was raining down on her these days.

She wasn't even sure how a person would go about faking the handprint bruises she had on each arm. Her own hand wasn't nearly big enough. The only way she could make that thought work was if her alter ego was turning tricks for the Jolly Green Giant and she'd pissed him off.

The one positive thing out of these last two days was that she had kept herself away from Zachary's bed, by flatly refusing him every time he asked to see her. And each time Allistair had come close he had touched her arm, causing her to wince and pull away. She'd been celibate for two whole days—a welcome change from the full-out slut she'd been channeling.

But as she stood at her sink on the third morning, glad that the bruises were finally changing from black and purple to yellow and green, she decided to go straight to her translator with this new message.

Vigilia prima venio ad te.

Work would be pointless. And besides, she was injured. At least there were casual clothes she could wear that would cover the bruises and not overheat her. Since she didn't own any of these casual clothes, she would have to go buy some of them as soon as the stores opened up.

Katharine meticulously copied the newest message onto a slip of paper, then copied it again. She would leave one with Margot at the library. Carefully, she stashed both slips of paper into the zippered pocket of her purse, then plopped onto the couch with a bowl of yogurt and granola. The TV had not misbehaved again, and she found herself flipping channels and winding up on a morning program.

She'd never watched weekday morning television before and found herself strangely mesmerized. So much so that when the phone rang she didn't break her gaze from the TV, just felt around off to the right, in the direction the sound was coming from. She still wasn't paying attention to the call when she answered it.

Her father's voice startled her. She didn't know who she'd expected, but it hadn't been him. "Yes?"

He didn't give her a moment to find her bearings; the man had never been concerned about anyone else's bearings anyway. And he surely wasn't calling to find out if she was okay, if there was a reason she'd been late to work so much and entirely absent so far today. No, he just started barking his problems at her. "Mary Wayne hasn't shown up for work in two days."

"Oh?" Katharine found that strangely soothing. At least she hadn't been subconsciously erasing the images of Mary walking by her at the front desk anymore.

"If she doesn't show tomorrow morning, then you go over to her house and we end this once and for all." He was red-faced, she could tell through the phone. "Hell, maybe you should just go today."

When it came to her father, Katharine was a seasoned veteran at getting out of what she didn't want to deal with, and her response was as sweet as sugar. "Yes, of course, tomorrow."

She hung up before she could get too mad about her father sending her off to confront an embezzler by herself. What if Mary was the crook? If she was leaving, then it was likely that she knew they were on to her. She might very well have a gun and a jumpy personality to boot.

Just as Katharine started to simmer over her father's casual disregard of the possible danger he was putting her in, her phone rang again. Still not on her A-game, Katharine answered it with a harsh "Yes?"

Her father's voice boomed across the line. "And don't do anything stupid. Take that assistant of yours with you when you go." Then he hung up, leaving Katharine to stare at the phone and marvel that though her father must have cared somewhat about her safety, he'd still managed to get in a good insult in the process. She set her cell back on the coffee table and allowed herself to be sucked back into the created drama of morning news programming.

Three hours later she had left and come home again, changing into the casual outfit she had bought at a high-end store. She found herself being surprised again at how soft the fabric was. Within minutes she was out the door again, heading off to the library on foot. As she walked the mile in her workout sneakers, Katharine tried to come up with ways to keep from having to tell Margot just how she had found the words she needed translated.

By the time she was facing the large double doors with the stained-glass insets of falling books, she hadn't invented any better excuse than a random stranger using the U.S. Postal Service. Katharine pushed through the doors.

This time, Margot's face looked up from the book she was reading the instant Katharine approached. Maybe before Katharine hadn't been worthy of her attention—until she brought in the mystery of the Latin stalker. Upon seeing the look on Katharine's face, the librarian's brows came together and the corners of her mouth turned down, probably a reflection of what was on Katharine's own face. Margot used her library voice, but that didn't mask the severity of her thoughts. "Did you get another one?"

Katharine nodded, already pulling the slip of paper from her purse. She slid it silently across the desk until it was practically under Margot's nose.

With a brisk nod and faster movements, Margot stood and started toward the reference section with Katharine trailing behind like an obedient puppy. Her head was dipped toward the slip of paper, which obviously held a fascinating mystery for her, but her feet followed a sharp line toward the back of the large room.

Half an hour later Margot was on the floor next to Katharine, both of them stumped. Though Margot was clearly concerned with the message, Katharine was wondering if Margot always sat on the library floor with her patrons.

"I can't get it. It's much more complex than the last two."

Katharine frowned. Sure, the first message was only one word, but the second had three. This one only had five words, and two were short. How much more complex could it be?

She didn't voice her doubts, but they must have shown, because Margot spoke up. "Look, we translated the last message wrong at first because we weren't paying attention to the grammar of the language. When I was going over it, I looked up a bit about it and realized there was way too much I didn't know. But I was able to muddle through that one. It was fairly straightforward. And I only *think* I got it right, or at least close enough."

The librarian finally took a breath, then continued. "This one has verb and noun forms—I'm guessing that's what they are—that aren't listed in the dictionary per se. So I'm going to have to study the whole language more before I can translate this." She huffed as if not being fluent in Latin were a personal failure.

Katharine nodded and started to roll herself up off the floor. Margot put a hand to Katharine's arm to stop her. It was only when she looked Katharine in the eye and waited that Katharine sat back down. "What?"

"You have to go to the cops."

"I can't." She shook her head and started to rise again. Maybe it had been a mistake to—

The hand on her arm tugged her back to her seat on the floor. Aside from grabbing Katharine, Margot hadn't moved a muscle. "I'm assuming there's more here than what you've shown me. I agree that it's odd to have threats delivered by mail in Latin. But the cops should do more than just see it as odd—maybe they'll act on it."

Katharine tried not to squirm.

Margot spoke again. "Also, I noticed that you've never brought the original note here, not even a photocopy. You've always written them out for me. It might be helpful to see the original. Did you save it? Maybe you should put the notes in Ziploc baggies to preserve any evidence."

Katharine nodded, "I already did. They're at home. In baggies." She paused. "And you're right, I should take them to the police. This is the last straw." *The last straw?* She never said things like that.

Apparently Margot noticed something, because her voice suddenly changed to low and soothing, like she didn't want to scare a deer. "Okay, you aren't going to the police. I get that. But you don't have the notes in baggies either. Where are they?"

Katharine pulled back, a small movement of self-preservation. "What? What are you talking about? I'll go. I said I would."

The thin face widened into a true smile that made Katharine realize Margot was actually pretty. Her shoulders moved and she relaxed completely, leaning forward as if confiding to a friend. In that moment, it hit Katharine that she didn't have any. Friends.

Katharine felt herself leaning in to hear what she would say. "Look around," she whispered conspiratorially. "I'm surrounded by books and I love to read. About a year ago I got cheated on by a guy I thought was *the one*. First I got mad. Then I studied up on liars. And you aren't a very good one."

At least Margot seemed contrite delivering that last line. But the fact that she wasn't a good liar wasn't news to Katharine. She sighed and sucked it up. "I'm sorry about your boyfriend."

Margot waved her away. "Turns out it was for the best."

For some reason, she felt compelled to tell Margot the truth, or at least part of it. Maybe because the woman had been helpful for no reason at all. Maybe because she seemed genuinely concerned for someone she didn't really know, someone who had just showed up in her library. Maybe because she had leaned in close and confided in Katharine, just a little. Or maybe just because Katharine was getting scared. "I can't take the notes to the police. I don't have them."

Dark hair moved at the librarian's shoulders as she shook her head. "I can see being pissed and throwing out the first one. But how did you lose all three?"

Her shoulders pulled up into a shrug. She didn't know how to explain this, how to explain any of it. "I never had them."

At Margot's frown she continued, compelled to purge herself of the lie. "They were on my mirror."

The librarian's mouth hung open. "Someone got into your house!?"

"Condo, but yes."

"And you still don't want to report it?"

Katharine shook her head, vehemently this time. If the librarian could spot her lies so easily, then the cops would have her confessing everything within ten minutes. Which would mean she was only thirty minutes from a padded cell.

"You cleaned the writing away?"

Katharine nodded rapidly.

"Okay, so you didn't . . ."

Damn! How had she seen the lie in that? "I washed one of them off, but the others just sort of disappeared."

That stumped the woman for a moment. She glanced around and dropped her voice before urging Katharine to scoot to one side as another library patron—perhaps with legitimate business in the reference section—came through the narrow aisle.

Her voice was lower than a whisper. "Was it like the old steam trick? So you see the words when you get out of the shower?"

A quick nod, and her own lowered voice responded. "Just like that."

"Do you know who's doing it?"

"Only in a roundabout way." Katharine shook her head, trying to get her thoughts to fall into place, trying to double-check everything she said before she said it. "Look, if I go to the police, they'll write me off as crazy. My house has been locked from the inside the last two times this has happened, and I don't have any proof. The notes are long gone."

Her frown had grown worse while Katharine spoke. Margot's hand had migrated to the middle of her chest as though she had to hold her heart in. "You got the locks changed, right?"

"Wouldn't help."

"But if they had the key—"

Katharine was already shaking her head. "There are three locks on the front door, one of which is a deadbolt that throws from the inside only." She shrugged. "It's L.A."

Taking advantage of Margot's confused silence, Katharine stood and finally took control of the conversation. "I have to go. Will you tell me when you get that one translated?"

She was shaking her head at her own rudeness—acting as if Margot were here just to translate for her—when the woman nodded that she would.

Feeling truly grateful for the first time she could remember, Katharine simply said "thank you" and walked away from the library not having told Margot anything other than the two pitiful words.

. . .

Katharine had skipped work entirely that day, not quite able to bring herself to go in after she left Margot at the library. She just couldn't convince herself it was worth it to go home and climb back into the hot long sleeves and fake smile that covered her cuts and bruises.

The writing on the mirror had disappeared by the time she got back to her condo after sitting in the coffee shop, nursing an iced coffee and reading through a fashion magazine she had picked up. Her afternoon was a couch marathon of TV show after TV show, a good remedy for keeping her mind off anything important. Katharine was amazed by what she saw. Did people really live like this? Surely the soaps were a blatant exaggeration, but the people on the talk shows seemed to believe what they were saying.

She fed herself the food that had magically appeared in her freezer the previous Thursday, thankful that none of the people who came through her place had encountered anything while they were here. But that thought, too, quickly passed out of her brain as Katharine purposefully fed it more empty television. By the time she rolled off the couch and into bed, she had wrapped herself in a cocoon that was comfortingly empty of real thought. Insulated from reality, Katharine quickly fell deeply asleep.

And instantly came sharply awake, sitting up to inhale a great gulp of air as if she had nearly suffocated in her sleep.

Her head spun as the oxygen rushed through her system, restoring her blood flow and slowly centering her thoughts.

It was there.

In the room.

With her.

Tired of being afraid, and more afraid of not knowing what it was, Katharine turned to see the beast. Again it sat in the corner, shadows pulled tight around it to conceal the truth. Deep eyes blinked slowly, as though the creature studied her the same way she studied it. Silvery skin moved with a grace unknown in this world.

But this time, it only watched her.

CHAPTER 12

Long, clawed fingers beckoned her to come closer, but Katharine didn't move. She didn't know whether that was because she had decided not to or because she was unable to move at all. For a long time, they stayed that way, merely staring at each other. This time she didn't feel afraid—she wasn't certain she could move, but it didn't seem to be due to the paralyzing fear she had felt the last time she had seen the beast. Maybe, finally, she had simply run out of fear.

Her brain didn't work, her body didn't work, yet she was awake, held in some kind of trance, likely caused by the beast itself. She wanted to laugh at it. It wanted her to come, beckoned her closer, but she was unable to do what it wanted because of it.

They stared at each other for an eternity and eventually Katharine blinked, noting the sudden bright light coming in around her blinds. Her head rested against her pillow and the ceiling filled most of her field of vision. Quickly enough to make a small cracking noise in her spine, Katharine whipped her head around to see her empty bedroom. The corner was as vacant as the rest of it. No soot, no shadow, nothing but the lingering memory of what must have been another bad dream early in the night.

As she pushed back the covers, Katharine realized that her body felt well rested for the first time in a long time, adding credence to her theory that, for once, the night visitor had truly only been a dream.

Walking barefoot to the bathroom, Katharine stretched the way she used to, before she had become afraid of the mirror and the soot. Though she had braced herself for something—told herself she was ready for anything—the bathroom mirror was blessedly blank. She turned, checking one last thing. Her clock said she was on time.

Her bruises had faded to the point that no one would see them unless they were looking for them. She had to shake her head. It all seemed . . . normal.

And she hadn't had "normal" in what seemed a very long time.

But Katharine embraced the almost lost memory of life as she used to know it. She ate a yogurt with some granola mixed in, her body thanking her for the familiar food, or maybe just thanking her for not shoving fast food down her throat or skipping breakfast entirely. Pulling a slip from her closet, she chose a suit based on what she wanted to wear, not what would cover her marks or make her look less tired. She hoped a T-shirt, instead of her usual blouse, made her look like a woman who owned at least some casual clothing.

She made it in to the office without incident and was smiling behind her desk, working on a request that had shown up in her absence, when Allistair came in. Aside from a fast hello and an even faster smile, she ignored him. Her research was more important. There was a machinery company in Japan whose stock was mirroring another company's that had taken a meteoric rise the previous year and had created a huge windfall for Light & Geryon. But aside from the money—the getting in and getting out at the right times—it didn't appear that anyone had checked the company's holdings. This time Light & Geryon would know. Katharine checked the employee pay records, matched them with the posted budgets, then cross-referenced that with the strength of the Japanese yen.

She was back-checking the company's average annual salary by the payroll budget and the number of employees they claimed to have when she realized Allistair had been standing beside her for some time.

Trying to hide the fact that his presence annoyed her, Katharine looked up at him. She knew she had no right to be annoyed with him. After all, he had been doing his job—which was actually her job—yesterday while she had been mysteriously absent. Still, she felt irritated, and if it showed on her face, Allistair graciously ignored it.

"Your father spoke to me yesterday."

What? Had she been turned in? Was Allistair in league with her father? Was he now watchdogging over her?

"And?" The word came out as hard and rude as she intended it.

"He asked if I would accompany you to see Mary Wayne. He was aware you have been ill recently"—somehow he managed to deliver the line without a trace of irony, without smirking that he had thrown the boss-lady off her game by laying her over her own desk—"but he still wanted you to go. He also thought we would be safer and more likely to get her to just turn the money back in if we showed up in greater numbers."

Now she felt chastised. She always did when she was thinking the worst of someone who was only doing what they had been told or, worse, had her best interests at heart. Still, she couldn't muster an apology. "So the two of us are supposed to be enough to make her roll over and give us all the codes to her offshore accounts? Will she escort herself to jail, too?"

Allistair moved his head side to side, neither a yes nor a no. "Well, yesterday your father made it clear to me that recovering the money was more important than punishing her."

"What?" That didn't sound like her father at all. For a brief moment, a thought flashed through her head that not only were there strange creatures in her condo, but the people around her were getting possessed as well.

"He said we should offer not to prosecute her criminally if she agreed to give us the money today. He suggested we already have the paperwork drawn up before we go. I did it yesterday." Allistair rocked back on his heels, his hands tucked behind his back as if he had nothing better in the world to do than wait for her reply.

"Did my father seem completely insane when he suggested we not prosecute her?" She tried to keep her jaw from scraping the nice plush carpet. She tried not to show her disbelief, or how mad she was that her nice normal day was getting all fucked up. And she tried to be indignant at the situation for making her think in swear words.

"No, he seemed completely rational. He said he was going to sue her into the ground in civil court and that he had enough control in the business world to make certain that she had real difficulty finding another job."

Katharine let out her breath. That, at least, sounded like her father. Though the thought was comforting, her voice was still wry. "Did he suggest a time for us to visit her?"

Looking chagrined, Allistair nodded. "If she wasn't at work today, then ASAP." He didn't have to be asked. He simply tacked on, "And she's not at work today."

"Did he lay out our wardrobe? Write us a script?" She knew her voice sounded snotty, but she didn't care.

And she was glad that Allistair had the sense to only shake his head no and press his lips together to hide the smirk that threatened to break free.

Katharine tried to shake the feeling of having her day interrupted. She stood and swept up her jacket from where she'd hung it on the back of her desk. So much for looking casual; what she needed to look like was a real ball-buster.

Allistair trailed her down the corridor, not saying anything when she told Lisa they'd be out for a while. His feet matched the rhythm of her steps as they walked the long hallway. He stood sentinel-like in the elevator, his hand brushing hers accidentally a few times at first, but then he pulled away and stood still. When they reached her car, he slid into the passenger seat and waited quietly while she put in the address for Mary's beyond-her-means home in Brentwood.

He said nothing, made no knowing facial expressions all the way there. *Smart man*, Katharine thought to herself. But when she opened her door and began to climb out, he put his hand on her arm. She was about to rescind her opinion when he asked, "How are we playing this?

Do you speak while I just nod and try to look menacing? Are we doing good cop, bad cop?"

Katharine sighed. He was right, they needed a plan before they went in. "I was thinking more along the lines of 'bad cop, worse cop.' She took our money. I don't want to be nice. Maybe I talk and whenever you feel you can, you jump in with something even worse than what I'm suggesting."

He nodded. "Works for me. Can I take just a minute to put on my menacing face?"

She bit her lip, but ultimately couldn't help herself. She had to look away as she busted out laughing. As she giggled, her eyes darted back and forth across the street. She didn't think any of the windows at Mary Wayne's big house would let her see this far down the street. With a physical shake and a quick breath in, Katharine got herself under control, but as she turned to nod at Allistair she saw he was fighting to keep his own mouth from quirking.

Slamming the car doors shut, they headed down the sidewalk under the cover of old-growth trees that had risen up higher than the houses and in most places touched over the center of the street. The whole street was its own little enclave. It was as though they were no longer in Los Angeles. This was half the reason this neighborhood was so expensive.

Katharine found herself blinking as they got closer. The sight of the house emerging from the shadows of the trees was beautiful. Old, deep-red brick served as both walkway and small retaining wall. It led through trimmed bushes and lush grass, right up to the clear, and surely bullet-proof, safety door. Behind that, displayed for all the world, was a hand-pieced stained-glass panel with just enough wood trim to hold a knob and be called a "door." Katharine stared at it, admiring the artistry until Allistair must have gotten tired of waiting and raised his hand to knock.

The sound was a dull, hollow thud from the plexiglass safety shield. Looking frustrated, he pushed the doorbell. The sound of actual chimes being hit rang out from behind the brick façade.

Katharine waited. Nothing happened.

She looked at Allistair. He looked back at her.

There had been no contingency plan in case Mary wasn't home. Katharine hadn't really thought about it. To her, work and home were really the only two places to be. Aside from the occasional evening out, they were where she always was.

Allistair rang the bell again and they waited while a jogger ran past on the street behind them. Katharine turned to see if the person was going to be nosy, but her ears had white wires headed into them and it was clear that her mind was elsewhere.

Without speaking, Katharine and Allistair nodded their heads at each other a few times in telltale gestures, making the decision to go around back and check the place out.

The way Katharine figured it, they'd either look through a window and see that Mary Wayne had already left for Panama and early retirement, or else the woman would meet them at the back door with a loaded pistol and kill them. Given the way her life was going, the third option was . . . well, Katharine didn't want to consider that, so she followed Allistair, trying to be sneaky in high heels and wishing she'd just worn the same comfy pants she'd had on yesterday.

The backyard was even prettier than the front. Guarded by bushes that the two of them slipped through, it housed a swing and a tea table, a small fountain, and, in the back corner, a hot tub. Making the most of the L.A. weather, bright blooms climbed the fence that separated Mary's backyard from whoever lived on the other side. It seemed the best neighbors were the ones you never saw.

The back door was as guarded as the front, which Katharine thought was a good idea given the ease with which she had gotten back here. And she wasn't even sneaky.

Allistair was way ahead of her, and he didn't bother knocking at the back door, just gave it a tug. Katharine was close enough behind to see his surprise as the door swung wide. When the inner door gave easily too, they both became suspicious and a bit more cautious.

Now that she thought about it, Katharine had no desire to meet

Mary Wayne on the bullet end of a gun, and she called out the woman's name as they entered.

There was no answer, but by that point Katharine really hadn't expected one.

Cautiously, they stepped in, entering a wide kitchen, the deep brown rock countertops glistening with the look of money that Mary Wayne shouldn't have. The tile sparkled, and the window in one long wall opened into the living area. All of it was spotless.

Katharine called again, holding back as Allistair slowly made his way into the larger room, the frown marring his perfect features indicating more confusion than anything else. Katharine knew her face mirrored his, and as she opened her lungs to shout again, she nearly gagged on the smell.

As if it had rolled in like fog, the smell enveloped her. Rank and overripe, it crawled into her senses and held on, refusing to let go. Katharine pulled her sleeve down over her hand, tucking her nose and mouth into the crook of her elbow as if that might stop the odor.

It didn't come close.

Allistair was standing in the middle of the living area in front of the couch. His back was straight and his face uncovered. Looking at him through eyes that threatened to water, Katharine took a few moments ,absorbing what she saw.

He put his hand up, palm facing her as though to ward her off. "Katharine, don't look at this."

But it was too late.

She could see around him. Not all of it, but clearly enough to know what the smell was coming from.

Slim feet in cute, sensible shoes lay one on, one off the couch, as though the legs had been flung there. A hand, in a shade of gray that was distinctly un-human, hung near the leather dust ruffle, rings still sparkling, one fingertip just brushing the plush carpeting.

The hair was brown and curly. It had once been neat and freshly set, but now it was messy. It was mostly the hair and the rings that told Katharine she was looking at Mary Wayne.

Just not all of her.

Still, it took a minute to understand what she was seeing. The woman's throat was missing; internal organs that Katharine couldn't identify were exposed to the air and rotting in plain sight where her belly had been laid open in great gashes. Katharine stepped around Allistair, disobeying even as he repeated that she should leave. She could see that some of Mary's bones showed where her chest had been ripped. It looked as though the body were made of loosely held-together limbs. The arm with the hand that still bore the rings was hanging by a sinew.

Her senses overtaking her, Katharine at last turned around. Gulping, she fought for breath, but there wasn't any to be had. All the air was tainted with the cloying smell of decay.

Stumbling toward the kitchen and trying to make her way out the open back door, Katharine grabbed at countertops and chairs as she passed, trying to keep a grasp on which direction was up and, most importantly, which way was out. When she was finally sitting on the back steps, on the beautiful walkway that led down to the red-brick deck and the built-in barbeque, her brain began to process what it really hadn't been able to just a minute earlier.

Mary Wayne was dead.

Mary Wayne was torn apart. Throat ripped open, body torn limb from limb, the pieces barely held together.

Mary Wayne had been shredded by long razors, several long razors set about two inches apart.

Katharine tried to breathe, but she couldn't. Her own arms hurt again and she wondered how long ago Mary Wayne had died. They hadn't just missed her by minutes—Mary had been dead a while. And Katharine was now certain she was crazy, just as certain as she was that Mary Wayne had been killed by the beast that had visited her. By whatever was writing on the mirror.

She didn't know when she finally began to focus on her surroundings. But she saw that Allistair sat beside her, his jacket and his arms draped around her shoulders. She didn't remember either of those things getting put there.

After her vision focused, a sound broke through into her thoughts, the wailing of a siren practically in her ear. The medics were coming across the backyard, but they didn't go inside. Allistair directed them to her, and Katharine became confused. They needed to get Mary Wayne.

In the background of her jumbled thoughts she heard Allistair's voice saying she was in shock and probably needed fluid.

Time passed, but she wasn't sure how much. She sat on the back step with the medic on one side of her and Allistair on the other. She answered questions about her medical history, though her words sounded slurred and mixed up even to her. After a while she was given a shot but couldn't even be bothered to ask what it was. Surely Allistair would have stopped them if she shouldn't have it.

Eventually, she was asked to stand, and she heard Allistair saying he'd stay with her that night and watch her. She simply felt too disconnected to protest.

She stood at his side, a blanket around her shoulders and her mouth shut, while the police asked him questions and he answered for both of them. Eventually, it began to grow dark and Allistair herded her toward the car, taking the keys from her as he folded her into the passenger seat.

Later, it felt as if she had woken up, although she didn't remember falling asleep, and she was at her front door with Allistair. He wanted to come in, but she wouldn't let him. Her thoughts were too confusing to make that kind of decision. And there was something in the words he said, something that had made her wary. He had known a lot about Mary Wayne. He had told the police all kinds of things she hadn't known herself.

He thought Mary Wayne had died a while ago. And Katharine wondered how he could have known so much. Allistair had spoken to the police for a long time, or at least her drug-muddled brain seemed to think it had been a while. He'd told them all kinds of things she didn't want to process.

He had shrugged when the cops asked about knives. But he'd seen Mary's arms, hadn't he? He should have connected it to the cuts on Katharine's arms. But he didn't. In fact, he told the police he thought Mary had fallen in with a bad crowd. Like a teenager gone a little wild.

How could he have missed something so obvious? Was he covering for someone? Himself? Or did he think he had to cover for her? She tried not to tax her tired brain too much when she knew she'd think more clearly in the morning.

She crawled into her bed, disturbed by how the covers rattled, and her thoughts skittered away and evaporated, like water on a hot pan. After several efforts to straighten her brain, she realized the covers rattled because her hand was shaking.

She should call Allistair back. He would come take care of her. He would know what to do.

But instead she slid down and pulled the comforter up around her neck, happy for the void that was coming on. With one deep breath her thoughts slipped away from her and she fell asleep.

. . .

Allistair stared at Zachary.

They stood beyond the veil, looking down at Katharine as she slumbered on in her drug-induced darkness. This time she didn't see him—didn't see either of them.

Zachary had gotten pissed. Allistair had made a move. He had stolen some of Katharine's precious time. While Allistair was proud of the move, Zachary had been bound to fight back. It was against the grain to let the other get ahead. In a war like this, getting the edge meant everything, and losing it meant retaliation.

But Zachary didn't make a move. He simply sat, as Allistair did, watching the woman they fought for. Waiting for a chance to get ahead.

Although they would have liked to have gone for each other's throats, they couldn't. They were evenly matched; there was no clear victor to tear out the other's entrails as had been done to Mary Wayne.

So they stared, each knowing what the other knew. Each knowing that they could make no moves now. But neither would be the first to step away. Neither would leave Katharine alone with the other if it wasn't a necessity of the charade.

They could have gone on like that forever.

But Katharine heard her phone ring and began to stir.

Allistair shivered and began backing out of Katharine's space. She had been seeing more than he expected. Let her find Zachary there.

Maybe his opponent didn't know about the drugs that would still be in her system. Didn't realize that the change in her consciousness would let her see through the veil, see them as they were. Two beasts, one black and deep as oil, the other silver and liquid-skinned.

So Allistair fled the scene, pissed again when he felt Zachary fade out just a split second after he had. That meant Zachary knew about the drugs, and that meant he had been following them earlier today and Allistair hadn't known.

He cursed his stupidity and wished for a solid wall to hit.

The need to hit something only depressed him more. It meant he'd been spending too much time in human form already. And there was nothing to be done for it.

He let the anger rip through his brain and swore one more time, knowing full well the power of the words he said. He only took a brief moment to contemplate the ripples his anger sent out into the world. The job at Light & Geryon was both blessing and curse. He was able to be close to Katharine, but on days like these when she wasn't in, he was still expected to show up as Allistair. And he had only a small window of time to make the change.

He cursed again.

. . .

Katharine held the phone to her ear, trying to look casual. "No, I really can't right now, but thank you." Though it didn't really address what Margot had said, it would get the point across.

There was an audible sigh on the other end of the line as the librarian gathered a protest. "You need to meet with me. It's about the messages."

"Later then. That would be great." Katharine faked a smile, even though she could practically hear Margot simmering .

"No!"

Katharine's head jerked back a little. She hadn't expected that from a research librarian. Unfortunately, the move caused Allistair to look up from his work, his frown asking, "Is everything all right?"

Katharine gave him a benign and reassuring smile as Margot's words filtered in.

"Look, I translated the last message, only I'm too late. Were you even okay when we talked this morning?"

"When we talked? When did we talk?" Katharine didn't pay attention to what she'd said and immediately worried what Allistair would think. But that concern was quickly yanked from her thoughts as Margot spoke again.

"This morning, early."

"No, I was asleep."

Margot sounded like she was beginning to put a few pieces together, but Katharine wasn't. "That's what you sounded like, almost like you never really woke up for the whole conversation."

There was a pause, then Margot continued. "You said something about the messages you've been getting, and it matches what I found."

Katharine put a hand to her head, no longer trying to cover for anything. A cold river snaked through her. What had she said? The drugs they had shot into her had worn off when she woke up this morning, but apparently she had talked to Margot while she was still affected. And she had no memory of it.

Margot's voice pulled her back to reality, or what passed for reality these days. "Where do you want to meet?"

"My place?"

She gave Margot a quick set of directions, then grabbed her jacket and headed out the door, barely saying good-bye to Allistair and Lisa.

Margot awaited her in the lobby of the building. Katharine spotted her just as the guard was starting to tell her she had a visitor.

All she needed was a wave of her hand, and Margot was up on her knock-off designer heels and following. The flat expression on the librarian's face wasn't a comfort.

Just as the elevator doors closed, Margot turned and began asking what felt like a thousand questions. "What were you saying on the phone this morning? It sounded like you had seen something. Did you—"

Katharine cut her off. "I live here. Please be quiet until we get to my condo."

Not that there was anyone else in the elevator, but Katharine was good and ready to add paranoia to her list of complaints for when she finally caved and checked herself in to the psych ward.

After she shut and bolted her unit door behind them, she shed her jacket and threw it across the arm of the couch, a place she was certain it had never been before. Margot gently laid her own coat on top of Katharine's as Katharine began firing her own questions. "What did I say this morning?"

With her hands planted firmly on her hips, she attempted to stare Margot down. It didn't work.

Although she was answered, Katharine knew she hadn't intimidated the woman.

"You said you had found a dead woman. And that she had been ripped open. That it looked like it was by the same thing that had cut your arms a week ago. And you said it so matter-of-factly that it made me go cold."

Katharine wasn't sure what to say to that. It was all true. It was all due to the drugs.

But she didn't need to speak. Margot took up the conversation again. "I tried to reach you all day yesterday, but you weren't answering. It sounds like you were out finding dead bodies. I got the translation of the last message, even though yesterday was already too late."

"What do you mean 'too late'?" Katharine waited, her hands on her hips putting forth the only power she had right now.

"The message says 'I will come in the first vigil of the night.'" Margot picked up her purse from the couch and dug a scrap of paper out of her purse from where she had set it on top of her jacket. As though the paper was proof of the message.

Looking at it, Katharine asked, "What does it mean by 'vigil'?"

"It's a Latin term." Margot was in her element now. She knew this stuff and wanted to share. "The night is divided into vigils; the first is from dark to midnight and so on."

Katharine nodded, somehow not preparing for Margot's next question.

"So, did he come?"

CHAPTER 13

Katharine looked at Margot like she'd grown a second head. "What?"

"It said, 'I will come in the first vigil of the night.' You said you had gotten the message the morning that you saw me. So that would have been two nights ago. That's why I know my translation was too late."

"No. He didn't." Katharine turned around, but it didn't prevent her from hearing Margot.

"You're a bad liar, remember? So, he came." There was a long pause. Maybe she was waiting to see Katharine's face, but Katharine wasn't going to give her that. "Are you okay?"

She caved. She had to give Margot something. "He came, yes. He just sat there, wanted to show me that he could break in. That's all."

"But he's not human."

Katharine's whole body snapped around. She had no idea how a normal person would react to that, but she tried to fake it. Once again, she tried to lie her way out of it. She frowned at Margot as though the woman were suggesting they make mud pies in the street while wearing feather boas.

But her face was as bad a liar as her voice was.

Margot's voice confirmed it. "I thought so."

Neither of them had been prepared for that. After the instant of satisfaction at being right, Margot crumpled to the couch, landing in a ladylike position though she appeared to have no control over her limbs.

Katharine found herself grateful that she didn't have to speak; Margot read her well enough that there was no need to say anything. So she calmly walked to the couch and sat herself on the other side. Her mind blanked. Although she knew she should be asking questions or throwing the librarian out, Katharine didn't seem to be able to do either.

Quietly, she stayed still, hands folded in her lap, wondering whether the librarian could read her, whether she could see the thin stream of relief that was somehow widening to a river. Katharine could only guess the relief was due to the fact that now someone else knew, someone who, at least on the surface, seemed and sounded sane.

Long moments passed while the two women shared space but not thoughts, each as shocked by the revelation as the other. As they sat there, Katharine realized that Margot had thrown the crazy statement out there knowing Katharine was unable to lie. But she hadn't expected to be right.

Finally, although she was uncertain when she'd decided to tell Margot everything, Katharine started speaking. "How did you know?"

For a moment there was only a deep sigh. "Seriously, I've never heard of a stalker who writes you notes in Latin but leaves no trace of his presence. Who would bother to threaten like that when you don't even understand the messages and would have a really hard time finding someone who could even translate them? It's not a curse or a spell, meaning it has no value other than as a threat. And you said something about a 'thing' that might have cut you. So either you are the target of a seriously deranged, overeducated, and black-ops-trained man or . . . Well, I tried to think of who could get through triple-locked doors and speaks Latin."

Katharine didn't say anything. What could she say? That she was impressed that she'd clearly given away too much information even in the little amount she had indulged?

"The only people who speak Latin these days are priests, and I figured I would go to the cops if I had a priest stalking me. But you didn't."

She shook her head. "Anyway, a demon is the only thing that made all the pieces fit, as crazy as that sounds."

Margot still didn't look at her. This was some bizarre territory they were covering.

But somehow Katharine found her backbone and renewed her resolve to save herself. She'd need to know everything she could, including what Margot knew. So she forced herself to ask, "Why does a demon fit the profile?"

A long sigh came out before the words. In a way it was reassuring that this other woman found the subject as odd as she did. It indicated that Margot wasn't a nut job out looking for evil and finding Katharine as a ready target.

But as fast as it soothed her, Katharine felt the chill seep in. If Margot wasn't looking for demons, then it became more likely that was what she was actually dealing with. Sucking in a deep breath, she forced herself to wait until all the evidence was in before she panicked.

"It's the Latin. In many texts, it's the main language of demons and angels. Also, you had asked me if the first message was in Aramaic. So I thought that was what you were leaning toward."

"I was." Katharine didn't know what else to say. She didn't know where to put her trust, what would get her institutionalized, jailed, or killed. But if she had a demon, it was a lot stronger than she. And she had never been strong. Not physically, and certainly not in any other way.

Sitting on her couch, with the afternoon light filtering through the blinds she'd only partially opened that morning, Katharine surveyed her thoughts. She pondered the familiar condo that she was used to but not certain that she loved. The new boyfriend she felt passionate about, and the man she was cheating on him with. The job she had loved and only recently seen for what it truly was. The fact that, at age thirty-two, she was only just now realizing that she didn't agree with everything her parents had taught her.

She stood to lose all of it, good and bad, solidified past and open future.

So she had to trust someone, because there was no way she could keep her own head straight about what was happening. In that split second, she chose Margot. The woman was the least involved, had no reason to lie, and could give Katharine objective advice—which wasn't true of just about anyone else in her life. The people in her life were few, but even Lisa, whose only relationship to Katharine was as her assistant, held some sort of sway. Besides, for some unknown reason, Katharine found she already trusted Margot. "Promise you won't tell anyone?"

The librarian didn't speak right away. There was no childish, immediate swearing in. Somehow that made the answer more valuable. "I won't tell unless you are in immediate mortal danger."

That sounded fair.

Katharine began talking.

. . .

"They said you did something that made you look suspicious."

Though Zachary's voice was mellow and his tone soothing, his words were anything but. And he knew it.

Katharine wouldn't dare ask him what she had done to catch the eye of the police. But he was certain she had a sneaking suspicion of her own—she was a bad liar and she *did* know more about the case than she should. He hadn't seen her in the flesh since two days before when he'd taken her home from the police station after holding the snarling officers at bay. And it was only just now that he—her lawyer—was able to get back to her with any info about the case.

It took her a moment to shake her head and shrug in answer to his statement, as if she couldn't fathom why the police would be suspicious of her.

Zachary responded in kind, "I gave them the usual runaround and they took it because they had to. But it bought you some time without them pestering you. The last thing I heard is that they have new evidence that takes you and your coworker out of suspicion."

If he had his way, he'd shine the bright light on Allistair. Making that fool sit in jail for a night in human form would be fantastic punishment. It would take forever for him to recover from holding shape for that long. And if he failed at it—if he couldn't hold form—he'd simply disappear from the jail cell. That he was a person of interest in a bizarre and grisly death would mean a massive manhunt for the man who could escape and leave locked doors behind. Which meant Allistair would have to at least abandon that persona and he'd have to start all over again winning Katharine's trust.

Zachary smiled. What a nice, tidy move that would be—to take Allistair out of play by human rules. Unfortunately, that particular move was off the table.

Zachary knew exactly what had killed Mary Wayne. He understood far better than what Katharine suspected. But for now, he smiled at her and soothed her. He needed to let it be known that he was here to help and that he was helping. "Don't speak to the police without me. Even if you just run into one of them on the street."

She stiffened immediately in his arms. "I thought you said I wasn't a suspect anymore."

"You aren't." He laid his hand against her shoulder and, with a little pressure, brought her down to rest against him. "But they will still want to talk to you. You're a witness, and they'll want to know everything you saw and everything you know."

She nodded at that, and he felt her relax into his arms before he told her his next piece of information. He needed to see how she would react. "While you're off the hook, your father's company isn't, yet. And they'll want to question you about that, too."

He'd kept talking even though she'd stiffened again at the mention of Light & Geryon. She would have blurted something out, but he'd railroaded her just a bit. Then it came, exactly what he'd been expecting in his almost-human brain.

"Why is the company a suspect? Who in the company? I don't get it." She was turned to face him now, her warm little hands pressed against his chest to prop herself up, her confused and angry face looking to him for answers, for comfort. This was good. This was where she needed to be.

He smiled, again placating her. "Of course they suspect people at the company from which she stole hundreds of thousands of dollars—they have to. The question is: how many people knew she was a thief? That will narrow their scope a little bit."

"Um . . ." It seemed to be all she could get out. She looked away, breaking eye contact with him, as though there were something to hide.

Interesting. He hadn't thought she was capable of hiding much of anything from him. At the very least, *she* believed she could. Still, he used the fumble to remind her of the severity of the situation. "Look, I'm your lawyer. Anything you say to me as your lawyer, like now, is kept in complete legal confidence."

He was curious what she would reveal now that she believed it wouldn't go anywhere.

Katharine began talking. "There were only a few people who knew about her. My father alerted me to the missing money. My assistant helped me trace the missing funds back to Mary. There was a PI, but she's not part of the company. It wasn't her money that was missing. And I have no idea who told my father and Uncle Toran about the missing money in the first place. Maybe someone in accounting."

Zachary nodded. He had made sure the accountant had spotted the missing funds, as he had been well aware of what Mary had been doing. To Katharine, he only said, "Don't worry, we'll get it taken care of. None of this is going to come back on you."

She pushed farther away from him. "No, that's not really what I'm concerned about. I didn't kill that woman—"

"I know." He smiled sympathetically and tried to pull her back, but she resisted.

"No! It's not about me."

He looked at her now, wondering what she was going to offer him, what juicy piece of humanity would float to the surface of her.

"There were only a few people who knew about the theft. And of those people, only four would be really upset. My father and Uncle Toran, because it's their company. Uncle Toran's nephew, who is supposed to inherit the Light side of Light and Geryon. And me. If it's not me, who do they suspect?"

Zachary did his best to look concerned. Then he planted the seed.

"What about your assistant?"

"Allistair?" She frowned as if she hadn't even considered it.

"Isn't he one of the people who knew?"

"Yes, but . . . he has no vested interest in the company."

"But I thought . . . Never mind." Zachary just smiled at her and nodded. He didn't want to be too obvious. It was just a tiny seed.

But that was the beautiful thing about little seeds. They grew.

. . .

Katharine had ditched work yet again and was headed toward the coffee shop to soothe her once-again rattled nerves when her phone started singing at her. It was the ring she'd assigned Margot.

Unsure if she wanted to know what Margot was calling about, Katharine looked at the screen for a moment. She kept walking down the street. Though the day was beautiful, it was still just a touch on the chilly side, and no one was on the street. As she passed a storefront, she caught a glimpse of her reflection and saw herself as the coward she was. Being a coward would only harm her from here on out. So at the last moment before the ring died and sent Margot to voicemail, Katharine pushed the button and answered. "Hi."

"Thank goodness, for a moment, I thought you'd decided not to answer."

"No, I just couldn't find my phone in my purse."

There was a brief pause. "You didn't have trouble finding your phone. You just debated whether or not to answer it."

"Is it okay if I hate you?" Katharine said in as pleasant a tone as she could muster. And then before it settled and Margot got mad at her she added. "That's really annoying, you know? My father always falls for that one."

There was a small pause. "Then maybe he hasn't paid the slightest bit of attention when he's around you. I've never seen anyone with a more organized house, purse, life, whatever than you."

Like a hit to the belly, Katharine realized that, as usual, Margot was right. Her father paid no attention to her whatsoever. For the first time, Katharine could see his always placid expression for what it really was—glossed over. His eyes failed to notice everything he might see in her if he just looked. Shouldn't he have seen that she'd been tired, drained, scared these past several weeks? He'd patted her hand and told her they'd known it was coming when her mother died, but had only hugged her once. Somehow she'd grieved for her mother all alone and had never gotten upset at him for leaving his only daughter to herself. She'd just accepted it as the way it was, even though she now knew better.

"Are you still there?" As Margot's voice came over the phone, Katharine realized it was still pressed to her ear and she was a little farther down the street.

"Yes." Although she was even more certain now that there was nothing Margot could tell her that might be even remotely good.

"Look, I want to ask a few more questions." Without waiting for Katharine to concede to being questioned, Margot launched into what was apparently quite a list. "Have you seen anything hovering or flying around your room? Or pecking at you?"

"Oh God, no!" That quickly brought her out of her thoughts. So it could be worse? They might peck at her? "Why?"

"There's a lot of demonology that says that's what they do. That's really been linked recently to hallucinations caused by rye mold—lots of scientists think they broke the whole Salem witch trials wide open when they discovered that the conditions were perfect for this particular kind of rye mold the years the persecutions went on. But there's still a lot of lore prior to that, and it says demons do this kind of thing, so I was curious."

"Nope, no pecking. No Goody Proctor haunting me." Katharine turned the corner to where the street ended and the shopping area began. The foot traffic began to pick up a little and she shared the sidewalk with another person here or there.

"That's a good start." After a brief pause, and while Katharine wondered what could be coming next, Margot started up again. "Do you hear voices? Telling you what to do?"

A laugh erupted from her. "Lord, Margot. If I heard voices I'd probably be glad to do what they told me at this point."

"All right then, no voices."

There was another pause and Katharine heard rustling noises in the background as she waited her friend out. She imagined Margot sitting at the library desk, turning huge pages from some gilt-edged tome she'd pulled from some far, dusty corner of the library.

As she passed a large plate-glass window, something caught her eye. Gasping slightly, she turned to see what it was.

"Katharine! Are you okay?"

She laughed again at Margot, thinking she hadn't laughed much at all in her life, because who would she laugh with? "I just saw the most fantastic blue suede pumps. They're perfect for you."

She leaned in, her breath fogging a small circle on the glass. The shoes were the color and texture of fog over the ocean, almost gray. Straps crossed over the top, giving the simple shoe elegant lines. As she stepped away from the window, about to ask Margot what size she wore, the reflection in the window changed. Katharine took a step back and frowned. It seemed the lines from the shoe were growing—extending wide. It took only a moment to realize the line was moving, and it wasn't the shoe. Without thinking about it, she stopped looking through the glass at the shoe and started looking at the window itself, her eyes tracing the dark forms reflected there.

She frowned as the lines converged at the tip of a long, oily wing. Subtle movement gave life to the thin membrane. Frozen, but still not comprehending, Katharine followed the reflection of the wing to where it joined a body. As deep and inky as the wing had been, the body looked even darker. Muscle flexed, crawling under liquid skin, as the creature rotated. Clawed fingers clenched and released as Katharine looked it over.

She followed the long and steely lines up past a neck far too solid to snap, past disturbingly long teeth that breath eased in and out past. Into hypnotic wells that passed for eyes.

In those eyes, something screamed soundlessly, and something deep and sinister drowned it out. In those eyes, she could see into the depths of something she never wanted to see. But she couldn't look away.

Even though she realized the creature was standing right behind her.

"Katharine? Katharine!"

She started. It didn't sound like the first time Margot had said her name. Somehow she forced out a "Huh?"

But still she couldn't tear her gaze away from the beast reflected in the window. Margot's voice tied her to reality—or at least what she hoped was reality.

Finally, getting a cold dose of some sanity, Katharine dropped the phone and screamed as her chest clenched and the utter fear poured out of her.

. . .

Katharine heard two strong knocks before she saw Margot push her way through the condo door. She nodded absently to her new friend, thinking that Margot's knock was what her mother would have termed "manly." But Margot, even with all her assertiveness and backbone, was definitely feminine.

If Katharine was up against what she thought she was, she was going to have to grow her own backbone, and really damned fast.

"So." Margot gracefully dropped herself into a dining room chair and crossed her long legs. "It sounds like you're having more of the problems on my list."

That, finally, got Katharine to lift her head and look at her friend. "You have a list of my problems?"

Margot laughed. "No, I have a list of problems that might be due to demons." It seemed the subject matter subdued her, and her expression turned more serious. "I tried to keep away from problems that were due to possession, but there may be some overlap."

With this, she frowned and started scrounging in her bag for something, presumably the list.

Katharine, her soup forgotten and her hands long past the shaking-like-a-seizure stage, pushed herself to her feet and headed down the hall to her closet. That black bag Margot carried bothered her no end. It was battered and scarred, and it had been cheap and styleless even when new.

"Katharine?" Margot's voice called from the living area. For a librarian she sure could make her voice go a long way.

"Just a minute." She continued to dig in the closet until she came up with a large black bag that revealed hints of purple when the fabric folded. Grabbing it, she marched back into the living room. "If you want it, this is for you."

Margot looked up from a sheaf of papers she was rifling through and blinked. "It's beautiful." She looked almost stunned as Katharine put the bag into her hands. "And I'm sure I can't afford it. Don't you want it?"

Katharine shook her head. "I love it, but it's too big for me. My mother gave it to me a handful of years back and I never used it. So it's just been sitting in my closet all this time waiting for someone who needed it. It's perfect for you."

Turning it over several times, Margot felt the material and checked inside, looking in all the little pockets. "As long as you're sure . . ."

When Katharine nodded, Margot smiled and simply said, "Thank you."

For just a moment, Katharine stopped where she was and felt

something form inside her. There were a thousand other things she had kept just because her mother had given them to her, so there was nothing particularly special about this bag. And she was never going to use it, but Margot would enjoy it until it was nothing but threads. She shook her head. "Thank my mother."

Katharine ate the dregs of her now-lukewarm soup while Margot busily transferred things from her old purse to the new one. It was nice to enjoy a moment with her friend that didn't involve discussing various things that could kill her. Painfully.

But after a short minute, and a chance to see everything Margot carried with her on a regular basis, Katharine was directed back to the list Margot had made.

"You said you saw something while you were talking to me."

Katharine grinned. It was all she could do. "Yeah, I saw the perfect shoe for you."

Margot just looked at her, waiting her out.

So she gave up and continued. "Then I saw a reflection, and as I looked it over I realized it was a creature. Somehow that didn't bother me until I saw its eyes." She couldn't suppress a shudder at the memory. It was almost as though just the remembering created a new link between herself and the creature. So she pushed it away. "The eyes were . . ."

Margot tipped her head, trying to catch Katharine's eyes. "This sounds like one of the questions I was going to ask you." She looked down at her list and added a check mark.

Katharine fought a shudder before she came back to reality. "What was the question?"

"Whether you were seeing things out of the corner of your eye or in reflections."

Dejectedly, Katharine nodded. "Well, I wasn't until then, but now, yes. What were some of the other questions?"

For a moment it seemed Margot wouldn't respond. When she did, it was to say that she wasn't sure she should ask them.

Katharine tried to be stern. "Tell me."

Only after a big sigh did Margot start speaking again, this time in a cold, rote voice. "Have you seen things crawling or moving along or under the walls or ceiling? Have you awoken above your bed or been held somewhere by an unseen force? Have you found cuts on your body that you don't remember getting? Is there anyone new in your life? Anyone special? Anyone particularly charismatic?"

CHAPTER 14

Allistair watched the door like a hawk, but Katharine didn't come through. Being her assistant had been a fantastic idea when she was a die-hard workaholic, but this whole mess had upset her rigid schedule and turned it into mush. He had no idea whether she would show today or not.

He needed her to show today. He needed to give her the news and he needed to give it to her in an offhand manner. If he called her in, told her she had to come, he would lose the apparent casualness he needed. He would lose the thrust of making certain that she saw the connections for herself. He would lose so much. And she wasn't here.

He rolled his spine, enjoying the way the bones slid against each other. He flexed his fingers and toes and moved his legs beneath the desk. He had already collected enough material—files, reports, random notes—to appear that he had been working all morning.

He walked back and forth across the office. The door was closed and no one would see him. If Katharine came in, he'd just say he'd been pacing, maybe waiting for her. Worried because she was late, again.

The motion in his legs felt good, even if it didn't necessarily help him hold form. Still, he'd incorporated on a day when he wasn't certain he'd see Katharine, so he used it, he moved. And while he moved, he plotted.

What if someone else told her? It wouldn't be delivered the same way, but then he wouldn't have to be the bearer of what would turn out to be truly catastrophic bad news. Since she'd been gone all morning, she might have heard. But she might not have. How would he figure out whether she knew without giving it away? And if she had already heard, wouldn't she have called him? He should be at the top of her list to contact in a case like this. But she probably didn't have a list at the ready for a case like this.

The phone at his desk rang, a deep buzz that wanted to slide under his senses and go undetected. But he picked it up anyway. "Yes?"

There was a cold pause at the other end—Lisa's general warning that she didn't really like him, and didn't like that he had gotten the job she felt was rightfully hers. "Katharine let me know she won't be coming in today."

Only a hair after the end of the sentence came the click of Lisa putting the phone back in its cradle. It was good that he didn't have anything to say back to her. All he had to do now was get out the door and stay gone for the day without raising suspicion.

After a few minutes he put on his jacket and tugged the sleeves straight. Making his way into the hallway, he stopped at Lisa's desk and leaned over her just a little. It was obvious from the way she pulled back that she didn't like it, but in a moment she wouldn't remember that part anyway.

His finger reached out and touched hers, making that all-important contact, and he told her he was going out to lunch, he'd be back later. But he walked down the hall knowing that Lisa wouldn't expect him back at all that day, and that she wouldn't find his absence at all unusual.

Now, if he could just find Katharine.

. . .

"No! That's just not possible!" Katharine heard her voice rise, but it didn't hit anywhere near the decibel level she wanted. Her body needed to screech like twisting metal. She wanted to let it all out, to rail against the utter wrongness of what she was hearing, but years of training worked against her. By force of will she was able to remain fairly calm, given the circumstances.

"But that's what the police say, baby." Her father stated. The added "baby" was an indicator that he knew she was stressed. That would be as much as he offered. There would be no other comfort forthcoming, just the one word that only she would recognize as the acknowledgement that it was.

"But I saw her last week." Katharine sucked in air. Her back stayed rigid, and only someone right next to her would have caught that. Not that it mattered. She was alone in her apartment, holed up for another day after Margot had asked her those stupid questions. No, she hadn't been held hostage in the air high above her own bed. No, she hadn't seen the walls move, and she hadn't had any flying hallucinations pecking at her—which was a damn shame, because that was often merely due to rye mold, so, no, of course she didn't have that problem. But she did have a new man in her life, a very charismatic one.

And that nasty little bit of information had plagued her all the way up until her father dropped this bomb on her. Katharine was still fighting it. "Okay, *I* didn't actually see Mary, but we have video of her, coming and going from the office. Call the security guys." At last she seemed to break some ground here, and her father replied, "I seem to remember something about that. I'll check with them. It would be really disturbing if we found video like that."

If? If? She wanted to scream it. What did he mean *If?* He was the one who sent her to get the footage in the first place.

But he hung up quickly, off to make the call to surveillance. Well, he'd set Sharon to the task anyway. But surely within a short while they'd have proof to take to the police and all this would be righted.

Katharine sighed again at the thought of her ruined day of rest. She'd taken the day off to recover from yesterday, but she wouldn't be able to take tomorrow off to recover from today. At least in a little while she'd hear that the tapes were in the coroner's hands and all would be resolved. Because there was no way Mary Wayne had been dead for over two weeks when they found her.

Yes, the smell had been really bad and the body had already started decaying, but that didn't mean two weeks. They really should fire that coroner, and maybe they would after the tapes proved him wrong. Part of her wanted to hop online and look up decay rates, just to add further fuel to her righteous fire, but a more sensible part of her realized that was a can of worms she really didn't want to open.

With a few deep breaths she sat back down on the couch and steadied her nerves.

Then she stood back up and paced for a few minutes.

She tried to eat something, but nothing would go down, not carrots or crackers or soda. And when she couldn't even get herself to eat a frozen Thin Mint from the last Girl Scout cookie sale, she realized none of it was working.

Finally she gave up, picked up the phone and dialed a number. "Margot?"

. . .

Katharine fought her racing heart. Her day of rest was now a complete bust. In fact, she was more worked up than she'd been yesterday. She hadn't told Zachary about following Mary Wayne, so he didn't know anything. Not that she had wanted to talk to the charismatic new man in her life. Still, she couldn't reconcile the idea that the beautiful Zachary could be a demon.

Betty in payroll remembered Katharine coming in and asking about Mary Wayne, and she remembered her answer. But did she remember actually seeing Mary over the past two weeks? Well, things were just so busy, Betty really couldn't be sure.

Katharine was nearly willing to let someone try some illegal interrogation techniques to *make* her remember.

Her father and Uncle Toran both told the police they had turned the whole matter over to Katharine. They said they knew Katharine had been sent to look for Ms. Wayne, but they didn't remember what Katharine had found out. So, no, they couldn't say whether Mary Wayne had been around in the past few weeks. Jeff Grason in security was out with a bad flu and no one had talked to him.

Katharine wasn't about to pick up the phone and check with him; she was growing ever more certain Mr. Grason would claim to have the mysterious fuzzy memory disease everyone else seemed to have caught.

So she sat on her couch and sucked in deep, bracing lungfuls of air. It didn't really brace her for anything, or stop her arms from quaking with fury. But she kept at it, hoping to inhale some zen on one of these breaths.

She hadn't told Margot anything about Mary Wayne other than the basics—she'd been looking for a thief, she and Allistair had gone to see her at her house, and they'd found the woman dead—well, shredded. So all Margot could do was corroborate that Katharine had been telling ongoing tales of seeing a woman who was already dead.

Patricia Sange, the PI, could only produce paperwork showing the accounting evidence of Mary's fraud. There were apparently no photos, and Ms. Sange hadn't actually seen Mary, even though Katharine had thought the woman had been tailing her, but even she couldn't remember for sure.

And then there was Allistair. Allistair had gone hunting for Mary Wayne himself. As Katharine's sidekick, he had searched out the woman, too. But Katharine couldn't get him to return her phone calls. It was like he had vanished now too.

Worst—by far—the video data had all been erased. It was standard company policy to erase data after a week if there hadn't been anything reported. And nothing was reported. There was no record of Katharine's visits with Jeff Grason or any of the other security guys. All the evidence was just gone. All simply disappeared, with easy, practical explanations.

The deep breathing wasn't working, so Katharine practically threw herself backward onto the couch. Staring at the ceiling, she decided maybe she didn't want to know if Allistair remembered seeing Mary Wayne. He would be the only one left to say she wasn't clinically insane. And at this point it was beginning to look prudent to keep her mouth shut.

. . .

Allistair watched as the colors turned the corner. Dread rolled off Katharine in waves, and as usual, her emotions reached the room long before she did.

The feelings themselves didn't swamp him, not unless he touched her. But even from a distance he could always sense her—her emotions had a habit of sneaking under his skin in a way that was certainly wrong but that he wasn't certain he disliked.

Today she was edgy. A subtle shimmer of nerves laced itself in with the concern, and he seemed to get a hint that it was all about him.

Cool and collected on the outside, she gathered her messages from Lisa and came in as she would have any other day—as if she hadn't just disappeared two days ago and was only now reappearing without dropping a clue about what had happened. If he'd been human, he would have thought she didn't even realize she'd been gone.

She said hello to him with a warmth that resembled her usual greeting, but the colors around her revealed the emotion to be entirely fake. Then she hung her jacket on the back of her chair. Without paying him any more attention than that, she got to work.

He took a few deep breaths while he perused his own computer screen. He felt edgy now too, although he wasn't sure if it was caused by Katharine's presence or his own knowledge.

It was a full hour later before she decided to speak to him. In that hour he had amassed and hidden a good bundle of work to cover for any upcoming days he might need to miss. He'd even found a potential investment out of the pile he'd been assigned to sort through—a pesticide company with new methodologies and stronger chemicals that would produce higher crop yields in South America, where the standards weren't so strict. So at least the time hadn't gone wasted.

"Allistair?"

Everything except the anxiety radiating off her looked calm and casual. "What?"

"Did you follow up on the Australian gem mine?"

"Of course."

For the next twenty minutes he kept up the pretense of a work-based conversation. He told her that Light & Geryon had invested heavily in the mine despite her written rebuttal to the original proposal. Apparently the information she had dug up about the movement of money in and around the mining company only made it look better to the investors.

Then he sat back and watched her quietly seethe. He didn't have to wonder what it would do to her to know that her argument against the abuse she'd found had only pushed her father's company toward it. She couldn't hide anything from him. Besides, the company would be hers one day. The question was, would she get fed up enough to leave before her father signed it over?

The anger only slowed her in her tracks for a moment before she righted herself and went back to her original goal. "I was wondering if you heard what the coroner said about Mary Wayne."

Not sure if what she said was a real question, Allistair just shook his head like he didn't know exactly what she meant.

Sure enough, she spelled it out. "The coroner said she'd been dead for two weeks when we found her."

"Huh." He tried to look impressed.

"Did you think she'd been dead that long?"

He wanted to laugh, but kept his voice even. "What do I know about that sort of thing? The average guy on the street could come up to me and tell me my assumptions about how long she'd been dead were all wrong, and I'd have to believe him. Do you know anything about forensics?"

"Well, no."

He cut off the "but" that was clearly perched on the end of her tongue. "Why do you seem to doubt that she was?"

There, she'd have to say something. He'd know in just a moment.

"I thought I saw her here in the week right before we found her. Didn't you?"

He shook his head. Not with his human eyes he hadn't. He moved the subject just a little left of center. "I thought you couldn't get a hold of her. Aren't there tapes? Or discs, or however they store that kind of info these days?"

She shook her head, clearly bothered by it. "I thought there might be too, but it's all been wiped."

The fact that she'd checked on the footage meant she believed Mary Wayne had been here. He nodded in sympathy.

She turned to him, once again looking calm and collected. "I also thought people said she'd been in at work." Katharine shrugged.

Allistair rolled his shoulders and looked to one side, as if he had to think about it. "I don't really remember. What people?"

Her eyes darted away as she threw his own words right back at him. "I don't really remember."

Liar.

Well, that made two of them.

She settled herself behind her desk and aimed her eyes at her computer screen.

With the conversation clearly over, Allistair went back to randomly clicking the keys on his keyboard. In his mind, he made a list. Katharine was denying the fact that things had been turned upside down. She'd seen Mary on video days after the time of death the coroner had given. She had seen plenty of records and had a handful of eyewitnesses who placed Mary at work on those last days before they'd found her, mutilated, in the beautiful house.

And yet she was beginning to believe that her own perception was wrong. That things were right because of something as simple and wrong as the number of people who professed them as truth. She was being swayed from her own beliefs.

Allistair was disappointed in Katharine.

Her failings would become his failings. And he couldn't afford to fail.

Katharine was proving to be as weak as she had been when he'd started with her. Though her eyes had been pried open, in often painful ways, her backbone hadn't gotten any sturdier. And if he was going to get somewhere with this, he would have to take what she wouldn't give him voluntarily.

In the end, he would need her permission. He would have to back her into a corner to give it, because if she turned herself over to Zachary first, he'd have hell to pay. But before he could claim her permission, he had a few other vital pieces to collect first.

The easiest to get would be her breath.

. . .

Katharine washed the coffee mug instead of just setting it in the sink like usual. Anything to keep her hands busy. Anything to keep from interacting more with Zachary, to keep from looking at him, from touching him. Having him this close made that difficult at best.

Her voice was a little unsteady, and she hoped he would believe it was due to the subject matter. "It's just that all that time we were looking for her, she was dead on her couch."

The image itself sent cold fingers walking up her spine. But the addition of the man at her back chilled her more.

She didn't like the way he had talked her into spending the evening with him. She felt manipulated—pushed even—when he'd made it sound like she was the one who was off base if she didn't want to invite him in. Yet she still wanted him, still had to keep her hands busy to keep them away from him. Margot's words rang in her head. Was Zachary her demon?

"Weren't there tapes?"

The factual question caught her off guard, and she turned, not sure whether she felt safer looking at him or having him behind her. "They were erased."

"Erased! That's ridiculous!" As the words left his mouth she found herself almost forced to agree. It *had* been nuts. And here she was, having to defend it.

"Actually, there aren't any tapes per se. It's all saved as computer data and the drives get erased after a week to make room for more. It's all full speed and there are cameras recording all over the building, so the data storage—even for just a week—is massive. Anyway, apparently a week is the statute of limitations on any Light & Geryon problem. Too bad, so sad."

Even as she said it, she felt bad. She knew it wasn't true. The data-storage problem was a legitimate one.

"Still"—he sounded almost personally affronted on her behalf—"with this case going on and the kinds of theft you were investigating, you would think they would find some extra storage."

She was getting into a snit, reacting to him being upset. She was defending the company's actions again before she was really even aware she was doing it. "Well, I don't think anyone projected this kind of scenario here. And there were no new missing funds. So by the time we even found that the money was gone, that data had long since been erased. Besides, it was all done on computer. There wouldn't have been any damning tapes of Mary dressed in black, hauling heavy bags of stacked bills out the back door."

Zachary laughed—and something about the sound put her a little more at ease. His response did too. "You seem tense. Is it me?"

She shook her head no as a languorous feeling washed over her. There *couldn't* be anything wrong with Zachary, no matter what Margot had read. Zachary broke that chain of thought, telling her to come sit by him, and she did. His kisses drugged her and she gave herself to him willingly. The feelings of his hands on her and of his body naked beside her became a hazy whirlwind around her, while inside a warm feeling of home took root and mixed in with too many other things to count.

No, she realized while he took her that he wasn't the problem. She knew it. She just felt it inside.

They talked a little while longer, wrapped in her sheets and tangled together like puppies. The words rolled out of her as though she were helpless to stop them. He asked about her father, about Allistair, about whether she was really okay after this latest blow in the Mary Wayne incident.

Of course she was.

And as she said it, she found she meant it. As drugged and sated as she felt in his arms, how could she be anything else?

Katharine didn't remember him leaving.

It was only later, when she woke—cold and alone—that she began to wonder where he'd gone.

Was it love? Was that the heady feeling in his kisses? Did she give herself so willingly because he was her soul mate? Or was it something far more sinister?

. . .

Katharine fought her way through the next day. Margot called early asking for further descriptions of anyone Katharine thought pertinent in the ongoing investigation into her sanity. Margot also relayed that most of what she was finding in her research was the usual: God made the angels; some of the angels fell and became demons. It was the standard heaven and hell mythology, and Margot was apparently quite horrified that she worked at a library that was so skewed toward the Judeo-Christian point of view.

Katharine was almost as horrified that Margot's diatribe made her late for work yet again. As she walked through the back doors from the garage she realized her consistent tardiness of late should have had someone hauling her ass in and firing her. At the very least she should have gotten a warning. Maybe it was because she was the boss's daughter that no one was willing to shove her in front of the board. Or maybe they just assumed it was okay for her to break the rules.

But it wasn't. Her father had made that clear from the day she was born. Rules were meant to be followed—to the letter. His rules at least. And that went doubly at work. His primary rule was that all employees sold their souls at the front door when they came in for an interview—Katharine included.

The metaphor made her shudder. But still she wondered why he hadn't called her to the mat on the issue.

She was so hung up on why she hadn't been confronted that she didn't recognize Allistair from the back of his head as she followed him down the hallway. It was only as he took his place in the elevator and turned to smile at her that she realized she hadn't felt him.

For the first time it dawned on her that she was used to feeling him, that there was something about him that moved the air in a way she always seemed to recognize. So why hadn't she recognized him now?

She offered a brief smile and made only the most rudimentary of small talk on the elevator. The way she had looked at him at first, assessing him, wondering why she hadn't smelled or felt him and how she had somehow gotten so close without knowing it was him . . . the others in the elevator must have seen it. They must be wondering about the two of them.

So she bordered on being rude to him before she thought better of it. She was entirely out of sorts. Her night with Zachary, the call from Margot, the fact that she was far later than she normally was, and now sharing an elevator with Allistair and all these other people . . .

Why were they here?

There should have been next to no one in the elevator at this time of morning. But it was packed.

She glanced at her watch.

"Do we have an early appointment?"

His voice startled her. And though she bristled at the way he assumed the appointment would belong to both of them, she just shook her head, suddenly even more confused.

She was right on time.

How was that possible? She'd gotten up on time, but the phone call had pushed her back. She had lingered, listening to Margot tell all the history of the earth even as the librarian denounced it. But here she was, just a few minutes early.

Allistair didn't push the issue. Whether he sensed the porcupine quills she was projecting or merely didn't care beyond the fact that he wasn't late for anything, she didn't know.

The packed silver cube stopped at almost every floor, letting loose some of its cargo each time the doors opened. As people pushed their way to the front, the remaining riders would reshuffle themselves. Allistair stuck close to her. A few times she could have almost sworn he had sniffed at her like a dog, but surely the other riders would have said something or looked at them strangely. Katharine knew most of the other people in the elevator with them.

There was Ted from accounting. Betty from payroll. Janine in research. For some reason Jeff Grason from security was in with them too—maybe he was reporting back after his long absence. He wasn't her favorite person these days, what with his convenient loss of memory of her seeing Mary Wayne go right past her on the tapes. When she'd called him at home, he'd said there were so many things he saw that he just didn't remember that particular incident. It was hard to hate him for it—it wasn't like he was the only one. Even Allistair had forgotten what she so desperately needed someone to remember.

In that moment, she realized she didn't really know any of these people on the elevator. She knew names and faces, but nothing about them. Did Jeff Grason have a wedding ring? She couldn't see his hand. He might have seven kids. Betty? A family? A hobby? Even Allistair she didn't really know. She had let him peel her clothes away and take her on her own desk, and she still didn't know anything about him. Nothing of any importance, anyway.

The melancholy stayed with her all the way into her office and eventually overrode her while she was sitting at her desk.

Her fingers worked; her computer registered that she was doing something. But even when she answered the phone she wasn't fully engaged. And her brain kept coming back to the fact that on the surface she had a cushy job and knew a lot of people—a lot of the "right" people, in fact—but she didn't *know* much of anything about any of them.

Only Margot, with her lying ex-boyfriend and need for a big handbag to carry all her things, came through in full relief. Somehow Katharine wasn't surprised when Margot called a little later in the morning to see if she wanted to meet for lunch.

"Did you find something else, a different"—she couldn't say "mythology," so she made a quick substitution—"angle?"

"No."

It wasn't the answer Katharine had expected, and neither was the line that followed.

"I just wanted to see if you wanted to grab lunch together. Just as friends. I thought it'd be nice to see you and not talk about all that."

Even though Margot's tone was warm and inviting, Katharine responded with her rote "That sounds fine" and was silent, until she realized what an ass she was being.

Here she'd been handed exactly what she needed today—the knowledge that she had a friend—and she was answering a genuine overture with standard, and probably cold-sounding, politeness. Not really sure how to be warm and friendly, she quickly gushed to fill in the space. "That's great. It'll be good to just have lunch with a friend."

There was a moment of silence on the line as it probably hit Margot that Katharine had no clue how to be a friend. Just as Katharine started to respond a third time, Margot's voice came through. "I know a place just down on the beach—we can walk. It's beautiful out."

They made plans as Katharine looked out her window, only now seeing the day in slim stripes beyond the blinds neither she nor Allistair had ever bothered to turn.

After hanging up, she stood and made a point of opening them all the way, for once enjoying the view that helped make the property value so high.

Half an hour later, Margot called her cell from the sidewalk downstairs, and in minutes Katharine was there beside her.

"How long do you have for lunch?" Katharine asked, as she came out the front doors.

Margot smiled. "However long I want. I'm not at the desk today, so as long as I put in my hours, it doesn't really matter when."

Having lost all concern that morning after her musings about not being fired, Katharine simply shrugged it off. "Me, too. So come this way with me first."

She tugged Margot over to the store by the coffee shop, the one with the perfect shoes and the demon reflection in the window. Her pace slowed as she approached, but she wanted Margot to see the shoes, and she wanted to face the window again without screaming. Even more, she wanted to look at it without seeing what had made her scream.

She hadn't been able to face it by herself, but Margot was the perfect buffer. She alone would understand if Katharine saw something. And if Margot saw it, too, then Katharine might just sleep a little better at night, even though Margot surely wouldn't. But instead of giving in to the shivers that wanted to overtake her, she said, "I saw this pair of shoes you'd love."

Margot frowned at the red patent leather pair that had replaced the pumps Katharine had seen. But her words weren't about shoes. "Is this where you saw the reflection?"

Katharine nodded. "But we're back for the shoes."

"I'm not really the 'fuck me' red type."

Katharine's mouth dropped open at the term, then she laughed out loud. "No, stupid. There was another pair in the window then."

She tugged the door open and led Margot inside.

After some serious shoe shopping, they strolled down the slim sidewalks leading to the beachfront walk that extended for miles. If they followed it, they would end up at Venice Beach, fighting off swarms of midday rollerbladers. And didn't Allistair live down that way?

Katharine pushed the thought aside and enjoyed the weather and the idea of being simply a part of the large crowd. They ate cheap sandwiches to make up for the money they had spent on the shoes, which were tucked in folds of tissue in the bags that hung on the backs of their chairs.

They talked between mouthfuls of bread and meat about old boyfriends and living on their own. About how the weather had finally turned and how neither of them had ever been rollerblading. They made a date to come down on a weekday when it wouldn't be so crowded and embarrass themselves trying.

On the way back, a phone call sent Margot off to head straight back to the library; there was some sort of emergency among the stacks.

Katharine was so lost in her own thoughts, so abhorrent of going back into her soulless cube of an office, that she lingered in the walkways through the houses. Footpaths replaced the front street and houses were stacked five deep. On the other side of the road, the land again pitched into the water, this time in a controlled, man-made way, the maze of boat slips packed to the gills. The spots that were empty belonged to those who had managed to call in sick or just brush off the land for the day.

She almost literally ran into him, surprised again that she hadn't sensed him. For some reason, she felt that was a right that had been snatched from her. He spoke her name, seemed surprised at meeting up with her, but she was looking Allistair over rather than really paying attention. Dark hair, dark skin, deep brown eyes. Was this a human incarnation of the creature with the oily black skin that came to her at night?

Working to cover her thoughts, she automatically turned away. Before he could ask why she was acting strangely, she reached down and plucked a dandelion from the untended yard that rolled up to the sidewalk. She held it up to him with a forced smile that said she had in no way been contemplating his lack of humanity.

His smile was quick and sure. And this time she felt him, felt whatever it was that made her let him do the things he did to her. The smile she returned was just as genuine as his, and for a moment her thoughts turned to Zachary. Here, in the light of day, with Allistair at her side, it seemed far more likely that this man was the human and Zachary the plague that had been visited upon her. "Making a wish?"

She nodded.

And wished it would all go away.

She wished she didn't know either of them. She wished she didn't know about the people at the receiving end of MaraxCo's firing pins or about the children in the gem mines. She wished she didn't have soot in her apartment and a fear of her mirror. So she looked at him and wished it were two months earlier, that she could wake up in the past and go on with her life the way it was, before she knew.

Holding the puff of dandelion in front of her, she blew the seeds right at him. With a natural sense of humor she hadn't quite expected, he smiled at her as the white fluff danced around him like falling feathers.

He was heading out to a late lunch and she was going back in, so they said a quick good-bye and went in different directions. But as she walked away, she found it harder and harder to shake an odd, nagging feeling that he'd taken something from her.

CHAPTER 15

Katharine ran. She screamed. And though she knew it was just a dream, she found she still couldn't fight her way out. Even asleep, she had begun to wonder whether her dreams were more than mere wisps of her subconscious. Perhaps the other reality of deep sleep, whether confined to her mind or not, had heft and value.

So she ran from what chased her. She couldn't let it catch her, especially if this wasn't "just a dream." Her legs worked furiously, though she knew she stood no chance of getting away from what chased her. It was far more powerful than she. And in the dream, she understood for the first time that it was far older, too. Being malevolent didn't prevent it from being wise. And she felt it pull back, as though it would just let her run herself into the ground, like a small rat, mindlessly working toward its own capture.

Not knowing what to do, she fought for a burst of speed and instantly smacked into something in the dark. Solid and feral, it brought her to a dead stop. It didn't need to engulf her or grab her—she was in enough trouble already, having run herself right into it. It pulled back and waited.

As she breathed in and tried to see through the darkness that came and went like fog, she realized she could smell him. And that it was Allistair. With a sigh of relief, she dove for his arms, hoping she could find the needed shelter there. But in the same instant that she started the movement toward him, she suddenly jerked back.

Here. Right before her all along, was another charismatic man who had invaded her life. Another new player in her story. Another who had drawn an unsuspecting Katharine in as easily as if he held puppet strings.

With that, she jerked wide awake in her room.

In a second or two her eyes adjusted to the little light that came in past the blinds and the faint glow from the nightlight in the bathroom. She had never left the overhead light on; part of her had always been aware that light changed nothing in her scenario. Nothing of her dream lingered in the physical space. There was no one here. And it was just her room. But she wasn't just Katharine.

No, she was shifting. Becoming.

. . .

Zachary jerked back, startled at Katharine's movement. She had stopped in the hallway that led to the garage. There, all alone, she had turned her head and looked right at him. Then she'd turned back and gone on her way.

She hadn't been tense. He would have seen that she radiated nerves, and these days she often did. It was his job to help smooth out those feelings, to help her stay as peaceful as possible. She hadn't been afraid either. That, too, he would have seen and done his best to prevent.

But, no. He'd stayed here, just on the other side of the veil and watched. He was apprehensive about calmness this morning. He had waited for the ripe smell of Allistair to hit him as it washed off her in waves. But it didn't. It seemed both of them had left her alone last night.

So he'd been shocked when she'd turned and narrowed her gaze to exactly where he stood.

She couldn't have seen him. If she had, she would have screamed, run, done something. Even if nothing physical had occurred, he would have seen the changes brought on in her thoughts had she managed to actually focus on him. Seeing through the veil was terrifying for humans, no matter what they looked at. They had no point of reference, no system of categorization, and no way to process any of it. Some were closer to what they might call "enlightenment," but Katharine wasn't.

Her car pulled out from its parking spot and she drove off to work.

Mary Wayne was still giving her trouble, he knew. Katharine was the only one who remembered seeing the woman there at the office after she had died. All other evidence had been erased. But Katharine had been unaware. She had told the police things in her drug-confused state—things that she couldn't have known—making her a "person of interest" in the investigation. And the state of affairs over Mary Wayne had gotten very ugly. The only point in Katharine's favor was that the police had almost stopped asking themselves who killed Mary Wayne; at this point, most of them had switched to the question of *what* had killed her?

But Zachary had been listening to see what they found, and the few holdouts for a human perpetrator—those who didn't think there was a crazy feral dog on the loose, or perhaps an escaped pet tiger—had put Katharine on their list to watch.

That was a dangerous place for her to be. If they saw her as insane, that would only serve to build the case, especially given the manner in which Ms. Wayne had been dispatched.

Zachary sighed. He could save Katharine from the police. And he needed to do it. She needed saving and he had to be the one who came to her rescue. It was the only way she would be safe from the cops and safe from Allistair. She needed to side with him.

Unfortunately, his human form didn't yet have access to the information that would stop the police investigation into Katharine's life. He would need to "discover" it in a purely human way before he could use it to free her from scrutiny.

He looked further, past the condo building and into the depths of Light & Geryon. Allistair looked up from where he sat hunched over at his desk, looking and acting all too human. Allistair was supposed to become more human the longer he stayed. While he didn't seem to notice all the other comings and goings beyond the veil, he pissed Zachary off by being able to find him the second his opponent turned his focus to Katharine.

Zachary decided to let it go. She was with Allistair now, and for the next several hours there would be nothing he could do. It wouldn't be prudent to try to get to her with Allistair right there.

So Zachary relinquished his attention. When he felt Allistair relax far away, Zachary turned his thoughts to the police. He regretted mixing himself up in police affairs. After all, this was supposed to be about Katharine. But he needed this, and so did she. With a nudge, he moved the thoughts of several of the officers—not enough to make anyone frown or wonder where it had come from, just enough to change the trajectory of the idea.

Patiently, he listened and he pushed. Just a little. One officer here. Another there. Until finally the detectives agreed. "I think we need to interview the Geryon daughter again," said one.

Zachary didn't want them on her trail. Unfortunately, sending them to her was the only way to get them off.

. . .

The knock at the door startled her.

For two whole days, she had managed to stay out of the clutches of either of Allistair or Zachary. She had felt pulled to each of them, both in her dreams and in her waking life. Before she opened the door, she steeled herself, reminding herself to tell either of them no, no matter what they wanted.

Taking a deep breath, she pulled the door open, ready to turn away anyone—except the people she found at the door.

Two officers flashed their badges, even though she already recognized them from the Mary Wayne investigation. One of them spoke. "Miss Geryon, may we come in?"

The refusal she had prepared wouldn't be a good way to start this. Feeling startled and out of sorts, which was probably how they wanted her, she said, "Of course. How can I help?"

In a few moments, they were seated around her dining table in a scenario the officers had obviously contrived to make her feel "comfortable." She braced herself for an interrogation, but it didn't come.

Instead, Officer Dashel shook his head. "We're at a bit of a loss, and we're hoping you can give us some information, anything, that will help clear this up. After all, you found her."

He seemed sincere and vulnerable, but Katharine was sure it was all an act. After all, why would the police really need her help? They had set up a neat little trap for her. If she didn't answer, she was hiding something. If she called Zachary, as he had told her to do, she was hiding behind her lawyer, which would only make her look guilty. If she just answered their questions the best she could, they could lead her into a corner. And without her lawyer there to help, they could probably do it fairly easily.

She hated this. She had studied some law in college. But tax law and theory didn't prepare one to face down what looked like it just might be a sugary-sweet assassination of her character. She could be sitting across the table from the perfect setup right now.

Something caught her attention from the corner of her eye, and she turned to look at it. Of course, there was nothing there—except maybe another new level to her craziness. Several times she thought she had seen movement and then turned to see what it was, but it had been nothing each time. She hoped the cops would interpret her sideways glances as unease at the memory of finding Mary Wayne's corpse. Maybe they would finally believe that she couldn't have done it.

Since she couldn't call Zachary, she had to save herself. So while she told them the truth, she lied.

Dashel leaned forward. "When you saw the body, what did you think?"

Katharine was startled. She wasn't a medical professional or an investigator—what did her opinion matter? And she asked just that.

It was Detective Leaman who answered her. "We don't expect an analysis. But a lot of times an untrained observer sees something we don't."

She didn't buy that for a second, but acted like she did. "I thought she was the wrong color. The . . . rational part of myself told me she was dead, but I hadn't really accepted it. So my thought was that she was the wrong color, but I knew it was Mary Wayne because of the rings and the hair."

"You're familiar enough with her to recognize her rings?"

See? There was the first corner they were trying to get her into. "Not really. I trained her when she first came to us. She seemed to like big rings. They were hard to miss."

Leaman pressed again. "It didn't seem odd to you that someone on her salary would spend that kind of money on expensive jewelry?"

"No. Honestly, I don't think they were expensive. I thought they looked a bit tacky. That's why I remembered them." Actually, she had thought they were just the kind of thing her mother would call tacky.

"Did you remember these rings from the recent times you saw her?" Dashel spoke this time. Were they tag-teaming her?

"No," she lied. "I honestly don't remember the last time I saw her."

"Can you narrow down the dates for the last time you did see her?"

"Probably not." She hated this and was beginning to hate them. She hadn't killed Mary Wayne. Nor had she wanted to. She hadn't even wanted to believe the woman was embezzling funds. But here she was, trying to keep herself out of the loony bin. Maybe she even belonged there. But she didn't want to go. Medicines and group therapy wouldn't help her. And so she pushed on, trying to answer the cops in a roundabout way that didn't seem roundabout. "I know I said that I saw Mary Wayne, but you do realize that it was only on the tapes. I didn't see her in person. And I was looking for her. So I guess it's entirely possible that I saw someone who looked like her on the recording."

Something shifted in Dashel's expression. He seemed to think he had her here. "You seemed very certain that you had seen her when we spoke before."

"Yes, I thought I had, on the tapes."

"But you aren't certain now."

She wanted to snap at them. But she couldn't. All those years of training held her frustration back. "How could I be? It seems she was dead before then. And, honestly, I don't think I've slept well in a month." The truth and a lie, all in one.

"You haven't been sleeping well?" Dashel pushed.

Katharine smiled and stifled the sharp retort that burst into her brain. She shook her head. "I haven't even been making it into work on a regular schedule. I keep sleeping in trying to make up for bad nights."

"Why haven't you slept well?"

She shrugged. "I've been sick. And the neighbors make noise."

Leaman was writing notes on his little pad of paper, clearly not having moved into the current millennium with everyone else. "And you reported this to the building super?"

"No, sir. The management didn't get a complaint from me." She paused while she mixed fact and fiction. "I have a new boyfriend and it didn't seem wise to report someone else." She left it at that.

By the time the two left, she felt drained.

Propriety almost insisted that she thank them for visiting, but her new backbone, weakened as it was, told her not to. She didn't wish them a good evening, or offer to help. She simply mentioned that she had been on the way to bed when they called on her, since she hadn't been sleeping soundly.

Most of that had been the truth. As she threw the bolt, she thought of Margot telling her she didn't lie well. She hoped she had thrown enough truth in there to keep the officers from seeing what her friend saw. Oh, well.

Katharine hauled herself off to bed and hoped for a few hours of rest before anything decided to bother her .

. . .

Five days. Katharine reveled in near bliss. Five days with no messages on her mirror. Five nights of solid sleep. Five times she had been able to tell Margot that there was nothing to report.

The only even slightly odd thing that had occurred was that she was catching visions of dust out of the corners of her eyes. She would see movement and turn to look at it, only to see that there was nothing there. In fact, it probably wasn't anything unusual; she likely saw the dust catching light out of the corners of her eyes all the time. She had probably always seen it but ignored it. Only now, as jumpy as she was, her brain was signaling her to look. So aside from feeling like an idiot for always falling for it, Katharine tried to pay no attention.

She had woken up feeling like she had slept. She'd arrived at work on time all five days, making a lie out of the truth she'd told the detectives. But she had skipped out to have coffee with Margot.

Yesterday the weather had been perfect, and the two of them had eaten a hasty lunch and rented rollerblades at the little shack along the beach walk. They wound up looking like utter idiots and laughed themselves silly for about half an hour before they decided neither of them was cut out for the sport.

Katharine returned to her office, and Allistair, flushed.

He hadn't pushed her to tell him where she'd been or why she was being distant. It was as though he could sense she didn't need it or that she had changed her mind about him. Or maybe her new backbone was showing. Whatever it was, she was grateful. Her backbone was growing. It just probably wasn't strong enough to resist him yet.

Still, when she walked into her condo that night, she braced herself. Each day, though she enjoyed the reprieve, she became just a little more tense. Because each day she was aware that it had to break, and soon. It wasn't until she got into her bathroom and forced herself to check her reflection in the mirror that she realized she'd been holding her breath.

But the mirror was clean. Her house seemed empty. And she was just letting herself take a second deep breath when there was a knock at the door. Katharine barely suppressed a yelp and then immediately chided herself. She had seen so much worse. A knock at the door shouldn't startle her so.

Still berating herself, she walked back and threw the door open wide. There was no stopping what might be coming through, so she and her backbone decided to greet it full on.

It was Zachary, hands in his pockets, looking at her from curious eyes. "I wanted to know if you would come out with me tonight."

He looked uncertain, almost vulnerable. Katharine's heart went out to him. But she stuck to her earlier decision. "I think I'm staying in tonight. But thank you."

The polite part of her wanted to add, "Maybe tomorrow." But the smart part of her held the Miss Manners part in check. There were strange things going on in her life. She smiled at Zachary, and when he nodded she merely closed the door.

As she threw the bolt, her knees weakened. Wondering what this was, Katharine stumbled to her couch, where she sank into the cushions and took a few deep breaths. She never flat-out refused anyone anything. If she said no she was schooled to offer a polite alternative. But tonight she'd just said no and nothing else. She couldn't remember the last time she'd done that, if she ever had.

That, in and of itself, was a revelation. She'd told her father her opinion of how the company spent its money. But it was only her opinion. She hadn't said no in any real way. And what she did give him, she'd given only after she'd done what he asked exactly the way he requested. She'd given the reports, both the first and the second, because it was her job. She'd been invited to do the research and create the company recommendation.

When had she ever not done something she was invited to do? When had she ever just said no?

She couldn't think of anything beyond her playground years, when she had told a boy not to pull her pigtail. But that was it. When she turned down a date, she always softened the no with an alternative—maybe another time, I'm not available, but I know someone who is . . .

Katharine didn't know how long she sat there on the couch, trying to recapture moments of strength from her life and failing miserably. Not since she was a child had she stood up to anyone or anything. She hadn't even done it much as a kid. But she did have distinct recollections of her mother and father drumming those instincts out of her. And she hadn't fought that either. She'd acquiesced. Just like in everything else, she never even protested to say that she should be able to protest.

Finally, she stood to . . .

She found she didn't know.

Maybe she was hungry? Katharine looked into the fridge and the dwindling weekly supply of dinners. She was down to a fish plate and a pasta dish with vegetables. Neither was her favorite; those two dishes always lingered until the end of the week. Had she never told the service to stop bringing them? She really didn't like them. Was she going to hurt the chef's feelings if said she didn't like zucchini in her pasta?

How had she lived like this? She was sharp and on the ball at work . . . but was she really? Had she ever protested a single one of those dozens of departmental transfers foisted on her? She had never asked what the master plan was for her. She hadn't negotiated her salary. Nor had she pressed the real estate agent to look further after she'd found this place. She'd just taken the first condo that met her needs. She'd been looking for a house but had even allowed the agent to convince her that a condo would be just the right thing.

The phone rang, making her jump again.

Picking up the receiver and again wondering who she would get, she said, "Hello?"

"Katharine!" Margot's warm voice flooded the line and her. "Have you eaten yet? I just got out of work and don't want to eat at home. Will you come out with me?"

Katharine considered it for a moment. She hadn't eaten. She didn't want to eat what she had. But did she want to go out with Margot? She needed to decide for herself. When she thought about it, she found that Margot's words were something foreign to her own system. Margot was forward. She had nearly forced her translation services on Katharine that first day in the library. She called Katharine, even though they'd only known each other a short while. The librarian hadn't waited for Katharine to reach out to her. In fact, when had she ever reached out to Margot? When had she invited her out?

"Katharine? Are you okay?"

"Um, yes. I'm here." Taking a deep breath, she announced her decision. "Yes, I'd like to go out, but nowhere nice. Someplace casual?"

That last had come out as a question when she'd meant it as a statement. Maybe she needed more training.

Margot didn't seem to notice. "Then I'll need to change. Can you meet me at my place?"

They made plans. Katharine threw on her jeans and headed to the address Margot had given her. Margot's place was nearly eight blocks off the beach, just beyond Lincoln Boulevard, the main road that separated the beachside houses from the cheaper rents. Still, the house had that beachy look to it, and when Katharine found the number, she saw that her friend had the top unit of three and a balcony that looked like it had a full view of the ocean.

Inside, the unit was bohemian-looking, not quite in keeping with the more uptight Margot that Katharine knew from the woman's work clothes. Her home was not dictated by her job, clearly. The walls were each painted a different color, and an area rug that incorporated each wall color and then some covered a real plank wood floor that was not in the best condition. The furniture had more colors from the rug and something about the lines in it looked more like refurbished older pieces than new ones.

Margot stood in the middle of it all, fitted jeans, new blue shoes, and a shirt to match. Her hair was down and her wide smile balanced her long face, and Katharine realized she had been too quick to judge the woman the first time they had met.

But none of this assessment seemed to faze Margot. She just chattered. "I'm so glad you were fast. I was afraid you were going to be one of those women who takes forever to get ready. I'm starving."

"Me too." Katharine felt her stomach heading toward earthquake mode.

"I know a great Indian place down the street. There's Chinese next to it and pizza and beer on the next block over. All within walking distance. What do you want?"

"I've never had Indian, and I think I'm too hungry to try something new. Just in case I don't like it."

"Good plan."

Katharine started to shrug, but then stopped herself. "How about Chinese?"

They walked about ten blocks to the restaurant. Being right at the coast meant that the days often ended very quickly, and though it had been just at the end of light when they started the walk, it was almost full dark by the time they got there.

Margot was right, the place was fantastic, even if it looked like the Chinese version of the local greasy spoon. The fried wontons had been perfectly crisp and the American-style orange chicken dripping with extra sauce. It was all over a spicy rice noodle that Katharine had never had before, and she was stuffed before she knew it.

Margot too nearly moaned and commented on how she had eaten too much. She swore she was going to pay her body back with an extra half hour of running in the morning.

"Do you have a treadmill?" Katharine asked. She had a gym in her building, but in recent years she'd fallen out of using it.

"I run along the beach. A friend usually meets me and we run together."

A sharp pang hit Katharine in the gut. Of course Margot had other friends. Katharine realized that she wasn't so much upset about sharing Margot with others; she was jealous that her friend had a richer life than she did, that a Santa Monica librarian had a house full of colors and friends to run on the beach with.

They hadn't talked about any of the craziness going on in Katharine's life, and she was grateful, even if the reprieve was mainly due to being in a public place. She hoped they would continue to ignore the subject for the remainder of the evening. Maybe they would talk about it tomorrow. Maybe Katharine still wouldn't want to.

Aside from a few restaurants, most everything was locked up by the time they made their way back to Margot's house. They hadn't paid any attention on the way over, with both of them starving, so on the return trip the two of them window-shopped, peering into darkened glass to see what was on display.

Katharine saw a cheap knockoff store that featured dresses that looked too nice for anything in this part of town. A shoe store held super-high heels and over-the-knee boots in patent leather. She didn't look any further. At the fourth store, she saw pet collars and dog clothes, none of it useful to her. The thought of a pet started to take root, but she put the decision off until later.

Her mother had convinced her as a child that pets were too much work and left hair all over everything. Somewhere in the back of her brain, she began questioning that. Maybe a puppy would have been too much work for her mother, but was it too much work for her? She'd have to leave work at lunch to walk it. Should she move? What about Zachary?

She needed to see him again, in a capacity other than as her lawyer. It was the only thing they had talked about the last time they had gotten together. The police wanted to talk to her again, and he wanted to set it up so he'd be there when it happened. He said he wanted to help defend her against any accusations the police would try to level at her. He wanted to keep her from getting tangled up in leading questions.

Katharine almost had to shake her head to come back to the present. Margot was saying something about a dog, but Katharine had missed the first part of it. Something had grabbed her attention in the window, and she turned back to the plate glass to get a better look at it.

Her lungs froze, and she clawed at Margot's arm, grabbing her friend tightly enough to cause instant alarm. "What is it?"

Katharine worked her mouth once before she managed to croak out, "Do you see it?"

"No, I don't. What is it?"

There was no way for Katharine to answer that. She couldn't say what it was. But it sat back on haunches and still it towered over them. Long arms revealed thick ropes of muscle flowing like water under the skin. Reflected in the shop window the way it was, it had to be sitting very near the two of them.

Suppressing a shudder, Katharine let her eyes travel up its body. The wide chest was stronger than anything she had seen. Though the creature sat silently, it was clear from its build that killing would not be a hardship. Slaying the two of them like Mary Wayne likely wouldn't even give it pause or cause it undue effort.

The mouth looked as though it couldn't close. Long rows of sharpened teeth overfilled the gap between its jaws, leaving the creature looking like it was ready to bite as easily as it blinked. Farther up, the eyes were huge and luminous, staring back at her from the reflection in the window. They looked through her and into her at the same time, and Katharine knew that her thoughts were no longer her own.

At her shudder, she felt Margot's hand tighten on her arm, though she had no idea when Margot had grasped her.

Unsure how long she stared, she couldn't move, couldn't look away from the eyes. She was pinned, as effectively as a bug on a board. She knew she should feel violated, but she couldn't feel anything.

Out of the corner of her eye she caught a movement and had only the briefest of moments to wonder what it could possibly be when she was already staring at the beast.

The creature moved like molten silver, its eyes breaking contact and rolling to the side.

Released from its spell, Katharine too looked where the creature had. Behind her, reflected in the glass, a second creature approached, its legs bent at unusual angles. Its wide black feet splayed out on the sidewalk like thick oil puddles as it neared the first creature.

The arms moved in heavy counter-cadence to the walk, and heat rolled off it as it came.

Its focus stayed on the first creature, and without appearing to hurry, it closed the gap far too fast for the silvery beast to turn and face it.

The black creature hauled back a massive arm and swung out. Just as bright long claws cut through liquid silver skin, the beast let out a furious attack cry.

Katharine stumbled as the ground shook beneath her feet.

For a moment she was shocked that Margot too had braced and felt the earth move.

Katharine squeezed her eyes shut, but she could hear the cry of the first creature in response. Whether it was from pain or anger, she had no idea. She was no longer watching.

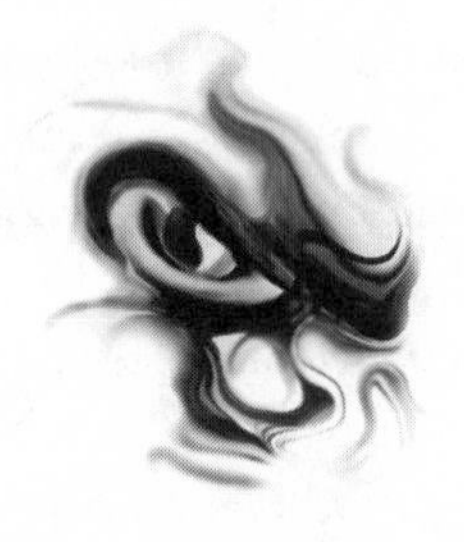

CHAPTER 16

Zachary worked hard to tamp down his emotions. They got in the way, destroyed rational thought, interfered with the way things must be. He was supposed to be more than this creature driven by emotions.

Still. What had Allistair been thinking?

It was quite obvious that Katharine had seen the two of them. Though it had been in a reflection and not straight on, the fact that she could look through the veil at all was a sign that she was growing, getting stronger. And that's what she needed. She needed to be more than she had been.

Of course, having him and Allistair around so much was certainly helping her to see further. But Allistair shouldn't have been there.

Slowly, slowly, Zachary pushed down on the flare of anger. He could not afford to show it in front of the others. It was base, and he wanted to be better than the deep urge that had grabbed him and made him react.

He had to dismantle his feelings before he saw Katharine. Before he became human. If he transformed and had any anger in him, he would carry it into his human self, where it would fester and grow. Humans were a prime breeding ground for deep-rooted emotions.

He didn't breathe—at least not until he became human. So he blanked his thoughts and waited for the anger to pass.

Then he waited beyond the veil in his own room. It was his as much as any person could own anything. But the idea that it was *his*, bought and paid for, would keep anyone from coming in while he changed. When he felt ready, he began.

First one piece, then another. He braced against the burn of forming flesh. To the extent that he could feel anything, he enjoyed the outcome if not the process. When at last he had pushed through, he waited for the air to clear of the tiny sparks of the sealing rift. He waited for the ionized air to still, for the smoke to settle or drift away. Then he took a deep breath.

As was becoming routine, he walked through his apartment naked, re-familiarizing himself with human senses as he cleaned up after his entry. He vacuumed the soot from the carpet, wiped away the tiny bit of ash the air-conditioning vent had blown over to the wall. Then he carefully dressed so that he would look like he had been simply relaxing today, then he sat on his couch, folded his hands together and waited for the call.

A minute or two later the phone rang. He could almost hear her emotion through the line. Katharine wasn't frantic yet, but she was definitely on edge. Zachary picked up the line and answered, "Hey! I'm glad to hear from you."

He listened as if he didn't already know what was coming, as if he hadn't seen it all forming and changed just for this. At her request, he agreed to come over to her unit, as her boyfriend. Because she needed a lawyer even though it wouldn't look good for her to have one there. Luckily, it was perfectly acceptable for her to have her boyfriend over. It would be a different story if this looked official.

The police buzzed in just a moment after Zachary hung up, and he made sure they got delayed in the elevator on the way up. They would find every button lit up, forcing them to stop at each floor along the way. So he had a moment to go over to Katharine's before they arrived at her door.

She let him in while she looked up and down the hall for the police. She looked guilty, and that wouldn't help her case at all. Zachary needed her out from under the cops for all that he had in mind. And now was the time to clear her, if she would just do as he told her. "Katie, take a deep breath."

He demonstrated and waited while she did it. Once, twice. Then, finally, when she didn't appear so frantic, he poured her half a glass of juice and made her take several sips from various sides of the glass. He wanted to be sure it looked like they'd been like this for a while. Then, he sat her on the couch with her glass and took a space next to her.

Within moments, there was a knock at her door. It seemed the police were anti-doorbell. Zachary motioned for her to stay put. "I've got it, Katie."

He opened the door to the officers in the capacity of boyfriend. Then they introduced themselves, and Zachary acted like he was getting new information.

Detective Leaman turned to Katharine, and his tone was almost accusing. "You didn't say you weren't alone."

Inside, Zachary smiled. His Katie pasted on a confused face. "You didn't ask. Is it necessary?"

Wandering around the room as though he hadn't seen the place before, Dashel stayed out of the conversation. Leaman looked at Zachary this time. "Are you here as her boyfriend or as her lawyer?"

Though he knew it wasn't at all what the detective wanted to hear, it was what Katharine needed. "If you're asking that question, then I'm here as her lawyer." He immediately took a seat on the couch next to where she'd stayed put and let him lead.

The officers took a moment to rearrange things. They pulled over chairs from the dining set and let Katharine and Zachary stay on the couch. It may have been an attempt to put them at ease, but Zachary didn't think it boded well for the line of questioning. He had seen enough to know they didn't have anything on Katharine at all really. They just thought she was suspicious. And in a case where they had nothing really to go on, they would latch on to the suspicious person and squeeze until they had a confession or a solid lead.

He didn't like the idea of them digging into Katharine's life. He had to turn them away and do it now.

They asked all about the company, about the missing funds, about Mary Wayne. Zachary steered the conversation as much as he could, but he didn't like the way they lined up the questions. They made it look as though Katharine were involved in the death, when he knew for certain that she wasn't.

Holding his hand up, he asked the officers to stop for a moment. "Look, my client doesn't know anything more than what she's told you about Ms. Wayne. For your sake, and so you can get a reasonable timeline here, Ms. Geryon can go through the whole course of events. But then I'm going to have to ask you to leave her alone."

The officers didn't agree to the "leaving her alone" part, but did let Katharine tell her side of the story. They interrupted periodically for the dates and times of various incidents, but that was all.

As he had known they would, the officers found the dates didn't match. Mary Wayne had been dead before Katharine had solidified the woman as a suspect. She hadn't known Mary Wayne's address until well after the date the medical examiner had declared as the latest possible time of death.

He was proud that she didn't lie about thinking she had seen Mary on the tapes, but she did say that clearly she had been looking for the woman in hundreds of faces and that she had surely just mistaken her. Zachary knew that Katharine still believed she had seen Mary Wayne long after she'd been dead, and he knew she was right—she had seen the woman.

Dashel spoke, making one of the first comments he had during the entire interview. "Ms. Geryon, you have to understand that your actions aren't typical given the situation."

He waited for her to respond. Good girl that she was, she just looked at him, confused.

"I'm sorry. I didn't know there were typical responses." She shrugged and moved as though to shrink just a little further inside herself. "Is there a standard scenario for this? I mean, my mother died from cancer several years ago, and that was reasonably peaceful. Other than that, I've never seen a dead body. Let alone a shredded one." She flinched a bit as she thought back to what the body had looked and smelled like. "And at the time, I did believe I had seen her recently. I had no reason to believe otherwise. So I don't understand."

Dashel sat back and Zachary suppressed a grin. She had done well. With the dates not matching and Katharine having a legitimate reason to believe she had seen the woman long after she had died and started to decay, the officers really had nothing to go on, nothing to justify coming back and questioning her again, at least not in the capacity of a person of suspicion. So he didn't point that out. He'd use it if he had to, but he didn't want enemies. He'd just let the good officers figure that part out for themselves.

At last, the policemen declared themselves finished. As custom dictated, they thanked the two of them, shaking hands. "Miss Geryon, Mr. Andras."

Then they were gone.

After the door shut and they heard the elevator doors close, Katharine sank back onto the couch. Small shakes hit her arms and legs, and he could see the tension begin to roll off her. She had held it in tight check while the officers had asked questions, and now she let it go.

She needed him now, and he held her close for a moment while she curled into him, breathing deeply, her nose against his shirt. When she seemed to shake a little less, he stood to pour her a glass of wine. She needed to calm down. The wine would help. So would the words. "You were fine. Great even. I know you don't know anything. But you have to realize they don't have anything on you."

"How do you know that?" She sipped at the merlot and leaned back into the cushions.

"I'm an attorney. I know the ADA. They aren't anywhere near arresting anyone, let alone pressing charges. The word is they have no one, so they're going to pester you and your assistant until they can come up with something."

"But we didn't do anything. We just found her."

"Sure, but they have nothing else. And they are looking for any little lead you can provide." He sat next to her, touched her arm, willed her to drink a little more. It would calm her down. "But don't worry. The dates you gave. They may ask you more questions, but next time they really will be looking for you to help. Not to try and catch you at something or trip you up in any way."

"Thank God." She leaned back and closed her eyes.

. . .

Katharine woke up in the middle of the night and immediately ran to the bathroom and vomited.

After emptying the contents of her stomach, she sank to the floor and huddled against the wall for a moment before she realized she was naked. On weak legs, she stumbled to her dresser and pulled out soft cotton pants and a T-shirt. But one look at the bed sent her scrambling to the commode before her stomach turned all the way over again.

Nothing came. Her stomach was empty and she barely made it the two feet from the toilet to the sink, where she braced herself on shaking arms as she forced deep breaths, as though that might calm her. Still, his scent lingered. What they had done together hung in the air. She tried not to breathe too deeply.

Eventually, she thought she could move enough to stand while she splashed water on her face and brushed her teeth. There was a rancid aftertaste of wine in her mouth that she desperately wanted to get rid of. Even after her mouth was clean and her arms only shook in intervals, she could not make herself turn and leave the bathroom. She looked down at the sink so she didn't have to see the bed behind her, didn't see the covers rumpled and silent. But they told her that she had been with Zachary.

She had drunk a glass of wine—or was it two? Three? She didn't remember—after the detectives had left. And Zachary had . . . stayed? She didn't really remember. Clearly, she had fallen asleep. Naked. She had vague memories of the all-consuming sex that she usually had with him.

What had happened?

She hadn't planned on sleeping with him again. Not after Margot's ideas about the creatures and the new men in her life.

Katharine had been dismissing the things she'd seen in the store window the other day. It was a sad state of affairs when she *wanted* to be hallucinating things. But she had seen a creature, dark and frightening, staring back at her. The first creature she had grown to be able to handle. No, it was the other creature, something from the realm of the first, that had walked into the reflection. Even darker and worse than the first, it had not looked at her.

Its deep and missing eyes had looked only at the other beast, and it had attacked with a speed and drive that had held Katharine motionless with its ferocity. Somehow she had picked herself up off the sidewalk, employed some of the grace her mother had drilled into her, and let Margot help her back to her apartment.

Somehow she had slept. She had compartmentalized the images and her body had taken over, probably exhausted just from the tension. She had gone into work and deftly avoided Allistair. They talked, he invaded her personal space, but she didn't let it go further than that.

But Zachary . . .

He had felt so safe. She remembered that. She had wanted to fall into him. And she hadn't been sober. The wine, coupled with the toll of the police interview and the undeniable relief at the outcome, had left her heady after a very small portion.

And with that her trust in her judgment had returned.

Zachary had taken away the last of the wine, turned down the lights, and walked her to bed. Had she been the one to initiate things? Had she asked him not to go? Begged?

Katharine wasn't sure. She had no strong memories save one.

Most of the night felt like an alcohol-hazed blur. But those short minutes ago, when Zachary had stood to leave, Katharine had awoken. Maybe she shouldn't have. Maybe she wasn't supposed to.

Still, she had seen.

As Zachary walked away from her bed he had the slightest limp. That's what had made her look closer, what made her change her vision from satisfied fuzz to sharp inspection.

The man had grabbed his shoulder with the opposite hand while he walked away and rolled the shoulder as though it hurt. The moonlight caught the pale skin of his arm, his biceps and triceps in perfect relief. But the shadows were wrong.

Frowning, Katharine had leaned in for a closer look and seen the bruising.

His right arm was healing from a wound. It looked several days old, not as fresh as if it were from something just a single day ago. But she trusted nothing now. Nothing.

And it was in the right place.

There were bruises everywhere. Subtle shading differences on his skin that would have been clear in broad daylight. His legs, his back, his neck.

Though she had stopped watching after seeing the reflection of the first hit in the store window, Katharine had listened. She hadn't been able to close her ears as she had her eyes. And the fight had been vicious.

Would a creature like that be able to walk away unscathed? Would it heal fast? Fast enough to appear as though it was a full week after the brawl rather than a mere day later?

She had no answers, but the questions were enough to imprison her thoughts and scare the crap out of her. Who had she just slept with?

Fighting to corral the wayward musings of her mind, Katharine had to consider the ideas that Margot had been planting. They were taking root and growing.

If her friend was right, then Katharine had to ask a very different question.

What had she just slept with?

. . .

Allistair waited in human form. He was in the office he was supposed to share with Katharine, in the role that had ultimately not afforded him the level of interaction with her that he'd planned on.

No, he was stuck here waiting for her. Trapped in his human body. Weakened by the expenditure of energy just to get like this. A victim of his own design.

Again, Katharine was late.

Through his human eyes the veil was virtually impenetrable, the solidity of objects nearly absolute. Even though he knew it was as much illusion as reality, he couldn't see further than the walls of his office the way he was.

Finally, he decided it didn't matter what Lisa thought of him. Maybe if he closed the door now, when Katharine wasn't around, it wouldn't look so suspicious when they closed it while they were in the office together.

As he felt the latch catch, he moved his thumb and locked the door, too. With his back to the door, in case someone had a key, he breathed deeply of the air around him, then shifted slightly and allowed some of the change to come.

As usual, it would cost him. Always in the growing there was a time where you weren't strong enough, where you had to invest more than you really had to move beyond your level. Allistair wasn't strong enough to shift without loss. Not yet.

Opening wide and bottomless eyes, he looked around at the world as it truly was. The walls were ephemeral, as were the desks and floors. The people beyond them had reach far beyond their arms as peals of color and light and darkness curled out and licked at the world around them. They didn't even know they did it.

Still, he didn't see Katharine.

He looked further, pushing down the irritation he felt at being denied. There was something about her. She held him in a thrall, even though it was supposed to be the other way around. He watched the yellow tendril unfold before him and knew that it was his. In his human form, he gave off human signals. And he was blessedly grateful that humans never saw it.

The yellow was a beacon to all the others like him, to anyone who saw. A changing signal of his fear and his frustration and his failure. For the moment he ignored it. Humans were blind to it, and the others that did see it . . . well, they had likely seen it long before he did.

His human overlay breathed again, and his eyes looked further.

He could see Katharine's room as clearly as if he stood in it. The covers on her bed were rumpled, mussed by two human bodies rather than one, and Allistair felt his human stomach turn at the thought. But he pushed the feeling aside, told himself it was merely the by-product of the form he was partially in, a vestige of a lesser being.

Katharine was not in her room.

The smell of her was strong; she had been here recently. The smell of Zachary was also strong in the room, though Zachary, being what he was, would create far more charged tracers of himself than any mortal could. Allistair ignored the anger that he saw bloom in front of him and tried to be logical.

The scents of both Katharine and Zachary in human form were equally strong. That meant that Katharine had been there very recently and Zachary had left a while ago.

Perhaps . . .

A quick scan for the other told him that his opponent was not near, not on either side of the veil. It was of lesser consequence to know where he was than to find Katharine.

Though he used his real eyes, he was shackled by his still-human form. It was plenty strong, something that caused equal measure of love and loathing in him. He shook his head, a physical manifestation of his desire to rid himself of a thought process that wasn't working.

Just looking for Katharine in the places he expected her to be wasn't working. Instead, he pulled back, deep inside himself, wondering if he would be able to find her so easily in this halfway form he was in.

A scratching noise in the hallway startled him.

He turned toward the door, then quickly turned away. That had been stupid in the extreme. Had he faced someone coming through the door, what would he have done? He didn't know if the person's brain would even comprehend his face. Katharine was starting to be able to see. But, then again, she'd been through hell in the learning of it.

Luckily, the door didn't open. And though he was grateful for the luck, Allistair hated his need for it.

He searched faster now; he needed to finish this, to find her, to know what to do next.

Closing his eyes, he stopped trying to guess where she was and simply searched for her.

And that was it. So easy. With just the thought of her, there she was.

And he would not have thought to look for her there.

Katharine climbed a set of weathered, wooden steps up the outside of a three-story building. For a moment she hovered in front of the red front door, waiting for a heartbeat before she knocked. Then she stepped back, looked around, and leaned against the railing. After a moment she knocked again.

A small smile played at his lips. She wouldn't like knowing that he was watching her. But he enjoyed it. He liked the way she wore her new confidence, incomplete as it was. He liked watching the new Katharine peek out from behind the façade of the old. She was unburying herself from years of propriety and dogma.

She knocked one last time before giving up and turning quickly to head back down the stairs.

That she was disappointed was clear. What she was hoping would happen at the door was not.

Unable to look away, he followed her progress back along the street to her pretty, shiny car that was a bit out of place among the others on the street. They looked like they belonged to people who lived in proximity to seawater, like the owners didn't have the money to keep them pristine or had decided to spend it elsewhere.

She was easy to keep track of, now that he had attached himself to her in a way rather than looking frantically in the places he would guess she might be. Why he hadn't thought of that before was a mystery to him.

Her car turned on Lincoln, then headed toward Marina del Rey.

She was coming straight toward him. Perhaps it wouldn't be a wasted day, after all.

And the closer he could physically get to her, the more he hoped to loop the two of them together. Maybe he could track her all the time.

And tonight, he would keep his eyes open for Zachary.

. . .

The hair on the back of her neck stood up.

Something was wrong.

Katharine ignored it. It seemed lately something was always wrong.

Zachary walked with a limp; his shoulder hurt; he had bruises.

Allistair had seemed to know she was coming even though he couldn't see her. He had called as she turned into the drive for Light & Geryon and said something about "in a minute, when you get here" as though he knew exactly where she was.

And the hair had stood up on the back of her neck this morning even before he'd said that. It seemed she'd spent the entire day feeling as though someone or something were watching her.

So she discounted the feeling as portending doom. She had plenty else telling her that. Hell, she practically had "Something wicked this way comes" written over her front door.

She turned the key in the lock to her condo and the door opened with a click. A part of her was waiting for the day when the key didn't fit and her family and coworkers didn't recognize her. But it seemed that wouldn't be tonight.

A quick survey showed her that the carpet appeared clear of soot; no burning smelled lingered in the air. And she looked no further, just took the bag of cheap Chinese food to her table and sat down to eat.

She broke the chopsticks apart and spent a minute picking at the strings. When they were finally not likely to cause splinters on her tongue, she pulled out the food and realized that she'd have to give in and get a spoon for the hot and sour soup.

She'd eaten alone at this table any number of times. Not like this though. Never cheap, carryout Chinese. Never with disposable utensils. And though she'd always been alone, she had never felt it so keenly as she did tonight.

When Margot hadn't been home at lunchtime, Katharine had texted her. She'd already tried the library and hadn't found her friend at any of the usual haunts. Some part of her had wanted to just bump into Margot. Maybe because she didn't want to believe she was running screaming to her friend about what she'd seen last night. And about what she'd done.

But no. Her friend was out of town until tomorrow, visiting family in Las Vegas.

She could no longer turn to Zachary, not to the new and far-too-perfect boyfriend she was glad to have. That too had been a mistake.

Even Allistair seemed like he would have been good to turn to. But she didn't trust him now. That, though, was just a general distrust.

It was Zachary she needed to be wary of; she knew that now.

The wonton got stuck in her throat when she thought about what she'd seen. Her stomach turned and she set the spoon down.

She'd had sex with him. And if Margot was on the right track, then he was something she couldn't even recognize. Maybe not even human.

Just a short while ago, none of this thinking would have made any sense. Katharine hadn't been one to believe in what she couldn't touch or smell or see. But that had been changing rapidly. First, the animals, then the messages. Then the things she was seeing in reflections . . . that had been too much—like a glimpse into a world that was beyond anything she could fathom.

Her appetite had fled, but she picked up the chopsticks and started eating again. She wouldn't let all the things around her change this. She wouldn't let it stop her from eating. She needed sustenance. She had fainted recently, likely more than once. She needed to be as strong as she could be. And if that meant eating when she didn't really feel like it, then she would suck it up.

Katharine wasn't going to hand any part of her life over easily. Not her sanity, not her job, not her home, and not even her dinner.

She picked up a piece of orange chicken and bit in. Her appetite had returned with her determination, and the bite was sweet and heavenly.

She ate another and another, not sure when to stop. It seemed her determination was possibly as out of control as the rest of it.

Eventually, she stopped eating. She cleaned up the lonely meal and didn't save any of it. With just a brief thought to the starving children around the world, she scraped the rest of it down the sink. Her brain flashed with an image of a landfill as she stuffed the trash into the bin. She wasn't even recycling. Like it mattered—half of it was Styrofoam. She was an environmental hazard on top of everything else.

She needed sleep. That was for sure.

Tomorrow she would go into work. She would get more comfortable with Allistair. She'd see where that relationship was going. And she'd avoid talk of Mary Wayne, if at all possible.

Though he lived next door and was still in her life, and though she was still afraid, there was something comforting in having found out. She would avoid Zachary. If she could.

She could arm herself with Allistair. Maybe another man would be enough to change things.

But that was enough decision making for one night. She took herself off to bed and pulled down the blinds, shutting out the very last bit of light filtering in from across the Pacific.

She slept soundly, until the pressure on the side of the bed woke her.

When she woke, it was to see a spotted leopard sitting beside her legs. It did nothing but look at her, its green eyes blinking.

Katharine hoped she was hallucinating, but too much time with Margot dispelled that notion. When she reached out and touched the creature's leg, it felt real too. Her friend had informed her that it was highly unlikely she would hallucinate in three senses at once. So she probably wasn't hallucinating the leopard as she could see it and feel it and hear it breathing.

In fact, she could smell it, too. It smelled far away, loamy and slightly fetid, just a little off.

The leopard looked at where her hand touched its leg. Then, with no warning, it leapt out the window, seamlessly flying through the glass.

It was Katharine who was bound by earthly science. Her hands flew to the pane, but as she had been certain would be the case, they did not go through.

She was just convincing herself it was a dream when she turned and saw the mess of the covers, the crumpled spot where it had leapt, pushing off with its powerful back legs. She could still feel the jolt as it had propelled itself.

No, it had not been a dream.

Somewhere in the back of her senses, the smell tickled her memory.

CHAPTER 17

When she walked into the office the next morning, Katharine discovered that though her night had been interrupted yet again, she had actually slept well.

That was almost disconcerting in and of itself. She shouldn't sleep well, not with the things she had seen. But at least she had one thing she could grab onto. No, two. Margot would be back today. Katharine would be able to meet with her friend and tell her what she'd figured out. Second, she could see what was going on with Allistair.

He stood up to greet her as she came in the door.

"You look good today." His words were tinged with shyness, and Katharine wasn't surprised when she thought about it. She had rolled on the floor with him and followed him to the beach, then she had done nothing. So she didn't know what to say. But he did. "You look like something is different. I can't put my finger on it, but . . . maybe just the way you were walking."

She smiled. He was right. "Actually, I can put my finger on it. I . . . realized something." Katharine struggled for a way to say what had occurred, because, even though he had seen Mary Wayne's shredded body, he hadn't truly seen what was going on. She needed human terms for him, but then she latched onto something. "I broke up with my boyfriend."

"You did?" He sounded surprised.

Well, so would Zachary when she actually said it to his face. And she had to pray that it would stick. She'd drunk too much the other night and wound up with him anyway, when she was supposedly working at not being with either of them. But she told Allistair the semi-fib anyway. "Yes, I did. He wasn't right for me. I'm starting to see him for what he is."

Allistair looked amazed, as though he had known all along and was stunned that Katharine had figured it out. Of course that would mean that he had thought from the start that Zachary was a cheater or an ass or . . . well, probably not something that would sneak into her condo and leave messages in Latin on the mirror. Maybe Allistair had sensed a general "bad egg" thing all along. Maybe that was why they'd had that staredown in the hallway on one of the very few occasions they had been close to each other.

"Katharine, wow."

Before he could go further, she shut the door and started talking. Never mind that the whole embezzled funds investigation was over, meaning there was no legitimate excuse for closing the door. She did it anyway. "I'm really sorry about the way I treated you."

"Don't worry about—"

"I don't know what I was doing with Zachary. He messed with my head. I thought everything was perfect and I . . ." She shrugged. There was no way to tell him what she suspected. Not Allistair.

He cocked his head to one side and looked at her with disbelief. "You really thought everything was perfect? You thought that, even though you were with me on the side? How did that even factor in with the perfect boyfriend?"

There was no good answer for that, and she told him so. But then she said what she'd been driving at from the beginning of the conversation. "I was out of line with you. And I don't know how you feel about me now. Maybe, if you wanted, we could . . ." It was hard to say. Hard to apologize and offer herself up to someone she had really liked in the space of several breaths. In the end, she chickened out. "Whatever you want, I'm open."

Then she ducked around behind her desk, offering a small half smile, half apology before she stared at the monitor and got to work. Allistair simply nodded as though he were confused and wandered slowly back to his chair. Since she didn't know what to make of his response, Katharine chickened out again and did nothing.

Two full hours passed with Katharine training her gaze at her computer. She didn't want to glance over at him, didn't want to be disappointed by what she might see. But finally Allistair came around behind her desk and leaned over her, his hands on either side of hers, caging her in.

Katharine's heart beat faster, knowing what it wanted, but not knowing what he wanted from her. His head came down, his mouth near her ear. And all she could do was wait.

His voice was low, "What did you mean when you said you were open? Did you mean like the way we were before?"

She could feel the heat of him, he was so close. Fighting not to swallow, not to take a deep breath, not to give herself away, though she feared she already had, she managed one word: "Yes."

He straightened, and the loss of his presence from her personal space was like a blast of cold air, or maybe of reality. She had tossed him aside with no explanation before, and here she was wanting to pick up where she had cut him off. She knew his cold response was perfectly warranted.

In slow, sure steps, Allistair made his way back to his desk and sat down. He said nothing, simply began typing. He shifted folders. Made a call. And let her sit there and feel supremely foolish.

But it wasn't long before he spoke. "Could I bring dinner to your place tonight?"

The tight bands around her chest loosened. "Yes. That would be great."

She would have deserved it if he hadn't asked. But she was more than glad that he had.

When he asked for the rest of the afternoon off, she granted it immediately, only asking when she could expect him.

Katharine spent the next several hours of her day feeling normal for the first time in a long while. She ate yogurt at her desk for lunch, then topped it off with a granola bar. She worked in the office by herself. And since she wasn't tense, waiting to see what Allistair would say or do, she got a lot of work done.

She checked a paper mill in Kansas and found that there was an abnormally high incidence of a certain chemical in a nearby city's water and that several agencies believed it to be caused by the plant. The plant denied all charges and demanded proof. Though they were making money in greater quantities each year, Katharine put the file aside and looked for another option to recommend.

When Margot called and asked if they could grab a coffee while she had a break, Katharine offered a hasty yes and cleared out for the day. Lisa looked at her a bit funny as she left, but there was nothing to say. She had been prompt every single day before these last few months had kicked in. She had stayed late, had done just enough financial research into a corporation to recommend it or not—exactly what was asked of her. She had been nothing but a model employee. Now, Lisa looked about ready to run an intervention. And she would've had good cause. Drugs looked like a good fit for Katharine's behavior. Sadly, drugs would have been an easier option to deal with.

The weather was beautiful, so she and Margot walked with their coffee drinks, which was probably a good thing, given the topic they landed on once they covered the details of Margot's visit with her mother and father. Katharine wouldn't have changed the subject, but she didn't have much choice.

"Something happened. Tell me," Margot finally broached the necessary subject.

She gave Margot all the details she had, right down to the shapes of

Zachary's bruises. Shaking her head, Katharine asked, "Do you think that's really what's going on? Some demon is chasing me? Or did we make up something to explain a prank we couldn't understand?"

Somehow her friend seemed to understand. "You can't just explain it all away as a prank. That's been the whole problem since this started, if what you told me is true."

"Yeah." Taking a long sip of her coffee, Katharine asked what she'd wanted to all along. "Do you think it will just go away now? I've identified the problem. I'm cutting myself off from him, I . . ." There wasn't much more to say.

"Who knows? I think we just wait." Margot shrugged and let it go at that.

But Katharine worried. What if it wanted something? It had proven that it could get into her apartment. The marks on her arms had proven that it could not just get in, but get to *her*. Would it just quit?

And, more importantly, what would she do if it didn't?

But she drank her coffee and changed the subject again. Margot would help if and when there was a need, and Katharine would cross that bridge when she got to it.

When Margot went back to run the evening shift at the library, Katharine headed off to her condo, then bolted herself into the unit. Then, feeling particularly brave, she squared her shoulders and inspected the carpet. After all, there was no ready explanation to give Allistair about that. Luckily, the carpet was clean.

She showered and primped, a little giddy at the thought of having him over. He was as much a drug to her as Zachary had been, but she felt safe with him now, in a way that she hadn't felt in the last several months.

He arrived as planned, looking relaxed in jeans and a T-shirt and bearing grocery bags.

Katharine watched as he produced chicken breasts, asparagus, and mushrooms. He had a small bag of flour and a carton of six eggs. Several clear plastic containers held fresh herbs. He loaded several additional items into her fridge before she could see what they were. She imagined the refrigerator was probably as startled as she was; she didn't think it had ever held actual ingredients.

He talked excitedly while he expertly chopped and seasoned the chicken. She offered to help, but when she admitted she had no usable kitchen skills other than opening wine, he produced a bottle of pinot gris from another bag and had her do the honors.

"It's already chilled." She was surprised. Somehow he had thought of everything.

"Of course, that's the way it . . . tastes best." A shrug dismissed the joy he was displaying. "I love food."

It didn't show. She tried to think back to the times they had eaten together, but nothing had foretold this. So she poured him a glass of the wine and leaned back against the counter offering conversation, really the only thing she could provide in a kitchen.

An hour later a covered baking dish holding dumplings, chicken, and many of the other ingredients he had brought was slid into the oven to bake. He offered her crackers and some cheese spread he swore by to tide her over while it baked.

He looked like a kid in a candy shop.

There was something about the way he was acting—the words slipped out before she thought about it. "Are we celebrating something?"

Immediately, she wished she could take it back. Instead, she braced herself for a deserved comment that they were in fact celebrating the end of her being a bitch to him.

Allistair smiled and said it in a much nicer way. "Yes. I never thought Zachary was right for you." He clinked his glass against hers. "This is to open eyes. And second chances."

When she smiled, she felt it clear through herself. It was no longer just a facial movement, but an expression of how she really felt. This time, he took her wine glass away and said before he kissed her, "All's fair in love and war."

They ate the sumptuous food he'd made, both of them practically moaning out loud at the taste. She had no idea he was such a good cook.

He laughed with her, freer than she'd seen him before. But then again, she'd only ever led him on as a cheap side deal to her acknowledged boyfriend.

When she kissed him hard and pulled him toward the bedroom, she thought for a moment that he might say no, but he quickly gave in. In a heartbeat, he became the lover she remembered from before, telling her how silky her hair was, how soft her skin felt.

She could be free with him, she told herself. And so she didn't hesitate to ask him to stay with her.

"I'll stay as long as I can." Allistair looked into her eyes and seemed to see the shadow of fear that was creeping in as time alone loomed over her.

Still, she let herself fall deep asleep in his arms, in her own bed.

Later, she awoke slowly, the dark surrounding her but the smell of him still permeating the sheets. Naked and warm, she was sure he must have just left the bed. With a smile, she rolled over and buried her nose in the sheets. They were new sheets she had pulled from the back of the closet in an attempt to remove Zachary in human ways.

Her lips tugged into a well-sated half-smile, and she curled back into the warm spot in the bed and waited. But she didn't hear anything. No running water, no sounds of someone stealing milk or leftovers from the kitchen.

Slowly, Katharine became aware of someone else in the room. In the corner, in the part that was shadowed. Had he sat at her desk and watched her sleep? There was something endearing about that idea. But still she wanted him with her.

Reaching out her hand to him, she called out in the dark, "Come back to bed."

When he didn't respond, she smiled. Surely he could see her; she was near the window and the light. Maybe he had fallen asleep at her desk chair. So she tried again. "Allistair?"

Finally, she heard a "Yes" in low and sleepy tones.

She reached her hand out just a little farther for him, her smile still layered on her face and even deeper in her soul.

But what reached back was dark and oily. Thick fingers, tipped in long claws, came at her as though to grab at her hand. She instinctively yanked it back. Into the small glow of the night came a heavily muscled arm with skin so inky it seemed to pull light from the air.

The name she knew tumbled off her tongue even as the gruesome face came into view. Its heavy breath infused the air and she fought not to breathe it in.

"Allistair?"

. . .

She couldn't go into work. She couldn't go down the hall.

Katharine was paralyzed with fear, and had been since the middle of the night, when she had screamed to wake the dead.

She'd nearly keeled over of a heart attack when the knock came at her door not ten minutes later. Naked, she'd gotten enough courage to check the peephole, thinking it was Zachary, since no one had called up. But since it was building security, she had to tell them she'd be a minute, and then scrambled to pull on some sweats.

It seemed the two uniformed men just wanted to know if she was okay. She had to step into the hallway, as per the building procedure. The idea was that if she was being held hostage in her unit, they would know by her refusal. Or, in the hallway, supposedly a safe place, she could request protection or pass a message. But instead, she had pulled off the best acting job of her life. It was just a nightmare, she said. She hadn't been sleeping well, and this one had been particularly scary. They had offered to search her apartment—also protocol. She let them, hoping they'd see the creature.

But it seemed it had truly disappeared when she screamed. The security detail didn't encounter it.

Later, the one contact she had made this morning was to call the front desk and ask who had reported her scream last night. She lied yet again and gave the excuse that she wanted to apologize in person.

Though she hadn't expected it, the attendant gave her the names. The unit beside her had called, as had the ones above, below, and one catty-corner to her bedroom. After thanking the girl, Katharine mapped out the calls in her head. Strangely, even though his unit abutted her bedroom, Zachary hadn't called.

Had he seen Allistair come in? Or seen him leave?

Had Allistair even left?

She'd been so wrong about Zachary. Maybe it was a good thing she hadn't gotten around to getting in his face and telling him what she knew—or thought she knew.

But now, how did she go into work and face Allistair?

Still in her sweats, she checked the carpet in the corner of her room. The sun was up now. If she opened the window, she could see the corner where the creature had been. She hadn't dared go near it to hit the light switch. But there was no soot, no marks, nothing that suggested the thing had even been there.

One deep breath was all she needed to get herself going. Though she'd never made real decisions for herself before, she was always strong on discipline. She could follow protocol to the letter and never break form. She could stay aloof and separate. She could live the life her parents planned for her. And now, she could apply it to what she needed.

Pulling on jeans and a thin top, Katharine brushed her hair, checking the mirror for messages and finding none. She pulled herself together and grabbed her fully charged cell phone. She was halfway out the door when she turned back, realizing the folly in her plan. She dialed Margot's library line from her home phone and shuffled her way through several steps in the automated system and even a person at the front desk before she reached her friend.

"Katharine! What's up?"

"I was wrong!" She again told the whole thing, trying not to shake while she spoke. The words coming out of her mouth were absurd. There was always the question of complete insanity. She'd seen movies where the character was so convinced of the hallucinations he or she was seeing that they'd made up a whole universe. Maybe Margot didn't even exist.

She tried to open her eyes and see the padded cell around her. Tried to feel the straightjacket or wrist cuffs that would keep her safe. But she could perceive none of it. Her greatest fear—that she wasn't crazy—seemed to be the truth. So she had to do something about it. And she told Margot her plan, even though her friend didn't think it was wise.

This time, when she headed for the door, she went through.

She kept her eyes peeled for Zachary in the hall and then in the parking garage. Katharine was grateful not to see him in either place; she really wasn't ready to talk to him yet. But soon . . .

Four blocks away from the office, she called in and asked for Allistair, but only his voicemail picked up. A second call to Lisa told her that he wouldn't be in this morning, and Katharine tried not to wonder why that was. Frustrated, but by no means ready to give up, she called Allistair's cell phone and again got no answer.

She was driving to his place to confront him there when her phone rang. The display name was clear.

"Hello?"

"Katharine." His voice was low and seductive, but with a hitch. It was as though he knew something was up.

Well, he did know, she thought angrily. And right then she realized it wasn't wise to meet him at his house. She shouldn't deviate from her plan. She'd originally intended to meet with him in a public place, and for good reason. Margot was expecting her to be there . . .

"Katharine?" His voice cut through her thoughts and she worked to get it together.

"I'm driving, I'm going to pull over." She tucked the small car into an illegal spot that she hoped she wouldn't be in for long. She was still four blocks off from the beach-walk houses where Allistair lived. She was in front of someone's driveway, but she had bigger concerns than moving the car. Once she had the engine off, she started talking. "Can you meet me at the Coffee Bean in . . ."

She was going to say, in front of the Light & Geryon, but she didn't want anyone she knew to see them there, to maybe butt into the conversation. She tried again, checking her phone for the address of a different coffee shop closer to his home.

As soon as he agreed, she clicked the call off and sent a message to Margot that she had changed the location and gave her the new address. Starting the car, Katharine headed off to find the place and stake her claim on a table. He said he'd be a few minutes, but that was fine with her.

She was waiting at a patio table with two drinks when she saw his car pull up. She took deep breaths as she watched him find a parking spot. He emerged from the small car, all fluid grace and good-looking male. She didn't want to believe what she now knew. But that was part of the problem, wasn't it? She hadn't wanted to believe it was Zachary either.

Had Allistair done something? Set her up to go running back into his arms, just as she had yesterday? Her chest ached with the fact that she had trusted him. She had been an idiot. But she was remedying things. Right now.

He smiled as he approached, and though he didn't notice, Katharine saw the lone woman at the far side of the patio give him a once over. He was in jeans and a T-shirt, and Katharine figured she had an idea what that meant.

As he spotted her and began to make his way over, she held out the drink she had bought him. It had begun to melt in the warm day while she waited, but that was too bad for him. Her drink was equally melted, as she had only been able to bring herself to sip it while she waited. He expertly wove his way past the empty tables and chairs. There was only the one woman out here, and Katharine had been pleased it was mostly deserted. There were enough people around that he wouldn't be able to do anything, but it was sparse enough that she could say what she needed to.

And Margot was sitting at the sidewalk tables in the restaurant across the street. Margot wouldn't let anything happen. Katharine was banking on that.

His fingers closed around hers as he took the drink. The feeling of his skin on hers was deceptively alluring, as it always had been. Margot had warned her about this, but Katharine took a deep breath and transformed the want into anger.

He was sitting across from her and smiling by the time she made herself look him in the face. But she saw his smile had an edge to it that indicated it was forced, and his eyes didn't look quite at her. They tracked around her and focused right in front of her, and something flickered there, as though he was confused. Finally, he looked her in the eyes. "What did you want?"

"I want to talk about what I saw last night."

This time his smile was warm—it sank into him, well below the surface—and for a moment, an answering depth flickered in her, too. But she twisted the feeling back where she needed it.

"What was that?" He took a sip of the drink, and she wondered if it cost him anything to appear so casual.

"I saw your real face last night."

She had intended to let it hang there. To let the words speak. But the jolt in his expression was too much. He knew. He was scared.

As she watched, he worked his expression back to looking calm. "What do you mean?" The words came out as slick and smooth as he was, and she was ready.

"Later, after I thought you had left . . . I saw you. I saw what you are."

Again, for a moment he looked afraid, and again he pulled it together. "I don't know what you mean. I'm just me."

"That's a convenient way to put it." As she leaned forward she inhaled the soothing scent of him. But she wouldn't let it get to her. She said what should either set her free or condemn her. "You aren't human. You change. I've seen the animals in my apartment."

"I . . ." He seemed at a loss. Feeling she had him, Katharine went further.

"I've seen your real face before, and you've scared the crap out of me. But last night, I finally realized it was you." She sat back. She waited.

"What? What did you see last night?" He looked worried, very worried. He faked it well.

"What you really are." Her heart was about to beat out of her chest, and he could probably sense that. Hell, maybe he could hear it or smell the fear on her. But she sat there, holding what ground she could, refusing to give in.

His mouth worked like a fish out of water. She waited.

Finally he spoke again. "Katharine—"

But the sound of her own name on his lips was enough to push her over the edge. "I don't know what you want from me, but I won't give it to you—"

Katharine stopped herself mid-thought. Her voice had gotten just enough louder for the woman at the other table to look over at them. So she pulled herself back just a little.

He leaned in. "I don't know what you saw last night, but—"

"Yes you do! I saw you! I see what you really are." Her nerves had been held so tight they finally frayed. Though she outwardly appeared in control, she had snapped. "Do it! Do whatever you are going to do to me! Just get it over with!"

His face softened. He sighed and took a drink from the now almost totally melted mocha. "I can't do anything to you, Katharine. No one can."

He might as well have stabbed her. This was worse. It left her hanging. Had he transformed into his real self and shredded her, she might have felt better. She thought she would end up sliced by those wicked talons after that last comment. In fact, she had almost counted on it. Instead, he didn't give her anything.

He spoke again, softer this time. "The only way is for you to agree, Katharine. To join. It's really up to you."

Her chin snapped up. "What about Mary Wayne? Are you saying she *agreed* to what happened to her?"

"In a word, yes."

Katharine's gasp elicited another long stare from the woman at the far table. She would have to tone it down or she'd be remembered. She knew she didn't want to be remembered. Or was that just some old buried part of her that had been trained to be part of the wallpaper? Maybe it would be okay if this woman remembered her face, and that of the almost too-handsome man across the table.

And Margot would remember. But Margot couldn't hear what he'd said.

And Katharine had no idea how to respond to the statement that Mary Wayne had said yes to what happened to her. Finally, she figured out what she needed to ask.

"And if I say no?"

He leaned forward, looking around her and slightly in front of her again. She was distracted by it, wondering what he was looking at. "You can say no. But when you say no to one thing, you say yes to another. The question is, what will you agree to?"

Something about the way he said it sent cold chills down her spine.

CHAPTER 18

This time Katharine told Margot everything. About the slut she had been, about how she had felt, and, finally, about what she had accused Allistair of at the coffee shop.

Margot nearly sloshed wine on her couch. They had the sliding door to Margot's balcony wide open, and they were listening to late-evening traffic with a slight overlay of the tide coming in. "He said that? He virtually admitted to slaying that woman the two of you found?"

Margot shuddered, while Katharine took another drink. Before she could talk, her friend jumped in again and asked, "Was it creepy?"

Katharine thought for a moment. "Surprisingly not. I was afraid some, but mostly I felt strong telling him what I knew. And he never really seemed threatening. I mean, we were in a public place and all, so he couldn't really do anything. But then again, who could stop him if he did? That creature is huge." Now as she sat here and thought about it she was creeped out by it. But she was grateful it seemed to occur only after the fact.

With a nod, Margot changed the topic. "While I was in Vegas, I did a little research at the local library."

"While you were visiting your family?" Katharine was shocked. Not so much that Margot would visit a library—clearly, they were like magnets to her—but that she would leave her family during a visit.

With a smile and a shake of her head, Margot asked, "Don't you get tired of your family when you are there with them day in, day out?" Then her hand flew to her mouth. "Oh! I'm sorry, I shouldn't have said that."

"No, it's okay." She thought back to the visits when her mother was alive, and how much the woman could act the part of the smothering mom. "I did feel that way, but I didn't leave. I guess I didn't know I could."

"Well, I just make sure I get out when I can. It really cuts down on the number of fights I see, and the number I'm involved in." Standing suddenly, Margot walked while she talked and grabbed the wine bottle from the kitchen counter before heading back to the living room and topping off both their glasses. "So at the library, I checked out all the mythology of demons I could find. It was pretty interesting."

Katharine settled back. "So, educate me."

"Well, there's a darn lot. A lot of the Judeo-Christian ideas believe that demons are fallen angels. Therefore, they have the same powers as angels do. Almost all religions have some kind of demon creature in them, though not all consider them malevolent. But most do think they are bad, if not evil. I avoided the idea of the 'mischievous spirit' because that clearly isn't what we are dealing with here. And I tried to find anything I could using the description you gave, though it does seem to change a bit."

Margot took another sip of wine. "If what you told me about Allistair is true, then change is the name of the game. According to a lot of the demon legends, he can change into whatever he wants, even become human, so the rest is no surprise. In the end there was just a lot of the standard evil, burn in hell, freeze in hell kind of stuff. A lot of it traces back to Dante's *Inferno*. But it wasn't helpful. I guess the only thing that did seem to help was one thing I came across on the web."

She stood and looked at her wine glass, as if wondering how it had gotten so low, then grabbed a second chair and placed it beside the first at the computer desk tucked into the far corner of the room. In a moment, she had pulled up a link she had emailed herself and had Katharine standing over her shoulder, sifting through the information.

"Look at this."

It took a while for her to read the whole page, but she could see why Margot had liked it.

There were hand drawings of beasts similar to the things she had seen, and Katharine pointed that out.

"Yeah," Margot said, "but a good number of sites had depictions or at least descriptions that were pretty close to those. I'm sorry, but your demon doesn't seem to have many distinguishing characteristics."

"You mean I just have a garden-variety demon?" That made her laugh. That for all the trouble she was having, she was just dealing with a pest? Maybe she'd had too much wine. Allistair's statement that Mary Wayne had agreed to what happened to her was well out of Katharine's scope. If her demon was just a small one, then she should be glad.

She read further, then looked up. "So, this is what? An anarchy theory of hell?"

Shrugging and nodding at the same time, Margot answered, "I guess. The idea being that hell is just a landfill for the unwanted. I don't know if they are heaven's unwanted or not. But the attached article also seems to say that those the demon gets to are also sent there. He travels in and out at will, unlike the poor souls who got left there."

Of course Margot had read the attached article. She'd probably cross-checked its references, too.

"In the end it describes hell as a lawless, conscience- and moral-free zone. It seems to be a land of boredom run by the mightiest. I think it's an interesting concept, that hell isn't really for the bad, just that heaven is only for the good.

"One of the references is really thorough, though—why are you laughing?"

Katharine almost couldn't stop. "I was just sitting here . . . thinking that you had . . . likely checked the references to see if they were reputable."

Margot laughed too, but took both their wineglasses to the sink and offered up ginger ale instead. She kept talking while she poured. "Okay, so the reference was about crossing over, and that's what I thought was really interesting."

Katharine sat up straight, listening while Margot reached into the big purse Katharine had given her.

"I printed a copy for each of us."

"That good?"

"You should read it for yourself. I'm going to reread it."

Katharine didn't balk when Margot handed her a highlighter. There was going to be test on this material, and if she didn't pass . . .

She started reading.

. . .

Katharine hid out at the library the next day. She had called Lisa and flat-out lied—said she was ill and took a sick day. The first one she had actually declared as a sick day. Previously, she'd just said she wasn't coming in. She hadn't paid any attention to the need to log the time. And why should she? She was the boss's daughter.

Lisa had made a *hmmm* noise when Katharine called in and told her. It wasn't clear whether it was a sound of acceptance or disbelief or if she just thought Katharine would suffer no repercussions.

And she hadn't. So far. But if she did . . . if her father decided to get upset about it . . . well, then, it would be far worse than any pink slip Lisa could imagine. The disappointment alone would be great. If it weren't for something so huge, she never would have done it.

At least she was unlikely to run into any of her coworkers at the public library. She had Margot to help her, even if it was only sporadically. The librarian actually had to work, and it wasn't like she could call in sick, then show up at her job to do research for a friend. So Katharine mostly winged it with a little guidance here and there.

By lunchtime she was ready to report in, and she did so after practically inhaling a sub sandwich as they sat at an outdoor table at a mom-and-pop place around the corner. Margot ate steadily while Katharine talked.

After confessing that she'd spent over an hour looking up demon mythology only to find the same things Margot had found, she switched tacks. "I looked up transforming, specifically transmogrification."

The librarian raised her eyebrows.

"Yeah, I found it in the thesaurus. I knew what it meant, but it isn't one of those terms that readily springs to my mind—though it sure will now." She played with a pickle slice that had escaped out the back of her sandwich, but she didn't eat it. "A lot was about werewolves and witches' spells, but there were a few things that seemed important."

"That's what all the photocopying was about, huh?"

"Yeah. Okay, one of the pieces dealt with alternate dimensions. Not like 2-D or 3-D, but like overlaid realities coexisting in the same place. The higher-order dimensions can see into the lower ones. Naturally we are about the lowest. Time is different there, gravity, all of it. But some of the papers claimed there are ways to see through to the other levels, and—get this—one is to look into a mirror or a crystal. There was a mention that this is the real idea behind the crystal ball."

"That offers something at least about the reflections you've seen. In the shop windows."

Katharine nodded. "I thought of that, too. Given that it seemed to match what I'd seen, I kept reading. It basically said that things can come through the levels, and mentioned that colors are indicative of where the creature came from. Like they change as they change level, but it isn't really like passing down or up. More passing through, one overlay into another, and they change shade as they go. But, get this: when they pass through, they have to rip the barrier. That causes sparks, and burning."

Katharine didn't have long to wait.

Margot's head popped up. "And you have strange animals leaving soot on your carpet."

"Yeah. I think I'm on to something."

They sat there, thinking for just a moment, crumpled sandwich papers in front of them, a gorgeous L.A. day all around them. Cars honked as they went down Santa Monica Boulevard. People waited for parking spots.

It was Margot who voiced the fears they shared. "We are on the right track, but do we know what to do?"

Katharine shook her head. All she knew was that she wasn't completely and totally crazy. She'd read a few accounts of people who had encountered similar things. Most of them had gotten locked up—in the psych ward or a prison. Some of them disappeared. But none had a "I fought my demon and won" story. Still, the fact that she wasn't bonkers was a huge relief. "That's what I'm onto this afternoon."

"I won't be around much to help." Margot slung her purse over her shoulder as they began the one-block walk back to the large modern building. "It's the third Friday of the month, and that means a docent tour."

Katharine trailed behind. "Am I stupid if I don't know what a docent is? And why it's getting a tour?"

Margot laughed. "You aren't stupid. It's a word from academia, and I'm the docent. I give the tour. A docent is kind of a keeper of knowledge. Universities and museums and libraries have docents."

"Of course." Katharine added that into her brain next to *transmogrification* and wondered what the hell she was doing here.

Two hours later, Katharine left her friend a note and drove herself home. She'd gotten nowhere since before lunch, and there was something else she had to do today.

She tried to keep her brain quiet on the drive home, and was relatively successful. As she turned the key in her lock, she looked down the hallway, disappointed that she had again missed Zachary.

Not that she thought he'd be home at this time of day, but it would have been nice to see him. While part of her was disappointed at missing him, she was also glad to have a moment to get ready.

After her now-standard apartment check in all the closets and corners, she took a shower and dried her hair. Next, she threw on a blouse and jeans, ran downstairs and around the corner to the small takeout spot, and grabbed a salad and pasta with pesto. She took the folded brown bags back to her unit, where she grabbed a bottle of white wine and headed over to Zachary's door. She owed him a big apology. And for a moment she was grateful she had been too chicken to confront him when she thought he'd been . . .

He didn't answer when she knocked, but that was okay. She needed a moment to think up a better apology. How did you say, *I'm really sorry, I thought you were a demon. But then I found the real demon, and I'm glad it's not you*? That was not the way to keep the boyfriend who blew her mind. There wasn't much she could say. She didn't want to tell him about Allistair, not about what she suspected, nor what he had said when confronted. More than that, she didn't want to admit that she'd been sleeping with the man she now suspected while she'd been with Zachary. Not that he'd asked her to be exclusive.

The old Katharine would have said that was okay. He hadn't asked, she hadn't promised. But the new Katharine knew she was responsible for what happened regardless of what had been asked of her. She didn't think it was wise to name names, but she would admit she'd been seeing someone else, and now she wasn't. Maybe they could move things to the next level.

She knocked again, then turned and slid down the door. She'd be here when he came home, and she'd gotten food that would keep, since he wasn't expecting her. Her thoughts ran away with her for a while, but she worked to gather them back into the semblance of something logical. She thought about the artwork that Margot had found her, the paintings and sketches that, if nothing else, told her she wasn't the only one to see these things. Then there was the article about passing through the layers and leaving ash.

She and Margot didn't have anything more to go on. There was nothing that they had found yet that told them what to *do*. Nothing that even hinted at whether she'd survive all this. Nevertheless, she felt so much better. After confronting Allistair and learning more, she was ready. She had faith in Margot. It seemed Margot could find anything.

A noise behind her caused Katharine to start. Jerking around, she listened from her seat at the door. Was he in there? Had he not heard her knocking? Or was he avoiding her on purpose, waiting for her to go away?

A sheepish thought entered her mind. Maybe he had someone else in there. She couldn't fault him if he did. It wasn't like they had said they were exclusive or anything. She'd had someone on the side. And the way she'd been acting lately would have driven any man to get a new girlfriend.

But instead of grabbing her bags and heading back to her own condo, she turned around where she sat and put her ear to his door.

There was no feminine laughter, no voices. It sounded like he was alone. She frowned as she heard a motor come on. A few minutes later it went off. Still, she sat with her back against the door. Should she just wait? Or call off the dogs?

She was reaching for her cell phone, wondering why she hadn't thought of calling him all along, when the door opened behind her and she tumbled onto her back at his feet—his bare feet that led up to nothing but a towel.

He grinned. "I thought I heard a knock, but I was in the shower."

She couldn't help smiling as she righted herself. Dusting her butt just for show, and wondering where that move had come from, she got to her feet and simply said, "I brought dinner and an apology."

He stepped back and let her pass by. "Neither is necessary. But dinner is appreciated. Just let me get dressed."

She sighed. Part of her wanted to tell him not to get dressed. But even though he said he didn't need an apology, she needed to give it. It might even be selfish to do so, but that didn't change things. So she didn't stop him from entering his bedroom.

Her head tilted as he opened the door. "Is that a wet vac? Is that what I heard running?"

She pointed at the small red and white contraption on the floor. It sported an arm with a small brush and a water container.

"Yeah, I spilled a drink I had in here. I'm really concerned about the white carpet." With that, he pulled the door behind him, leaving a small crack that gave her a glimpse of a bed, perfectly made, and a bedside table with a single book and lamp sitting on it. The book looked new, and definitely nonfiction. She wanted to know what it was, but she pulled her eyes away.

As she did, she noticed that he was lying. He couldn't be really concerned about the white carpet. It was the same as the thick, pale, cream-colored pile she had in her own unit, but with random circles of gray. If he was concerned about the carpet, that concern was as far as it got. Whatever it was wasn't getting cleaned up well enough, that was certain. Either he or the wet vac wasn't working up to code there.

But it made her grin. He was such a guy. Her mother had always said that men wanted things to look nice, but wanted other people to make that happen. Something about the missing chromosome or some such.

She turned her attention to the food and wandered through his kitchen, pulling dishes out of their organized places in the cabinets. She checked the dishwasher when the drawers yielded no serving spoons and found it perfectly empty. Oh, well. A zap in the microwave brought the pasta back to life, and while she waited for the machine to ding at her, she rifled through the drawers again looking for a wine bottle opener. No luck there either. She frowned.

"What?" He was right behind her. She hadn't even felt him come up and her heart kicked a little as his voice startled her.

"No wine bottle opener."

"Oh, wait, I have one." He turned and went into the other bedroom, closing the door behind him. She scanned the place. He was definitely a doors-closed kind of guy. He had left the bedroom door peeked a bit, but that was it. In a moment, he emerged from the room, opener in hand, and closed the door behind him.

She reached for it. "I won't even ask why you had a corkscrew in your bedroom."

She almost didn't hear him speaking. The metal was so warm it was nearly hot to the touch. And it was just a basic corkscrew, nothing else. She'd have pegged him for the type to have the latest gadget version.

"That's not a bedroom, it's the office."

"Ah. Then I won't ask why you have a corkscrew in your office." The opener cooled right off and she pulled the cork from the wine while he set the plates and silverware on the table.

In a few moments, they were eating, and for a second her thoughts turned to the meal Allistair had cooked for her, how much more sensual it had been. Not sensual as in sexual, but as in real enjoyment of everything about the food. But that was the problem. He sucked her in. He made her believe things that weren't true. *This* was what was real, even if it didn't taste quite as good. Her sanity was worth it.

They talked about her day a bit, and she told him she'd spent some time at the library doing work research. She managed not to choke on the word *work*, which was the only lie in the sentence. She told him about her new friend, and he looked at her quizzically.

"A librarian, huh?" He sipped at the wine. "That doesn't really seem like the kind of person you would pick for a friend."

"I know. But I like her. I think maybe I was picking my friends wrong before."

"Like me?" He grinned.

"No, not like you." And there it was. The opening. The new Katharine dove right in. "I wanted to apologize for the way I've been acting lately."

"What do you mean?" His blue eyes glanced at her from the side.

"Disappearing for days at a time, closing the door on you. Not returning calls."

"You were sick, so I thought it was that. Is there more?"

How should she say it? How *could* she? She had been sick, in a way. "Yes, I was. But I didn't need to be so rude about it. I'm hardly ever sick. And I don't think I have been at all since my mother passed away. I was pretty grumpy through the whole thing."

"Then there's nothing to apologize for. Next time, I'll bring you soup."

She wanted to smile. She wanted to stop here. And he'd be okay with that. But now she wouldn't be. "There's something else."

He leaned back and waited. Katharine couldn't tell what his expression meant, whether he was waiting for the other shoe to drop or if he thought she was going to apologize for something as silly as being sick again.

She charged in. "When we were first seeing each other, I was seeing someone else, too."

He nodded. "Is that it?"

She stopped, surprised, then wanted to ask him if he'd been seeing someone else too. Instead, one small word came out of her mouth. "Yes."

His smile lit up his face, blue eyes twinkled, and he ran his hand through his blond hair, ruffling it just enough to not be perfect. "I figured as much."

"You did?" She couldn't have been more surprised. But then she settled herself back. It would come, the part where he said he was seeing someone else too.

"A beautiful woman like you? Katie, I knew I wasn't going to just walk in and have you all to myself. I was ready to fight for you."

Well, then, he knew more about her own life than she did.

When he looked her in the eye, she felt heat spread through her. Leaning in, he formed his next words carefully. "You said you *were* seeing someone. Are you finished with it?"

"Yes." The word almost felt as if it had been pulled from her. She couldn't look away.

"And you told him this?"

She nodded.

"So you're all mine now?" There was no smile on his face, only deep seriousness. His eyes held hers, and the little voice in her head said this was where she wanted to be. And, more importantly, where she needed to be.

"Yes, I'm all yours."

"Good."

. . .

Allistair was in shock.

Katharine told him she had seen his real face. She had. Several times, in fact. So why was she just now standing up to him? And why was the fight in her so attractive?

He sat on the beach in human form. He could have stood here on the other side of the veil, but he wouldn't have felt the sand or the wind. The sounds of the waves and the birds would have been something that came to him in pure knowledge, but he wouldn't have been able to experience them.

Since it seemed his time here was growing short, he wanted to feel all of it. The beach had a smell—the standard saltwater and biology smell, but in Los Angeles it was overlaid with the odor of industry and, where he could afford his beach house, the slight scent of human sweat. It came from the vagrants and street vendors, rollerbladers and skateboarders, and anyone who had been out for a while in the day that was getting just a little too hot. The smell didn't bother him. It was distinctly human, and somehow, though he wasn't supposed to, he seemed to enjoy all things human. It was a real shame that humans so rarely did.

He contemplated quitting his job at Light & Geryon, but that thought only lasted a few minutes. He would have no ready human access to Katharine if he quit. Especially now that she had rejected him.

That was still a mystery. Somehow she had wanted him so much one day, then called him out the next.

Zachary was probably responsible somehow. His opponent so often set Allistair up for problems. And it seemed that his bad luck was never just random; no, somehow, though others would lay the trap, Allistair's failures had always been by his own hand in the end.

With that thought, he changed his mind again. He wouldn't quit. He'd take a lesson from Katharine and stay in the game. It wasn't over yet. And he was determined not to lose her. He couldn't—the stakes were far too high. He would show up at work when she did, stay in the small room with her, get in her face. Anything to convince her that she couldn't choose Zachary.

As though the thought conjured him, Zachary was there. Behind him. Allistair could sense it, even without turning his human head and looking. He wished he was himself. Humans were vulnerable from the back, and having Zachary there made him nervous. "Yes?"

"She has chosen."

He felt the heat come around him, and with his extra senses working beyond human borders it was stronger than the wind. But he stayed still. His hand wasn't played out yet. "She may have decided for herself, but it isn't over yet."

"Close enough."

Allistair closed his eyes; they weren't necessary. "Did you think I would take her decision to be with you as the final say? That I would turn tail and run? Just quit?"

"Actually, yes."

He could tell from his tone that Zachary had thought exactly that. And that infuriated him.

He wanted to shimmer through and face Zachary on even ground. He could; he was more than capable. Going back was easy. But he was in the open on the beach. There were at least a hundred people in sight. Humans had rules, and one was that they didn't just disintegrate, which is how it would appear if he did pass through to the other side. And Zachary had put him in exactly that position. But then again, he had made it easy for his opponent.

He held himself stiff and didn't respond. Eventually, Zachary left.

But Allistair stayed there, unable to move, unable to anchor the angry thoughts that bounced through his head. He sat there in human form and acted like a human—mad that Zachary had called him coward. And mad that Katharine had rejected him. And even more mad that Zachary might just get her in the end.

. . .

Katharine had gotten only a glimpse of Zachary's place the night before. He'd wanted to stay at her place, but she had wanted to stay with him. Eventually, he relented.

She'd studied his surroundings as much as she could, wanting to know more about the man. But the doors remained closed. His closet, the office. The book by the bedside was new: *Why We Do What We Do: A History of Man*. The book itself didn't interest her, what interested her was that he thought he should read it.

All through the condo, things were immaculate and sparse. The dishes were stacked neatly in the cupboards—only the few they had used had been loaded in the dishwasher by her own hands. The counters were devoid of any of the normal surface clutter: no toaster in the kitchen, no toothbrush in the bathroom. Aside from the gray patches on the carpet, it was almost as though no one lived there.

But she hadn't had much time to wander. She was pulled to him, like always. Somehow she just went under each time he kissed her. It was wild and deep, and she always ended up satisfied but tired. She had fallen asleep immediately last night, and dreamed of bumps and heat from all over the unit.

In the morning, he had been gone. There was a note saying that he had an early meeting at work, and that there was milk in the fridge and apples on the counter. Sure enough, when she wandered out, they had been there. But the fridge was otherwise empty, and the apples were the only food available.

Katharine had done a full three-sixty turn in his living room. The door to the office was open, and she peeked inside to see a desk and chair. There was a thin, shiny computer setup and a shelf of sealed paper reams, a few books, and an atlas.

In the bathroom, there had been a toothbrush left out with a note with just her name. She found toothpaste in a drawer alongside another barely used toothbrush and brushed her teeth at his sink. There was a small thrill in being there without him, but she resisted the urge to do any real snooping. It was enough that he trusted her here alone.

Given that she had done a short and thankfully private walk of shame this morning—from his door back to her own unit—she had tucked a spare pair of underwear in her purse before she went out with him tonight. They were going to see a movie, then on to dinner. She intended to stay over with him again.

He kept her talking about the new developments at work, things she found she could only speak briefly about, as she hadn't been there enough to develop any knowledge of any depth. But soon he had her telling childhood stories in between bites of salmon and risotto.

He fed her a rich custard with blueberries and talked about their future together. It was the first time she could remember him saying that they would be together. That she could be with him . . . he even hinted at forever, and she knew that this was exactly what it was supposed to be.

He called her Katie and held her close, and she managed to talk him into letting her stay at his place again.

She was curled up beside him, naked and practically comatose, when she felt him jerk upright in the middle of the night.

Still groggy, she must have known deep down that she was with him, because she didn't startle to immediate wakefulness herself. But that only lasted a moment.

It was Zachary's low voice she heard as it ground out the words, "Get out."

And, while she slowly blinked to wakefulness, he came into focus. Sitting naked at the side of the bed, all smooth muscle, he leaned forward and faced what looked like a huge black wolf.

CHAPTER 19

Katharine had to go into work. She had to put in an appearance.

Her father had called and wanted to know why she was missing so much time. Was she really that sick? Why hadn't she seen a doctor? He asked question after question and the underlying tone all the time was "why do I have to tell you this?" Wasn't she grown up enough to figure this out for herself?

What Katharine really wanted to know was why he was so frustrated when it had taken him so long to notice her constant absences. She couldn't remember a day in her life that her father had taken care of her. Fathers didn't do that kind of thing. Of course, had she been allowed to watch TV like a normal kid, she would have seen that some fathers did, in fact, take care of others. But hers just asked her questions as if she were mildly retarded. And she had no defense; there were no answers she could give and still look sane.

She was left saying she felt better and she'd be into work. And she *had* felt better about the whole thing—*until* her father pretty much demanded she come back into the building daily.

Which meant she would face Allistair daily, too.

Sure enough, when she opened her office door, he was behind his desk, looking like a man who was simply working. She closed the door and stood there in her heels and suit and stared him down.

He didn't budge.

"Why are you still here?" She moved closer to him.

He looked her in the eye and his voice was even, if not happy. "Because I need to be."

"I'll fire you." She stepped forward again.

"You can't."

"Wanna bet?" She was nearly in his face, and pissed as hell. She was the boss's daughter and she'd never really used it to her advantage. Sure, she'd taken what was offered, but she'd never gone in with the idea that she'd get what she wanted because she was Arthur Geryon's offspring.

But she turned on her heel and stormed out of her office.

A lot of her steam got lost while she sat waiting for Sharon to say her father was free. It gave her time to think up why Allistair should be fired. She was armed with a great idea by the time she had finally cooled her heels and had been admitted to stand in front of her father's desk.

He, however, opened the conversation with an ambush. "I really like that new assistant of yours. You said he trained quite fast."

Her mouth opened like a fish, she was so surprised.

Her father talked to fill the gap she had left. "I think it's time to promote him. He should get his own office in research. I think the one next to yours is open."

This time she balked. "No! I actually came up here to tell you that you should fire him."

"For God's sakes, why? I thought he was great."

"No, Dad. I think he trained so fast because he used to work for Gottlieb. In fact, I imagine he came straight here from that job—and with their blessings. They're an investing firm and I think they planted him here. And foolishly, I just trained him how to get into all our systems. I don't think he was an errand boy there. I think he's . . ."

"Really?"

"Yes." That would do it. There was nothing her father despised more than underhanded tactics. Except, of course, if he could find a way to justify them for himself. He wouldn't stand for this. Katharine waited.

It didn't take long. "We can't have that."

"No." She smiled.

"Now that we've taught him what we know, we need to change tacks."

She faltered. And waited.

Arthur Geryon spoke again. "If he is checking us out and we cut him loose, he'll go back and tell them what he knows. We'll have to keep him here. In fact, I think you should keep working with him. He's in your office, isn't he?"

This was not going the way she wanted. But when she saw her father was waiting for her response, she nodded.

"You keep an eye on him. I didn't get that impression from him at all, that he was a corporate spy. However, if you think so, you stay on him and see if you can find some proof. Though I must say, I'll be very disappointed if you do."

She sighed.

Her father kept going. "In light of this, I think it best that we not promote him right now. So let's keep him right where he is. Don't say anything to him."

That was it. He had turned his attention back to the papers waiting on his desk and she had been dismissed.

Walking out, she felt like she had been hit by a stun gun. She had gone in with what she thought was a good plan and walked out with Allistair sewn even tighter into his position. Gaining some ire, she marched herself back down to her office like a good soldier. And a pissed one.

When she entered, she once again closed the door behind her but didn't say anything. Allistair looked up at her and didn't speak until she went to sit behind her own desk. "It didn't work, did it?"

"Of course not." Her head snapped up. How could he have known it wouldn't work? "I don't know what you did to him, but you stay away from my father!"

He nodded. "Your father is safe. You're the only one in jeopardy."

Her heart stilled. Maybe she didn't like speaking openly about this after all. "You say that so calmly, like it means nothing to you."

"On the contrary, it means everything. More than you can know." His eyes seemed to heat up as they looked at her, and that worried her even more.

She turned back to her work, even though she wanted to ask him, "Now what?" but she was too afraid of the answer. She was afraid he'd tell her the truth.

. . .

She didn't go home that night.

Allistair had been a perfect gentleman all day—in deed at least. As she thought back to the few times they talked, she got mad. He'd answered all her questions. He'd had a conversation with her—a frank one—and still, he'd never outright confessed to any of it.

She wanted him to say he did it. Say he killed Mary Wayne. Say that he was after her. But all he said was that she "needed to be careful" and was "in jeopardy."

Later, at Margot's, Katharine unloaded all of this while Margot listened patiently but couldn't come up with a good answer for her, or even a passable theory.

The patio was its usual soothing cacophony of city sounds. And Katharine tried so hard to enjoy it. "What's going on in your life, Margot? We always talk about my life. And I'm not being a very good friend. Plus, I desperately want to know."

It started with a shrug for an answer. "I got asked out today."

"That's only worth a shrug? I never get asked out. How can you shrug that away?"

Margot laughed at her. "I'd like to point out that you must be off base about never getting asked out, since there have been *two* men after you of late."

"Um, no. And, as best as we can tell, one of them's a demon." She wondered where her voice was carried to on the wind. But in Los Angeles there were all kinds of freaks and weirdoes—who knew what you might overhear? No one would think anything of it. "And only Zachary asked me out. Allistair just sort of . . . happened."

"Like thrall?"

"Must be." Katharine thought she could see a smidge of beach down one of the streets. Something about it called to her. She liked the ocean, but with some effort she pulled her thoughts back in. "It must be like thrall. When I'm around him, I just smell him and he seems so safe. It's so hard to resist him." She shook her head. "He said my name and reached out for me today, and I just wanted to go into his arms." She shuddered now at the thought of it. "I almost did."

"That doesn't sound like thrall."

"Doesn't it?" But Katharine knew she was about to get a breakdown on what the word actually meant. Normally, she found that kind of correctiveness annoying, but somehow Margot always made it seem simply informative, never meant to put down.

"Thrall is more like body control. Your brain doesn't want it, but your body obeys."

"Like the old dead-behind-the-eyes 'Yes, master' kind of stuff?"

"Yup."

Katharine shuddered. "Nope, not like thrall then. Thank God." She maneuvered the conversation back to where she wanted it. "So tell me about this guy who asked you out. How often does this happen?"

"Almost daily."

"You get asked out almost daily? Of course you do! You're pretty and smart and really good at being sociable without being pushy. And you're just a bit uppity—I bet that makes the boys beg."

By the time she was through, Margot's small laughs had turned into full-belly guffaws. "I can't say I've ever had the boys begging. I think it's just the job."

"It's not the job." Margot was pretty. Her wide mouth smiled in a way that was happy and inviting and with none of the coyness that most women displayed.

"Oh, please, it's the job." Margot was still laughing. "Every man has a librarian fantasy! That's all it is."

"Okay, I hadn't thought about the whole librarian fantasy thing, but it's not just the job. I bet the other librarians don't get asked out as much as you do." Katharine leaned back and watched as her friend absorbed the compliment. As teens at boarding school, the girls had complimented each other with the social understanding that a return compliment was expected in reply. This might be the first time she'd simply praised someone without expecting anything in return. "So what was this next-in-the-long-chain like? And why does he deserve a mention when you get asked out almost daily?"

All Margot could do was shrug and look off into the distance. "He was . . ."

"Did you say yes? Please tell me you said yes."

"I gave him my card and told him that if he was serious he knew where to find me."

Katharine didn't know if that would work. She hoped it would; something in Margot's eyes made her think her friend really liked the guy. But this was L.A., and there seemed to be a secret male pact to collect as many numbers as you could and never call.

It was Margot who turned the subject back around. "I think I found something workable today. Wanna hear?"

"Always." Katharine ducked inside and pulled a ginger ale from the fridge for Margot and a Sunkist for herself. She'd never tried Sunkist until recently when Allistair had introduced her, and she wondered if she should just ditch all the things associated with him or if she could enjoy the soda for what it was.

But Margot was motioning Katharine to join her where she now sat cross-legged in the middle of piles of photocopies in the living room. Katharine had needed to step over them when she came in, and she'd managed to ignore what they meant for a while. But now Margot sat amongst her research, wanting Katharine to focus. Most of the stacks were two to ten pages thick, with a neat staple punched into the upper right-hand corner. "All right, there are three routes I found: Catholicism, voodoo, or Wicca."

"What's the difference?"

"Smart question." With one long, graceful finger, she pointed to a tall stack of papers. "With Catholicism you have to go to the church—"

"I don't attend Catholic church."

"No, not attend, but you do have to go and petition them. At the central parish. Tell them you have a demon. Then they hold a committee meeting and decide if they should send an exorcist out for you."

Katharine felt her brows pull together. "That sounds like we could beg and plead and they could still say no. And do I really need an exorcist? I'm not possessed."

"That's my thought exactly. It doesn't fit what's happening here. Plus, you have to consider that, these days, most of the priests aren't trained in exorcism. Most of them don't even believe in it. I imagine that route would be an uphill battle with no good outcome. But it's there if we need it."

"So that's the Catholic pile?" She pointed to the largest stack, about three inches high and made up of smaller stapled packets. When Margot nodded, she asked, "Then what's that one?"

The next-biggest stack was voodoo. "While I imagine that there are voodoo spots in L.A., I don't know where any are, and I couldn't find anything that didn't look to be about as legit as one of those fake-fang vampire clubs. Plus, you have to pay the voodoo master or mistress to work your spell. It can get expensive."

"I have money." She might as well spend it on this as a new pair of shoes.

"It's not the cost. I'm just leery of any magic you have to buy. I don't think you should have to pay for it. I don't think anyone should be making a house payment from someone else's misery."

Katharine nodded. "So, no old voodoo lady selling me a gris-gris. That leaves Wicca."

"Yup. What I like best about it is that you can do it yourself."

"Isn't it better to have the high priestess do it? Isn't she super strong?"

Margot nodded. "But where are we going to find one? There are Wiccan enclaves all over L.A., but it seems that anything I've looked up, particularly on the web, isn't likely to be the real deal. We don't need a tree hugger, we need a demon fighter."

Katharine had to laugh. "And you choose me?"

"Well, us. But, yes." She leaned forward. "You're the most familiar with what you saw. I wasn't finding references to these creatures in any of the information here. We're starting to marry mythology and religion, so I don't know what would happen if we went to some priest and said, 'She's not possessed; a demon is just following her around.' You know?"

"So we do it ourselves." Katharine slugged back the last of the Sunkist as if the orange soda would give her strength. She started sifting through the spread-out papers, all with different ideas. She saw several packets titled *Binding Spell* or some version of that idea. But her fingers picked up the one that said *Avalon*. "What's this?"

Margot looked at the paper. "Oh, that's interesting. Avalon was the home of Morgan le Fey, sis—"

"Sister of King Arthur. It was an island off of England. I read about it in school." She started to catch on. "The island was trapped in mist and would disappear, and time was slower there."

"Exactly, at least in one interpretation. They had to cast spells to go back and forth to get to it. The idea was that the veil between the worlds was particularly thin there."

"Is it thin here? In L.A.?"

"Got me. It just seemed like it might lead somewhere. And it did." She picked up another article. "Halloween originated in the pagan holy day where the veil is supposed to be the thinnest. That's why you dress up as scary things, so the evil monsters don't recognize you as human, and therefore probably as tasty. According to the pagans, things from across the veil walk freely among us on that one night. Things like what you are seeing."

"So after Halloween we can lock him back up? That's too long to wait."

"I know. I just thought it might help. We're on the right track, and something here is going to lead us to exactly what we need."

"I know you're right. I don't mean to sound negative. I'm just impatient."

"No problem, I'd be impatient too, in your shoes. I did find a handful of binding spells." Margot handed a few over to Katharine. Two looked more like recipes than articles. "The idea is that you can stop the creature from harming others, and 'others' would include you. But your spell has to be more powerful than his magic. So that may be an issue."

Katharine nodded.

"The other option is"—Margot sifted through the mix—"a protection spell." She sifted more. "I had two of them. Together. Crap." She flipped papers and thumbed through the stacks of Catholic and voodoo information, her brows pulled tighter and tighter together while she looked. "I brought them with me . . . I thought."

After fifteen minutes of checking her bag and looking around the apartment, she declared the binding spells officially lost. She said she must have left them behind by accident. She had kept them out separate, after all.

Katharine leaned back on the couch. "So sometime tomorrow, we'll figure out how to protect me from him."

"Nah, let's go now."

"It's eleven. Even I know the library is closed."

Margot smiled and pulled out her keys. "But I'm the head librarian. I can get in whenever I want."

"Really?"

"Oh yeah. I should drive, so it looks less like someone trying to break in. It'll be my car in the parking lot. If anyone sees it, they'll recognize it's me. It makes the visit look more legit."

With her purse slung over her shoulder, Katharine followed her friend down to her car, uneasy about going into a closed building. She didn't think she'd ever done this before. It was a little too close to B & E, as far as she was concerned. But her friend seemed to think it was no problem. And Katharine's desperate need to know what was in those spells more than outweighed her concern.

It wasn't far to the big ultramodern building. Margot parked in an employee spot and walked up to the door just like it was 8:30 a.m. and she was there to start her shift.

Though there was a light overhead, it was dark at the doorway and she had trouble getting the key to fit.

"Margot, the cops are going to come." Katharine had never had a run-in with the police before recently, and she sure didn't need another. Not so soon.

"The police aren't coming, wimp. I have a master's in library science—surely I can work a key!" But it took another minute of Katharine sweating bullets and watching out for the boys in blue before the key worked. She probably looked even more guilty, the way she kept glancing around, but she couldn't help it. She was grateful to get into the building with the door closed behind her.

Margot led her into the office and looked around, then softly swore one more time. "Pam would have put all the papers left on the counter into recycling. I'll have to go find it again."

Though they put the lights on in the back where the offices were, Margot didn't want to light up the whole library or even just the reference overheads; it might alert someone driving by that they were there. So she grabbed two flashlights and started down the aisles.

It was eerie as all hell.

Katharine wasn't one to be skittish in the dark before this, but lately she had become more and more so. The quiet clicking seemed to be normal for the building, but though it didn't faze Margot at all, it was making Katharine jumpy.

Then there were the glass windows. They were high up on the walls, where the two of them were waving their flashlights, and she didn't think anyone on the street would see the lights. But that concerned her less than the thought that she might see something in the reflections.

Luckily, Margot had no designs on keeping them out in the stacks for long. Since she couldn't remember exactly which books she'd found the protection spells in, she started pulling whatever she could. By the time she was done, Katharine must have had about fifteen huge volumes stacked in her own arms and Margot was balancing almost as many.

They walked the books back to the office and set them down.

Methodically hunting for the spells they needed, the two women would periodically stop and point something out, then photocopy it. By 1:00 a.m., they had only one spell—but a huge stack of pages to read through later.

Katharine was getting tired and was about to ask if they could come back and try again tomorrow, when Margot grabbed her arm tight enough to make her wince. But her friend didn't notice. Katharine leaned in. "Did you find the spell?"

"No. Look." Turning the book around, Margot held up a two-page reproduction of a painting for Katharine to see. She didn't point, only spoke. "I'm thinking about what you described to me. You said it changed sometimes . . . not the animals, but the creature itself."

Katharine nodded. The painting depicted beasts like the ones she had seen, some black and tarry, the others silver and slick, long blades of fingers ripping at each other's flesh. They all bore wings, and some hovered overhead, held aloft by an unseen breeze on black or silvery membranes, like skin stretched taut enough to see through. Mouths barely contained sharp teeth that could only be made for tearing at each other.

Transfixed by the picture, her blood was running colder and colder. "Yes, that's what I saw."

Her beast had appeared to her in both ways, black and silver. And when Margot asked exactly that, Katharine could only nod.

This was what she had been seeing. This was not a similar idea or a pencil sketch. Some artist had seen just what she had been seeing, only he had seen legions of them. And he had depicted them with a near-photographic skill that took her breath away.

Margot's voice was so soft that she almost didn't hear it.

"Katharine, the painting is called *The War of Demons and Angels*."

THROUGH THE EYE

CHAPTER 20

Katharine sat stunned.

But Margot didn't. "Didn't you say Zachary had bruises? Right after you saw that fight in the shop window?"

Katharine nodded. "But he doesn't have them now. Maybe I imagined it."

"No, you didn't imagine any of it, and that's the problem." With a very troubled look marring her pretty features, Margot set the picture down across the desk in front of them. The book was huge, fifteen inches tall, and when open it was almost two feet across. The painting was horrific. "How could you have just imagined the exact same thing other people saw?"

Katharine was about to give some non-answer when Margot charged into the fray again. "Why did we suspect these guys in the first place?"

That she could answer. "You asked if there was anyone new and charismatic in my life. You read that a demon may appear that way. And I said there were two men like that."

She wanted to vomit. Somehow she had held it together when it was just a demon. Somehow, through all that craziness and all the unexplained things, she kept up appearances, even to herself. But now . . .

"Katharine! Are you all right?" Margot didn't wait for an answer, just pushed her gently into the nearest chair and ran to fetch a mug from the break room. "It's just tap water, so it isn't too cold, but you should drink it anyway."

She pushed the mug at Katharine until she was forced to take it and drink the lukewarm water that didn't taste too great. That was L.A. for you. She managed three sips before she started to break down again. Her voice came through in just a whisper. "I had sex with both of them . . . I didn't really think about that before. I just got mad that it had taken advantage of me. I kept thinking that at least one of them was the real deal, but now . . ."

"Take a deep breath." Margot breathed with her and pulled up another chair.

The seats were barstool height so the staff could work at the high counters. But right now Katharine just feared she would fall off and hurt herself. She feared a lot of things. But one of those things had hovered at the back of her mind for days. It was begging to be acknowledged. Only now, in the middle of the night, in a locked public building alone with Margot, could she bring herself to voice it. "What if I'm pregnant?"

"What!" Margot did almost fall off the chair. "Oh God, that never occurred to me." She straightened herself and began straightening the office, too. She gathered books and jotted down a few of the titles, then put them all in the drop-off bin. Then she took Katharine's hand and tugged her off the stool. "Let's get that first one taken care of right away."

After locking up the library, they drove around. Luckily, it didn't take long to find a pharmacy that was open twenty-four hours. Leaving Katharine in the car by herself, Margot ran in and came back out with a small box in a plastic bag.

Twenty minutes later, Katharine was lying on Margot's bed with tears running down her face. "Oh God. That had me so scared."

"Hey, at least it came out the way it did. I don't even want to think where we'd be if you were pregnant."

"We?" Katharine shook her head. "Where *I'd* be. I'd be the pregnant one. You've been doing all of this because you're just nice."

Margot laughed, and it occurred to Katharine that the librarian laughed more than anyone she'd ever known before. "I'm not just nice. *Nice* is why I helped with the first translations. Then I looked into it because I was curious—which is just a natural fault of mine. But if you were pregnant, it would be about where *we* would be. Because we're friends. Sometimes you act like you've never had one before."

That stopped Katharine in her tracks.

Surely she'd had friends before. There were a few girls from school that she kept in touch with. But when she thought about it, she did that because they were in the same sorority and their parents knew each other. They had lunch when they were in town; they caught up. But that was about it. She showed up to charity functions for her Dad, and even planned a few. She knew the women who fit in there, they had gone out for drinks. She'd gone clubbing a few times with some of her coworkers, but that hadn't lasted long.

No, she didn't think she'd ever had a real friend before. But she didn't say it.

Neither did Margot. Her new friend just handed over a soft, pink Victoria's Secret sleep tee and told her to stay where she was. Margot took the futon in her own guest room.

Katharine slept until sometime right before dawn, when she woke up, sensing that something else was in the room. She didn't flinch, even though it took a full minute to remember where she was. Then she was mad. It had come to Margot's home.

The faint light of dawn sifted in through the thin curtains, revealing a shape sitting in the middle of the floor. As her eyes adjusted, she saw that not only was it a panther, but it was stretched out as if it had made itself comfortable.

Leaning over the edge of the bed, she did her best to stare it in the eyes. Her voice was low and mean, and she said the words the way Zachary had when he had gotten rid of the wolf. "Get out."

This was the creature that had tormented her. It had toyed with her for months, showing up in her condo, disappearing, leaving traces of soot, and rearranging small things until she thought she would go insane. To what end? What purpose had all that served, except maybe to show that it could get to her? No more.

"Get out."

Just then, the door opened, throwing light across a sector of the room. Katharine jerked her head up to see Margot standing in the doorway. "I thought I heard someone—oh, holy shit."

She looked down at the panther. And as Katharine watched, it looked back up at her. Its head moved, almost as though to nod, and then it turned its gaze back to Katharine before sinking into the floor.

If she hadn't been so pissed off that it had come here, she would have laughed hysterically at the look on Margot's face. Her expression of horror went over the line of comical. But it didn't last long. As usual, her friend held it together. "So, that was the thing that visits your place?"

"Yes." Katharine was now sitting up on the side of the bed, legs dangling over the edge as she looked at the huge spot of soot the panther had left. She was just as pissed that she'd have to clean up the mess as anything else.

"Well, at least it's official," Margot declared. "You aren't crazy. I just saw a panther in my room and it sank into the floor."

"Amen to that. Do you have a wet vac?"

"No." Margot frowned at her. "Are you always this calm about it?"

"At this point, it has happened enough that recently, yes, I have been rather calm. I'll bring my carpet scrubber by later and clean this up."

"Do the animals always look like that?"

"Like what?" Katharine was puzzled. Black? Kind of silent? What?

"Its coat was black, but there were so many colors reflected in it. The way colors reflect in an oil slick. It looked solid and real but not quite like something I could look up and find in an animal guide." Margot's brows pulled together in the look that told Katharine she was thinking of how to say what she wanted. "Like we would find out that breed of cat doesn't come in pure black or something. Like something was just a little off."

"Yes, they do always look like that. Except for the leopard. I didn't notice anything unusual about it." She paused. "Except that it jumped out a plate-glass window without damaging itself or the window. But otherwise it was normal, I guess."

"But it was beautiful." Margot stretched the word out as if the panther was something to be admired. There was a hitch in her breath as if even just the memory of the animal left her awestruck. Then her voice changed tone completely. "Oh, crap! I thought it was beautiful! I'm in its thrall!"

That time, Katharine did laugh.

. . .

Zachary watched from a distance as the two women finally fell back on the bed. They shared the wide mattress this time, not wanting to be alone as they each tried to get a little more sleep before daylight.

Things were breaking.

Allistair hadn't turned and run like he should have, and it had turned out to be a good move on his part. But that didn't work in Zachary's favor.

The women were starting to put all the pieces together. They knew about both of them now. They knew there was a choice to be made. Margot was helping Katharine and it was speeding the process up.

If Zachary were greedy, he might have thought about bringing both of the women with him. After all, how often did a human wind up in Margot's place, seeing creatures from across the veil but not being courted by them? But he wasn't greedy, and he was smart enough to know that, though he could offer her all the riches and benefits that he was offering Katharine, he wasn't strong enough to carry two through the process. Yet.

Allistair had stayed there at the edge of Katharine's bed most of the night. The panther had staked its claim and made the point to Zachary that he could go anywhere he pleased—including Zachary's space, and anywhere Katharine might go. And he also did it to show Zachary that he could get there first.

It all pissed Zachary off. For one about to fail for the umpteenth time, Allistair had a knack for hanging on, for showing up just where he wasn't wanted. And that move the other night in his own condo was just too much.

Zachary had protected the place against Allistair when he first claimed it. And it had worked. Allistair himself had never been able to breach the boundary. But as the animals he could. Zachary hadn't thought ahead to protect his condo against all forms. Who incorporated as a creature? It was an old trick from lower orders, used before they became as powerful as they were now. Who would have guessed that Allistair would resort to it?

But he had resorted to it. And it had paid off.

Still, Zachary could get another move in before daylight.

. . .

"Holy crap!"

Katharine heard Margot's voice from the bathroom. "What?" But the question was unnecessary because she was already headed that way and Margot was already talking.

"There's a message on my mirror."

And sure enough, sparkling on the glass—as though ice crystals had simply frozen there—were the words *Mihi crede*.

Margot ran out of the room. At first, Katharine thought it was in fear, but in a moment she was back, pen and paper in hand and a faint gleam in her eyes. She wasn't afraid. Then again, it wasn't her life at stake, even though within the last few hours whatever it was had invaded her life.

Her friend copied the note twice, then checked the two copies against each other. She pulled her cell phone out from where she'd stashed it in the waistband of her pajama pants and snapped a picture. Margot turned to Katharine, still breathing a bit heavily from racing around like she had. "I got it. Look." She held up the cell phone.

But Katharine shook her head. "I don't see it."

Margot nodded sadly. "That's why I wrote it down first." Then she pointed at the mirror. "It's already fading."

Sure enough, it looked like the ice crystals were melting. But Margot had already moved on. "I'll get it translated first thing . . . I don't know about you, but I am going to be running on adrenaline and coffee today. I have to go to work. I need my paycheck and we need my access to the library."

The paper scrap was folded neatly and tucked into one of the pockets of her purse while Katharine just stood and watched, and then Margot walked off to get ready for work. Finally getting herself together, Katharine followed her out the door about ten minutes later. In the time it had taken her to put her own clothes back on from last night and grab her purse, Margot had gotten ready for a day at work.

Her hair was slicked up into a twist, she had on some makeup, and she was dressed. Katharine was pouring out two insulated cups of coffee for them when Margot emerged from her room, ready to go. Katharine was impressed. "Wow, you did that fast."

Margot smiled. "I'm organized. I had this whole outfit set aside for an 'Oops, my alarm didn't go off' day. This is the fastest hairstyle I know. Nothing to it." She took the coffee Katharine offered and they were in their separate cars, heading in different directions, before Katharine even realized that she had taken the cup from her friend's cupboard and driven off with it without even asking. But they both knew she'd bring it back. She didn't need to ask.

Friends knew that.

Something settled in her soul.

She had to head home first; she couldn't wear the same clothes again. She had to put a change of clothes into a bag and had to throw the wet vac into the trunk to take to Margot's that evening.

She didn't see Zachary in the hallway as she approached her door. She thought she might, given the early hour, but the hallway was thankfully empty.

The last she had seen of him, he had stared down the black wolf and told it to get out. Eventually, it had turned and walked out of the bedroom, and Zachary had followed it. Even though her heart was about to thump out of her chest, she had pretended then to be asleep.

Katharine had wanted to believe it was just a big dog. Zachary certainly hadn't acted like it was anything other than a pest in his bedroom. He had even muttered something about watching dogs. And she had thought maybe the fact that it had looked like all the other animals, as though this particular species didn't come in all black, was just a coincidence. It must have been a real dog. Otherwise, wouldn't Zachary have been as shocked as she had been the first time she'd seen an animal in her apartment?

She had tangled it all up in her brain. She'd concocted excuses—Zachary was dog-sitting, he was half-asleep and didn't realize he shouldn't have a dog in his unit, it was just a dog, she'd just had too much to deal with—but she couldn't write it off anymore.

Not now, when it made more sense.

Zachary had not been freaked out by the dog because he knew exactly what it was.

She had two creatures following her, and they appeared to be acquainted with each other. As she stood there in her own hallway, ideas bloomed in her brain. Puzzle pieces started connecting. The pissing match that had erupted between the two of them at Light & Geryon when Zachary came to get her for lunch . . . they had known far more than she at that time. The fact that the two had appeared almost simultaneously in her life. It was clear now they had known each other before she had known either of them.

She was putting more things together in her head when she got the last bolt undone and opened her front door . . . to utter chaos.

The TV was tipped facedown onto the floor. Her bookshelf was practically naked; books littered the floor in front of it, some with torn covers. Angry but unafraid, she stalked through the rest of the unit. Her bedcovers were tossed about, her clothing on the floor. Her lotions and toothpaste and all the little bottles and tubes that were on the counter had all been tipped. Most were piled in the sink.

There was no message on the mirror here.

There was no soot on the carpet.

Katharine went back out to the living room and lifted the corner of the TV to see if it was broken or just knocked over. From what she could see, it appeared intact. She set it back down.

She had thought the TV would be the deciding factor. If it were broken, she'd call the police, report a crime, and file an insurance claim. But even as she squatted down to lift it, she realized it didn't matter. She wasn't going to file this with any agency.

There was no way she wanted to see the police in conjunction with another crime. She'd been through enough. Nothing looked truly ruined except a few of the books. She realized then that, even if it had been bad, she still wouldn't have reported it. What good would it do? It would bring the cops. It would raise her insurance. And it would have tons of other people traipsing through her condo when she knew they wouldn't find a thing.

And her blasé attitude would only swing the cops right back around to the Mary Wayne case they still hadn't closed. Zachary had gotten them off her back, but they could get right back on so easily with something like this.

She decided to sort through the clothing for an outfit to wear to work. Coming from Margot's had put her on a short schedule, and finding her apartment like this had definitively made her late. Katharine sighed. She wouldn't be able to use it as an excuse at work because she wasn't reporting it. The last time she'd alerted someone that she wasn't reporting things, Margot had crawled down her throat and told her she had a demon.

She was pulling a skirt from under a pile of her things when Zachary appeared at her front door. Almost swearing under her breath at her stupidity, she realized she'd left it open.

His startled expression seemed genuine, but what did she know?

His voice carried to her as he picked his way across the mess to stand in her bedroom doorway. "You weren't home when this happened, were you?"

She looked him up and down, trying to figure what he was about. She had first believed him a demon and run straight to Allistair. Then she had believed the same of Allistair and run to Zachary, thinking he was human. But the timing and the painting had changed her beliefs. When she added in the encounter with the black dog, she knew that there was no safe choice—neither man was as he appeared.

She didn't look him in the face. Which was he? Angel or demon? She needed to figure it out, and fast. "Of course I wasn't home."

"Katie, you should stay with me until this gets cleared up."

She knew better and still didn't look him in the face. "I have a place to go. I don't think that will be necessary."

"Are you going to call the police?"

A slow calm settled over her and she felt her back straighten, felt the need to make her own decisions, no matter what Zachary might be. "No, there won't be any prints, and you and I both know it won't serve any purpose."

"We do?" He took another step into the room, either unable to sense that she was uneasy with that or simply not caring.

"Yes, we do." Holding an undamaged outfit from her fingertips, she looked up at him and this time met his eyes. Instantly she was beset with feelings of safety and concern. They washed over her like water, and she felt better. She wanted to stay with him; a niggling sensation at the back of her brain told her she'd be safe there. She didn't listen to any of it. "Please, leave. I have to get to work."

He turned to leave. But at the door to her unit he turned back to her. "Be careful."

"Always."

. . .

Allistair waited patiently for Katharine to show up at work. She couldn't afford to be late these days. She had to come.

So in human form he spoke with Lisa, walked the hallways to grab a cup of coffee from the break room, and said hello to as many Light & Geryon employees as he could. There was so much money controlled here, yet none of them knew how they were changing the world.

They had faces that were neither innocent nor happy, but they had their work ethic. And their paychecks. Like most people, their colors changed day by day, melding into the air around them. A few people maintained the shade unique to those who had found themselves. But very few of those humans worked here at Light & Geryon.

Slowly Katharine was becoming stable, no longer just floating along, reacting to the few things that happened directly to her and ignorant of the changes she made in the world by doing so. If he could get to her, he could change that. She could use this place, make its impact bigger, if she wanted.

Stepping into the men's room, he checked himself in the mirror. He could see the large eyes and long teeth shimmering just under the human form he kept remaking each time he incorporated. This shape had been the easiest; it was the way he had naturally formed as he passed through the layers to get to Katharine's level.

He was proud of his dark skin tone. It was darker than last time he'd had a human assignment, meaning that, in spite of his many failings, he had made some progress. His human eyes were dark too. Always a good sign of achievement. But his real eyes, the eyes of the creature he was, saw beyond all that. They saw his true self, the skin and the form and the muscles that would be called overdeveloped in human terms.

He was consistently right here in front of them, and they didn't see it. If you didn't look further, you missed what was there for the taking.

Just as Katharine had taken for granted that there was only one creature. Didn't she see that the black animals were different from the spotted? She had only just now recognized that he and Zachary had both showed up in her life at the same time—she was only now putting those pieces together. Though he was impatient with her, she wasn't really any slower than most other humans would have been. He left the restroom, knowing full well none of those around him would look further than the façade or try to see what was there under his seemingly innocuous surface. Shame on them.

He was pouring the coffee as his senses perked. Katharine.

She was coming up from the garage.

He stood there in the break room and tried to look as though he wasn't waiting. He sipped at the coffee, savoring the still, cool ceramic against his lip and the stinging burn of the bitter liquid on his tongue. He made sure to notice these things.

Katharine was coming around.

She was putting pieces together.

He wasn't long for this body.

CHAPTER 21

Katharine closed the door behind her as she entered her office.

Looking as innocent as she thought he could, Allistair sat on the edge of her desk, holding a cup of coffee cradled in his hands as though he enjoyed the heat. "Good morning."

"Not so good. My apartment was ransacked."

He appeared surprised by that, but this was the second time she had seen the same reaction, and by her math only one of the men could be genuine. He looked her in the eye and asked, "Do you know who did it?"

"I have a feeling." She stared back and waited.

For what, she didn't know.

Maybe she was waiting for the wash of feelings that invaded her when she was in Zachary's space, maybe for the yearning she felt for Allistair. But she only felt what she had been feeling all morning: the urge to confront him. The feeling that she *needed* to confront him. The feeling that she wasn't afraid of him.

A small knot inside her wanted to go into his arms and find the safety and comfort she had always felt there. Her brain told her in no uncertain terms that it was a false feeling. But even that strong warning didn't stop her from wanting it.

Allistair didn't say anything else. And a part of her appreciated that he didn't play it off as though he knew nothing about it. The concern stayed in his eyes, though. A very nice trick if it were indeed his work in her condo last night.

So she stood there with her back to the door and waited for him to get mad, to confess, to tell her something to piss her off.

When he spoke next it was so far from what she expected that it startled her. "How can I help?"

Katharine grasped for a response to that. "Tell me what you are."

"I'm not like you."

"I knew that!" She practically spat it. He hadn't given her what she wanted. He never did. "What about Zachary?"

"He's more like me than like you." Allistair shook his head as though he were as frustrated as she was. "It's all I'll say. Ask for something else."

"Then tell me about Mary Wayne."

He sipped the coffee, looking more human than he had a right to. "What do you want to know?"

"You said she agreed to what happened to her. How?"

With an open hand, he motioned her to sit down at her desk and pulled his own chair up to sit across from her before he spoke again. "She made a deal."

Katharine was glad she was sitting. The idea was so preposterous that her knees would have given out. Her words gushed out before she could think about them. "No one makes that kind of deal."

"We all do." He set the coffee mug on the edge of her desk and leaned back in his chair, gesturing as though it were his natural state. "We create reactions in the world around us. We agree to things that have ramifications, even if we don't see those repercussions when we agree. Think about the impact you've had just by recommending or withholding stocks."

Her whole body turned to jelly. It was as if he knew that her TV had gotten stuck. As if he knew she had figured out what happened with WeldLink and the firing pins. But then again, maybe both men already knew everything.

He leaned forward. "She tried to break her deal, Katharine. So be careful what deals you wind up making. Be certain before you make them."

"Why me?" It was the question she had been wanting to ask someone for so long. And now she finally could. But as soon as it was out of her mouth she wanted to swallow it back.

"Mary led us here, to you."

Her heart iced at the thought, and her next word was barely a whisper. "How?"

He shook his head, sadness shuttering his previously open expression. "I will do what I can to help you. I need you with me. But there are many things I can't tell you, Katharine."

Anger, righteous and strong, erupted through her. They could write on her mirrors, scare the crap out of her, ransack her condo, and *hurt* other people, but he couldn't tell her what she wanted to know, what she *needed* to know? "Why not!"

It was so loud that she was sure Lisa must have heard her from out in the hall. Allistair, too, looked toward the hall, worried. With a glance at her, he opened the door and peered down the hallway, then stepped back, leaving the door open as though everything was business as usual.

"We've all made deals, Katharine, and I am bound by mine."

. . .

Katharine called Margot before she showed up at the library, right before her friend's shift ended. Because she was on day hours, Margot didn't have much to do. But Katharine followed her around and, while they were within earshot of the other employees, made Margot tell about her day.

"Liam called."

"Liam?"

There was something shy in Margot's smile that wasn't usually there. Katharine caught on before her friend spoke. "The guy I gave my card to the other day. He asked me out . . . just for coffee!"

As if that was a bad thing. "It's a fantastic place to start."

"Yeah, he suggested maybe the coffee date could go on for a long time, so he picked a place in a mall with restaurants and a theater right there. I'm trying not to read too much into it." After she said good-bye to the other employees she turned to Katharine. "Oh, I made those other photocopies we wanted."

The protection spell. They had been too upset the night before. "Thank you. Do we have the stuff to make it tonight?"

Katharine tried to keep her words ambiguous as Margot was briefly introducing her to some of the other staff coming in for the evening as the two women made their way out of the building.

"No, but we can get it. I'm anxious to make a double batch after last night." She pushed her button to unlock the car. "Come with me. We can go out and get the stuff."

Margot kept talking as Katharine slid into the passenger seat. "I found a place to buy all the herbs and everything we need. Since it's experimental, I say we get enough for three batches. In case we mess something up. We need to get you protected, but if there's any left over, I'd like to do one for me, too. Especially after last night."

"Absolutely. You need it. I can't believe it came to your house." She held her thoughts back. There was so much to say. Instead, she moved the conversation back to something she could manage. "Where's this place? What is it?"

"It's a store for magic practitioners and witches and pagans."

Katharine didn't even ask how she'd found it. Margot could find anything. "When's this date with Liam?"

She watched as her friend actually blushed. Amazing.

"Friday after work. But I told him that I had a friend who was in a bad place and if I canceled last minute or even no-showed on him, he shouldn't take it personally . . . he said it was good I was being such a good friend."

Katharine sobered. Liam didn't know the half of it. "He's beyond right."

There was a pause in the conversation, and with a breath, Katharine dove in. "My apartment was ransacked last night."

"What!"

"Yeah, nothing broken. It didn't look like they were looking for anything." She shrugged and told her how Zachary had come by that morning and offered her the chance to stay with him.

Katharine had decided to clean it up and stay at her own condo, but Margot wouldn't hear of it.

"Margot! In the one night I stayed at your place, we got visited by something. I can't stay with you. This stuff is just following me wherever I go. But thank you for offering." After that, she deliberately changed tacks. "So there's one demon and one angel after me? Right?"

"That's what everything would lead us to believe."

She relayed everything she'd asked Allistair that day before he'd clammed up.

Margot finally made a left turn they'd waited through three lights for, then spoke. "It's all about making deals? Do they want you to make a deal? Like some weird devil-went-down-to-Georgia kind of thing?"

Bless her, Margot could make her laugh even in the middle of a terrible conversation. "It seems that way. But which one of them do I make the deal with? Allistair said he needed me with him."

"But if they've both already made deals, then they each need you for something. You're clearly a part of it." Margot frowned. "I'll feel a lot better when this protection spell is on you."

"On us," Katharine clarified.

They finally parked and entered the store. It was painted purple both inside and out, and it carried everything listed in the spell Margot had decided on. Katharine paid for all the materials and Margot insisted they do the spell at her apartment.

"I picked this one because it seemed hard to screw up. And it says to do it at a safe location. I think that means my un-ransacked apartment right now."

They picked up Katharine's car and then stopped for huge slices of pizza, each of them eating in the car as they made their way up the hill to Margot's. In twenty minutes they had all the materials laid out and were ready to start.

Flipping through the pages she had stapled, Margot read the whole thing through again just to be sure, and then they began. Katharine felt silly at first, sprinkling salt and saying chants, but Margot kept a straight face. However, it only took a moment before it started to feel like something right, something she needed to be doing.

It was fine until she put her finger in the salted water and began to stir.

"Counter-clockwise!" Margot reprimanded her.

"Does it matter?" Katharine moved her finger the other direction, against the tiny current she had made in the water.

"I don't want to find out" was all her friend would say.

At the end of the ritual Katharine was to blow out the big candle on the table, and she gathered a breath to do so.

Right on cue, the flame went out, and that was it.

"I don't feel anything, Margot."

"Everything I've read about pagan magic says you won't. You just sit back and have faith and wait for the changes you have wrought." She snapped on the light and began clearing the materials out of the way. Just as easily, she laid out a brand-new setup of salt and candle and settled herself behind the table in the spot Katharine had just vacated.

Twenty minutes later they had completed the whole thing again and wished each other a good night and sound sleep with no incidents.

The drive home afforded little traffic, and Katharine made it in quick time. As she parked the car in her spot behind the building, she noticed how serene she felt and thought about what Margot had said about rituals. That partly they worked because people had been doing the same rituals for eons, that others had put energy behind the spell that Katharine and Margot would tap into and add to.

In her own hallway, she latched onto that feeling of serenity and prayed it wasn't false, prayed that the protection spell had worked.

Margot had said the rituals had to be repeated or they wore off. That would mean it was at its strongest now, right?

She passed her own door and knocked on Zachary's.

He answered immediately. "I have been waiting for you."

Stepping aside, he motioned her in. The gray stains were still on the carpet and she wondered how she had ignored them. She saw them now for what they were—soot stains from his comings and goings, and not well cleaned. It was clearer now. So was her resolve. "Talk to me."

"Of course."

They stood in the center of the sparsely furnished room.

"Tell me about Mary Wayne."

Something flickered in his eyes. "She didn't listen, Katie. I tried to, but I couldn't stop her. She got herself into trouble I couldn't save her from."

It was virtually the same thing Allistair had told her. Trust came over her in a wave, as it always did when she was with him. But this time it passed right through her. It didn't root, she didn't feel it; she simply knew it had been there.

"Tell me about me."

He shrugged. "We each need you. But he can't give you what I can give you."

Her serenity fled, replaced with a simmering curiosity laced with just a hint of dread. "And what is that? That you can give me?"

He held his hand out to her, and though she waited for it to transform into something with sharpened claws, it didn't. It and he stayed entirely human-looking.

It took a moment for her to reach her hand out to him. She did as Margot said and put faith in the spell they had cast, believed that it would work, and she wondered if he knew she had done it.

His fingers laced through hers, bringing her palm into warm contact with his.

His voice ran like thick honey over her. "Close your eyes and watch."

Behind her eyelids, a world opened up. Something he was showing her, she knew. Light was everywhere, food was plentiful, and a sense of deep satisfaction told her that her wants would always be met. But there were faint shadows in the background. Katharine tried to focus on them, though they resisted, flitting just beyond her vision. With effort, she sharpened her gaze and saw that there were people beyond what she was seeing. They were hungry and cold and sometimes went without.

Her head shook back and forth a little as she tried to make sense of it. Though she didn't speak and neither did he, Zachary answered her question.

In her mind, she simply knew. These were the people who had not accepted. They had not sided with Zachary and his brethren, and so they did not live the gifted life he showed her.

At last she opened her eyes. "What is it?"

"It is the Kingdom."

Without another word she left, wandering back to her own apartment, still in awe of what she had seen. When she opened her door, she found that nothing was out of place. Though she had only straightened a little of the mess, her home now looked as if this morning had never happened.

After getting ready to go to sleep, she lay down in her perfectly made bed and let her eyes drift shut.

When she dreamed, she dreamed of the Kingdom.

. . .

Once again, Katharine found herself rushing to find Margot. She knew her friend would help her sort these things out. Her friend would keep her sane. Her friend was . . . her friend, and that was enough.

She pulled Margot from the library on yet another impromptu break. Katharine was glad she had a trust fund, as both women were likely to lose their earthly jobs over this one. She startled Margot by telling her right off that she had sent a document to her lawyer saying that a large amount would go to Margot should she die. She laughed a little when she related how she had started the missive with *I, Katharine*

Geryon, being of sound mind and body. "You're the only one who can contradict that, Margot. So if anything happens to me, you have to keep your mouth shut so I can make up for the fact that you lost your job because of all this."

Margot finally opened her mouth in amazement and laughed. "You really shouldn't do that Katharine, I'm not going to lose my job. They love me."

"Well, of course they do, and thank God for that." Katharine leaned back in the chair. They were at the coffee shop closest to the library, and her drink wasn't very good, but she couldn't tell if that was because it was actually bad or because she was still shaking from her conversation with Allistair that morning.

Margot knew enough not to ask while they were inside and surrounded by other patrons, but now that they were outside at the patio table, she leaned in. "What has you so shaken up that you're changing your will?"

She blurted everything she could about what Zachary had shown her, about the Kingdom and all that came with it. "I told Allistair, and he said he couldn't show me anything other than earth."

Margot looked thoughtful at that, but Katharine barreled on with the rest of it.

"He then asked me what I knew of myself. If I knew what it meant to be a Geryon." She was flustered just in the retelling. "I don't know what he means."

"That *is* an odd thing to say." She frowned and started rooting in her purse. "I want to go back to the branch and all my great access, but I worry what everyone will say if I bring you in yet again." She pulled out her phone. "This is a little slow, but I've done a bit of research with it before. We'll just see what it gives us."

Katharine nodded while Margot pushed a few buttons, presumably typing in something about her name. "What about their names? Does it mean anything that Zachary is 'Zachary'? Isn't Zachary biblical? Zachariah? God, I wish I'd paid more attention in church."

She took a sip of her drink to calm herself, but didn't remember until she tasted it that she didn't like it. At least the bitterness distracted her.

Margot was looking at the little screen on her phone and shaking her head. "I don't think your Zachary is the biblical Zachary. That wouldn't make any sense. Not that *any* of this makes a lot of sense."

"Yeah, I don't really think so either. I don't know where the name Allistair comes from, but . . . I probably shouldn't rely on that. I didn't even think of it until he asked about my name." She shrugged.

Margot looked up. "'Katharine' was easy. It popped right up. But 'Geryon' . . . well, you should look."

Warily, she took the phone her friend was offering. On the tiny screen was a standard picture of a devil. She looked back up at Margot. "The demon Geryon? Is he saying I'm part demon?"

"Who knows? But that's kind of interesting that you've had this last name all your life and never knew it was a demon name." Margot tucked the phone back in her purse. "And it's the first thing that pops up on the search engines."

"What did 'Katharine' mean? I never looked it up myself. I guess I was never curious." She mistakenly sipped the drink again before leaning over and throwing the almost-full cup into a nearby trash can.

"It means 'pure.'"

Katharine jerked back. "Like I'm pure demon? That just can't be right."

"No, it means pure as in good. Taken together as your name, it's contradictory, that's for sure." Margot stood and hiked her purse up on her shoulder. "I'm sorry, I have to get back to work, but we'll talk tonight."

"No, we won't!" Katharine stood and stretched her legs, grateful for the feeling of muscle and tissue. She didn't know how much longer she would have it. She had to make a deal with someone, and probably soon. Just look what happened to Mary Wayne when she made the wrong deal. Katharine turned her thoughts back to Margot. "You have a date tonight with Liam; you will *not* be talking to me."

There was a hint of a grin on her friend's face as they hugged good-bye. The hug was new. It meant both of them knew they were getting closer to the end. Closer to Katharine having to make a choice.

Within a few moments, she was in her car and headed back to work. Back to her office. Back to the space she shared with a creature that she knew wasn't really of this world. But what was he?

The problem was, he wasn't saying, and neither was Zachary. It seemed they couldn't. They were bound from telling her what they really were by these mysterious deals they had made. But did it matter? A demon would probably lie about what he was anyway. And she would still have to choose by her own wits. But how did she choose something knowing that it would kill her if she chose wrong?

That was the problem. She couldn't tell what was what.

She turned the car smoothly into the parking garage. The car seemed to move of its own accord; her thoughts were elsewhere. But she still noticed the Coffee Bean she passed just before the garage entrance. Avoiding the elevator, Katharine took the garage stairs to ground level and went into the small wood-paneled shop. She wanted to enjoy something. She wanted a nice taste, a nice texture, the feeling of a cold, iced cup on her hands. She would sit on the patio and enjoy the breeze. She would watch the people pass by and listen to snippets of their conversation.

For a moment, she would just be.

. . .

Zachary watched as the two of them sat in the sand.

He had been keeping a closer eye on Katharine of late. Too many things had been escaping his notice, and that needed to be remedied. The endgame was coming up on all of them, and quickly. So he had followed her most of the day, leaving her side only when he was called away or when she was asleep. Though even then he could move her forward if he chose. But she'd been out with Margot, talking about him—and about Allistair.

For a moment, things had turned mundane, and he had left, intending to be back soon. When he returned, he found her sitting at the coffee shop outside the Light & Geryon building, simply relaxing and enjoying her drink. He was worried about her, sitting there. She needed drive, ambition. Instead, she relaxed there, showing the exact opposite, and he was afraid that was due to Allistair's influence. How would she accomplish all that she could in this life if she sat still and watched it go by? But there was nothing he could do on the crowded street that wouldn't call attention to him or to her.

Though he could appear to her in any form, right there on the sidewalk, it wouldn't be wise. She might jump up and yell at him—a creature no one else could see. Though he could do damage control and erase the memories of those around, there were so many that it would be a horrendous cleanup job. He simply couldn't afford for Katharine to see him right now.

He didn't need Katharine to get any more attention than she had. The people at her job had already started to take notice. The neighbors had called about her screaming once, and they would more readily do so if they were bothered or concerned again. She already had enlisted her friend. No, she needed no more attention than she already had.

But in the end, Katharine would need to make her own choice, and it would be better if she could do it on her own.

So he stood back and waited, then followed her up to her office.

She had tried to confront Allistair again. She asked pressing questions, Zachary knew, because he was starting to get some of them from her, too. His rival balked at a few, and he waited for Allistair to slip up, break the rules, get yanked. His opponent had messed up too many times. But maybe he had learned something from it. Zachary hoped that wasn't the case.

Then again, maybe he simply felt Zachary watching over them.

When Katharine had finally gone into the office, Allistair had taken her hand and pulled her out the door and back down the elevator. "They'll never miss us." He showed her how Lisa didn't see them as they walked right past.

Katharine protested. "The cameras will see us!"

Zachary tensed as Katharine got closer to a truth. Allistair shook his head. "Yes, but cameras can be erased—edited—very easily."

"That's exactly how Mary Wayne got past me!" Katharine stopped dead and yanked her hand back, but Allistair grabbed her by the wrist this time and pulled her along. "Who walked Mary Wayne out of here? Who made her . . . invisible?"

Allistair stopped and looked her in the eyes.

Zachary waited. What would he say? And how would Katharine take it?

"Those are two different questions, Katharine. The first answer is 'no one,' and the second I can't tell you."

She got frustrated then, yanking her arm away from Allistair again and making Zachary happy. Every inch of distance she put between herself and that reject was another step in the right direction.

Though she didn't touch him, she followed Allistair along the sidewalk and three blocks over to the marina. She checked out the faces of people as they passed, marveling at how they seemed to somehow step out of the way without knowing she was there. Her face showed traces of both awe and confusion; she seemed to want to wave her hand in front of someone's face, to try to get someone's attention. But Allistair kept the pace just a shade too fast for her to do that. And he kept it up all the way until they reached their destination.

The edge of the water here was rocky, and there were only a few places where the coastline wasn't privately owned. But since no one saw them, Allistair seemed unconcerned about this. He settled them both on a dry patch of smooth pebbles and told her to ask what she would, and that he would answer what he could.

Zachary sat behind them, seeing the breeze in their human hair, seeing their words carried on the wind. He knew there was salt and pollution in the air. But none of it filtered through the veil.

Allistair sighed, and something about it told Zachary that his rival knew he was there, that he watched and heard everything. He waited to be snitched on, for Katharine to look around and try to see him after her officemate told her he was just behind them. But Allistair did no such thing, and Katharine didn't seem to sense him.

She simply started in with her questions, asking about her name and its meaning. She asked if the meaning had any real purpose in her life. So Zachary waited.

"Your names don't make you who you are; they just give you potential. Options."

She asked if there was demon blood in her.

"Somewhere back in the line, yes. That's how a human gets that last name." Allistair sifted his fingers through the rocks on the shore. He clearly loved the feel of it. It was pathetically human and Zachary started to feel the pinch of pity.

But he started at Allistair's next words.

"That's funny, Katharine. Look at your hands . . . you're rolling the rocks around, like me."

Her eyes widened. "Is that a good or a bad thing?"

This could be it. Allistair could ruin himself if he answered this. Any higher being with even a small amount of skill would not, but Zachary clung to his belief that Allistair would shoot himself in the foot.

He didn't take the opportunity.

"You have to decide that, Katharine. I can lead you, and I can ask you, and so can Zachary, but neither of us can make you do anything. As much as we would each like to, we can't make the choice for you."

They talked longer, and Zachary grew bored. Allistair told her a little about the veil, only confirming what she had already surmised with the help of her friend. He told her about the earth and how it really only existed on this level, as did the animals and people who lived there.

"But why do we have drawings of angels that look like people, if people are the only things that look like people?"

"Because you cannot see beyond yourselves, cannot imagine a creature so different from yourselves. Most cultures still have trouble recognizing plants as creatures. You cannot come to terms with us yet."

Zachary tried to wait while Allistair philosophized, but he was suffering the same inaction that he had accused Katharine of earlier. He gave Allistair one more chance to impress him.

Though Zachary was mad when Allistair leaned close to Katharine, the words were innocuous enough.

"If you want to know where a being is from, look into its eyes."

She nearly laughed at that. Good girl. "Windows to the soul and all that?"

"No." Allistair smiled, and Zachary watched as Katharine smiled back.

Damn him! He was charming her in entirely human terms. Zachary found himself angry with her; he had thought she'd gone beyond the usual frail human susceptibilities.

Rocks tumbling absentmindedly through his fingers, Allistair continued. The smile still played around his lips. "Eyes are the windows to your origins. Just think of the things you've seen. And think of people. Human eyes come in blues and greens and browns—sky and water and land." He waved his hand at the scene before them. "Earth colors. People are of the earth."

Frustration flowed through Zachary. If Katharine was falling for this, then there was nothing he could do about it, except let it play out. He would simply have to counteract Allistair later. Which meant there were things he had to do, and he couldn't do them here, hovering.

He was pulling away when he heard Katharine's next question.

"Can Zachary really give me the Kingdom he showed me?"

Tell her, tell her, tell her.

Stopping dead, he felt the very human idea surging through his brain. Allistair had to answer her truthfully. This was not forbidden.

He waited while Allistair hesitated. And waited.

Until his rival was forced to say it. "Yes."

Good. Allistair had just worked things in Zachary's favor. And if he played his cards right, Zachary could build on that. Sometimes, the deals they had made worked in his favor.

Now, now there were things to do.

. . .

Katharine returned to her condo that night thinking of Margot and her date with Liam. She thought about what Allistair told her, and about how she wanted to look this Liam in the eyes before she left Margot with him. She remembered the eyes of the two beasts and became even more convinced of which was which.

So that meant she could tell the two creatures apart, and she knew now not to be afraid, but she didn't know the rest. She was still no closer to knowing which man was which. Though Allistair had let her stare into his eyes for as long as she wanted, it had been to no avail.

She settled into bed without calling Margot. She was happy for her friend, but it was all moving so fast now that she wanted someone to talk to. Tonight. But she also didn't want to interfere with her friend's new joy, especially when all she had to offer were more questions and concerns.

Katharine drifted into sleep wondering what the next step was, what was in store for her now.

She didn't have long to wait.

She woke peacefully a few hours later, feeling rested and safe. As she sat up on the side of her bed, she saw the man in the shadows. Unlike the inky blackness of the past, he was outlined by light, though she couldn't make out his face.

She was learning, though. Maybe it was better that she couldn't see his face. She couldn't trust his face.

As she watched, he became lit from within, and gorgeous feathered wings unfolded to nearly the width of the room. His hand came out to her, palm up.

It wanted her to put her hand in his.

But still she waited, unsure.

A whisper echoed around the room.

Katharine, come with me, come with me, Katharine

CHAPTER 22

Katharine curled into the heat of him. Here was everything she wanted. *He* was what she wanted.

Here, with him beside her, was safety, strength. She sighed against him, into him.

He was thrill and comfort, all soothing touches, soft lips against her temple. This was what she had waited for, even though she hadn't even known she needed it or wanted it. It was simplicity wrapped in complex passion. In a word, love.

His hands stroked the sides of her face, laced into her hair, while his mouth wandered over her eyes, nose, cheeks—until his mouth found hers and he settled into kissing her, deep searching kisses of need layered with trust.

Beneath her palms he was supple muscle and smooth skin, moving against her not in the way of just a lover, but of someone who loved.

Deep inside her, soft heat built into a roaring inferno for him.

She wanted.

She needed.

Katharine.

Her name escaped his lips as his legs entwined with hers. The silk of her pajamas prevented her from touching all of him, but she wasn't quite rational, wasn't quite able to do the logical thing and simply take them off.

He didn't pressure her. He waited, kissing, tasting, touching her.

He caught her sighs in his mouth, and answered back with her name again.

Katharine.

She opened her eyes to see his as he watched her unravel for him. Eyes like bittersweet chocolate looked deep into her own, and for a passing moment she wondered what he saw.

His hand traveled over silk, down her side and across her hip, tucking her close, keeping her body flush with his.

His name came out of her mouth as a wistful sigh.

Allistair.

"Allistair!" That time she hissed it.

Her eyes flew open wide as she pushed at him, yanked herself back from him, wondering what he had done to her. Then not wondering, as she realized she had pressed up against him, that he had taken advantage of her while she slept.

"Katharine, don't—"

She shoved at him again, but he didn't move.

He protested again. "It isn't—"

Lightning fast, her hands shot out again, giving another quick push. This time she managed to catch him by surprise and he toppled out of the bed, sputtering her name. "Katharine!"

"Get out! Get out! Get out!" She yelled it until she was hoarse, until she was more angry than scared.

Until he stood, blank-faced, then turned and walked out of the room.

It took only a few heartbeats for her anger to drive her after him, to yell some more.

But as she entered the living area, she caught the last glimpse of the man as he lowered into the floor, leaving a pile of black ash in his wake.

For a moment, she stood there in shock and stared at the pile of soot. Then, as it sank in, she began to shake. Great, head-to-toe spasms shattered any sense of peace she had clung to before she'd gone to sleep.

It was simply too much. She couldn't take any more than she had. Keeping it together now took the very last of her reserves; she just might break next time. The tremors overtook her for a few minutes and she had to brace herself against the doorway, her hands against the jamb while she sucked in air and fought back tears. The scariest part was looking back at how much she had wanted him. She had needed him. And there, in her bed, the desire had felt so real.

Standing, shivering in her doorframe it no longer did.

After more deep breaths than should have been necessary, she turned to go back into her bedroom and cut her foot on a shard of glass.

. . .

"Margot, if Liam's there just please tell him your crazy friend needs you," Katharine pled into her cell phone as she drove the nearly deserted pre-dawn streets.

Though still a little sleepy-sounding, Margot's words proved she was alert. "He isn't here. I don't put out on the first date."

It hit Katharine then. "Oh, my God! I'm a total slut."

"No you aren't, you were . . . coerced in some way." She could hear Margot moving around the small apartment. Something clattered softly in the background. "That sounds really bad . . . just know that you aren't a slut. Do you want to tell me now what happened to get you up in the middle of the night, or do you want to wait until you get here?"

"Both." Katharine turned the key as she parked the car and was out and hobbling across the lawn and heading up the stairs before she managed the next words. "I'm already here." She clicked the phone shut just as Margot opened the door for her.

"Come in."

Katharine managed to half walk, half hop over to the couch and plopped down as Margot closed and bolted the door.

When her friend turned, the worry on her face couldn't be hidden. "What happened?"

"I stepped on glass."

"On my lawn?"

"No, in my bedroom." Katharine slid off her shoe and peeled back the Kleenex she had tucked in there to keep it from bleeding. "Do you have Band-Aids?"

"Sit tight." Margot went into the bathroom and rummaged around. All of this was amazingly calm of her, as she had to know there was something up. Something big enough to send Katharine running to her place at 4:00 a.m. with a cut that she hadn't even attempted to bandage.

Suddenly, Katharine realized she had done all this in her silk pajamas. This was it then—the moment when she realized she had snapped. That must be why Margot was being so calm. When Katharine was half a second from breaking down, Margot came back with a stocked white box with the big red cross on the front and Katharine nearly laughed. "Of course you have a full first-aid kit. You have everything."

"Actually, I got it last week. I figured we might need it, so I splurged and replaced my rinky-dink one with the biggest home kit I could find."

That explained why she had what basically amounted to a red plastic suitcase stuffed to the gills with rubber tubing, gauze, sterile wipes, and bandages of every size. She handed over one of the wipes and waited while Katharine cleaned out the cut, hissing between her teeth the whole time. A few moments later, a large cloth bandage covered the wound and Katharine began talking at about a mile a minute.

Margot was asking questions faster than she could talk, and certainly faster than Katharine could answer them. "It had feathered wings? What did you do? Did you touch it?"

"No, I threw my lamp at it."

"You did?" Margot was in awe. "Why?"

"Angels don't have feathers." Katharine shrugged. It had seemed so logical at the time. People thought angels had birdlike wings, but that wasn't what she had been seeing; it wasn't what had appeared in the painting at all. So, upon seeing the creature reach out to her, contrary to hundreds of years of belief, she had instantly grabbed something to throw at it.

"Did you hurt it?"

"No, it disappeared before the glass even got to it. The lamp shattered on the wall."

Margot absorbed what she could, then took a stab at it though she clearly didn't think all the pieces worked. "So then you stepped in the glass and came over here?"

"No, I went back to sleep."

"What?" Margot frowned at her.

"Yeah." Though it didn't make much sense at all now, it had seemed so logical at the time. What else was she going to do? She hadn't wanted to ruin Margot's date, so she hadn't called, hadn't told her about the false angel with feathered wings. Hadn't shared the latest detail at 2:00 a.m. She'd laid down to wait for morning.

But now she told her about waking up with Allistair, and even though she tried to explain what she had felt when he held her, she couldn't.

She didn't have the words to explain it to herself, let alone someone else. And she was too embarrassed to try to say how swept away she had been, how fervently she had wanted him, how clear her thoughts had been when she did. It was only later that she realized what she was doing—and who with—and had gotten so upset. But she'd known it was him even while she slept. She would recognize the smell of him and the feel of his body heat anywhere. And she'd wanted him.

She didn't know how to say any of that to her friend. But she did know how to say what she wanted. "We have to do the protection spell again. Allistair is more powerful. It worked with Zachary, but Allistair seemed to get through it."

Margot's eyes snapped wide. "It worked?"

"Yes, but I think only on Zachary."

"How do you know?" Her friend leaned forward, her grin growing wider. "How could you tell?"

"Because when I talked to him, I saw what I was supposed to feel, I *knew* it, but I didn't *feel* it. It just went past me. I don't think that makes any sense, but . . ."

"It does. I get it." Margot was nothing if not organized, and even as she was acting gleeful at their initial success, she was motoring around the apartment in her T-shirt nightgown and puffy, feathery slippers. In moments, she had everything they needed for the protection spell. They had bought three of each item, prepared to run the spell three full times if necessary. They had completely over-purchased. The herbs that were smoked and the candles, the salt—all of it was reusable. So it turned out they had enough materials to concoct protection spells until Armageddon. Or at least Katharine hoped they did.

They worked until the sun came up, doing the only thing they knew how to do to keep Katharine safe.

. . .

At 8:00 a.m. that morning Katharine had stood in front of her mirror and called Margot again.

She had swept up the glass in her bedroom and run the vacuum over it to get any small shards. She'd picked out a suit and laid it on the bed while she climbed into the shower. For some reason she had looked around before she climbed in, as though that would make any difference.

At least when she had turned the water on, she felt like she was alone.

When she climbed out, the message had been there.

So she'd copied it diligently twice—just like Margot. Then she had called her friend. After explaining all of it, telling her that this message was in the steam, and waiting through a small handful of questions, she asked one of her own. "Did you get the translation of the last message?"

"Oh crap!" Katharine thought she heard a horn blare in the background. Perhaps Margot was on her way to work? Margot sputtered, "I forgot to tell you. With everything else going on, I just forgot. It said 'Trust in me'. . . Or at least I'm relatively sure it did."

But who was she supposed to trust? Who had left the message? The black dog? The one who ransacked her apartment? Were they the same?

The only one Katharine really trusted these days was Margot. And she had known the librarian a shorter length of time than any of the others.

She didn't speak for a few minutes, just stood there looking at the almost too neatly written message on her mirror and wondering what *me paenitet et te amo* could possibly mean.

Surely, it didn't mean . . . no.

Te amo had to be something different in Latin. Not . . .

"Katharine! Are you there?"

Jostling her brain out of its wandering, Katharine assured her friend that she was there and that she was okay. But she still stood there with her hair dripping rivulets of water all around her, her towel tucked up under her arms. Her bare feet left imprints on the carpet while Margot talked.

"I also found an article about shape-shifting in demons. Who knows how true it is, but I found the same kind of information in several different unlinked sources. So I tend to think it's probably got the right idea at least."

Katharine waited silently through all of it, watching as the steam cleared from her bathroom mirror, taking the message with it. The words that certainly didn't mean what they looked like they might.

Margot's voice filtered through her thoughts. "It said they could shift into any kind of creature, but that they were forbidden to take the shape of another," Margot continued. "So they can appear as a kind of creature you know, like a dog, but they can't take the exact shape of your dog."

Like she cared—she didn't have a dog. And the words that clutched at her were almost gone.

She must have indicated that she was still listening, because Margot kept talking. "It means they can't appear to you as each other."

That, finally, got her attention. She had called to Allistair and the beast had answered yes.

"Can they answer to someone else's name?"

"I don't know." Katharine could practically see her friend shaking her head. "But it did say they could take the shape of a dead person."

"Oh, okay, I'll keep my eyes peeled for any dead relatives." It was meant to be sarcastic, but immediately she thought of her mother and wondered how she would fare if one of them came to her as her mom. Would she be able to resist listening to her?

"No, I was thinking of your coworker."

Her thoughts shifted immediately at Margot's suggestion, and Katharine shuddered.

. . .

Katharine was grateful that Allistair didn't show up at work that day. For eight hours she was given brief respite from the whirl of insanity around her. For just a while, she could pretend she was normal again. She wrote reports, pulled figures on companies, and did what she used to do before Zachary and Allistair had come into her life.

Even though her brain knew otherwise, she managed to keep up the illusion that nothing had changed. For lunch, she picked up a sandwich from a nearby deli and ate it at her desk. Then she went back to filing, informing, researching. She found good investments and recommended them.

She ate dinner at her dining table, by herself. There were plenty of frozen Tupperware dinners in the freezer, as she hadn't been eating them at nearly the pace she had before all this. The service had even left her a voicemail saying they'd noticed, and asking whether she wanted to cut back next week. She should call them back, but she didn't feel like it.

Katharine wanted to call Margot, but her friend was out on a date with Liam again. She'd been thrilled to find out that Margot had already met a few of his friends, and that they had known him a long time. He was nice and outgoing but not particularly charismatic. All of this made Katharine feel a little more secure about Liam.

She changed into loose cotton pants and a T-shirt and watched a sitcom on TV before crawling into bed, scared that something would happen, and just as disturbed that the fear would keep her up all night whether or not something happened.

Though she was afraid, she fell under right away and slept deeply and undisturbed the entire night.

The next morning, she went through the usual routine of getting dressed, putting on makeup, putting up her hair. Her mirror was clean and so was her carpet. The car started with a soft purr, as usual, and she drove to work in silence and on time. The guard waved her into the garage, and she said hello to two different people she recognized as they rode up the elevator.

For the first time, she wondered if others recognized her. People she didn't know, or people she had met but didn't remember. Would they remember her? Would they remember the boss's daughter, regardless of whether they knew anything of her or not?

She looked more closely at faces she passed in the hallway, wondering how many times she had seen them before and never noticed, and not finding any answers in any of them.

When she arrived, her office was deserted, and she hoped it would stay that way. Files were handed off to Lisa, calls were returned. Her morning was perfectly normal.

Until Margot called.

Her friend opened with, "He's a really good kisser. Do you want to do another protection spell tonight?"

The rapid-fire change in topic didn't faze Katharine in the slightest way, and she felt the beginnings of a smile on her face. "Oh no you don't. Spill. I need details."

There was almost a hum coming through the phone line; surely it was the energy Margot was radiating. "He's really great. At one point we were coming out of the theater, really late, and this gang was following us—"

"Gang?" Katharine's eyebrows rose.

"Yeah, about ten guys, faces low, looked like trouble, you know? And the street was deserted; it was just us and an empty parking garage. So as I'm trying to walk faster and faster, Liam tugs my hand and slows us down." Her words were nearly falling over themselves, and she sounded just a little breathless. "Then he turns around, and he kind of rolls up on his toes, like he's a predator or something. You know, that stance that only the best-trained fighters get but everyone can recognize?" She didn't wait for Katharine's answer. "He looks them point blank in the face and says, 'Can I help you?' They all just scattered. It was so . . ."

At the sound of the sigh on the other end of the line, Katharine supplied "Dreamy?"and then she laughed.

As the shards of her own joy pierced through her reality, she sat with her cell phone clutched in one hand and suddenly realized she'd gone right back to coasting through her old life the past few days. While she was grateful that things had been quiet recently, she had slipped far too easily into her old routines.

She'd done everything the way she always had—without actually experiencing any of it. She hadn't enjoyed her food, or even the silly TV show she'd watched last night. She hadn't even double-checked the companies she recommended investing in.

So now she changed what she could, and she took a deep breath in and dove into the conversation with her whole self. She wanted to know about Margot, about the date. She wanted to be a better friend. "He's a fighter?"

"Turns out he was elite military. But he can't tell me more than that or he'd have to kill me."

Katharine laughed again, this time from somewhere deeper. "What did you say?"

"That I'm becoming Wiccan and I'll cast a spell on him to make him tell me his top-secret military stories."

"Is that true? Are you becoming Wiccan?"

"I think so." Margot sighed and her voice lost the silly quality it had held just a moment before. "This is the first time I've seen anything work, and I have to say all this has changed my perspective from 'Go to church on Sundays and major holidays and pray you're in the right religion' to 'Step up and do something.'"

"You don't think we're messing with something we shouldn't be?"

Margot laughed. "I think it's messing with us! Besides, I always had trouble with a God who put temptation right in front of me but expected me to never go for it. That just seems like bad parenting."

"Yeah, me too." She sighed herself this time, and felt it in her chest.

"Do you want to come over tonight and bulk up the protection spell? We can grab supplies and do the binding, too, if you want."

It was an invite like she never would have thought she'd say yes to. And it was the best thing she'd heard in a long time. "Should I pick up Chinese on the way? Or should we just grab some while we're out?"

Katharine made plans and closed her phone, and finally took a good look around her office.

Her shoes pinched her toes. She kicked them off and enjoyed the feel of the plush carpet beneath her stockinged feet. It was a waste to have such thick pile when everyone wore heels.

The room was a little too warm. The shades were closed as they had been almost every day she'd worked there. She wasn't even sure what the view was.

The walls were a shade of cream that bordered on ecru—the same as every other office in the building. Katharine wanted to believe that she kept the color as it was because she would move offices when she moved jobs again. But the fact was, she wasn't one for making any waves, not even tiny ones.

Except it was turning out that she *was* one for making waves. She wanted an office with a color, a real color, not ecru . . . and open curtains, not blinds. Her desk was a sleek, standard mahogany that Light & Geryon used in all the offices. And really, she hated it. She didn't like ultra modern lines. She didn't like the nearly white carpet in her condo and the standard-issue paint color that she had just left on the walls there, too.

She didn't like anything she had.

And she was only just now seeing that there were things she did like and that they weren't out of her grasp. She could change the world around her rather than bouncing along in a world that everyone else had changed for themselves. She could be good or bad, right or wrong, or just different. But she could *be*.

Katharine peeked out the window and nearly gasped when her gaze skipped over the top of a nearby building and landed in the rolling waters off the coast. But she could only see it if she stood at the window. Still, she opened the shades and let the sun in.

Plopping down at her desk, she began writing up her latest paperwork in the sunlight that now spilled in around her.

She printed the report and delivered it to Sharon outside her father's office, refusing to go in. She just needed to leave the folder for him.

Feeling lighter than she had in a long time, Katharine tried to ignore the pinching in her shoes as she headed back to her own office and rounded the last corner.

Blue sky greeted her beyond the glass panes. She stared at the view outside her own windows for a moment before she spotted Allistair sitting at his desk.

Sucking in just a little air at her shock at finding him there, Katharine fought for composure. "You're late."

"No one will notice."

He was standing before the door swung closed behind her. Startled, Katharine turned to see it latch shut, just as if a person's hand had pushed it. When she looked back at Allistair, she lurched backward. He now stood right in front of her.

"Katharine."

"No." She didn't need to hear what he asked to know what her answer would be. She didn't want to hear any of it anyway. Her right foot snaked out behind her and she tried to step back.

Reaching out for her, Allistair clasped her hands. Lacing his fingers through hers even as she struggled to get free, he brought their palms together. "Don't fight, please."

But she did. "What are you doing?"

She tried to pull her hands away, but his grip was like iron. His face pressed close to hers and he smelled like something she wanted.

Why did she want him? Why was he able to get through? Was he just that strong? She found her voice for a second. "Stop."

"I can't, Katharine. I have to do this." There was something in his tone that made her look directly at him.

His eyes were tired and clearly far older than his years on earth appeared to be. But the sadness in them didn't change her feelings. "Please don't."

"I don't want to, but I have to." He shook his head a little and tried to claim her gaze again. She didn't let him.

"I want what comes from this, so I have to do it. Just watch."

Without her permission, her eyes fell shut. And just like with Zachary, a world opened up in her vision.

A police officer in a dirty, dusty town fought back against gunfire, until his own gun exploded in his face, blowing half of it off. The scene continued as he fell forward to the ground. The gunners grabbed several boys where they crouched, hiding, and hauled them away while their mothers screamed. One mother was shot for the noise she was making.

The scene that had intruded into her brain shifted to a family in the middle of nowhere. No father, only a mother and five skinny children who were clustered around her. Katharine listened as the two oldest begged their mother to let them work, promised they could do it, that they could bring in money. But somehow, even though she was only a visitor to this scene, Katharine knew what the mother would have to do to get her boys a spot in the mines. Her stomach turned as the mother agreed and they walked back toward the shantytown. But there was nowhere else to go.

Again, a new scene appeared. A mother and father, both in threadbare flannels and thick work boots, huddled against each other as the doctor gave them the prognosis for their child. There wasn't enough money for her care, and all the money in the world wouldn't cure her.

She watched as a man in his own home made his maid perform for him. Lewd things that Katharine had never wanted to see. Still the scenes changed. They got worse and worse.

Gangs stabbing each other in broken cities, children with no food begging from mothers who had nothing to give.

Katharine struggled, fighting to free her hands from Allistair's strong grip. Her stomach churned and she knew she was going to be sick.

Her breathing ratcheted up until her chest heaved and her bile started to rise. She twisted and yanked, trying to get away.

He released her so fast that she stumbled backward and would have smacked into the corner of the desk if he hadn't caught her. As his arms came around her and stopped her fall, he mumbled to her, even though her arms flailed out and pushed him away. She heard him whispering into her ear, "I'm sorry, I'm so sorry." But she shoved at him, then turned and made a fast grab for the trash can, just before she lost her breakfast.

When her stomach quit turning, she stood and grabbed the hem of her jacket, straightening it. She reached up to her desk for the bottle of water she had set near the edge, and after rinsing her mouth out turned to face Allistair, half expecting to find him gone.

But he remained right where she had left him.

In two steps she was at the right distance, and her arm swung up fast and hard and smacked him across the cheek, the crack surely loud enough to be heard several doors down.

But, of course, no one heard it. Even Lisa, right beyond the door, made no motion to come in and stop this.

Allistair had let her slap him. She knew that, knew that he'd allowed her the hit that had made his human head snap back.

Her hand throbbed and she must have made a motion to that effect, because he reached out to grab her fingers, splaying them out to look at her red palm.

Katharine would have pulled her hand back, but again she couldn't—his grip was simply too strong. This time she didn't fight it, just braced for what came next. But, though her palm practically sizzled when he pressed his hand to it, when he lifted his skin from hers, the redness was gone.

She would have doubted she had even hit him if it weren't for red welt on his face in the exact shape of her hand.

His voice was low. "I'm sorry."

She threw out the one thing that she hoped would hurt him the most and certainly more than any hit she could deliver. "Zachary showed me a kingdom. People were happy there, and they had what they wanted and what they needed. Are you telling me that he lied?"

"No, he didn't. He can give you that."

Her body quivered with frustration that she tried to keep at bay. She was on the very edge of tears and trying so hard to hold them in. "Then why would—"

"You saw them, Katharine, the others who weren't allowed in. The Kingdom isn't for everyone."

"It's for those who choose it! Why can't I choose it too?" This time when she yanked her hand away, he let her have it back.

His voice was nearly a growl when he answered. "Is that what you really want? A world of haves and have-nots? Why would you have to choose anything?" He flung his arms wide. "You already have that here!"

She was nearly yelling and she had lost the battle with the tears now streaming down her face. "It doesn't matter. Why did you show me this? Why?"

"You had to see what this firm does. What the ramifications are. How far-reaching and how big they can be."

"I already knew! You bastard! I knew!" She turned away from him and began crying in earnest. But barely a moment later she turned and faced him again, this time with renewed anger. She was yelling in a way she never had before in her life, full of fury and pain. "I also know that you can watch me any time you want. Even when I don't know you are doing it! And I hate it."

He flinched at that but let her keep going.

"So the one time it would be useful to have you watching, you fuck it up!"

He winced again.

"You asshole! You should have known! I already resigned!"

She turned away and cried even harder for a moment before she got herself together. She could sense him right behind her, and she could tell he was considering putting his arms around her.

He was smart not to. She might have snapped his hand off at the wrist if he had tried.

"Katharine." His voice was soft, as though he were trying to soothe her. "Katharine."

"Go away."

"I did know you resigned. You still had to see." She heard his sigh, then those same stupid words. "I'm sorry."

This time when she turned around, he was gone.

CHAPTER 23

That evening, Katharine had told Margot about what Allistair had shown her, but she hadn't given all the details, hadn't said how he'd made her cry. Or that she'd slapped him, and he'd healed her hand. But not his own cheek.

Was that because he didn't care about his face? Because he didn't feel it at all? Or maybe because he wanted her to see what she'd done? In truth, she'd been proud of the mark she'd left on him. But she didn't tell Margot that.

She told Margot only the basics of her encounter with Allistair and that she'd handed in her resignation and, because of Allistair, had left before her father had seen it. Not that he'd called. There was every possibility that he had put the folder aside intending to leave it until morning.

To add to her discontent, the magics store was out of binding tape. Katharine had read over the spell herself and wasn't sure that she really needed binding tape per se. But the guy behind the counter said that it was infused with herbs and salts and was particularly effective. If there was anything she and Margot needed, it was for the spell to be particularly effective. He told them the store expected another shipment in four days.

Katharine hoped she had that long.

Without a spell to cast, she and Margot had done their best to let it go for the evening. So they had watched TV, talked, and drank a glass of wine each, and then finally Katharine headed for home and crawled into her own bed.

Sadly, she was becoming accustomed to waking in the middle of the night to a sound or an odd feeling. It no longer startled her as it had in the beginning. So when she sat up and just knew there was something else in the room with her, she decided to take a good look at it.

A stunningly large leopard paced back and forth in her room, its shoulders rolling as it slunk back and forth with an unearthly grace. Every now and then, blue eyes flicked in her direction and made contact. But the cat continued its walk from one side of her room to the other, cutting her off from leaving the bedroom. She couldn't get to the door, or even her desk or phone, without crossing its path. So she waited.

For a long time she watched the creature, and it watched her. Still it made no move other than to walk one way and turn and go back the other. In a short while, she grew bored of the tireless pacing and she dozed as it continued its walk. Katharine didn't know how long she was asleep, but it happened more than once that she opened her eyes to find the cat still there before drifting back off to sleep.

She wasn't sure what the creature was doing there. Was it keeping an eye on her, afraid she'd do something? Was it watching out for her, afraid something would happen to her? She couldn't tell; she watched it for long, dull periods, but it *couldn't* have been long; nothing had changed. Even after several cycles of sleeping and waking there was no evidence of light coming from outside. For what seemed an eternity, nothing happened.

Then, in an instant, the atmosphere changed.

The wolf came through the doorway with a speed that defied gravity. Powerful jaws grabbed at the back leg of the leopard and sent it sprawling.

Blue eyes snapped around and in them Katharine saw that this was what it had been waiting for.

The leopard wrenched itself to the side, the wolf's teeth tearing the flesh from its leg. As the cat stood and faced the dog, the wound healed while she watched, flesh knit to flesh, leaving no marks on the animal. The only evidence that she had seen something real was a few drops of blood slowly darkening on her carpet.

A low growl from the black wolf shook the room, and Katharine pulled her feet up to her chest while she watched in horrified fascination, too terrified to move. An answering yowl came from the cat, and they circled each other slowly.

The cat lunged and missed. The wolf tried too. But neither made contact.

This time when the wolf went for the cat, he latched his jaw onto the back leg again, sacrificing his cover as he did it. The leopard turned its head, mouth gaping wide to reveal razor-sharp fangs. Howling as it bit, the cat cut a large gash in the wolf's side. But regardless of the damage he suffered, the dog's teeth didn't unlock; he kept the leg firmly in his grip. And as the cat thrashed, the wolf slowly backed away from the bed, dragging the howling leopard from her room.

Small red spots and smears appeared on the carpet as evidence of their passing.

Petrified but unable to sit still, Katharine stood and leaned over to examine the stains.

She was watching as a red smear turned to black when a horrific scream pierced the air just beyond the open doorway. Her head snapped up and she felt pulled to the sound as a second howl answered the first. Afraid, but too curious to do otherwise, she padded toward the living room, where the noises were getting louder and more discordant. They changed from yells of pain and surprise to the deeper primal sounds of anger and violence.

When she reached the doorway she saw that the creatures were no longer leopard and wolf. Trapped by the physical confines of her living room, two beasts fought for domination. Long claws took chunks out of each other in swift and sharp motions, arms sailing quickly through the air and dealing what should have been deadly blows. Even with the damage each sustained, their screams seemed to indicate rage rather than pain, and Katharine's ears hurt from the shrieking.

She slunk backward, cowering behind the edge of the door frame, occasionally peeking around to see what was happening—as though a mere wall of backer board and wood molding could keep her safe from the beasts fighting on the other side.

She watched as flesh was flayed open and then stitched itself right back together. It was almost as though the claws passed through warm butter rather than sinew and bone.

With her fingers in her ears, she huddled and cringed and waited. She fought off tears and gulped for breath and tried to keep herself together. She curled herself further and further into a ball, trying to be unnoticeable.

Katharine remembered nothing further when she woke in the morning, aside from a vague recollection of a warm man carrying her to her bed. The fight had gone on—and must have even ended—without her.

. . .

Zachary waited on her couch, his left ankle crossed over his right knee in a purely male pose. He had a glass of ice water in his hand, but he didn't drink it.

She was waking. She'd still be a few minutes after that. The bedroom had a private entrance to the bath and she would use that. She wouldn't come out and see him here until she'd probably brushed her teeth and her hair. Zachary wasn't quite sure what exactly she did in the morning, but he knew what humans in general did. Allistair would know exactly what Katharine's normal routine was, but that was because he liked to watch her, to linger on the other side while she did pointless little daily rituals. It didn't matter. Zachary didn't need the specifics; she'd be out in a few minutes.

Katharine lurched to a halt when she came through the door and spotted him there. But she didn't say anything.

She stood barefoot amid the spots of blood he and Allistair had left the night before in what was a truly stupid show of ego. That was all it had been. Neither had won. Both had walked away, injured but intact. And Katharine now had more reason to fear them both. Showing their true faces gained them no ground with her.

In silk pajamas she stood tall, staring at him.

He waited for her to ask about the Kingdom, to ask about the fight. Even the blood that likely wouldn't come out of her carpet. Ever. But she did none of this.

He reached out to her, pulled her to him with waves of trust that she would feel.

Though she clearly did sense them—she frowned and took a step backward as though she'd been tipped and needed to right herself—the waves didn't do what they were supposed to. The trust didn't embed itself in her.

He closed his eyes for a moment and tried to see beyond the human realm. The question was, could he alter his eyes enough to see what he needed—without her seeing that he'd changed them? Zachary tried.

Though his vision was not the same in this hybrid form as it was in his true form, he managed to see some of what she had done. Finally, he spoke. "You have cast protection spells."

She nodded at him in reply but didn't come any closer than the doorway. If she took just a step forward, she would see the soot pile from where he had come in. Maybe it was best if she wasn't reminded of how he got here, so he didn't pull her toward him. He needed her. And she needed him. He would work within that.

He continued. "It's good that you're doing these spells. They work—just a little."

She nodded at him, hazel eyes trying to look through him, trying to figure out which one he was.

"They aren't enough, Katie. You have to see that."

She nodded again.

"He got in last night."

He saw that she was going to speak before he heard the words. "You both did."

"I had to. Katie, I can't protect you much longer."

"No. You can't." She crossed her arms, and he realized he wasn't going to make the connection they had shared before. Scared of everything, she had shut them both out. But she was strong and stoic in the face of her fear. She didn't budge, didn't cry because of last night. Zachary admired that; Katharine would be a great addition to the Kingdom. She would be able to share her story with others, the story of how he had protected her. The story of the great joy she had found with those who had been chosen, and who had chosen. She was looking him in the eyes now.

And her words were a bit of a shock. "How did you get your condo?"

"What?"

"How did you get your condo?"

He shrugged, not sure what she was asking. "I paid for it."

Her mouth tightened. "I don't care if you bartered with chickens or just made people believe it was yours." Her arms tightened across her chest, too, showing her discomfort, whether she meant to or not. "This is an exclusive building. How did you get the unit?"

"It was open. I applied. They chose me. Humans like us. You're naturally drawn to us." *Damn it!* Where was she going with this?

"Why was the condo available, Zachary? Tell me that."

Oh, he knew where she was headed now.

And she tried to head him off. "They died, Zachary. Did you do that? Did you?"

He shook his head. "They were old, Katie. They were just old."

"You have to admit, it looks suspicious."

He shook his head again. "Just because it looks bad doesn't mean that it is."

"It still looks bad." She turned to walk away, and he knew he couldn't let her. She had to see.

"Katie!" His human eyes watered with emotion. "Katie!"

This time she turned back and looked at him.

"You're going to have to choose. And it will likely be soon. I can't keep you safe for too much longer. I just can't."

"Okay." Though she said the word, she didn't capitulate. "I'm going to go take a shower, and I expect you to be gone when I get out."

There was really nothing he could say to that. She had dismissed him. And the way things stood, he wouldn't be able to push her too hard. Katharine was still staring straight at him, so he nodded his agreement.

Only then did she turn to walk back into her room.

He had already started to pass back through the veil when she turned back to him. He ground his long teeth together and pushed hard to reincorporate so she wouldn't have to see him phase through.

"Are you going to leave a message on my mirror while I'm in there?"

"What?" He shook his head. What was she talking about?

"Never mind."

She closed the bedroom door behind her.

. . .

Katharine sighed with relief at Margot's words.

"It's not a problem. I'm not in until two today."

Katharine wasn't going in to work today either. What could they do about it? Fire her? Besides, she had a trust fund. Her mother had left her all the money from the Bariel side of the family. When Mariam's father had left it to her, he had stipulated that it be solely for her and for her children. So there was plenty there that wasn't tied up in Light & Geryon. Katharine just had to figure out what to do with it.

For the first time in her life, she felt free. Free to make her own errors, on her own time. She was getting to set her own standards and live by her own rules. She didn't want to give up her life by making a bad choice. And she didn't like her odds. She wanted—needed—to put as much into motion as she could to ensure her safety, to ensure that she got to live to see the things she wanted.

Margot didn't show up at the condo until close to eleven. She'd slept in on her day off and done a little research of her own. "There's another shop over in Hollywood, on Vine. I called and they have the binding spell tape in stock."

Her friend looked down at the carpet, noting the blood spots Katharine had told her about. "This is nuts. I want to send it to a lab to be analyzed, but I don't have mad forensic skills to even understand the results and I'm not all that sure I really want to know what's in it." Tentatively, Margot reached a finger out to touch a smear, but then she thought better of it and pulled back.

Katharine shook her head. "I feel really odd, driving all the way across town to get herb-infused tape for a spell, but . . ." She shrugged. "If it helps . . ."

"Anything that helps here is good. This stuff is too crazy to not take every precaution." Margot stood and headed out the door. "If what's been happening is half as crazy as you told me, then we need to do everything we can."

Out in the hallway, she waited while Katharine locked the bolts, and then looked her friend in the eye when she turned around. "And I suspect a lot of it has been twice as crazy as you've said."

Katharine only nodded. How was she supposed to tell Margot about all that Allistair had shown her? How was she supposed to describe how Zachary had cried this morning as he pleaded with her? He had looked and seemed so sincere, so worried. But she didn't know what was real anymore.

She changed the subject. "Zachary said he hadn't left me any messages."

Margot frowned just as the elevator made its soft ding to let them know it was there.

"On my mirror," she clarified.

"Oh, so the messages all came from Allistair?" That seemed to surprise her.

"*If* Zachary wasn't lying." Neither of them knew how big that *if* was. Or even if one or the other of the men would lie to her. Allistair had said he couldn't. But what if that was a lie? Her head hurt from all the possibilities, and her chest ached from the strain of the constant hum of fear.

They climbed into the car and headed out into the perfect L.A. day, only to get mired in traffic. The surface streets were all clogged and so were the freeways. As they sat there, they tried to reason out some of what they had.

"I got the translation on that last message, too. It's pretty interesting."

"Oh." Katharine wasn't sure how any one of them could be more interesting than the others. They were all pretty weird. "How so?"

"Listen to this: I'm pretty sure it said, 'I'm sorry, but I love you.'"

If she hadn't already been stopped in bumper-to-bumper traffic, Katharine would have likely slammed on the brakes. She'd been afraid that it was something like that. "He loves me? Allistair? Loves me?"

Margot didn't get a word in edgewise before Katharine's brain took off with her mouth again. "Or is this just another lie? God, what am I supposed to do with that?"

"Deep breaths." Margot's hand touched her shoulder, and it did help, just that someone was there. "It may take us some time, but we'll figure it out."

Did she have enough time? The game was escalating. Zachary had told her she'd have to choose soon, and she did not want to end up like Mary Wayne.

Her thoughts must have shown on her face, because Margot spoke. She didn't turn to look at Katharine, but she didn't have to. "That's what we're headed across town for. We're going to buy you some time."

At least the thought made her want to laugh a little—the idea that buying a roll of some kind of infused and blessed fabric tape would actually buy her time. But if the binding worked, it just might gain her a while to figure a few more things out.

The store had the tape waiting, as Margot was just a common-sense genius and had put it on hold. They were in and out in less time than it had taken them to pay the parking meter and walk the block over to the store. In just a few minutes, they were sitting in traffic again.

There wasn't enough time to go to Margot's and do the binding spell, not if Margot was going to make it to work on time. So they decided to stop along the way and each lunch at the California Pizza Kitchen just a few blocks off their path.

While she sat and ate her pasta, Katharine took stock. She had on cute and comfy sneakers, no pinched toes. Her jeans were soft; there was a mild breeze and a blue sky. And in spite of the pollution she knew was there, the air seemed fresh. The restaurant was full of colors and the chatter of people talking about everything from jobs and babies to apartments and movies. It was so different from the sterile, stifling environment of the office.

She had been here before, had been to loud and boisterous parties, had walked barefoot on the beach. But somehow, she'd never really felt anything before. If she died from all this, at least she had learned to enjoy the taste of good food and the presence of a close friend.

While they ate, they chatted about Liam. They couldn't talk about the rest of it in here. If someone overheard, they could be . . . well, they'd be thought clinically insane, that's for sure. And the simplicity, the normalcy of the conversation was soothing in itself.

Her phone rang halfway through the meal, and Katharine picked it up to check the number. She held the phone up and showed Margot, then hit the button to ignore the call. "My father."

"Oh." Margot paused, her fork halfway to her mouth. "That's gonna likely mean he got your resignation."

Katharine nodded solemnly and sighed. "I'll call him back when I get home. Then I'll do the binding."

"By yourself?"

"Yeah. I need to do it soon." Doing the binding all alone would be a nuisance—she was used to having help—but the blood spots on her carpet said she needed to forgo the ease and get it done. Returning her father's call could wait.

"Here. You need these." Margot pulled a handful of small sheets of paper from her purse and handed them to Katharine. "I did a color copy of the painting and cut out two of each. I tried to get ones that were whole, where one body part wasn't obscured by something else."

In her hand, Katharine held two tiny demons and two tiny, evil-looking beasts the artist said were angels. There was a part of a foot missing on one and a hand missing on another. Margot kept talking.

"I read through the . . . instructions and it seemed like it might work better if they were stiff. So I laminated one of each."

Katharine turned them over; the un-laminated copies were already beginning to curl. She'd read the spell, too, and it didn't say anything about whether the drawing should be on paper or cardboard, or even how it was done. It had suggested a photo, but there was no way Katharine was going to get that. The pictures should work as well as anything. The backs were plain white paper, but that wasn't addressed anywhere either as far as she knew. "It makes sense. We'll just see if it works."

Katharine tucked the little drawings into her purse as the server came up to give them the check. They paid the bill and made their way back to Katharine's, where Margot gave her a brief hug before climbing into her car and heading into work.

Katharine didn't see Zachary on the way up to her apartment, but now she knew to be just as wary opening the door. Clearly, either of them could get in at any time they wanted.

Her living room was clear. No men, no beasts, no new soot. Her mirror was empty, too. So she took a deep breath, sank down on her couch, and called her father.

Sharon put her straight through—not a good sign. She barely got a hello out before he steamrolled her. "Katharine, is this a joke?"

"No, Dad. It's not. I'm resigning."

"Why on earth would you do something like that?"

Her mouth quirked up at the edge.

This was why she had lived the way she had. She could have chosen her own friends, her own job, felt all the things around her. But before she could really do it, there would be hell to pay. She was starting her payments now.

It was all there in his voice, the implied idea that "why would she do something so *stupid*?" There was only his way, and he saw nothing beyond the borders of his own vision. As she was learning, there was much beyond his borders, beyond hers, beyond any she had known. And he was right too in asking "Why on earth?" Because she was on earth, and she needed to really be here, in a way she had never been before. She needed to belong to herself.

But there was no way to say any of that to him. He would never understand. "Because I need to build my own career. I need to make my name in my own right."

There was silence. No, he didn't understand that either.

At least she'd tried.

"You're convinced of this?"

"Yes, Dad." It wasn't like they were going to miss her at Light & Geryon. She only did everything . . . and nothing.

He was muttering. "You're just like your mother. Stubborn as hell sometimes."

That statement nearly made her head snap back, and she thought maybe it was a shame she hadn't done this in person, where he could see her. "Mom was less stubborn than a piece of silk, Dad. What are you talking about?"

"Every once in a while she got some idea . . . and she just wouldn't let it go." He was clearly still miffed about these perceived slights by a dead woman, and by Katharine continuing the tradition.

"You mean that once out of a hundred times she wanted something done her way?" Her heart hurt. Maybe she'd never been anything to the man other than a chess piece. She suddenly realized something, and she spoke it before it got away. "I want you to be proud of me, Dad."

"Well, I . . ."

"I need to make my own way. I think you'd appreciate that if I were your son, Dad."

"But you're not!"

Clearly. "No, Dad, I'm just me."

"Well, you can leave any time you need. You don't have to worry about staying the two weeks."

She wanted to believe the gruff tone in his voice meant he thought he was being helpful. But it didn't help her at all to know that he thought she was as expendable as she did. Katharine said good-bye and hung up the phone.

Part of her wanted to curl up into a ball and cry for a while, but a bigger part of her realized she didn't have that luxury. So she dried her eyes, rolled her shoulders, and worked the kinks out of her neck, then rummaged through her purse for the little cutouts Margot had made for the binding spell.

She took the special tape out of her purse and peeled off the paper wrapper it had come in. She turned the little spool over in her hands for a moment. It looked like normal silk ribbon, in a near blinding shade of white. She'd probably been ripped off. On a hunch she smelled it, and her eyes instantly began to water. It was potent, so maybe she hadn't been totally ripped off. She unwound the whole spool and cut it in half, laying the two pieces aside.

She pulled out her white pillar candle and the paper Margot had photocopied with the chant on it. After setting it all out on her table, she closed all the blinds in the room. In the back of her mind, she wondered if the spell would work if the names she used weren't their real names, but there was nothing she could do about it now. And the spell was too simple not to give it a try.

Sitting at her dining table with her back to the kitchen, she looked out at her darkened living room and took a deep breath. She agreed with Margot; the laminated pieces looked like they'd hold up to a binding better, and besides, they were the ones that were whole—no nicked off hands or feet.

After one deep breath, she forced herself to start. She picked up the inky black demon drawing first and began the chant. "I bind you—"

But she came up short. She didn't know what to say. Which one was it? She needed the picture for the spell to work, but could she just say "I bind you" and not use a name? It seemed the spell was linked to the name and the picture.

She breathed deep and started again. Katharine folded the white ribbon around the demon drawing and tucked the loose end in. Then, as she wound it round and round, she chanted. "I bind you, Zachary, from doing harm against me and others. I bind you, Allistair, from doing harm against me and others, I bind you . . ."

She felt silly, but she kept going. Maybe it would work. The protection spell had seemed to. Zachary had commented on it. Or he had seen them doing it and wanted to mess with her. Sadly, that was entirely possible.

The ribbon was long enough to get tangled, and she stopped winding for a moment to free the knots, thinking she could have cut it shorter. But she kept up the chant.

She was getting the first knot out when she heard the footstep. She faltered in her chant as she heard another. The sound had come from right in front of her, on the other side of the dining table. After the third footstep brought the sound around near the end of the table, she struggled to make her shaking hands and voice work again.

Katharine spoke a little louder this time. "I bind you, Allistair, from doing harm . . ."

The steps continued, though she couldn't see anything. She strained to see behind her as they passed just beyond the kitchen countertop. The sound of her own voice blocked some of the footfalls, but it sounded as if it walked right up to the kitchen sink and passed clean through the half-wall that separated the kitchen and dining area.

As she chanted, the footfalls came around behind her, beyond the wall just on her right. A little faster and heavier now, they completed a counterclockwise loop around her and kept going.

Becoming more afraid as she went, she raised her voice just a touch, and her determination more. The steps kept getting louder and faster and began to be intermingled with the sound of a deep and raspy breath.

The shaking in her hands tangled the stupid ribbon again, and the trembling in her fingers made it that much harder to get the twists out. But she didn't stop. Even when she finished the binding, she merely picked up the picture of the silvery creature, trying not to wince at the mouthful of fang-like teeth it too sported. She tucked in the ribbon and started over with the winding, even though her words continued on the same, both names interlaced in the spell because she had no idea who was who.

But she did believe it was the demon moving in ever-tightening, counterclockwise circles around her. And she wondered if the circles were some kind of spell of their own.

The ribbon tangled more as she went, rather than less. The breathing turned into growls, and it kept circling. She no longer turned as it passed behind her, just kept her head down and her eyes on the mass of ribbon that had obscured the little picture about fifteen loops ago.

Now the demon was passing through the table where she worked. Still she couldn't see it, but the surface rocked a little as it went by, making the flame dance just a tiny bit. She felt the air move as it passed, and any doubt about where it was had been eliminated; the growling noise had turned into something that sounded like the earth opening up to swallow her.

She was nearing the last small bit of ribbon, the end unbearably short now. What was she going to do when it was done?

She kept up the chant, partly so she could block the sounds from all around her now. It took three tries to tuck in the stray end. When it was tight, she stopped at the end of the phrase.

The demon was right behind her.

She didn't dare turn, too afraid of what she might see.

The noise, like the bowels of hell were yawning open, came from just in back of her head. Only this time her hair moved with its breath.

Though she sat very still, clutching the tiny, silk-bound pictures, tears escaped from each eye and rolled in fat, desperate silence down her cheeks.

The noise became deafening, and her hair blew forward with it, and she knew she was likely living her last moments. Thoughts of Mary Wayne's shredded corpse froze her from any action.

And just like that, it stopped.

The roar moved backward at a tremendous speed, though it still howled in anger. Another sound moved with it, overlaying the depth with a keening pitch. She finally moved—dropped the bindings and clapped her hands to her ears—but the sound didn't fade. She wasn't hearing it through her ears at all.

For several minutes, screams of pain and bellows of rage came from all around her. The building shook, tiny tremors that California residents wouldn't even consider an issue. Though she knew it was useless, her body turned toward the sound each time it moved—a quicksilver reflex for protection against things of her own realm.

Eventually, the noises faded, but she stood behind her table shaking like a leaf. Several of the chairs had been overturned, but when, she didn't know. She hadn't *seen* anything, and that was probably good. The knowing alone had been petrifying.

Katharine didn't know how long she stood like a zombie in her own home, only that when she came around to being cogent again, she had scrambled to gather the bound images. The spells said to keep them in a safe place. But she knew of nowhere that she could hide them from the creatures she'd bound. Keeping them with her at all times seemed the only option, and she carefully tucked one into each back pocket.

She needed a drink. A good stiff . . . something. But the last thing she needed was dulled senses and the chance of being caught unaware or slow. And she didn't dare risk the possibility that the alcohol would open some of her senses, making it easier to see things in the reflections or make sense of the swirling shadows in her life. Water was probably all she could handle right now.

She had turned, weak legs finding some strength to carry her the last stretch into the kitchen, when she heard a new noise.

Crackling and popping sounds came from behind her, across the living room. She didn't dare look, but her body was wired to jerk around at this new perceived threat. It turned, regardless of the message from her brain.

Electric currents arced and curved back in on each other, moving and changing as she watched. And while she looked on, frozen in place, a man emerged.

At last the cluster of small lightning strokes subsided and she could see him more clearly.

Her heart pulled her across the room, her mouth worked like a fish, but she couldn't get any sound to come out.

Deep gashes marred him everywhere and bright red blood oozed from every cut.

His chest bore four deep symmetrical cuts, and his hands looked like he had given as good as he got. He looked her in the eye, and her heart leapt into her throat.

He swayed once . . . twice . . . before collapsing on her carpet.

Katharine found her voice as she rushed to him.

"Allistair!"

CHAPTER 24

Allistair took a deep breath and looked up at her from where he lay crumpled in the middle of her living room.

Her instinct was to run to him, to put her arms around him and keep him safe.

But she didn't do it for several reasons.

Katharine knew she couldn't trust those same instincts: they were flat-out lying to her about at least one of the men, and possibly both.

So she stood for a moment, watching his naked form as he breathed. He had fallen to his hands and knees when he had come through to her living room, but in the moment after that he had crumpled forward. His weight rested on his right leg, which was curled under him at an awkward angle, and on his shoulder. It seemed he didn't have the strength to even change his position. He was clearly in pain.

Though Katharine thought about helping him, she just stood and watched over him for any changes she might see. Besides, what could she possibly do to help him? He wasn't mortal. She couldn't tend his wounds, didn't know what to tell him, and even just putting her arms around him would do nothing for him. No matter how much she wanted it to.

Still, she walked toward him. Blood was making small pools on her carpet where his cuts were oozing just fast enough to be dangerous.

But she reminded herself as she walked closer that though losing that much blood would be dangerous to a human man, no matter how much Allistair looked like a man, he was far from it.

Clearly exhausted, he breathed in deep and long and rolled over onto his back.

Vulnerable, he continued to look up at her, his hand resting on his chest as it heaved. For a moment, he looked like he was merely worn out at the end of a marathon. Katharine knew better and briefly considered grabbing one of her kitchen knives and pushing it through his ribs while he lay there.

"You wouldn't."

His voice was melodic and, though tired, confident in tone. Her body stiffened at the sound and for a moment she disbelieved her ears. "Wouldn't what?"

"Hurt me." The edges of his lips curled up in a half smile.

He could have guessed that, she told herself.

Breaking her thoughts, he spoke again, dispelling her notion that he couldn't see into her thoughts. "You wouldn't get one of your kitchen knives and skewer me."

"Don't you look in my head!" In the snap of anger she felt, she yelled it loud enough for all the neighbors to hear. Would Zachary hear it?

With great effort, Allistair shook his head back and forth. "Not trying to. You're projecting it loud and clear." He took another slow breath in and she noticed that his wounds already looked a little better, though he still sounded winded. "I'm not really in any shape right now to shut you out. Sorry about that."

Turning her back on him, she went to her hall closet. She would have explained rather than just walking away, but clearly he was listening in on her every thought. When she returned, she dropped the soft couch throw on him.

His breath hissed in this time and she felt it down to her bones. She didn't like that she felt these things for him. Nor did she like that it soothed her somewhat that his feelings were seeping into her, too. Still, there was nothing she could do about it; she was linked to him. And he was even more firmly linked to her.

There were a thousand questions swimming indistinctly in her mind, but she didn't ask any of them. In a few more minutes he'd be even stronger. She'd thrown him the blanket mainly because he was lying naked on her floor, not because he'd needed it. Though she wrestled with whether she should help him, she wondered if there was anything she could do.

Just as the thought passed through her mind, he smiled again. "Water."

Even as she fetched it for him, she considered the possibility that she was aiding a demon, helping the very creature that—as soon as it was well again—could conceivably drag her to hell.

She filled the glass with cold water, wondering if he would like it that way and then questioning why he didn't respond to that last thought. He seemed to be reading all the others so clearly.

As she handed it down to him, he worked up the energy to lift an arm and say, "It's perfect. Thank you."

The next thought simply fell out of her mouth as soon as it passed through her head. "If I choose Zachary, will he really give me the Kingdom?"

"Yes." He slowly pushed himself upright, being careful to not spill the water. For a moment Katharine found that disturbingly ironic given all the blood that he had already spilled onto her carpet. But she didn't laugh as he struggled to sit up just enough to drink without sloshing it and pulled the blanket tighter around him as though he were cold. Not that he would feel that, would he?

But it was his answer that pushed through her clouded mind, still numb and reeling from the adrenaline overload of the spell and the circling demon.

Katharine had to reconsider everything Allistair said to her. Was he wounded because he had fought the demon for her? Or was he wounded because he was attacked? Was he exhausted because he'd been running circles around her?

Still she had to ask. "Why would you tell me something that would make me choose him? Then why would I choose you?"

He shook his head and slowly, painstakingly stretched before sitting all the way upright and taking another lingering drink from the glass. His long legs now had scabs and scars but were no longer bleeding.

She blinked. Of course he was getting better. It's what they did. But still it was a shock to see that the blood that had started leaching through the blanket in small patches had stopped a while ago. His strength was returning and he smiled up at her, brown eyes laughing a little. "I'm sorry about your carpet."

"Yeah, me too. Want to fix that for me?"

Though his expression still danced a little, his eyes looked sad and he shook his head. "Can't. Have to save my strength for when it's needed. Carpet is far less important than you."

She didn't trust the implications of his words or even his tone—though she wanted to.

After several deep breaths of her own, she decided to start with what had been bothering her most. She sat down directly in front of him, both of them cross-legged, her knees touching his through her pants and the blanket. The contact was more than she should have allowed, yet less than she wanted. Even knowing she shouldn't want it didn't change the way she wanted it. It was a pull deep inside her, moving her against her better judgment and taking her will along for the ride.

"If Zachary showed me a place where the chosen are well and cared for and live in peace, then what did you show me?"

It took a while before he answered and she worked to be patient and still her mind, to wait for this one thing without getting sidetracked as she so often did around him.

"There are two questions there. And the premise of the first part is a good bit wrong, but I can't say more—"

"Why not! Why can't you say more?" she yelled, leaning into his face, again likely disturbing all the neighbors, except maybe for the too-good-looking one just next door. Her hand lashed out, grabbed the glass from his hand, and smashed it against the wall just to have an outlet for her anger. Though she wanted to, she didn't dare hit him.

Allistair waited her outburst out and didn't really react at all. It was as though he had seen the storm coming from far away and had prepared for her explosion. "I cannot. I am forbidden from telling you all you wish to know. And so is he."

She couldn't let that be all. She couldn't hang here in limbo, waiting for something to hold on to, waiting for an answer that made sense or something that she could prove to be true. Something to believe in.

Allistair seemed to understand that. So he gave her just a little bit more. "We lose if we go too far—"

"Lose?" Her heart fell through her, her hopes plummeting with it. "It's my life, my everything. It's all been turned upside down." Tears began to track down her face, and she shook her head. "I've disappointed the only family I have left. And it's all just a game to you?"

"No." His hand reached out to her, then pulled back as she leaned away from him. "It's not a game, but it is a system. This isn't just about you. This is often how it's done. One of them, one of us."

"But not always this way?" Was there another path this could take? Maybe she could change things. Hope reared its head again, though the tears still fell—she hadn't been able to stop them.

"No, not always. Sometimes a person only sees one or the other, and then the choice is just yes or no. Not much of a choice at all when you think about the kind of influence we have. You get to choose."

"I don't want to." She started to turn, to stand up and walk away from him. She pictured herself standing in the doorway, much as she had with Zachary last night. But before she could change position, his hands on her knees stopped her from going anywhere.

"What you want doesn't change things. Even though I am sorry about that. You will have to make a choice. And it will have to be soon."

Silently, she sat there for maybe a minute. He looked at her, and maybe through her, and while he could likely tell everything she was thinking, she couldn't read a thing off of him. But his arms had healed.

There were no more scabs, only thin white lines showing where the torn flesh had been. None of the scars were jagged, though she didn't know if that was due to his rapid healing or the fact that he had probably been cut by razor-sharp blades that would have left only clean cuts. In another minute or two he would be back to his beautiful, unblemished self.

Eventually, he spoke again.

"You humans have a flawed idea of what's beyond you."

That was not surprising. Clearly, Allistair was right. In all her early years of Sunday school and church every week, no one had even hinted at this. She didn't grace him with words—simply waited a bit longer.

"You have mixed up ideas of heaven and hell. There are two things confused in the names. The realm that I am from—"

He stopped himself. And Katharine sat, watching him and waiting.

He'd very nearly told her something of importance, something he shouldn't. He'd almost slipped up. Katharine leaned forward, even more alert. Because she knew he could hear it, she spoke it. "What happens if you slip up?"

"I'll die. And you'll default to Zachary."

She felt like she'd been slapped. "And if he slips up?"

"You'll default to me."

Fire raged through her. She was getting slammed from one end of the emotional spectrum to the other. "So, if either of you messes up, I lose my choice? It's really not in my hands at all?"

"It is."

She realized his hands held hers, though she didn't remember him grabbing them or holding them before this moment. Disgusted, she yanked her own grip out of his. She was being played more ways than she could count.

"Keep with it, Katharine. I think you'll prevail in the end."

"Why don't you just tell me?" Her voice was the one she hadn't heard from her own lips since she'd been a teenager, angry and petulant—only now it was laced with tears and fear.

"I can't . . . I don't know." He looked her in the eyes again and went on with what he'd said earlier. "There are realms where angels live. And you could call that heaven. And there are realms where demons dwell, and you could say that's hell. But it isn't what you think. That heaven where the angels reside is merely a place to be. It isn't a place of unending peace and clouds where all your loved ones meet you. It's just a place. And hell is just a place too. It isn't eternal punishment, or fire or ice. It's just a place where demons happen to be. I've been to both."

She looked at him, wondering where this was leading.

The blanket hung around his shoulders, revealing that the white lines had faded while she wasn't paying attention. If she hadn't known exactly where to look, she would never have seen these final remnants of the battle he had fought just a short while ago.

Now, all was still. Her phone didn't ring. The air almost didn't move. And he was just as he had always been, from the moment she had met him.

But she was so very different.

"The real heaven and hell are here, Katharine."

"What?"

"They're on earth."

"Where?" She looked in his eyes again, wondering if she could discern his origins in them. But she couldn't. They were just human eyes, even though she knew he was anything but.

"There isn't a specific place. They are both in many places, sometimes the same place. It's just here . . . part of the people. You can live in one and your neighbor in the other. Some people are caught in between. Some find heaven in the darkest times and others will be in hell no matter how the world is around them. Sometimes it's yours to find or to make. And sometimes it finds you. But it isn't a place you can go to. It isn't a place that either Zachary or I can send you to."

"Then what happens to me if I choose?"

"You'll live out your life. Until you are called."

Like Mary Wayne

The thought flitted across the outskirts of her thoughts, but was there nonetheless.

Still. She was still. Neither happy nor sad. Not afraid. She was simply still.

"And when I'm called?"

"You will go into service for whichever side you chose."

So she couldn't choose wrong. It was as simple and as complex as that.

He smiled at her, a sad smile that one would give a child, and he looked beside and past her as he sometimes did.

Something about the way his eyes moved made her ask. "What?"

"You've been casting spells."

"Can you just see them or something?"

"Kind of like that. Yes." His hand reached out and brushed the air beside her head. "Protection spells. That's smart."

Katharine shook her head. "I don't think it's been working."

"Why is that? They look strong to me."

"I still have feelings for you."

Once the words were out of her mouth, she regretted them. She shouldn't have feelings for him. She should have been able to get rid of them once she knew what he was. Angel or demon, he'd never love her back. He couldn't really want her. Not as she had wanted him. And she knew both creatures were simply toying with her. She was mouse to their cat. Yet she was still sucked in by him, still imagined leaning into him and curling up in his arms. Even though she knew it was very wrong. Even though another large part of her didn't want to give in to anything at all. So, though she spoke the words, she didn't do anything else.

While she could refuse to act on her urges, she was still haunted by them and disturbed by the fact that he could probably see right through her.

"So?" was his only response. At least he didn't look like he was trying to take advantage of what she'd just blurted out.

"The spells seem to have blocked Zachary. I'm no longer pulled to him. " As she said it, she realized Zachary might be toying with her—he might have stopped playing with her emotions simply because he wanted her to feel that her little spell had accomplished something. Or was it as she had originally thought? Was Allistair just so much more powerful that the spell hadn't stopped him at all?

What would Allistair's response be? And could she trust it? She kept talking, peeling back layers and exposing her soul in an effort to gain some knowledge, anything that would help her out. "Why is that? Why don't I still have feelings for him after the spells when I do still have them for you?"

"Because I didn't put them there."

. . .

Katharine came around, blinking in the bright light. From the amount of sunlight that streamed in through the open shades, it appeared it was midday, and she was lying on her living room floor—surrounded by bloodstains.

Sadly, there was nothing unusual about any of this.

The blood on the floor didn't really bother her. And there was only a fleeting thought in her brain that it wasn't even human blood. She didn't bother to think about trying to scrub it out. Let the cops figure out what would get demon blood out of a thick wool carpet. She wasn't up for that kind of challenge.

It didn't even really disturb her that she found it necessary to check the display on her cell phone to know the date, let alone figure out the time.

It was 11:00 a.m. on Saturday.

The last thing she remembered, she'd been talking to Allistair. They had been sitting cross-legged, face to face, right here on her living room floor. Then she had floated backward . . . and nothing. Not until now.

Wondering how much of it had really happened, she stood and walked around the condo, checking things out.

In the mirror, she could see she was wearing Friday's clothes and that she'd clearly slept in them for a while. That, at least, was easy to fix.

Her hair and the faint outline of carpet pressed into her cheek told her she should shower first. That, too, was easily remedied.

She needed to see how much she could remember, and find out how much of it was real. Had she cast the spells? The table said she had. There was the cardboard spool that had held the binding ribbon, empty now and on its side. It looked like it had rolled away from her at one point. The candle was there, too. But the bound pictures—

Her hands patted at the back pockets of her jeans in a panicked frenzy. Though she felt better to find there were lumps in each pocket, she didn't calm down until she had pulled them out and seen that she held them in her hands.

She needed to keep tabs on those. After the night in her pockets, the ribbon around the pictures was smushed flat, though luckily still intact. Katharine was surprised and relieved that they were still whole. Supposedly, just unwinding the ribbon broke the magic. Grabbing the pair and clutching them tight, she examined the table again, this time for signs of the demon.

There was almost nothing to tell of what had happened. The wood of the table and the backer board on the walls were smooth beneath her touch—there were no marks that gave any indication that the demon had passed through the furniture, the cabinets, the walls when he circled her the night before. But the tall pillar candle was burned about an inch deep, and the cavity the flame had left behind was slanted heavily to the right from where the flame had flickered hard and threatened to go out each time the demon passed by.

And there was all the blood on her living room floor.

Yes, there was evidence here.

Taking a deep breath because there was nothing more she could do except hit the shower, she looked around the room.

It was Saturday, the beginning of the weekend.

And for her, it was the first time in her life that she didn't know where she was supposed to go next, what she was supposed to do.

Everything loomed before her, open and exciting and scary. Her life was closing in just as it was ripening, full of possibilities for great success or abject failure. And those were just her career options, never mind if she chose poorly about her life.

And that thought put it all into perspective.

For the first time in her life, she took a moment to realize that the wealth she had been born into was not just a set of chains tying her to the easiest route through life. It was not just a system whereby her father wielded such great power and her mother such status that she would never be able to carve her own way and make anything of value of herself.

It was also a great gift. A gift that most didn't have, and never would.

She had the chance to not look for work—to take time and decide for herself. What did she want to do? Did she want to work for someone else? For herself? In the same market? Or choose some other career path?

Katharine had no idea.

But, first, she needed to take the time to figure out what to choose.

Everything rode on this one decision.

Feeling a bit too needy, but nevertheless grateful that she knew who to call, Katharine picked up the phone and dialed Margot's number.

"Katharine!" The voice washed through her. *Friend.*

"Hey, how was last night? Oh my God! Is Liam still there? I didn't even think I might be interrupting!"

"Ha! I told you. I'm not a total slut. He left last night." But Margot was laughing in that pleased way.

And that made Katharine smile, and wonder. "Are you a partial slut?"

"Um. Yeah."

Katharine laughed. It came from deep in her belly and shattered all the problems around her like thin glass. They would rebuild themselves again later; something would happen and it would all come back to her in full relief. But for the moment, the laughter was welcome and all-encompassing. "Want to tell me about it over lunch at the beach?"

"That sounds like a plan. And it sounds like you didn't have anything too exciting last night then. Did the spell go well?"

Katharine sighed and waited a moment. "We'll have to take the food down to the beach and I'll tell you all about it. I should shower first, then I can swing by and pick you up in about an hour."

It seemed, for once, to all go according to plan. No messages on the mirror. No one waiting in her living room when she got out. No animals. Nothing.

She dried her hair most of the way and decided to give up. Looking out into the distance, she whispered, "Sorry, Mom."

It seemed she wasn't her mother's daughter, at least not the one her mother had intended her to be. And she wasn't to be her father's either. She had spent far too long belonging to everyone around her.

Katharine stopped dead in the middle of the room. She had apologized to her mother in that soft, to-the-ether way a thousand times before. But this time she spoke in her full voice and added: "Be proud of me, Mom." It wasn't a question. Though it was only to the air, for the first time, rather than simply agreeing with what her parents thought, she had told one of them what she needed. Another piece settled firmly into place.

She turned to her closet and pulled out a pair of Bermuda shorts and a soft white T-shirt. She slipped on a nice pair of flip-flops that were beaded and slightly elevated. She'd bought them a few days earlier, after seeing a similar pair on Margot.

Her closet looked as foreign to the old Katharine as the rest of her life did.

But to the new Katharine, it was starting to look familiar.

She made it to Margot's right on time, and they swung by a sandwich place to get overloaded subs, grilled and melting in the bag.

As they walked to the beach, Katharine waited to tell Margot about the binding spell. About what Allistair had said.

Margot didn't wait, though. "Do you know yet which is which? Did talking to Allistair help?"

"Not unless any of it becomes clear to you from what I repeat." She sighed, enjoying the edge of salt that came in with the air. "What he said makes sense, but it violates so much of what everyone believes."

She shrugged. The idea of his heaven and hell was so different from all she had been taught.

Margot nodded. "There's something that feels wrong about going against eons of religion. Even with reason."

"Yeah. And as good as it sounds, can I trust it?" But she answered her own question. "I'm not ready to trust either of them. They've both deceived me, and everyone who came in contact with them, just by showing up."

She didn't want to say more while they waded through the people crowding the cement trail along the beach. They watched for a break as the beach traffic went by, skateboarders, bikers, and rollerbladers who were far more skilled than the two of them put together had been.

But as the sand and waves beckoned from the other side of the trail, Margot found another tack while they waited for the traffic to clear in both directions. "I think I found something more. About how they come in. Remember I had that piece about changing color as they incorporated? How it depended on the level they were from? I think I have something that may get us more information."

"Will it help me figure out which is which?" Katharine saw a gap in the flow of people and stepped onto the pavement.

Margot followed. "I hope so. But I don't have it yet. Just an obscure reference that I found in another reference."

"Both of them have been telling me that I'll need to make a choice soon," Katharine spoke softly as she walked. "It's the one thing I think I can trust to be true, since they're both saying the same thing about it." Her foot passed off the opposite side of the walkway and sank into sand. The grains climbed up and over the soles of her flip-flops and under her feet. With each step, the sand shifted, creating new patterns as she went.

Margot joined her in the sand, somehow managing to kick off her sandals gracefully and balance her sandwich bag and her drink in one hand while she scooped the shoes up with the other.

Katharine must have been eyeing her oddly, because her friend immediately grinned and said, "I waited tables through college."

Yet another skill Katharine needed to acquire. "Do you think you'll find it soon—the information on the colors?"

"I'd guess it will take a good four days. A lot of the old stuff isn't scanned and I'm waiting for it to be shipped."

"Doesn't shipping take longer than that?"

"Interlibrary loan is actually pretty fast."

They walked toward the beach, Katharine trailing slightly behind so she didn't have to pay attention to where she was going.

The sun came down on the day, giving it that glow that made L.A. famous. It was just hot enough to be obnoxious, but the breeze off the ocean made the difference. She felt the slight prickles in her scalp as her hair was lifted and played with by small winds.

There were sounds of people behind her, wheels going by on the walkway, the slap of sneakers in regular rhythm. There were voices, all mingled together in a single tide of sound that rose and fell in a pattern less regular than the waves before her.

She could see that the water receded just a little each time, not reaching quite as far, not coming quite as close to claiming her as it had in the previous wave.

Margot picked a spot and sat down, settling her sandwich bag in her lap and pushing her Coke into the sand to steady it. She didn't even wait for Katharine to get situated.

"Talk."

CHAPTER 25

Sunday had come and gone in reasonable disappointment.

Margot had given Katharine the update from the library, and sadly it was that there was no update. There was nothing new to learn about what was happening to her. Nothing happened at the library on Sundays. No interlibrary loans traveled. Hopefully, nothing would happen to her either. There wasn't anything to do but wait until Monday.

She cast her protection spell again, this time prepared for the demon to visit. She worked the entire spell with her muscles clenched in anticipation of noises, fire, men breaking through the air in front of her, something, anything. But nothing happened.

Margot was busy. Katharine wouldn't call her father. Where before she might have picked up the phone and called Zachary, or even Allistair, she now knew better than to do that.

So she'd spent her day online, trying to be the researcher Margot was—or even a tenth of the researcher Margot was. But she didn't get anything they didn't already know and she did get a lot that was patently untrue according to what she had already seen and learned.

Katharine tried to watch TV for a while, but wound up merely marveling at the amount of programming she had stockpiled on her TiVo. She usually spent some of her evenings just watching what she liked. But lately she hadn't kept up. As bizarre as it had been, lately she'd had a real life. And she was finding herself willing to do almost anything to keep it.

She was ready to fight for what was hers. Willing to make a stand. And yet she was sitting around in front of her TV—there was nothing she could do about it with nothing happening.

She'd handed over everything she knew to Margot, and was waiting on whatever information her friend could bring. Unless Zachary or Allistair started something, there was nothing to do but wait. She tried to focus on the TV, but when even that failed—it was so much less interesting than the things swirling in her mind—she gave up and decided to at least try for a good night's rest.

Katharine slept the night through, unencumbered by dreams or interruptions.

Monday, she got up late, thought about what she wanted to do with her life over a bowl of oatmeal, and then called her Dad.

He answered as soon as Sharon put her through. "Katharine! Did you change your mind?"

"No, Dad." She walked a small, circular path around her living room. "I was actually wondering what happened with my trainee. The guy I was working with?"

"You were working with someone? Wouldn't HR know about that?"

Yes, Katharine thought, *except you gave him to me personally.* "Oh, you don't remember him? Allistair West?"

"The name doesn't mean anything to me." She could hear him shrugging in that way that discounted her when he didn't understand. And that was it. He asked about her plans. Harrumphed when she said she was still figuring them out, and insinuated that it was stupid to quit a great job when she didn't even know what else she was planning on doing. It was all so very typical, and this time Katharine didn't kowtow to his wishes or let him reason her back into his way of thinking.

Katharine tried to let it all roll off her. She wasn't as good at it as she'd like to have been. But she did try. And before she hung up, she flustered her Dad by saying, "I love you."

But given her father's almost non-reaction to Allistair's name, she called Lisa, and then HR. No one seemed to have records or even any memory at all of an Allistair West.

For a moment, Katharine wanted to double-check her sanity. Though Margot believed her, her friend had never met either of the men and, at this point, probably didn't want to either. That meant that Katharine was operating on a lot of information that absolutely no one could verify. She wanted to declare the whole thing a figment of a crazy mind and be done with it. Maybe even get some medication that would make it all go away. But she'd been down that road before. There was no shaking it. She'd see it through to the end.

All day there remained no word from Margot, and it seemed that Liam would have her friend's attention for the evening. So Katharine watched a few more shows and, rather than be upset that she was by herself, enjoyed her comfy couch and the smooth slide of ice cream down her throat.

All in all, Monday had turned out dreadfully dull.

. . .

Zachary watched. Katharine was doing nothing.

Though he had made it clear that she would have to make her choice soon, she had spent the last two days doing nothing to move anything forward. She had told her father that she loved him. Maybe that was a last-ditch "just so you know, in case I die" kind of thing. But that was the only move of any value she had made.

It seemed, if things were left up to Katharine, she would continue this into her old age, watching TV and living off her trust fund.

It was going to be up to him to drive this forward.

He had to do something. And it appeared Allistair was about to make his own move.

. . .

Allistair stood at the edge of her living room, his human form feeling more his own than ever before. His heart beat within his ribcage as he watched Katharine sleeping on her couch, and he enjoyed the steady surge of blood through his veins. He was in more trouble than he could imagine.

Even if Katharine chose him and his, he was still stuck with all that had changed in him this time around. He'd not only done the one thing he wasn't supposed to do; this time he was so tangled that he couldn't stop himself.

In a purely human gesture, he walked across the room and scooped Katharine up from where she'd fallen asleep while watching TV. She rolled into him, her weight both a blessing and a burden. The soft sigh she let out as she curled further into his arms nearly undid him.

In her bedroom, he laid her down on top of her covers and straightened her out. Up until the very last minute, he only intended to leave her there. He meant to make her more comfortable and then walk away.

But as he looked down at her, he found he couldn't look away. He'd been so wrong to get so involved with her. He'd left her messages, though he'd known she wouldn't understand the words, and he'd tried so hard to get through to her. And somehow she had understood part of it. She'd gone out and proved herself resourceful. She'd found someone to help her. And she'd found a real friend in the process. He was proud of her, even though he shouldn't be.

He was so many things he shouldn't be.

In a moment of sheer weakness, he leaned over and kissed her sleeping mouth.

There would be no more.

No more touches from Katharine, and no more textures, scents, sounds, any of it. He had to get himself under control. He had to start pulling away. Had to let go of all the things that were so seductive to him and start the journey back to what he should be.

But he lingered, the taste of her on his human lips too sweet and too seductive to step back. He brushed her hair off her face and whispered a few words before kissing her one last time. He forced himself to turn away.

Walking a straight line in the opposite direction from where she lay, Allistair pushed himself straight through the wall in frustration at his feelings and at what he had to do. He went right through to the other side, only to find Zachary had been watching.

He stared his opponent in the eyes for just a moment.

Endgame.

. . .

Katharine awoke to several things at once.

Her phone was ringing, though it was clearly still the middle of the night.

She was on her bed, though she didn't remember getting there. She was certain she'd fallen asleep on the couch.

And heavy footsteps were walking away from her bed. The icy chill of fear flooded her as she smelled the edge that clung to the air. Somewhere, just beyond her five senses, was the odor of rot and the soft lick of something evil. Not something that hated her or was after her. No, it was far worse. It was a feeling that this thing wanted . . . something. She was in its way. And she was completely unimportant other than that.

It would toss her aside, step on her, shred her as she screamed. And it would think no more of it in its attempt to reach what it wanted.

Katharine's instincts had her sitting very still, breathing shallowly and trying to calm her racing heart like the rabbit that prays the hunter won't see it.

But, like the rabbit, she gained nothing with her tactic.

She couldn't see the creature, didn't even see its outline or form, but she knew exactly where it was. There was a change in the air quality where it stood, even though there was nothing she could point to. She heard the footsteps slow and come to a stop near her doorway, but it was something else—some other odd sense that she'd never exercised before—that told her it had turned and was looking right at her.

Her breath caught in her throat and everything in her jerked to a standstill.

Though she couldn't see it, smell it, hit it, anything, she knew it could do all those things to her. And worse. So she waited.

It continued to stare at her, for long enough that she began the long, gradual inhalation through her nose that would keep her from passing out. Once she had ever-so-slowly filled her lungs, she began to let the air out just as slowly. And still it stared. Katharine didn't move, but continued her nearly invisible breathing and began to wonder what it was thinking. What it had planned, for surely it was planning something. She was just a rabbit. No, she was less than a rabbit. The rabbit was food to the wolf, and food was important. She wasn't even that.

So she sat still and tried to give it no ideas.

Though she had no concept of the time it stood there, eventually it turned and walked away, the footsteps fading near her front door.

Even then, she waited to hear the door open and close, then remembered that the door wasn't necessary; this creature wasn't constrained by her human boundaries. She would have to trust her instincts that it was gone. Even so, she waited a full minute before she let out her breath and sagged on the bed, staring at her carpet, hoping not to see anything else. But when she did look up she saw that Zachary was striding through her living room, visible through the open bedroom door.

He was coming back to her on the same path the demon had just walked and, though she only just now noticed it, the phone was still ringing. Or ringing again.

As she gathered her thoughts and straightened out her breathing, she held a finger up to him and reached out to grab the phone. "Hello?" A call this late couldn't mean anything good.

"Katharine!" Margot's voice came through clearly. "I found it! I'm on my way over."

"Yeah, come on over, I'm up now. What did you find?" Katharine's eyes remained on Zachary, though he seemed unconcerned that she was inviting her friend over with him standing there in front of her. She desperately wanted Margot to see him, to see and validate at least some of what was going on. Zachary's nonchalance began to worry her, but Margot's voice through the line pulled her back into reality.

"The thing about the levels. After Liam went home I wasn't tired, so I started reading. I have it."

She sounded excited about it, and Katharine felt her lips lifting up at the sides. Until she looked up.

Now Zachary broke into the conversation. "Is she coming over? Tell her no. It's not safe."

He was grabbing at her hand, trying to tug her along while she was trying to explain what Margot overheard him saying.

"Katharine!" Margot sounded frustrated. "Is he there?" She didn't specify which "he" and then ignored her own question and kept talking. "I need you to answer a few questions about what they look like. Maybe look at a few things in this book, then we'll know which is which. It's still a bit of a crapshoot, but . . . I think I know how to figure it out."

"Really?" Katharine sat back down on the edge of her bed, yanking at the hold Zachary had on her. It should have bothered her more that he wasn't letting go. But she'd been lulled by the fact that she didn't have feelings for him anymore. By the idea that the protection spell was working. Though she was very afraid of her future, she was no longer afraid of him.

He pulled her back to her feet. "Get off the phone. He's coming! You have to get out of here."

This time she ignored the phone and looked right at him. "Who's coming?"

She needed to know what Margot was going to say before she went anywhere with him. Had Margot really found it?

"Allistair." Zachary didn't shout it; he didn't sound afraid. And maybe the one word was more ominous because of it.

He took advantage of her momentary confusion and took the phone out of her hand. "It isn't safe here now. Tell her not to come."

Katharine still looked at him askance, but did as he instructed before he shut off the phone and tossed it onto the bed behind her. She heard only the first part of a word as Margot was cut off.

His urgency grew. "We have to go. We have to leave now."

But she didn't trust him—didn't trust him to be what he said, didn't trust him to keep her safe from the evil that was after her. She didn't trust either of them, and didn't trust herself to make any decisions at all right now.

She wanted Margot. Wanted to know what Margot knew. But Zachary had her on her feet and was pulling her headlong toward the living room when they ran into Allistair.

"Zachary, Katharine." Allistair was cool and calm, his dark coloring in direct opposition to Zachary's blonde hair and beautiful pale eyes. Katharine was thinking about Allistair and his earthy good looks when she felt a tug.

Still cuffing her wrist with his hand, Zachary turned to her and looked right into her eyes. "It's time. You have to choose." His breath heaved in and out as though he had run a great distance to get to this moment, as though this were very important to him.

But Katharine wondered. Was it really important? How bad would it be for him if he lost the game? As bad as it would be for her? As bad as it had been for Mary Wayne?

She looked at both men. "Why do I have to choose now?"

Allistair's face didn't belie any expression. "Zachary got called."

"What?" Her head whipped around to look at him, just as Zachary's did. But Zachary didn't loosen his grip on her wrist and Katharine didn't fight it. There were more important things to do now.

"He has been called to another assignment." Allistair's voice was as calm as if he were announcing that the day would be partly cloudy and warm. As if it were of no consequence whatsoever.

From her feet to her head, fury boiled up and over. "And so that's it? You're done with me? Game over?"

Allistair opened his mouth to respond. "You have everything you need."

But Zachary spoke over him. "You have to decide now. Allistair is manipulating you."

Katharine watched the conversation rocket back and forth between the two of them.

Allistair simply looked her in the eyes and shook his head no.

Again, Katharine wasn't sure she could trust that.

Tugging her hand along as he gestured and spoke, Zachary stared Allistair down. "You were here earlier tonight. You carried her into her bedroom."

He didn't ask it, he stated it, and Allistair didn't make any denials. Katharine waited.

"You said something to her. You have been trying to tell her something." This time Zachary let go of her hand and stepped back as though to present her in a grand gesture, leaving Katharine standing between the two men, facing Allistair and waiting. "Tell her now."

But Allistair didn't. Couldn't. Wouldn't.

Attempting to gain some measure of control of the situation, Katharine stepped back. It was really all the same, wasn't it? No matter what he said or what she did to make him say it. No matter how the two men prodded at each other, it would all come down to her.

As Zachary stepped in to fill her field of vision, she automatically turned to hear what he would say. "Come with me, Katharine. You deserve the Kingdom. You won't have it right away. There's still more for you to do here, but you'll find your time here is filled with riches. Katharine."

He held his hand out to her. His perfect hand. Pale and soft and unused. And he waited.

Allistair's hands remained in his pockets. She knew what they were like, didn't have to see them. Even in his short time here, he'd used those hands. He was starting to get calluses. Though the small cuts he got healed quickly, he was always shoving his hands into the pebbles on the beach, trailing them along fences and siding, getting them dirty, nicking them as he tried new things. He didn't say anything to her now, and though he tried to look as though the decision was all hers, he looked worried. At least she thought he did.

Katharine looked back at Zachary, his hand still out to her, waiting for her to accept his invitation. His expression said he was offering her everything if only she would come. She then looked at Allistair, hands in pockets, a small frown forming between eyes the color of rich soil as he stared directly at her.

Someone was about to win.

And someone was about to lose. And there was every possibility that the loser would be her.

For an eternity she stood there, both men watching her and waiting.

Her brain and her heart fought.

She felt things from Allistair, the pull of him that she knew was just because of what he was. And she fought against it. Fought to stay rational. Though she began just then to wonder if being rational was the right thing to do? What had it gotten her so far?

It was Zachary with his Kingdom that appealed the most. And maybe that was the problem. But how could she choose Allistair? He showed her so many things that scared her, too many bad things to count. How could she knowingly pick that?

She wanted to call Margot, ask for help. She needed to know what her friend had found out.

Maybe Margot was on her way here already. Maybe if Katharine just held out long enough, she could wait until Margot arrived. Then she could really make her choice, and make an informed one. She didn't like the guess she was being forced into.

Zachary shook his head at her. "She won't get here in time. You can't call her."

Allistair at least looked sympathetic. "It was always this way. You have always had to make the decision on your own."

Katharine stood there and waited, not really knowing what to do, but never questioning that they had both responded to thoughts that she hadn't put into words. It was more important to think that maybe they were wrong. They couldn't stop Margot, could they? Katharine did nothing while both men watched her. She focused on the second hand of the clock on her living room wall, and went away in her head for a few moments.

The clock had been her mother's and had belonged to some long-ago grandparents before that. It was old and out of keeping with her taste. She didn't like the clock. She'd just been told that it was hers, and so it had been. She watched the second hand sweep and wondered how many other things she had and did that were just the things she had been told were hers. And she wondered how she was going to fix all those things. Then she realized that it didn't matter. Unless Margot got here soon, she wasn't going to get the chance to fix much of anything.

As the second hand passed the twelve again, Katharine watched for the minute hand to make its tick. Sometimes at night, she could hear the sound as the hand lurched from one minute to the next.

But it didn't do that now.

She watched again as the second hand swept all the way to the bottom, then up to the left and past the top again. And still the minute hand didn't move. Again. Again she watched it do this.

At last she turned to look at the two men.

Zachary's eyebrows were up. There was nothing she could do.

At least Allistair looked a bit apologetic.

Katharine saw then that they had been right, Margot would never make it.

There was no time, and yet there was all the time in the world.

They were right—she had to choose. And she had to choose on her own. With only what she already knew. There would be no more information coming from the outside. She had only herself and the two of them.

Of all the things she hadn't sorted out, there was one thing that bothered her more than the others. She had woken that one night, right after Allistair had left her bed, and she had called out to him. It was the demon that had said yes.

If it had truly answered to its name, she would have to choose Zachary. She needed to know what had happened. She had to at least ask.

"Allistair." She pleaded, praying this would solve something, get her closer to what she needed to know. "When you answered to your name . . . do you remember? . . . Did you . . ."

She struggled several times to ask it, and he waited patiently while she didn't get it right. Finally, she just retold the story and asked if it was him.

"Katharine." His eyes were sad. "I can't tell you that. I can't tell you what I am or what Zachary is. You have to choose based on what you've already seen, on what you feel." He shook his head. "If I answer that, you will belong to Zachary, because I will have broken the code."

With tears in her eyes, she nodded, hating it but understanding.

She was so afraid and so cold. As she started to shake, tears began running down her cheeks in earnest. She sucked in air, and both men came at her, sympathy in their eyes. But she shook her head at them. One was fake, he was plying her . . . or both were.

Her chest clenched at the thought, and she took a step back.

Her body forced a deep breath in.

Zachary had showed her the Kingdom. Allistair had sucked her into a whirlpool of emotion, an all-encompassing cloud that defied reason and only wanted, leaving no room for rational thought. Zachary had befriended her, called her Katie and . . .

Zachary.

Zachary of the light blue eyes. Margot said they changed as they moved. Allistair was dark.

Allistair had said eyes showed origin. And Zachary's were beautiful.

In a moment of serene peace, she opened her mouth. She prayed she was right, but felt that there was nothing more to do. She had chosen and she would live or die with the consequences. "I—"

"No, Katharine!" Allistair came toward her with his hand outstretched. "Don't!"

Again she stepped back, angry and scared all at once. "Do you know who I'm going to choose? Do you hear my thoughts?"

"No." He shook his head, and in his eyes she saw the reflection of her own fear. "I just see that you are about to choose. I have to tell you—"

Zachary's voice broke into the conversation, his gaze aimed laser-sharp at Allistair. "Don't you dare." It was low and full of venom.

Katharine sucked in air. Had she chosen wrong? Zachary looked vicious and ready to strike; that he was striking out at Allistair rather than her didn't change how she felt at all. And she was suddenly very afraid of him.

Allistair.

Allistair, who had shown her only the truth. Who told her things she didn't want to hear, but that she needed to. Allistair, who somehow, right or wrong, she had fallen in love with. She saw it now. The overwhelming feeling that he swore he hadn't pushed on her. It was hers.

Could she have loved a demon?

And if she did—if she loved him—would it really matter what he was?

With open eyes, Katharine turned back to Allistair. And this time she saw him, bright and shining. Again she opened her mouth to choose. She knew she had to state her choice out loud, and she had to do it before Zachary advanced on Allistair.

Zachary's deep voice cut through her thoughts and pierced her plans.

All his intense focus was on Allistair, who stood solid in the face of his enemy. Zachary leaned toward him, his eyes on fire with anger. "You can't."

"I can." Allistair gave no ground, just put his hand out on Zachary's chest and pushed.

Katharine gasped. It was the first time she had seen them touch each other in human form. The hiss and smell of burning flesh was suddenly everywhere.

Zachary was forced back, small curls of steam rising from the middle of his chest where Allistair's hand had made contact.

"You don't." His hands came out to latch tightly onto Allistair's shoulders and arced small currents in the air around them. He pushed back.

Though muscles strained, neither man made up any ground. They stood there, locked in a struggle that was evidenced only by the malice on each of their faces and the spitting noises of the air as it crackled around them and seemed to sear their skin.

Then, with one great push, Allistair broke free.

Desperate and fast, he turned to Katharine.

Despite everything, despite what she had just seen on both their faces, despite what he might be, when he reached out for her she reached to him.

For a millisecond she worried that her skin too would hiss and burn with his touch, but it didn't. Instead, he closed his hand around hers, making contact, and talking as fast as he could.

"You have to choose—"

"I know, and I—" She interrupted him, only to have him interrupt her back.

Zachary stood watching, seething, as though something about the touch linked her to Allistair and he knew he wasn't able to break it.

Allistair caught her attention, looked her in the eyes. "You *don't* know. There's another option."

"You wouldn't. You'll cost us both." Zachary's warning pricked at her in a thousand places, and as Katharine glanced around she saw tiny drops of blood welling all along both her arms.

Her breath sucked in, and the sting began to radiate through her. How had he done that? She had to say it, had to say Allistair's name. She tried to get enough air to speak, but the cuts were as frightening as they were painful.

"Katharine." Allistair pulled his attention back to her. He caught her gaze and held it with his own. "Look here, look at me, listen to me. No matter what he says or does."

She nodded. She had chosen, and her eyes locked with his, the same way they always had when she was with him. Whatever he was, she was with him.

He began speaking rapidly, and although Katharine was trying to pay attention, it cost so much to tune out Zachary and his painful protests that she only half heard what Allistair was saying.

"You have to choose. But there's another way. There's a third choice. You can decide against both of us. You can choose neither. You can choose you."

"No!" Zachary's voice lashed out and caught her unprepared.

Katharine would have bent over, folding in half, if Allistair hadn't been holding on to her. The tiny pinpricks on her arms opened to small cuts everywhere. Her blood began to ooze out. She felt it on her neck, her face, everywhere that was exposed to the sound of his voice.

Allistair pulled her close in an attempt to protect her. He growled at Zachary. "I told her. It's done, it's over."

"It isn't." Zachary came toward him, the sound and feel of his footsteps vibrating through the floorboards like a heavy machine.

Allistair's voice was sharp in her ear. "Say it. End it. Katharine. Choose."

CHAPTER 26

She huddled in Allistair's arms, bleeding from a thousand open wounds on every exposed surface of her flesh. She wanted to choose him, but he didn't want her to. Not any more.

His voice came from right beside her ear and inside her head at the same time. "Choose you. Katharine. Do it. Now!"

He pulled her closer as Zachary approached.

She had believed that maybe Zachary wouldn't be able to break the bond that Allistair had formed by touching her. But that wasn't true; he had broken it with his voice alone, leaving her huddled there, oozing blood from all the little cuts the shards of his voice had opened. And he was striding toward them, furious, coming to tear them apart.

Katharine fought to breathe. She had trouble finding her voice; it was the one thing she needed now. It all depended on her saying the words.

Allistair huddled over her and around her, his voice strong and almost angry sounding. "Now, Katharine. Say it now."

With one great gasp, she blurted it out. "Me. I choose me."

Does that work?

The thought raced through her mind and was gone before the air had even cleared.

Zachary had stopped in his tracks and stood stock-still. For just a moment he did nothing but look stunned.

Then, with a speed that seemed to stun Allistair, too, he did something that looked like he was inhaling. Less than a moment later, all his anger burst out of him in one pulse, slicing through the air. It radiated out, like a shock wave. The roar of fury that emanated from him rattled her down to her core and would have knocked her over had Allistair not held on to her so tightly. He was as solid as Zachary. He could withstand what was thrown at them, and so she clung to him.

The force of what Zachary had unleashed passed through them, and the building seemed to shake beneath and around her while Allistair held her close and steadied her through the onslaught. Huddling into his arms, Katharine waited for cracks to form and the building to start to give way underneath them. Surely it couldn't hold up against that kind of force. But she took two more breaths before she believed that they were still there and not buried under piles of rubble from the shaking.

Then Zachary stopped and stood still again, his anger a presence in the room, but no longer active. He seethed while she started to breathe just a little again.

Though her arms and face still stung just a bit, when she looked, the cuts had faded. With a tentative smile, Allistair rubbed his fingers over the blood there, smearing his fingers but revealing the healed skin underneath. "You'll be okay now."

With one last venomous look on his too-attractive face, Zachary turned to Allistair. His voice was somehow serene as he spoke just two words. "You'll pay."

Allistair set her aside like a doll he had been holding. Nodding at his enemy, he accepted what had been said. "I know."

Then Zachary was gone.

He didn't sink into the floor. There was no crackle of electricity, no change in the air, just a moment of nothing in the place where he had stood. Only a pile of soot on the floor gave evidence that he had been there.

Katharine sank back into Allistair's arms, letting herself feel completely safe for the first time since the whole thing had started. As though she belonged there, even if she didn't really know what he was, his arms curled around her, holding her tight against him. And for a few breaths and a handful of heartbeats she didn't worry.

Then, just as she leaned all the way into him, fear wound around her heart. She had ended it, but she hadn't . . .

Her eyes snapped up to his. "What about you?"

Allistair shook his head. "I'll be fine."

"But I thought I had to choose you. For you to win."

"Don't worry." As he took her hands, the look on his face changed from one of contentment to one of acceptance. "You have what you need. You've seen what you are capable of."

She cringed. He had shown her that: all the devastation, all the things she'd had a hand in funding, the evils that she hadn't caused, but had helped along their way.

Though she hurt over the thought of the consequences she would have to deal with, he simply smiled at her. "No Katharine. All that you have caused is done and cannot be undone. Even Zachary and I cannot undo what is. And it was never my intention to make you feel guilty, just to make you see."

She understood. Finally. "The TV, the night it was stuck . . ."

He nodded. "The animals. Just to wake you up. Make you look, make you see."

"But what I've done—"

"Is done. You need now only look to what you are capable of. Think of all that you can do if you pay attention. Think of what you can do if you aim that focus the right way. The way you intend."

Her heart tightened with shame at what she had been doing, at all that she'd unknowingly caused, but at the same time her burden lightened, and for the first time in her life she simultaneously felt both free and strong. He was right. She could do so much . . .

Allistair's eyes flicked to the side, suddenly wary. His body tensed as he went on alert from something she didn't sense. Katharine knew enough for his reaction to frighten her, and her muscles tightened to brace for what Allistair sensed. She didn't get a chance to ask him about it, though.

As she opened her mouth, she began to hear the sound at the base of her brain—a wail from another world.

He stepped back, away from her, looking both afraid and resigned.

"Allistair!" She dove forward, reaching out for him, hoping to grab him and hold onto him in some way, but his hand came up, warning her off.

Something in his eyes made her stop, even though she wanted nothing more than to throw herself at him. So she stood, helpless, as he changed.

He didn't want it. She could tell.

He seemed to know she was more comfortable with his human form. And he fought the metamorphosis, struggled to fend off what was happening against his will. But it was clearly a losing battle.

This, then, was what he really was.

And, though she watched the change and in her head knew it was Allistair in there, it scared the crap out of her. She was riveted to the spot, unable to move forward, to offer any help, even while she knew her help was of no consequence in his world. Although she knew that this was what he really was, that she had been seeing a façade, she still didn't want to see the real him. But her eyes wouldn't close and she couldn't make herself look away.

His skin lost the texture of human cells, changing on the surface while his basic shape morphed as well.

"Katharine." He beseeched her in a voice that altered and deepened even as he spoke the single word. He said it again, this time a pleading sound wound through her name, as if he begged her to look away.

But she couldn't. Wouldn't. He had faced Zachary's wrath for her. She could look him in the eyes, whatever he turned out to be.

Slick and shiny, his skin turned to something more like mercury than anything else she could compare it to. His muscles moved and flowed under his skin with an unearthly grace. The claws that grew from his fingers didn't frighten her as much as they once had, and not as much as the fact that he was changing.

He was so tall her head tipped back to look up at him.

His wide, deep, black eyes revealed eternity—all that he had seen and all that he had been.

His origins were there—endless fields full of food, an embrace of the cycle and rhythms of nature, deep seas in constant motion, and something far beyond all of it. Peace.

Though it was there in his eyes, their blackness revealed sadness, too, and Katharine began to wonder what it was.

"*Me paenitet. Me paenitet et te amo.*"

His mouth moved with the sounds, but the voice came from far away. "Allistair?"

He shook his head. "*Cavē.*"

His English was gone with his human form, it seemed. The fear that had wrapped around her heart squeezed tighter, cutting off her air.

Her hands reached out but got no closer to him. "Allistair?"

But this time he didn't respond.

The wailing she had heard before grew louder and he looked around, up, back over his shoulder, beyond where she stood.

At last he looked at her. Towering over where she stood watching, helpless.

"*Eras incolumis.*"

The voice was deep. Afraid. Resigned.

"Allistair!" She screamed it. But it was too late to worry about the consequences of her actions, and too late, period. She might have accomplished something had she done this just a moment ago. If she had touched him when he was changing. If she had understood and not let his desire to keep her within her human comforts of his familiar form dictate her actions.

She ran across the few steps separating them and threw herself into his arms, not knowing what she would find, not knowing whether he would be solid, soft, cold, welcoming. But she knew that he was still

Allistair, and so she hurtled herself at him, knowing that whatever she found would be him.

But just before she would have touched his new skin, something yanked him backward with a speed she could not have foreseen.

He was ripped from the air with a blast of cold wind and a noise like fabric rending a thousand times over. She barely caught the expression on his face as the space around him crackled and glowed with electrons popping and altering in that glimmer of a second. Then he was gone.

She landed all alone on her own carpet in the space where he had stood a fraction of a moment before. Slivers of wispy silver ash floated down around her, the only thing left of his passing.

Katharine gasped in the now frigid air.

She fought against her own sobs, her shock the only thing holding them at bay. But her lungs expanded, and her body fought for life, for oxygen, even though she was left with nothing. Where had he gone? What had happened?

The wailing had stopped, leaving the air with a stillness more unearthly than anything she had seen or felt so far.

But Allistair had looked resigned to something right before he was pulled away.

She wanted to cry, but was still too stunned to do even that.

Eventually, she looked up at the clock and watched as the second hand swept around again, still not cueing the tick of the minutes. The whitish pieces of ash drifted slowly down around her.

She was beginning to gather pieces of thoughts into something mildly coherent when she heard the footsteps and saw the sizzle of the air in front of her. Small currents arced as something started to push through the space in front of her, and Katharine's heart and hope leapt into her throat as she watched.

The smell and a surge of desolation washed over her as surely as a wave when Zachary pushed through the rip he had created. He waited while she looked him up and down, his human self just as she had always seen it. His beauty was colder and farther away than it had seemed before, obvious to her now that it was nothing other than the shape of his eyes, the line of his nose, the curl of his mouth. He stood still under her unflattering assessment until he caught her eye, and then he laughed.

Fear traced through her heart, followed by weariness. What had he come back for? What could he do to her now?

Was he here to break the rules and take her now that Allistair was gone?

Somehow she found air, even though breathing meant she breathed in the feel of him, sick and rotted and crawling with the knowledge of what he was. In her knowledge, she found her voice. "You lost."

He nodded. But it didn't faze him. He kept walking toward her.

She spoke again, hoping to stop him. Knowing she wouldn't. "You both lost."

Again, he nodded.

Finally, he stopped of his own accord, his feet a few inches away from where she had fallen on the floor. He knelt down and put his blue, blue eyes level with hers.

Though he looked completely human, his voice was his own, a deep gravel of horrible thoughts rubbing against each other as he spoke. "I have lost time, but time is nothing. I have lost face, but I will get it back. I have lost status, but I'll climb up again."

He stopped.

She waited.

He blinked.

His eyes changed to the color of an oil slick, they swirled with things she'd rather not see, but this time it wasn't her choice; she was horribly unable to look away.

When his mouth opened this time, his teeth were longer, a thousand pointed razors that threatened her just by their very existence. "I have lost. But he is dead."

"What?" His words froze her completely.

He curved his mouth into a gruesome imitation of a smile. "No matter what I am, I cannot lie. I could have given you the Kingdom. You could have helped us."

In that moment, she made the mistake of looking right at him. Somewhere in the depths of his eyes, of what he was, she saw that he was what had ripped Mary Wayne to pieces. But she didn't have time to worry over that.

He spoke again. "This was his last chance. He failed. If you had chosen him, you could have saved him, or at least bought him another chance, more time. Instead, you killed him."

"What?" Her breath sawed in and out of her. Regardless of the source, she felt the truth in what Zachary had said. It had been there in the wail all around Allistair those last minutes. It was in the forced change, when he would have rather stayed human. In the way he had been ripped from her, from here.

He was gone.

Her eyes betrayed her in front of Zachary. Pain pushed at the back of them, pulled at the edges of her jaw and the back of her throat. It shot through the core of her in cold sharp spikes. Emptiness set into her bones, a hard frigid weight that kept her pinned where she sat.

Zachary's smile nearly finished her as he said the words again. "You killed him."

With that final stroke, he stood.

As she watched, he stepped back and again disappeared beyond the air. Only this time she watched as it happened. She was looking directly at him as he passed through, and for a moment she saw through the veil. She saw the black beast, the oily skin, the power and the teeth and the claws and the intent.

And then he was gone.

The air settled around her as she sat, unmoving, in the middle of the silver ash that was the only evidence that Allistair had been there. That he had saved her.

Her eyes went wide, glazed over with the pain that shot through her, continuing to get worse each moment even though she was certain she could not bear it. The room became a photo before her, flat and unmoving, something to look at, but of no consequence. She watched it, waiting to for the pain to cause something physical to happen to her.

The minute hand moved on the clock with an audible tick.

CHAPTER 27

Katharine was still sitting on the floor in shock when Margot found her.

Her friend was breathing quickly as she came through the door, her words coming out in breathy gasps. "Thank God you're okay! Your building looks good. I didn't see any cracks, but I was rushing up here to get to you."

Katharine looked up, confused, but couldn't move from her spot on the floor.

According to the clock it had been about three hours since Allistair had disappeared and Zachary had left. The air in her home had a different quality than it had had for the past few weeks. She breathed in a mechanical fashion, not really wanting to go on, but her biology made it inevitable.

"Katharine?" Margot got down on the floor on her hands and knees, waving her open hand in front of Katharine's thousand-yard stare. "Are you okay? Did you feel the earthquake? Katharine?"

Margot must have realized that something had happened. She just sat down next to her and hugged her friend.

Sometime later, though her pain had made it impossible to tell time, Katharine found her voice. "I chose."

She could feel the change in tension in Margot's arms, but was grateful that she didn't waver.

Margot's voice was monotone, but that didn't disguise the fear in it. "Who did you choose? Are you okay?"

"Me. Allistair told me that I didn't have to choose one of them. That I could just choose to be me. To live my own life. I'll deal with my own consequences and belong only to me."

"Good for him." Margot's breath whooshed out of her as she seemed to realize that maybe it was over.

Margot's presence and the small conversation forced Katherine into herself, and she began seeping back into reality. "You knew it was him, didn't you? You figured it out?"

Margot nodded. "I found a reference that said when they come in, they darken as they change levels, as they move through earth, toward the demons. They lighten as they go in the other direction."

Yes, of course. After the fact, when it was far too late, it all made sense.

Margot kept talking, as though simply putting sound waves into the air would help anything. But maybe it did hold some of her sadness at bay for just a few more minutes. "So your angels will naturally incorporate darker. The further they have to come to get here, the darker their skin and hair and eyes will appear."

Zachary, with his beautiful light blue eyes and pale skin had come the other way to get here. He was from somewhere far below.

Katharine leaned her head against Margot's shoulder. She was so tired that all she could do was breathe and listen.

Margot's hands stroked her hair, like she was a child. "I was coming here to tell you that when the earthquake hit."

"There was an earthquake?" Her own voice coming out was still a shock. How could she sit here and speak relatively calmly with her friend after what had just happened?

With a glance up at the clock, Margot answered. "Three hours ago. It was big. I'm surprised you don't remember it. But then again, maybe I'm not surprised . . . There's a lot of damage."

Margot sucked in a breath before she continued. "It took me the entire three hours to get here. I was on my way when the quake hit. My car jumped over a whole lane. I was ready to make an exit and suddenly we were all slammed over about ten feet."

Katharine scrambled, turning to face her friend. "Are you okay?"

Margot nodded rapidly. "But it clogged the roads. Trees fell. There's debris everywhere. That's why it took so long to get here. And I couldn't call, the cell towers were all jammed, so I was listening to the radio. A lot of the buildings have some bad damage, but one completely collapsed. . ."

What wasn't Margot telling her?

Her friend looked at her, watching Katharine's face as she delivered the news. "According to the radio it was the Light & Geryon building."

Katharine felt her breath suck in as her lungs hollowed out. "How many . . . were there people inside?" Katharine grappled with her thoughts, trying to make sense of yet another incomprehensible thing on this horrid day.

Margot shook her head. "There were some inside. A lot got out. Apparently it took a few minutes for the foundation to give way after it had been cracked. The radio said they are waiting for better reports from there and from a few houses where trees fell, too. There's an apartment building that's in bad shape. They're checking the residents."

Her father.

Her thoughts were stilted and incomplete.

"The building?"

Again Margot shook her head. "They're saying it was built cheap. Not quite up to code." She shrugged and started to stand. But an aftershock shook them and she sat back down, waiting out the few seconds that seemed to stretch for minutes.

The two women sat side by side, silent, just being.

Finally, Margot asked, "What are the feathers?"

That, at least, earned a half smile. "They aren't feathers—they're ash." Katharine picked a piece up and watched as it disintegrated in her hand, and then her smile fell apart. "Something yanked Allistair out of here, and this is all that's left. Zachary came back just to laugh at me and tell me I had killed Allistair. I didn't choose him, so he didn't win. . . ." She barely held on. "He told me not to choose him."

It was then that she cracked in half.

She fell into Margot's arms then and cried. Maybe for hours, she didn't know. Her body shook with her sobs, sometimes making her wonder if aftershocks were shaking the building or if it was just her grief. It wasn't important enough to ask.

CHAPTER 28

Somehow, three days later, Katharine was still alive.

No one had been able to find her father. He hadn't answered his cell phone when she frantically called. No one had seen him since the earthquake; all anyone had been able to locate was the GPS on his car, and it was sending signals from the bottom of the rubble—right in the garage.

If his car was in the garage, he had most likely been in his office. He practically lived there since her mother had died. It seemed likely that he had died there, too.

Katharine resigned herself to the fact that he was gone.

Margot had taken a handful of days off work, not unusual in the aftermath of a large earthquake. She spent some time helping to reshelve all the books, but her main job was to oversee the damages and file the insurance claims. She could do those things mostly from home, so she spent a good portion of her time helping Katharine try to find out anything more definitive about her father. Margot's own family was far enough away to not be in any kind of danger. Liam was safe, but had gotten himself on a volunteer cleanup crew, which kept him pretty busy. And Margot had other friends she'd checked on.

Katharine had too. Though she might not have called them friends, there were a surprising number of people to call, to ask if they would call her if by chance they saw her father—and to let them know that she was reasonably certain he had fallen with the building.

It was on the third day, as she and Margot pulled up to look again at the rubble, that a worker came forward to talk to them. From the look on his face, whatever he had to say couldn't be good. Katharine squeezed Margot's hand while she heard the news.

Her father's body had been pulled from the ruins. The only consolation in his death was that it had likely been quick, from a blow to the head.

And now she had something to bury.

Standing there, looking over the spot where the building had once stood, she could see beyond it and out to the ocean. The marina waters lapped in, coming up on the rocky edges of the land, meeting up with slips packed tight with boats both small and large. The sea was beyond the man-made barriers that bordered the marina, and it pushed and pulled out there. Inside, in the calmer, protected waters, they didn't see or feel it that much.

The space left by Light & Geryon suddenly revealed all that it had kept hidden by its sheer size. Katharine wondered what else her father's firm had tucked away from view all those years.

Blue sky and open water that was the same shade of mixed green, blue, and gray as her eyes beckoned to her. This was where something in her had come from so long ago, according to Allistair's theories.

Though she was still cold and numb from all that had happened—she hadn't felt anything since the freezing, blinding fear of Allistair and Zachary standing in front of her—she suddenly knew what she had to do.

Margot still held her hand tight in support as Katharine took her first real deep breath in days, as she thought for the first time of something beyond the demands of simply surviving the present. As Katharine began to plan, she smiled at how fitting it was that her friend was right beside her. But she didn't say anything, just stood and watched the sea.

. . .

Hollow to her core, Katharine went through with the funeral for her father, with Toran Light at her side the whole time.

Uncle Toran hadn't been at the building the day of the earthquake, but his world had been shaken anyway. He seemed not to know what to do without her father there—not with the business and certainly not with himself.

Katharine waited politely until the last guest, and even Margot, had cleared out after the reception before she sat him down and began talking. "Are you planning to reopen Light & Geryon?"

He simply looked at her, and from the way he did it, she knew he had already planned out what to say. And somehow it still surprised her.

"Only if you are the 'Geryon' part."

She hated to break his heart, but she did it anyway. With a deep gulp of air, she took the plunge. "I can't."

He'd always been alternately grandfatherly and corporate. It was part of his charm, and how he'd accomplished most of what he had in his life. Now he seemed genuinely perplexed by her response. "But it's what you know. It's what your father would have wanted."

She leaned back on the soft white leather couch. The very expensive couch. "Uncle Toran, I loved my father. But I am no longer doing what he wanted me to. I was finally becoming my own person, just before all this happened. I can't change that because of this tragedy."

"Yes, I remember you quit." He, too, leaned back, and if he'd had a cigar, she was sure he would have rolled it between his fingers. "I thought you were just mad at your father. Maybe just being rebellious."

Yes, he would think it was like that. He would believe that her leaving was her own flaw, obviously. It had to be a barb at her father; it couldn't possibly be a rational, well-thought-out decision. Not if it didn't agree with the two old men. And so this was where it got dicey.

"Did you know what we invested in, Uncle Toran?"

"Of course," he blustered. "Everything went through your father and me for approval."

"Then you knew about the diamond mines that were putting out families with no food and nowhere to go. They were working kids, and in unsafe conditions, too. Did you know we dumped a ton of money into cheap firing pins for guns? They tended to explode in the hands of the person holding the gun. We supported a paper mill that was poisoning the water and giving people cancers in three nearby towns. In each case, we made a ton of money."

His face was red before she'd even finished talking. "What are you talking about?"

"I'm talking about what Light & Geryon really did. What we funded, the things we made happen."

As though a magic wand had been waved, his features suddenly smoothed over and his tone became condescending. "You're mistaken, honey. That didn't happen."

"It did. I have evidence. And it's why I won't work for Light & Geryon again."

She waited. Wanted to see what he would do. What offer he would put on the table. From what he'd said earlier, her refusal meant he was out of business too.

"I just don't see any of that happening. If it did, I certainly didn't know about it and neither did your father." His hand ran down the front placket of his shirt in an absentminded gesture. All of it—the tone, the movements, the smooth assurance—said that if he hadn't known about it, then it had nothing to do with him or his company. It couldn't possibly be his responsibility.

She wanted to tell him more if not all of it. She wanted to say that her father *had* known, that she'd been there, had told him, and had been summarily dismissed. And when she thought about it a little more, she wasn't sure how much she really trusted Uncle Toran. Not that he would lie to her—she didn't think he would do that, didn't think he could look her in the eye and outright tell her something he believed to be untrue. But it was the belief part that got her these days.

He would never be able to look at the house he lived in and see that it had been built on the backs of the children in the mines and paid for by the families who had lost loved ones in firing pin accidents and to cancers from the contaminated water near the mill. And even if she pressed the issue, produced evidence, he wouldn't believe it.

He was closed. And he was comfortable that way. Unlike her father, he still had his wife and his life. When he surveyed his holdings, all of it was as he wanted it to be. And because of that, she would have to disconnect herself from his work as well as from Light & Geryon.

When she'd come here, she'd harbored small hopes that he would be outraged by the things Light & Geryon had helped happen in the name of money—but he wasn't. He was sad about losing his friend and his business. He didn't have the drive to do anything more than ask her to help him rebuild. But she couldn't do that. She couldn't make Light & Geryon into what it once was. She wouldn't make a success out of little maneuvers that, in and of themselves, weren't bad, but that had disastrous consequences. She couldn't disengage herself from the end result like he did. She didn't even want the name resurrected. Didn't want anyone to think they would get the same thing they had previously gotten at Light & Geryon.

She was trying to figure out what to say to Uncle Toran. She wanted to tell him the truth about her father. But he would find it disrespectful. Her father was dead. He wasn't causing damage now. Not that he'd caused it in the past; he'd simply done what so many do, which was to let things slide past him and be unconcerned by what he allowed. And his company was defunct. So that was at an end, too.

But even though she wanted Uncle Toran to know the truth, she wasn't sure what it would accomplish now. By the same token, she found she wasn't able to say anything about the company or its work that wasn't true. She couldn't tell the white lie and let him believe that she believed it was all okay.

She was trying to figure out how to say what she needed to when he started the conversation she had been waiting for.

"What do you plan to do now that you're out of investing?"

Katharine sucked in a breath. Here she went. "I'm not out of investing. I'm opening my own firm."

He leaned sharply forward at that. "What? You won't work with Light & Geryon, but you're going to go into direct competition with us?"

"Uncle Toran, Light & Geryon doesn't exist right now, unless you reopen it. There's no building and we have no idea where half the employees are."

"The money is still there. It's still invested." He clasped his hands together and leaned back again, smug. It seemed it was always about the money.

"But without the people to manage it, what could you do?"

He deflated. "I'm not sure I have it in me to rebuild by myself. I find it entirely distasteful, though, that you seem bent on going into direct competition with your father's firm."

"It's not direct competition. It's quite different." She shook off the idea that he would call her actions "distasteful" after all that *he* had done as part of the firm for all those years. Then she leaned forward, wanting and needing him to tell her that she was right, that she was doing something solid and good. She knew she likely wouldn't hear that praise, even if it was just about striking out on her own. She told him anyway. "We'll vet our investments through all stages, and only invest in things that improve the quality of life somewhere."

He waited but didn't say anything, didn't offer the pat on the back that she still wanted even if she didn't expect it..

"I don't see how we could possibly be considered 'in competition.' We'll be getting a different kind of return on the investment. We won't likely generate the same kind of monetary returns that Light & Geryon was getting."

"Then what's the point?"

And that was exactly the point. Sadly, he didn't see it at all. What she wanted was so far outside of the scope of what he could imagine, what he believed, that he couldn't even comprehend it. Moreover, he thought she was crazy or stupid—or worse.

But she knew.

She let the conversation turn to other, trivial matters and later, when she was ready to leave, hugged him, and told him to be well. Asked him to keep her up to date on what happened with Light & Geryon. It seemed he agreed to that only because legally, she was heir to her father's half of the company. He remained deeply disappointed by what he saw as her defection from the family business, but Katharine stood her ground.

Though he only made halfhearted statements about attempting to reopen Light & Geryon, Katharine remained greatly concerned about that. She couldn't be party to it continuing on the way it had. But she steeled herself to wait for his decision, and she breathed a sigh of relief a week later when she picked up the phone to hear him say he had decided to dismantle the company.

It was a good thing she'd been in her condo and by herself, or he would have seen her trip over her own furniture when he told her that her share of the sale of the investments would probably be in the tens of millions.

Katharine sat on the floor open-mouthed for about an hour after that.

And slowly, while she sat there, unmoving, she realized how she could use that money to do what she had been planning. She thought and figured and counted in her head. Then, several hours later, she dashed down to her car.

. . .

"Margot!" Katharine nearly ran up to the reference desk at the newly re-shelved and reopened Santa Monica Library.

Her heart was beating faster and her eyes were wet. She'd opened the windows on her car and let the air blow in as she'd raced over as fast as traffic would let her.

She was excited.

The world was opening up. And despite the deep ache she was beginning to think she would always carry, she wanted something.

"Katharine." Margot looked at her askance, then went back to helping the man at the desk who was puzzled and in need of help with some huge book.

When Margot finally turned back to her, Katharine was breathless. Patience was not her strong suit today.

"Margot. I need you." She felt it in her cheeks and her eyes and it wove throughout her limbs. "Come with me. Let me explain. . . . Um, take lunch or a mental health break. Please?"

With a stray nod, Margot got someone over to cover the desk and took her lunch hour.

Katharine managed to hold her excitement in until they were sitting on the beach in the patch of clean sand she had come to think of as their spot. The wind and water were calm today, as though they too were waiting to hear what she would say.

"My Uncle Toran is dismantling Light & Geryon. Do you know what the company was worth?"

Margot shook her head and then dropped her mouth open as Katharine told her. But Katharine didn't stop. "Half of that is mine. In my bank account, inside of a month after all the legalities get taken care of."

"Wow. What are you going to do?"

"Well, I had decided that I had enough money to start a very small fund of my own. I would get others to invest with me. A little here, a little there, until we were big enough to go public."

"You want to go back to that kind of investing?"

Her hands flew, trying to fill things in faster than she could talk. "That's just it. I *know* investing. I know it head to tail. I want to invest in things that need it. Green companies, small business funds in underdeveloped countries, sound mining practices. Who knows? The return will be smaller in number of dollars, but bigger in other ways."

Margot nodded. "That makes more sense."

"But with this infusion, I can start a corporation now. I have enough to do more than just invest my own trust money. I can hire a few people, start a real fund right off. It still won't be huge, but it's enough to go public."

Margot broke out in a huge smile and threw her arms around Katharine. "I'm so happy for you. This is great news—"

"No," Katharine pushed back. "Maybe you can be happy for *us*. I need a researcher. Someone I trust, someone who can find anything—follow the business trails through to the products and the ramifications. I know where to find people who can count the money, but I need you to make this work right."

Margot stilled as the idea hit her.

"Don't say anything yet." Katharine held up her hand. "I don't want you to be an employee. I want you to be my business partner. I'll invest the money, but the business will belong to both of us. You probably need to think about it."

"Wait. What?" Margot's eyes glazed over.

Katharine waited a few moments. Though she just wanted her friend to say yes, she knew better. But it didn't last long. "I don't want you to be my employee. You're my friend. And honestly I'm scared of running the whole thing by myself. I know how to run this whole business. But I need another logical brain to help out. Fresh eyes. Good ideas. I don't think I should be the sole decision-maker. I don't know that any one person should be."

She watched as Margot started to think. And sure enough, about five seconds later, well-thought-out questions began coming one after the other.

"Are you sure you can put only your money into this and have me as a partner? Maybe I should just have a small percent. Even that would be huge for me."

Katharine smiled. Margot was working out details. That probably meant she'd eventually agree.

"Yes, I'm sure. And no, you're in fifty-fifty. Not even forty-nine–fifty-one."

"I don't have any money of my own to invest. It doesn't seem right."

For a moment, Katharine was somber. "I don't really have the money either. I know how Light & Geryon earned that money. I thought long and hard about just giving it all to the United Way or the Red Cross or something like that. I don't want it. Even the money in my account is the same thing. It's not quite blood money, but it's close. I can't keep it for me. I wouldn't feel right living off it. But I do like the idea that it could do something good. Something important starts with it. Something that you'll help me make into something bigger than the damage that started it."

"Holy crap." Margot sighed, and Katharine laughed. "When do we start?"

"When can you quit the library?"

"I need to give two weeks' notice. It will take me that long to train someone up and get the new person oriented." This time her sigh was smaller. "I love that library."

"I know. And I'm really grateful."

This time Margot looked at her dead-on. "You don't know me well enough to give me half of your multimillion-dollar corporation."

"It's just money. And, yes, I do."

For maybe the first time ever, she reached out to hug someone for no other purpose. It wasn't a quick pat on the back or a loose-armed, go-to-bed-now social expectation. It wasn't romantic or sexual or leading to anything else. And she didn't even once think that it would be rejected.

She simply draped her arm around Margot's shoulders and pulled her friend close. Margot hugged her back, and they sat there, heads touching as though they might be transferring thoughts, staring out at the calm waves rolling up, and grinning like loons.

The soft sounds of the ocean were periodically punctuated by Margot saying, "Holy crap."

. . .

It took Katharine two weeks to sell her condo. She hadn't yet started the company.

But she had already filed the initial paperwork, and she kept a running tally of her thoughts for what she believed the company should do. Where they should start. What they needed to avoid.

She'd asked Margot to write down her ideas too. Three days after Margot had come in from her lunch break and handed in her resignation, they had sat down to compare notes. Liam had been hanging around and had laughed that Katharine came in with a laptop and spreadsheets, while Margot appeared with a yellow legal pad and a handwritten but truly elegant mission statement.

Katharine shrugged at him. "It's why she's my partner. A mission statement hadn't even occurred to me. And mine would have had bad grammar anyway."

They created homework assignments, Margot found an artist to design the logo for Green Sea Investments, and Katharine found a web designer.

She worked harder than she ever had before. Uncle Toran had called several times to let her know how disappointed he was that she was starting her own company instead of reopening her father's. He also saw fit to let her know that her father would be disappointed in her too.

She tried to let it go, but the barbs burrowed deep and stuck. And they hurt. But they didn't change her course. Nothing was strong enough to get her to change her course.

She got other calls asking her to vacate the condo so the agent could show it. After one such visit where she'd been too engrossed in her spreadsheets to remember to leave, she decided to stay for all the walkthroughs.

She didn't like the people that had come to see the place. And she realized after sitting through several more walkthroughs that those were the only kind of people her unit seemed to attract. After one particularly snotty couple came by and complained about everything from the color of the walls (too garish a beige) to the quality of the bathroom tiles (clearly not handmade), Katharine cornered the agent. "How do we get nice, decent people to come look at it?"

"Is that what you want? I was wondering why you kept turning down good offers." The agent had offered a soothing hand on Katharine's arm. "You know, you won't live here after you sell. You don't have to like these people. You won't know them."

"But I want to like them. What do I have to do to get someone good in here?"

The agent practically snorted. "Drop the price by about two hundred grand!"

The woman had looked at her, horrified, when Katharine said, "Okay, do it."

It had taken three days and the promise of a commission on the original asking price before the new listing went into effect. Katharine saw four young couples, a single lawyer, a junior businessman, and an older couple in the space of the next four days.

She sold the unit to a family who came through with a little boy. He wanted a dog, and the mother said they didn't have enough to redo the carpet. She had noticed the incredibly faint soot stains that had never quite come out. The blood had entirely disappeared, but the gray stayed, just a bit.

They offered twenty thousand less than the asking price and Katharine took it. She then left them an envelope with a check for another twenty thousand to get a puppy and paint or retile or whatever. Writing that check had felt better than most anything she'd ever done.

So she took the money from the unit and gave it to Margot—who promptly told her to stuff it. Then she tried to say it in a nicer way. She ended with "I'll buy my own house, thank you."

Well, she'd overstepped. Luckily, Margot didn't hold it against her.

Katharine had already bought herself one of the little houses on the walks up from the beach. It was small and homey and had the smell of sea air in every room. Though it was in Santa Monica rather than Venice, it reminded her of Allistair's house. Well, it reminded her of the house where he'd taken her while he'd been here.

She painted her walls in bright colors, gave her old furniture to Goodwill, and bought new pieces. When she looked at her new living room set and realized it looked amazing but was too uncomfortable to sit in, she discovered she hadn't been paying enough attention.

Instead, she put a mattress on the floor in her bedroom, telling herself she'd wait to find just the right things. Most people took time to acquire their homes. She should too.

She spent her first night in the new place sitting on her hard sofa and wondering if she could keep up this pace indefinitely, if she could stay one step ahead of the heartbreak that dogged her heels even as she ran from it.

And she knew she couldn't.

Why had she even thought she could?

She'd been too slow all along. Too slow to see. Too slow to choose.

And her inability to see what was in front of her had killed someone who had twice told her, "I'm sorry, but I love you." Who told her to choose herself, even though it would mean the end of him and all that he was. Someone whose last words to her Margot had translated as "You're safe now."

CHAPTER 29

Katharine sat back, a wide smile on her face and a silly hat on her head.

The world outside Margot's windows had gone dark for the night, but at this time of year that didn't mean it was late yet. The dark, barely held at bay by the thin panes of glass, was more than made up for by the birthday cake that sat in front of her, the top of it a little sloped and the writing close to illegible. She was pretty sure that Margot had written "Happy Birthday, Katharine." Or she had meant to. The loops hadn't fallen where they were intended to, and it looked more like "Haggy Bidhclay, Kathanne." However, to Margot's credit, and due to her considerable drive for proper grammar, there was both a comma and a period for Kathanne's Bidhclay.

Katharine just said thank you and left it to Liam to point out that cake decorating might not be Margot's strong suit. Everyone else at the little get-together had kept their mouths shut about the cake too. No one wanted to hurt Margot's feelings. For a few of them, Margot was their boss, and so the cake drew no comments other than that it tasted great and was colorful. Both statements were true.

Katharine had grinned at that. She was happy again. Mostly.

She had watched Margot and Liam together for several seasons now. Margot was happy too—only her happiness went all the way down.

Katharine tried not to be jealous of her friend, but some days that took more effort than others, and it didn't always work.

Margot and Liam would get married soon. They hadn't said anything, but it was there for everyone to see if they looked. It was in the casual affection that made it seem they'd been together much longer than they actually had. The simple way they communicated. The fact that they sometimes fought, and though Margot complained to Katharine about the fights themselves, she never once complained about Liam. Never called him an idiot or an ass or any of the other things she could have called him, given the disagreements. Katharine had no doubt that Liam afforded Margot the same respect. He loved her; it was as complicated and as simple as that.

She watched as the two of them met up in the kitchen and talked about something. She didn't know what, and she decided not to listen in. Instead she checked out the lopsided birthday cake.

It was probably the saddest-looking baked good she'd ever seen. And certainly the ugliest she'd ever been given. But it was by far the most beautiful, too. Margot had made it for her—for Katharine, who had been raised to believe that appearances were everything and perfection was important. That anything and everything should be made by a professional if possible, and that it could all be bought for a price.

She hadn't even had a cake in years. Grown-ups didn't have cakes. Her eighteenth birthday had been the last. That cake, like all the others, had been ordered from whatever bakery was *de rigueur* that year. Those birthday cakes had been tiered and themed and lavish, and looking back, they had been laughable in their pointlessness.

It didn't matter what this cake looked like, or even if it had tasted like cardboard. This year, someone had cared enough to do it themselves.

In addition to being presented with an imperfect cake, Katharine didn't think she'd ever worn a pointed grocery-store birthday hat either. But here she was, with Liam and Margot and a handful of others, all of whom had been in her life since the earthquake, and they were celebrating. These were her coworkers and a small handful of real friends. She didn't have many, not like when she and her mother had ruled the social scene, but these friends were real. One was even the daughter of one of her mother's friends, and she too had gotten out of the game her parents lived in. So much had changed since the earthquake.

And that was how she had thought of it—just as "the earthquake," because she couldn't withstand the pain that came when she thought of the other things that had happened that day.

In the end, only the Light & Geryon building had fallen; everything else in the city, even the things right around the building, had stayed upright. In fact, it had later been determined that the structure had collapsed not so much due to poor construction but because it had been at the exact epicenter of the quake. It seemed her father had built on a small fault line that no one had seen before, running right through Marina del Rey.

Katharine still wondered sometimes whether Zachary had caused it, whether in his anger he had done more than roar his fury and had actually destroyed something. She probably wouldn't ever know, and wasn't sure she wanted to.

It had been a long year, and she really had nothing by which to mark where she'd been at the beginning of it. She hadn't even celebrated her last birthday. But in that time things had changed so drastically.

She'd lost Light & Geryon, both the building that had stood as an icon in her life and the people who had made up the company. And she'd lost her father; she'd somehow thought he'd always be there as stalwart and unchanging as the brick. She was glad she had told him that she loved him.

There had been a handful of fights she'd had with Uncle Toran about her business this last year. And even more that she hadn't. She had bitten her tongue so many times knowing that telling him what she thought was a waste of her breath. But he started some of the arguments anyway. Each time he learned more about what she was doing, what she was trying to build, he told her in no uncertain terms how stupid an endeavor it was, and how it would never work. People wanted money. But she had stood her ground, sad that she had to fight so hard for it, and glad that it was hers to hold. And still, she had fought to push all the arguments and hurtful words aside and told him, as often as she could, that she loved him.

He had only offered a nod at that. But it was the best he had to give, and Katharine had come to accept it. He wasn't going to pick her up and swing her around and tell her he was proud of her. Aunt Lydia had stood by his side, clearly showing her support of her husband's opinion, but at least she'd stayed silent, neither berating Katharine nor lauding her. And later, Aunt Lydia had stood still and proud at Uncle Toran's funeral, then sold their stately home and moved back east with her sister. Katharine hadn't seen or heard from her since.

Her own beach house now had all the rooms painted. She had a better couch, soft and comfy and even a little worn-looking. Sunk into the corner of the soft pillows, she had a nightly habit of curling up and reading, and all too often falling asleep there.

Though she had found the perfect headboard and frame for her bed some time ago, she often didn't crawl into it until three or four in the morning, and she rarely slept the night through. She was plagued by nightmares, and it seemed for a brief time each night that things were worse than they ever had been during the waking horror she had lived.

She watched Allistair get pulled from the air over and over in her dreams. Each night she lost him again. Sometimes she was in his arms when he would be ripped away. Sometimes she smelled singed flesh and watched as he screamed. Sometimes she did.

In one version she plunged a long sharp knife into his chest while Zachary looked on and smiled. No therapist was required to figure out what that was all about.

After a while, Katharine had finally learned how to make her own friends, as evidenced by the small but true turnout to her first real birthday party. The first one she'd had where people were invited only because they liked her and wanted to celebrate the year. But even so, there was no boyfriend. No one she was even interested in.

Katharine had not yet figured out how to make that connection. And she wasn't sure she would figure it out either. Margot had held back and not pushed her, seeming to sense just how painful that would be.

But the year had brought other interesting changes. This house was Margot and Liam's. As of a month ago, they jointly held the mortgage. Green Sea was not making money hand over fist, nor were investors lining up and beating down the door. But each month brought a few more. Each advertisement or drive they did found a few more people with a few extra dollars who thought those dollars were worthless unless they did something good.

Green Sea had propped up a work-study college that had started to fail. The students and graduates had rallied, but so many were liberal arts majors and employed as social workers that the alumni alone had not been able to save the school that had saved them. Green Sea had done it. And a handful of the grads and professors had in turn joined the investment pool.

The company had poured money into an inventor who had developed a disaster setup that he planned to sell to every fire station, ambulance owner, and hospital around the country. Green Sea had gone all in, because his invention not only sped up triage setups and saved lives, but his business plan had provided for a free kit donated to an impoverished area in another country for every ten units sold. They were still putting money into production, but Katharine had hopes that when it went on the market in two months, they would see the predicted turnaround. And maybe even more investors. It was now a game of wait and see.

Some of the people at the party worked for her and Margot. Jeff had leaned over and wished her a happy birthday, regardless of what Margot's cake said, as he put it. Then they had all sung to her. It was the first time the song had been performed for her by amateurs rather than a hired band. Well, she thought the song was for her even though they had all warbled, "*Haaaappy Biiiirthday, Kaaathannnne.*"

Over her laughter and the last line of the song she thought she heard Margot protesting. "It says 'Katharine'! Katharine!"

The candles were lit in front of her, and they all cheered and cat-called, and a voice somewhere in the back shouted out, "Make a wish!"

For a moment, while the candles flickered in front of her, she thought about what to wish for.

She wanted to sleep at night.

She wanted to not feel guilty.

She wanted to not miss him, and not miss what she hadn't seen clearly enough until it was far too late.

She wanted . . .

So, just as Allistair had told her it would work, just as Margot had found that spells were often powered on a burst of human breath, Katharine closed her eyes, held tightly to her thoughts, and blew.

. . .

It hadn't worked.

The thought had passed through her mind as Katharine stood there in the coffee shop in the middle of fifteen people, all more alert than she was. It seemed she had that thought about once or twice a day.

She had never slept well after the earthquake, and the well-meant but apparently poorly executed birthday wish had done nothing to help. In fact, if she had to pinpoint a time when things had changed, it had been just after her birthday party when the dreams had escalated. Now, each night she saved Allistair. She chose him. She grabbed at him and pulled, knowing that he was about to be yanked out of her world and fighting to keep him with her. Each night, in her dreams, she did something that prevented the wailing that had ended with the end of his life.

But as soon as they shared a sigh of relief that he was safe, she would kill him. Sometimes by stabbing him, sometimes by burning him at the stake, or shooting him, and worst, by recanting and choosing Zachary.

She had never lied to herself about that—that she had been less than three seconds from choosing Zachary. She might be her own person, but her own person had spent the past year not sleeping well.

Hearing her name called out, she absently reached up to grab the coffee. She'd gone for the brewed stuff rather than the blended throughout the winter. This morning, the weather had changed. It was nearly eighty at 8:00 a.m. and hot coffee wasn't going to wake her up. This past week, the dreams had gotten even more persistent; so many times, even during a single night, she would see Zachary. He would come up to her, his beautiful face changing, his breath going fetid as he closed the distance. She never could really run or even back up in the dreams. She always cringed, with his sharp teeth threatening just inches from her cheek or mouth. He never said anything other than the same three words: *You killed him*. Most of the time, in the dream, he laughed.

Perhaps even harder to deal with were the dreams where she saved Allistair and the two of them stayed together. They lived a life as a couple. Normal. Buying a house. Making dinner. Playing with a child that she couldn't quite see clearly but knew was theirs. It all seemed so real. And because of that, when she woke up, she was devastated anew each time.

She tried to come fully awake and gather her thoughts. What was the worst was that they were just dreams. Zachary wasn't there. And neither was Allistair. She remembered when he had been. She knew the difference. And this was just her subconscious trying to tell her something. Unfortunately, if it wanted her to understand, then it would need to let her get some sleep so she could process things. Clearly, it had other plans.

So this past week she'd been having the coffee shop guys add an extra shot of espresso to her drinks.

In a little while, when the caffeine kicked in, she'd be happy to be at her job, glad to be controlling where all the money went. But right now it was a two-shot morning. So she wasn't really surprised when she reached up to grab the cup only to have someone else's fingers brush hers.

As she raised the cup to her lips, he spoke rapidly. "Um, that's my coffee."

"Huh?" Well, she hadn't slept in about a week really. Clearly, she wasn't going to be eloquent today. She turned the drink around and tried to study it without spilling it. The cup was the right size, the marker scrawled across the lid looked like what she had ordered.

She was turning it the other way to look for a name as he spoke again. "I'm Aaron."

She blinked and looked briefly at him, but only got the impression of clear green eyes and blond hair before she turned her attention back to the cup.

He was right that it wasn't her coffee, but . . . "You're E-R-I-N?"

This time she did look up and he grinned a little abashedly.

Her brain kicked in as she wanted to laugh and then realized she shouldn't. "I'm sorry. It *is* L.A., and I shouldn't judge."

When he laughed, she decided she could too. Maybe she hadn't made that big an ass out of herself. She could hope.

"No, I'm Aaron with the standard A." He reached up to the counter and turned the other nearly identical cup around. "And you are . . . Catherine?"

She shook her head. "Almost." She spelled out her name with a shrug.

"Hey, at least they got yours gender-appropriate." He switched the two cups, gently lifting his out of her hand.

As she looked at her fingers oddly, thinking that it had been really dumb of her to stand there and talk to him about his coffee while she continued to hold on to it, he carefully slipped her drink into the curve of her hand.

"Thank you, Katharine with a K. It was nice to meet you."

He nodded at her slightly, then went on his way.

Katharine made her way out of the coffee shop, sipping her drink through the purple straw and starting to come just a little more awake as the caffeine and the wind off the ocean both hit her brain at the same time. The Green Sea office was just down the street. Close enough to the water to smell it, but far enough away to save the rent money for more important things.

She had two new employees coming in today, and grabbing someone else's coffee from the counter wasn't a good indicator of how she would fare in educating the newbies. But she was happy they had two new people. They needed them. Things had been slowly picking up speed since that emergency services device had hit the market. The current investors were seeing real profit in addition to the good feelings promised when they signed up with her firm. And the profits were bringing the investors' friends on board, too.

They'd learned early on that Katharine's connections into moneyed families had meant relatively little. Aside from the occasional relative here or there, old wealth didn't have much concern about the air or the seas or even other people. And those occasional rebellious cousins usually wound up getting themselves disowned. No investment money there. No, they'd had to start from scratch.

And just under a year into it, they were beginning to break even. They worked day and night sometimes. Too many times Margot had been the bearer of bad news—namely, that a really good investment was involved in something they didn't put money into. A new incubator for underdeveloped preemies was getting marketed at such a high cost that it was bankrupting the parents of the babies who needed it and lining the pockets of the manufacturer.

And that had just been the last disappointment in a long line. It was rare to find something worth her money. Something that would make the world better. So when they found those things, the whole office celebrated. And on the other days, they worked to find the investors who wanted to put their money into those things.

Margot grabbed her and started talking as soon as Katharine came through the door.

That was something else she had learned this past year. She'd never really been a morning person before. She'd just done the morning thing like everyone else in her office. But Margot was the real deal. She was up and around by six, seven at the absolute latest, and cheery-eyed to boot.

This morning, she was waving a stack of papers and no doubt knowing that the diamond on her left hand was glittering as she moved it. Liam had gotten her a princess-cut solitaire. And Katharine guessed that he had liked it because it was square. She didn't doubt that the one sitting with military precision on Margot's ring finger was perfectly even. And she knew it had come from upstate New York, not Africa or Australia. Someone had gotten a decent wage, plus hazard pay and benefits, to get that thing out of the ground.

Margot's voice twinkled like her shiny rock. "Guess what I have?"

"A much better morning disposition than me?" Katharine wrinkled her nose and looked at her friend. The world still looked a little blurry.

"That, and a company that does eco-friendly oil spill clean up."

"You followed them all the way through?" They had to know what the ramifications were, had to be sure of exactly what they were putting their customers' and their own investments into.

"I wouldn't be this happy if I hadn't."

That was debatable. Katharine thought her friend always seemed overly chipper in the mornings. Of course, Margot not only slept at night, she slept beside Liam. But Katharine's thoughts didn't get much further than that before Margot was speaking again.

"They are not only clean, they are green. As in give-back green."

"That's fantastic." She spontaneously hugged her friend and was instantly glad that her coffee had a lid. Then she made her way into her office where her two newest recruits were waiting.

Today, exactly one year after the earthquake, her world was very different than it had been.

. . .

That was her routine.

Sleep poorly, drink espresso shots mixed into something to dull the taste, and work her days away.

She was waiting on her standard morning drink a few days later when she saw the cup go up on the counter and a hand reach over her shoulder to get it.

She looked at the cup, then up at the guy behind her. "Hey, they spelled your name right." She smiled.

He grabbed a second cup and handed it down to her. Apparently, hers had been sitting there and she hadn't seen it come up or hadn't heard her name called. Well, that's why she was back up to two shots today. Well, that and the crying jag that had hit her at 4:00 a.m.

His voice cut through her attempt to not feel sorry for herself again.

"Sadly, they did not get yours right. You could tell them 'Katharine with a K.'"

She shook her head but didn't look up. The not-feeling-sorry-for-herself wasn't working. For the last week the dream had been different. In it, she was lying in bed, and the doorbell would ring. When she answered, it would be Allistair. Waking up from that one was painful in the worst way. And she couldn't seem to get to sleep again. Katharine pulled her thoughts back to the conversation in front of her. "What's the point? They'd get the K but give me an E in the middle."

She shrugged at the same time the tears started flowing. She shouldn't miss him this much still, should she? But somehow she did.

"Oh." Aaron looked down at her, not seeming to know what to do. "It's not that bad. The coffee's good even if they never spell your name right."

This time when she looked up, she made real eye contact with him.

She'd seen him only enough last time to recognize him again today. But now she saw that he was tall, a bit older than she was. She probably wouldn't have called him handsome; in fact, he looked a little battered, like he'd lived more than maybe he'd ought to.

"I'm not crying about the coffee." She sniffed, embarrassed at the tears that were somehow escaping and running down her face. "I had a really great dream last night."

His eyes narrowed at her. "Okay, this I have to hear. Come outside."

His expression was compassionate as he turned and grabbed her by the hand not holding the coffee. He was pulling her through the crowd, so he didn't see her eyes widen at the jolt she had felt when he touched her.

Her brain snapped itself alert and her own eyes widened, though she had no idea what had caused the current she'd felt.

The crowd barely moved to let them pass, and with each step they took she tried to look at him. Really look at him, through him.

It only took a moment to assess that he wasn't otherworldly. He was human. The jolt hadn't been strong enough for him to be more than just what he appeared to be. He didn't have the beauty that the others had come in with. It just didn't fit. His body had been born and had grown this way; it wasn't knit by a power beyond her.

But that jolt.

She'd never felt it from another person before.

And while she was trying to figure out what he was, he had seated her at an outside table and had taken the chair facing her. "You're looking at me weird."

"Sorry." Tears were still absently rolling down her cheeks, though she suspected it was mostly from exhaustion now.

Leaning a little forward, he looked right into her eyes. "Do you recognize me?"

With that, the spell was broken. She immediately jerked back and felt her face flush. She was acting like an idiot. It was L.A., she'd seen a handful of people on the street that she thought she knew, only to realize later that she'd seen them on some TV show or in a movie. She was really glad she didn't make a practice out of walking up to people and saying, "I think I know you from somewhere."

So she scanned Aaron's face, trying to put it and the name together. But that didn't work. She concentrated on just his face, knowing that he may have told the guy behind the counter his name was Aaron rather than having someone call out something akin to "Brad Pitt!" when the coffee came up. After a moment she gave up. "No, I don't recognize you. Should I?"

He shook his head even as she asked him, "Are you an actor?"

"No."

"Then why would you ask me that? Do you recognize me?" Now she was just puzzled.

He sighed. "No, I don't, but it's a long story. And this is your turn. How did a really great dream make you cry? Oh, unless it's a sex dream; then I don't need to hear about it."

At last she laughed. "Unfortunately, no. It wasn't a really great sex dream. I wish." She looked far away, at the sky and the clouds tripping past in the wind. She didn't know why she told him, but she did. "I dreamed about an old friend. I dreamed he was here . . . He died. And I'm partly responsible."

"Oh." But he didn't look away. Somehow he didn't get uncomfortable and didn't make her uncomfortable; he just exuded sympathy. "That's a lot to carry around."

She nodded, realizing for the first time that he was right. As much as she wanted to, she couldn't change it. She was changing what she could, everything she could, in every way she could. But she couldn't change that, couldn't fix it. And she was struggling under the weight of it. "I was so happy, until I woke up and realized it was all just a dream. And that he was still gone. Then I cried for a while, and I haven't gotten enough sleep, so that doesn't help much, does it? And that's probably more than you bargained for."

He grinned. "Actually, I'd say you bargain for quite a bit more than that when you ask a beautiful woman why she's crying in the coffee shop."

CHAPTER 30

She didn't tell Aaron much about Allistair. What could she say, really? Somehow, she had managed to avoid getting locked up through the whole ordeal. She wasn't about to give a near stranger enough ammunition to have her involuntarily committed now.

Still, she told what she could. That her ignorance and bad decisions had led directly to this man's death. It wasn't the usual get-to-know-you conversation. But she wasn't surprised when he turned up next to her at the coffee shop the following day.

At least this time she wasn't crying. The same dream had woken her up again the night before, and she told him so. She also told him that she had somehow managed to get back to sleep after it. A first for her.

Aaron tapped his plastic coffee cup to hers in a mock toast and congratulated her on the extra three hours of sleep.

They sat there at the metal mesh table, and he waited a beat before he asked her last name and told her his. He was Aaron Brown, and though the name was common enough that she thought she should have recognized it, he was still mildly disappointed that she didn't.

This time she made him explain.

He confessed to being a cocaine and heroin addict, as well as an alcoholic. And he added in that he didn't remember any of it.

Luckily, Margot wasn't expecting her at any particular time. They'd agreed that Katharine would come into the office when she could and that if she got the opportunity to sleep in, she should take it and not worry about the company. There were no pressing meetings today, so she sat and drank her coffee and continued to listen to his story even after her cup had been empty for a while.

He remembered only the last half year of his life. Apparently, he had done so many drugs that he'd messed up his memory. However, he could recall everything with perfect clarity from one day about six months ago.

Aaron had woken up after a drug-induced cardiac arrest in a hospital in Michigan. He'd been half crazed from the drugs in his system, and the detox had been terrible. He'd been a John Doe then, his brain too warped to even remember his own name.

His sister had found him. She had been looking for him for a while, and she had narrowed down her search to a general area where she thought she might find him. According to what she said, he'd been homeless for years, living only for the next high. But she'd been trolling the hospitals regularly just in case he came in. She'd been ready when he did.

Fingerprints had proved he was her brother. He sure didn't recognize her.

The family had rallied around him, even though he didn't remember anything about a single one of them.

When he paused in his story, they walked down to the beach and watched the traffic on the walkway go by on skateboards, bikes, and rollerblades. Katharine confessed that she didn't rollerblade. Aaron had no idea if he did. He'd only been in L.A. for a week, and there wasn't much rollerblading in the winter in Michigan.

She told him about Light & Geryon and about Green Sea.

He said he was impressed she'd turned her tragedy into something good.

They had talked long enough that part of the day had passed, and he pulled her into a small Thai place a few blocks up from the beach. It was an interesting mix of smells and textures, linen napkins looking out of sorts, folded neatly on sparkly seventies Formica tabletops. Katharine didn't think they were modern tables in an old style; they were worn enough to look like the real thing.

The food was served on cafeteria-style scratched white china plates. And as she watched, Aaron savored each bite, traded pieces with her, and inhaled the scent of each new item before he rolled it on his tongue. The man clearly enjoyed his food.

By the time they had finished, she knew he'd come to L.A. because he thought he'd been here before, though he had no idea when, and he wanted to see if he could find anyone who could tell him anything about his past.

For her part, she'd fielded a call from Margot, who had grown worried when 1:00 p.m. had come and gone.

Her friend had laughed in her ear when she said she'd met a guy and was hanging out for the day. "Katharine, if you met someone you *want* to spend your day with, then *please* play hooky. We don't mind at all."

She'd hung up before Katharine could say anything. So Katharine held the now blank-faced phone up to Aaron. "Apparently, I'm now playing hooky for the day."

"You're the boss, right?" He sat down in the sand and motioned for her to sit beside him. He leaned back and breathed in the salt-laden air. "I really love the sea. I think I need to see the Atlantic, too."

"You've never been?" Even as the words left her mouth, she regretted them.

But he didn't seem to mind. He shrugged. "Not that I remember." He looked out over the water as he absently shifted the sand through his fingers.

"Do you think you'll go? Do you have a plan for when?" She took off her shoes and buried her toes in the cold grains. Though the day was warm, the sand hadn't heated yet. That wouldn't happen for another month.

"I don't know." Something in the middle distance held his attention.

"I just picked up and came here, you know. Looking for something or someone who knew me. I didn't expect to find you."

It didn't scare her that he said it that way. And when he asked if she wanted to go with him, something calm settled inside her and she nodded. "Someday. I'm booked up the rest of this week, though."

His grin matched the one spreading across her own face. "It's a date then. Maybe for your birthday."

This time she laughed as she shook her head. "My birthday's in November, not a good beach month for the Atlantic. At least not the North Carolina part I'm familiar with. We'll have to go before then."

Somehow, here she was making plans with the man she'd met in the coffee shop three days ago.

His fingers reached out and snaked through hers, and it felt like they belonged there. She'd gone back to sleep last night. He'd told her that she was carrying too heavy a burden, and it had lifted a little. The earth was shifting underneath her again. And finally in a good way. It felt more solid and less sad with him here. Even though she didn't really know what he was, and he didn't seem to either.

His eyes crinkled at the edges and his voice turned her back to the conversation. "Ah, a Thanksgiving baby?"

"No, the sixteenth. Earlier than turkey day, but close enough to be obnoxious." As the last words came out of her mouth his expression changed. He was looking at her oddly. "What?"

Aaron tried to shake off the strange expression, but it didn't quite work. "When on the sixteenth? What time of day?"

"Around four in the morning." She started to add that her mother joked she'd been contrary from the beginning. But that had always been her problem: she'd never been contrary. So she didn't say it, and instead asked him again. "What is it?"

What could he possibly tell her that was stranger than that he had no memory?

She found out.

"When I overdosed, apparently I killed myself. I died on the table. I was dead for about fifteen minutes. Then they shocked me back. It was on November sixteenth."

Oh, that was weird. "At 3:54 a.m.?"

"No. Not even close. Well, aside from the date." His fingers tightened around hers. "It was at 9:07 in the evening. I remember everything after that. And nothing before."

She heard his voice as though from a distance.

9:07 p.m. in Michigan was 6:07 here. At 6:07 p.m. she had been at Margot and Liam's, sitting in front of her lopsided birthday cake. Ever the organized one, her friend had brought the cake to the table at six, just as she had told everyone she would, but it had taken a few minutes to get the candles ready and get everyone singing. At 6:07, Katharine had likely been blowing out the candles.

Oh, dear God.

Her breath came faster and her chest worked to get air as she looked down at their linked hands.

Thoughts slammed through her mind.

The jolt the first time he'd touched her.

The look on his face when he smelled the food and how he seemed to enjoy it so much.

The way he absently ran the sand through his fingers.

"Aaron?" Katharine fought through all the images that were rolling back on her. She could practically hear the links finding each other in her brain and clicking together. She forced herself to look at him, to look into his eyes as he looked up at her from where he lay back on his elbows, waiting for her to tell him something of importance.

"What?" The clear, open shade of green told her everything she needed to know.

She had missed it at first.

Just like last time—she hadn't seen what was right in front of her. But she did now.

She did recognize him.

OTHER NOVELS BY AJ SCUDIERE

Resonance

Earth is Overdue...

Vengeance

There are a million ways to die,

some are just more fun than others

Available at www.AJsAudioMovies.com

Follow the making of AJ's fourth novel, Phoenix, at
www.PhoenixTheBook.com

8-15

DISCARD